NORDIC SPECULATIVE FICTION

This volume brings together scholarly theories and practices on speculative fiction from the Nordic countries, including Denmark, Finland, Iceland, Norway, and Sweden, that are all rooted in similar values, culture, and history yet are independent and unique societies. The book exhibits both the convergences and the diversity of the Nordics in fiction and fandom as well as in research.

It traces the roots of Nordic speculative fiction, how it has developed over time, and how the changes in Nordic environments and societies caused by overhanging shared global issues – such as climate change, mass migration, and technological acceleration – find space in speculative practices. The first of its kind, this book allows for deeper insights into the unique characteristics that make Nordic literature and art recognisable and allows for a better understanding of the place of the Nordics within wider global culture systems. The chapters range from literary critiques, film and television studies, creative works by three Nordic creative writers, transcultural text comparisons, and contributions on speculative art to theoretical and methodological discussions on fandom, worldbuilding, and semantics.

Part of the Studies in Global Genre Fiction series, this book contributes to connecting Nordic speculative fiction scholarship to the wider global community within the field. It will be of interest to scholars and general enthusiasts of speculative fiction and those with interest in Nordic fiction; film and television studies; literary, culture, or media studies; comparative literature; and cultural history or art-based research.

Jyrki Korpua, PhD, is a researcher of literature at the University of Oulu, Finland.

Aino-Kaisa Koistinen, PhD, is a poet, freelance writer, teacher of creative writing, and university researcher at the University of the Arts Helsinki Research Institute, Finland.

Hanna-Riikka Roine, PhD, docent, works as an associate professor of digital culture at the University of Bergen, Norway.

Marta Mboka Tveit is a PhD candidate with the CoFUTURES research group at the University of Oslo, Norway.

Studies in Global Genre Fiction

Series Editors: **Bodhisattva Chattopadhyay**, University of Oslo, Norway, and **Taryne Jade Taylor**, Embry-Riddle Aeronautical University, USA

Studies in Global Genre Fiction offers original insights into the history of genre literature while contesting two hierarchies that constrain global genre fiction studies: (1) Anglophone literature and other global language literatures and (2) literary fiction and genre fiction. The series explores the exchanges between different literary cultures that form aesthetic concerns and the specific literary, sociopolitical, geographical, economic, and historical forces that shape genre fiction globally. A key focus is understudied genre fictions from the "global South" – where geographical location or language often confines works to the margins of the global publishing industry, international circulation, and academic scrutiny, even if they may be widely read in their own specific contexts.

Contributions to this series investigate the points of disruption, intersection, and flows between literary and genre fiction. The series analyses cross-cultural influences in literary classifications, translation, transcreation, localisation, production, and distribution while capturing the rich history of world and global literatures.

Editorial Advisory Board

- Takayuki Tatsumi (Keio University, Japan)
- Dale Knickerbocker (East Carolina University, USA)
- Pawel Frelik (University of Warsaw, Poland)
- Joan Gordon (Nassau Community College/*Science Fiction Studies*, USA)
- Amy J. Ransom (Central Michigan University, USA)
- Farah Mendlesohn (Anglia Ruskin Centre for Science Fiction and Fantasy, UK)
- Rana Issa (American University of Beirut, Lebanon)
- Alexis Brooks de Vita (Texas Southern University, USA)
- M Elizabeth Ginway (University of Florida, USA)
- Aino-Kaisa Koistinen (University of the Arts Helsinki Research Institute, Finland)
- Helge Jordheim (University of Oslo, Norway)
- Abhijit Gupta (Jadavpur University, India)
- Suparno Banerjee (Texas State University, USA)
- Isiah Lavender III (Louisiana State University, USA)

Books in This Series

Science Fiction Cinema in the Twenty-First Century
Transnational Futures, Cosmopolitan Concerns
Pablo Gómez-Muñoz

Nordic Speculative Fiction
Research, Theory, and Practise
Edited by Jyrki Korpua, Aino-Kaisa Koistinen, Hanna-Riikka Roine and Marta Mboka Tveit

For more information about this series, please visit:
https://www.routledge.com/Studies-in-Global-Genre-Fiction/book-series/SGGF

NORDIC SPECULATIVE FICTION

Research, Theory, and Practise

Edited by Jyrki Korpua, Aino-Kaisa Koistinen,
Hanna-Riikka Roine, and Marta Mboka Tveit

LONDON AND NEW YORK

Designed cover image: Getty Images

First published 2025
by Routledge
4 Park Square, Milton Park, Abingdon, Oxon OX14 4RN

and by Routledge
605 Third Avenue, New York, NY 10158

Routledge is an imprint of the Taylor & Francis Group, an informa business

British Library Cataloguing-in-Publication Data
A catalogue record for this book is available from the British Library

Library of Congress Cataloging-in-Publication Data
Names: Korpua, Jyrki, 1977- editor. | Koistinen, Aino-Kaisa, editor. |
Roine, Hanna-Riikka, editor. | Tveit, Marta Mboka, editor.
Title: Nordic speculative fiction: research, theory, and practise / edited
by Jyrki Korpua, Aino-Kaisa Koistinen, Hanna-Riikka Roine and Marta Mboka Tveit.
Description: Abingdon, Oxon; New York, NY: Routledge, 2025. |
Series: Studies in global genre fiction | Includes bibliographical references and index.
Identifiers: LCCN 2024030199 (print) | LCCN 2024030200 (ebook) | ISBN
9781032602363 (hardback) | ISBN 9781032910475 (paperback) | ISBN
9781003561101 (ebook)
Subjects: LCSH: Speculative fiction, Scandinavian--History and criticism. |
LCGFT: Essays. | Literary criticism.
Classification: LCC PT7083.5.S64 N67 2025 (print) | LCC PT7083.5.S64
(ebook) | DDC 839/.5--dc23/eng/20240812
LC record available at https://lccn.loc.gov/2024030199
LC ebook record available at https://lccn.loc.gov/2024030200

ISBN: 978-1-032-60236-3 (hbk)
ISBN: 978-1-032-91047-5 (pbk)
ISBN: 978-1-003-56110-1 (ebk)

DOI: 10.4324/9781003561101

Typeset in Sabon
by Deanta Global Publishing Services, Chennai, India

CONTENTS

FIGURES

CONTRIBUTORS

Caroline Elgh is an art curator and PhD researcher in gender studies at Tema Genus, Linköping University, Sweden. Elgh's work within feminist environmental humanities and posthumanities explores postdisciplinary processes at the intersection of art, science, ecology, and speculative fiction. Previously as a curator at Bonniers Konsthall in Stockholm, she curated exhibitions such as *Cosmological Arrows* that examined contemporary arts relation to science fiction.

Michael Godhe is an associate professor and senior lecturer at the Department for Culture and Society, Linköping University, Sweden. His research concerns, for example, Critical Future Studies (CFS); see "Beyond Capitalist Realism – Why We Need Critical Future Studies" (co-written with Luke Goode), *Culture Unbound*, 2017:1 (9), and the thematic issue of *Culture Unbound*, 2018:2 (10) on CFS (co-edited with Goode).

Line Henriksen is a senior lecturer in Literature and Creative Writing at Malmö University, Sweden. She is co-author of the monograph *Feminist Reconfigurings of Alien Encounters: Ethical Co-existence in More-than-Human Worlds* (2024) together with Nina Lykke and Katja Aglert, and her research interests include monster theory, hauntology, and creative writing as method.

Aino-Kaisa Koistinen, PhD, title of docent, is a poet, freelance writer, teacher of creative writing, and university researcher at the University of the Arts Helsinki Research Institute. Koistinen is the former chair of *FINFAR*

– *Finnish Society for Science Fiction and Fantasy Research* (2018–2020) and former editor-in-chief of *Fafnir – Nordic Journal of Science Fiction and Fantasy Research* (2016–2018).

Jyrki Korpua, PhD, title of docent, is a researcher of literature at the University of Oulu. His books include *The Bible and Literature* (2016, in Finnish), *Tolkien and the Kalevala* (2024), *New Perspectives to Dystopian Fiction* (2020, edited with Saija Isomaa and Jouni Teittinen), and *The Mythopoeic Code of Tolkien: A Christian Platonic Reading of the Legendarium* (2021).

Pekka Kuusisto, PhD, is a university lecturer of literature and director of Transcultural Encounters Research Center (TCERC) at the University of Oulu, Finland. He has written on Dante, literary encyclopedism, science fiction and fantasy, and co-edited the recent TCERC volumes *Humans in Change*, 2018), *Debate! Language, Culture and Information in Interaction* (2023), and *Discourses and Regimes of In(ter)dependence* (upcoming in 2025).

Claudia Nierste holds a master's degree in language diversity from the universities of Greifswald, Germany, and Tampere, Finland, with a focus on Finnish language, literature, and translation and a special interest in Finnish morphology as well as Finnish speculative and climate fiction.

Laura Piippo, PhD, title of docent, is Senior Lecturer in Finnish Literature and Director of Narrare: Centre for Interdisciplinary Narrative Studies at Tampere University, Finland. Her research and publications focus on the places, forms, and value of book objects, print literature in digital environments, and the poetics of contemporary experimental fiction. She is the co-editor of several volumes and special issues on these topics.

Juha Raipola, PhD, is an independent researcher hailing from Tampere, Finland. Raipola has a keen interest in Finnish speculative fiction and has published articles on a variety of topics in the fields of narratology, genre studies, posthumanism, and ecocriticism.

Oskari Rantala is working on their doctoral thesis in the University of Jyväskylä, Finland, researching medium-specific narrative strategies and medial self-awareness in the comics of Alan Moore. Their research interests include medium specificity, (inter)mediality, comics, and speculative fiction. Currently, Rantala is the chair of Finfar, the Finnish Society for Science Fiction and Fantasy Research.

Hanna-Riikka Roine, PhD, title of docent, works as an associate professor of digital culture at the University of Bergen and leads the project "Imagine

Democracy! Narrative Fiction as a Tool for Imagining Democracy in Finland" (2023–2026) in Tampere University. Her research interests include literature as a technology for imagination and digital media from the perspective of our engagements with the possible.

Maria Ruotsalainen, PhD, works as a post-doctoral researcher in the Centre of Excellence in Game Culture Studies, University of Jyväskylä. Her research focuses mainly on gender in games, gaming, and esports. She has published in journals such as *Men & Masculinities, Game Studies, Games and Culture,* and *Television and New Media*, as well as co-edited the book *Modes of Esports Engagement in Overwatch* for Palgrave Macmillan.

Jenniliisa Salminen, PhD, is a university lecturer at the University of Helsinki. Her current research interests include contemporary Russian literature and transnational cultural connections between Finnish and Russian literature, especially fantasy and translations of Slavic folktales.

Kasimir Sandbacka, PhD, is a literary scholar at the University of Oulu. His research interests include late modernism, postmodernism, and metamodernism, as well as irony, nostalgia, and utopia. His current research project, "Post-war European history and metamodernism in contemporary Finnish literature," is funded by the Finnish Cultural Foundation.

Maria Dorothea Schrattenholz is a Norwegian poet, translator, and editor. She's the author of the two critically acclaimed sci-fi poetry collections *Atlaspunkt* (2015) and *Protosjel* (2021).

Marta Mboka Tveit is a PhD candidate with the CoFUTURES research group at the University of Oslo. She researches climate futures in Norwegian and African speculative fiction.

Josefine Wälivaara, PhD, is a researcher at Umeå University, Sweden. Her research on speculative fiction focuses on normativity, temporality, and representation informed by theoretical perspectives such as critical disability studies and queer theory. After finishing her dissertation on sexuality, queerness, and (hetero)normativity in audiovisual science fiction in 2016, she has examined the relationship between (dis)ability and discourses about the future.

Sophie Wennerscheid is an associate professor of Nordic literature in the Department of Nordic Studies and Linguistics, University of Copenhagen. Her latest book publication is *Sex machina: Zur Zukunft des Begehrens* ("Sex machina: On the future of desire," 2019). She is currently completing a book manuscript on farming, food, and the environment in ontemporary Nordic literature and film.

Ruth S. Wenske is a senior lecturer in the Department of Foreign Languages and Literatures at the Ben-Gurion University of the Negev. Her research focuses on contemporary Anglophone African literature, with a secondary research interest in the interconnectedness of literature, literacy, and language in East Africa.

MARS (A POEM)

Maria Dorothea Schrattenholz

"MARS" (UTDRAG)

Maria Dorothea Schrattenholz

men solen har blinde flekker
og de yngste spør meg:
hvorfor må du reise fra oss?
vi har alltid vært her
alle husker det samme
vi kan hamre ut fuglemasker
av blått metall
legge dem over huden
bore hull til øynene
legge hodet tungt på skakke

åpne nebbet og skrike
skrike
vi kan leke
at vi ikke lengter

men jeg er valgt og svarer dem: vi må reise
jeg vet at vi må reise
tilbake og grave, lete, finne
det som kan gjøre det gamle nytt,
alt vi ikke har sett

DOI: 10.4324/9781003561101-1

puste asken inn, grave i den med hendene
gni den mot huden
tenk på alt vi kan få se,
og dere senere

jeg lener ryggen mot veggen
løfter hendene mot vakuum
som er der oppe, holder
grensene på plass

"MARS" (EXCERPT)

Maria Dorothea Schrattenholz

the sun has blind spots
the smallest child asks me
"why do you have to travel?
why are you leaving us?
we have always been here
everyone remembers the same"

I hammer out a bird mask
as all the others do
drilling eye holes in the blue metal

to see
as I do, I flop down
on my back and scream

"we can only pretend
that we don't long
long for what we lost"

but I am chosen and answer them: we must travel
I know we have to travel
back and dig, search,
find that which can make the old, new
all that we have missed
it's there,

inhale the ashes, dig into it with our hands
rub it into our skin
think of everything
we can rediscover

I rest the back of my head
against the side of the dome
raise my hands up
so they contain the wide martian sky
a vacuum which the limits of this dome
hold in place

Excerpt from poetrycollection "Atlaspunkt" by Maria Dorothea Schrattenholz (2015), originally published by Oktober in Norway. Second excerpt from English-language version, translated by Eyra Dordi and Charlie Getter. US Publisher: Brandon Loberg / seven7h tangent. Used by permission.

INTRODUCTION

*Jyrki Korpua, Aino-Kaisa Koistinen,
Hanna-Riikka Roine, and Marta Tveit*

The preceding poetry excerpt by Maria Dorothea Schrattenholz arguably describes a longing for a home, a home that no longer exists. A similar longing might be experienced today when encountering ecological problems such as melting glaciers, changing forests and highlands, and absent snowscapes. Furthermore, imagery of cold, inhospitable environments; resilient, taciturn characters; and a gloomy tone ornamented with a thousand shades of wistfulness might be described as "typically Nordic" features, popularised recently by the Nordic noir genre. What, then, are the specific characteristics that make Nordic speculative fiction recognisable, perhaps as its own geographical sub-genre? How are the changes in Nordic environments and societies, caused by climate change and other environmental or societal phenomena, negotiated through speculative fiction? These are some of the questions that sparked the creation of this anthology.

We are proud to state that the book you are now reading is the first definitive research anthology on Nordic speculative fiction and the first one written in English. It brings together the discourses of research, texts, and bodies of work from a region previously underexplored in the fields of speculative and science fiction and fantasy studies: the Nordic.

What we mean here by *Nordic* is the geographical and cultural region of Europe that consists of the nation-states Denmark, Finland, Iceland, Norway, and Sweden. In addition to these states, the Nordics include the Åland Islands (an autonomous and demilitarised region of Finland), the Faroe Islands and Kalaallit Nunaat or Greenland (which form part of the Kingdom of Denmark), and Svalbard (which is protected by the internationally acknowledged Svalbard Treaty but is under Norwegian sovereignty).

DOI: 10.4324/9781003561101-2

There are also other specific areas within the Nordic countries, with their own rich cultures and traditions and some degree of autonomy, such as Sápmi, the region traditionally inhabited by the indigenous Sámi people, which stretches across northern Norway, Sweden, Finland, as well as the Kola peninsula in the extreme northwest of Russia.

In this publication, the emphasis is on Finnish, Norwegian, Swedish, and Danish work, and perspectives, which, to our knowledge, reflects the current state of research on speculative fiction. Despite our efforts, we were unfortunately unable to attract chapters showcasing speculative fiction research and perspectives from Iceland or smaller cultural areas of the Nordics such as Indigenous communities. We hope that these shortcomings will be addressed in subsequent anthologies. We also acknowledge that Finland is overrepresented in this publication, something which is owed to the fact that speculative fiction research in the Nordics is similarly Finnish dominated. This dominance was also very much reflected on the responses to our open call for papers when compiling this anthology. However, we do our best to also showcase research on Danish, Norwegian, and Swedish speculative works.

Finland has a larger fandom, creative, and academic community orbiting speculative fiction, with longstanding traditions, than the other Nordic territories. There, we find large-scale conventions and research conferences, and societies like Finfar – The Finnish Society for Science Fiction and Fantasy Research, which publishes the open-access journal *Fafnir – Nordic Journal of Science Fiction and Fantasy Research*, now central to the Nordic research community. In 2020, *Fafnir* became the first academic journal to win a World Fantasy Award, one of the leading international awards in speculative fiction. There are also a number of annual speculative fiction awards in Finland, such as the Tähtivaeltaja Award, which is awarded for the best science fiction book released in Finnish, and the Atorox Award awarded to the best science fiction short story (more on Atorox can be found in Chapter 15).

What, then, is speculative fiction? In our understanding, it is a broad umbrella term for texts that include elements that do not exist, or do not exist in the form in which they are portrayed, in the referential known universe (e.g. Selling 2004, 21; Korpua et al. 2021, 11–12; Koistinen & Mäntymäki 2020; Koistinen & Mäntymäki 2022). This includes most works in genres such as fantasy, science fiction, magical realism, supernatural horror, alternative history, weird fiction, slipstream, New Nordic Magic (see *Kosmorama* 2021), the Russian wondertale (as discussed by Vladimir Propp), and more, not simply falling along the lines between "genre" and "mainstream" texts (Suoranta 2023, 16). Beginning with the premise of posing the question "what if" or suggesting the reader/viewer/player to "imagine if," these works use speculation as a strategy to reveal something new and relevant through engaging them into addressing the premise (Roine 2016). Furthermore, speculative fiction can be argued to be a genre in which the structures of storytelling and forms of worldbuilding are put self-reflectively on show (Polvinen 2023, 11) and thus a means for addressing contemporary reality through the acknowledgement of the creative artifice of any attempt to organise the world into a narrative form (Kraatila 2021, 52).

One of the most known authors whose work (or some of it) is typically categorised under the umbrella of speculative fiction, Margaret Atwood, has argued that the genres that speculative fiction encapsulates all draw from the same deep well: "those imagined other worlds located somewhere apart from our everyday one: in another time, in another dimension, through a doorway into the spirit world, or on the other side of the threshold that divides the known from the unknown" (Atwood 2011). Another influential author, Ursula K. Le Guin, has beautifully described speculative fictions as the realism of a larger reality, "perhaps trying to assert and explore a larger reality than we now allow ourselves" (2007, 87).

Although this anthology concerns itself mainly with Nordic speculative fiction from the twentieth and twenty-first centuries, the histories of speculative fiction in the Nordic countries are long and diverse. Folklore, fairy tales, myths, sagas, older literature – "Northern Myth," as J.R.R. Tolkien called it (Flieger 2005, 27–37; Whittingham 2008, 37–38) – and the cosmologies of ancient Norse religions are testament to the longstanding and strong traditions of visiting "worlds located somewhere apart" and exploring "a larger reality."

In recent decades, Nordic speculative fiction has blossomed, emerging explosively on to global markets, quickly becoming its own recognisable "brand." From Norway, Maja Lunde has reached unprecedented levels of success with the novel series *Climate Quartet* (2015–2019), now translated into 40 languages. From Finland, for example Emmi Itäranta has had great international success with the novel *Memory of Water* (2022). Both Lunde's and Itäranta's works are discussed in this anthology. Moreover, the Danish short story collection *Sky City* (2010) and the Icelandic poetry-collection *Dimmumot* (2019) by Steinunn Sigurdardottir (in English "Dusk," about glacier downwasting) have made an impact outside of Nordic borders.

There is also a thriving Nordic fandom community as well as large communities organised around games and gaming, Live Action Role Play, transmedial art, and fan fiction, all more or less overlapping with speculative fiction fandom. The fandom community is especially active in Finland, of which the selection of Helsinki as the site of Worldcon, the World Science Fiction Convention in 2017, is yet another proof. Furthermore, Finnish video game developers have enjoyed extraordinary international success since the beginning of 2010s, and many of the well-known video games incorporate elements from speculative fiction. These include, for instance, the action adventure game *Alan Wake* (2010, Remedy) and its recent sequel (2023), which make use of the survival horror genre; a platform roguelike *Noita*

(2019, Nolla Games), which references Finnish mythological creatures and the *Kalevala;* and *Returnal* (2021, Housemarque), which is discussed in this anthology. In the latest Nordic Game Awards, the big winner was *Skábma – Snowfall* (2022, Red Stage Entertainment), a game by Tampere-based indie game studio and inspired by the beliefs and folktales of the Sámi.

Within Nordic television and film, "new nordic magic" is currently in vogue, and an increasing number of media productions have begun to reach for the speculative toolbox (Hellstrand, Koistinen & Orning 2019). To mention but a few examples, films such as the Finnish surreal thriller *Apeiron* (2013, dir. Maria Ruotsala), based on Leena Krohn's novel *Umbra* (1990), and the Danish dystopian time travel narrative *Qeda* (*Man Divided*, 2017, dir. Max Kestner), set in Denmark in 2095 and 2017, showcase emotionally and cognitively engaging Nordic speculative fiction. Moreover, Swedish *Gräns* (*Border*, 2018, dir. Ali Abbasi) serves as a prime example of speculative political imagination in film as it deals with the boundaries of gender and humanity. In television, the Swedish science fiction series *Äkta Människor* (*Real Humans*, 2012–2014) tackles the relationship between humans and human-like robots in an alternative Sweden (see Hellstrand, Koistinen & Orning 2019) and Icelandic *Katla* (2021) hints at Stanislaw Lem's classic novel *Solaris* (1961) with its uncanny doppelgängers (that raise timely questions of ableism among other things).

Often, speculative fiction and crime fiction are combined (see Koistinen & Mäntymäki 2020; Koistinen & Mäntymäki 2022): for example, the Norwegian *Okkupert* (*Occupied*, 2015–2017) blends dystopia and crime thriller in a storyline where Russia attacks Norway (that currently seems less speculative than before), the Swedish *Jordskott* (2015–2017) blends together fantasy and a traditional police series, and the Norwegian-made international HBO success *Beforeigners* (2019–), also discussed in this anthology, seasons the crime story with time travel.

There are, of course, examples of the speculative in Nordic film already before, with forerunners like Benjamin Christensen's fictive documentary on witchcraft, *Häxan* (*Häxan: Witchcraft through the Ages*, Sweden & Denmark, 1922), or Erik Blomberg's horror-fantasy *Valkoinen peura* (*The White Reindeer*, Finland, 1952). In television, a forerunner in speculative fiction is Danish Lars von Trier's *Riget* (*The Kingdom Exodus*, re-made in 2022, original series 1994–1997) that plays with both horror and fantasy and enjoys a cult status.[1]

We argue that the recent boom of Nordic speculative fiction should be given more attention within academia. What work is speculative fiction doing in the Nordic societies today? What does the increased popularity of genre fiction perhaps tell about recent technological, economic, political, environmental, and social developments, and about the ways in which these developments received, both within the Nordic societies and beyond them? How do the creators and fans use speculation as a strategy to negotiate global and regional issues such as climate change and mass extinction, migration and xenophobia, war (in Europe and beyond), and the continued struggle for queer and transgender rights? Some of these questions are discussed already in this anthology. Future studies should, however, take these discussions further.

Nordic countries are often praised for equality, such as in terms of gender. The praise is deserved to some extent, but many gendered problems, structural inequalities, harmful assumptions, and violent practices exist in the Nordic context. In this anthology, we have attempted to do our part in the struggle for gender equality by championing the use of inclusive language. In the spirit of the Finnish gender-neutral personal pronoun "hän" (in Finnish, there are no gendered personal pronouns, just "hän") and the Swedish gender-neutral pronoun "hen" (introduced alongside the two binary pronouns), we have encouraged all authors to, when applicable, use the pronoun "they" when referring to people. That said, specific genders are, of course, mentioned, and specific pronouns utilised when gender identities are known, or gender is relevant to the analysis. In terms of inclusivity, we have also chosen to keep a very light touch while standardising language, allowing the authors to maintain their own, personal style of writing.

As mentioned above, this anthology was compiled through an open call for papers. Consequently, the structuring of the anthology into four thematic sections follows from our aim to draw out some recurring themes in the field of Nordic speculative fiction. These themes are prominent not only in research and theory but also in speculative artistic practice in the past and present alike.

The first section, titled "Strategies of Speculation," kicks off with Hanna-Riikka Roine's chapter on speculative strategies used in narrating the future of Finnish democracy. With the case study of an anthology of short stories commissioned in 2021 by the Finnish Innovation Fund Sitra, Roine lays out the elements of speculation as a strategy and argues that speculations both draw on and have the potential to shape their social and cultural contexts. While Roine analyses the relationship of speculation to narrative, Laura Piippo examines its intersection with the experimental in the three novels by Finnish author Jaakko Yli-Juonikas published between 2009 and 2015. Drawing on the discussions on the relationship between the postmodernist novel and science fiction, Piippo shows that the connection between literary experiments of the contemporary avant-garde and speculative genre fiction is very much present in the Finnish context.

Michael Godhe then discusses possibly the first Swedish science fiction novel, Claës Lundin's *Oxygen och Aromasia: Bilder från år 2378*, published in 1878. Departing from the interdisciplinary field of Critical Future Studies, Godhe deconstructs Lundin's novel and shows that while Lundin's usual progressiveness is more ambivalent in this tale, the novel both widens the scope of possible futures and shuts down imaginative possibilities. The first section closes with Pekka Kuusisto's chapter, which presents a reading of the structuralist critical tradition of the literary fantastic in terms of its generic encyclopaedism and how literature theorist Tzvetan Todorov's predecessor Vladimir Propp's criticism of the Finnish school of folklore studies (e.g. Julius Krohn, Kaarle Krohn, and Antti J. Aarne) links structuralism with the Northern tradition of nineteenth-century philology.

The second section focuses on different forms of "Uncanny and Ecological Impulses." In the first chapter, Jyrki Korpua analyses uncanny experiences created by Swedish-speaking Finnish author Tove Jansson's five short stories written between 1935 and 1991. Korpua argues that Jansson uses at least two distinct kinds of motifs, those of the sublime and horror, to evoke such experiences in readers. Next, Sophie Wennerscheid examines the contemporary trend in Danish speculative fiction where the boundaries between human and nonhuman, familiar and unfamiliar, as well as past and future are renegotiated in darkish visions of possible futures. By making use of the concepts of the uncanny and speculation, Wennerscheid argues for speculative literary practices as a means of opening up for unknown dimensions of reality and for possible futures that might unfold on premises we still do not know.

Juha Raipola's chapter considers the speculative cross-genre of Finnish Weird (*suomikumma*) as a platform for environmental themes in the works of Leena Krohn and Johanna Sinisalo. In Raipola's analysis, Finnish Weird is approached as a specifically Nordic subgenre of weird fiction which has more generally been construed as notably well attuned to the portrayal of the disturbing effects of global environmental crisis from a non- or anti-anthropocentric viewpoint. Continuing with the environmental theme, Claudia Nierste's chapter wraps the section up, examining references to the primary world in the contemporary Finnish climate fiction written by Emmi Itäranta and Risto Isomäki. Nierste's analysis finds that not only the connections between the novel's storyworlds to the primary world serve a variety of purposes, but even direct references to the primary world do not fulfil a solely mimetic function. Instead, they provide powerful communicative tools and building blocks in the storyworld.

The third section is centred around different "Border Crossings." Kasimir Sandbacka focuses on the tension between a historical past and a speculative present in Finnish author Jani Saxell's *Europe* series (2010–2017). Sandbacka proposes that the key narrative device Saxell's series deploys to represent such a tension is dream narration, a form of metamodern in-betweenness that contributes to the reconstruction of historical understanding and utopian imagination after an era of postmodern deconstruction. Jenniliisa Salminen, then, explores the two first novels of Susanna Hynynen's and Dess Terentjeva's fantasy trilogy *Neonkaupunki* (2020–2024) within the wider phenomenon of introducing Russian culture to Western fantasy readers. In particular, Salminen analyses how the novels use elements of the fantasy genre and of Russian culture to build and negotiate the identity of young Finland Russians and to mediate Russian culture to Finnish readers.

For its part, Marta Tveit's chapter discusses extractivism in Norwegian author Maja Lunde's *Blå* (2017) and Mame Bougouma Diene's African speculative fiction novelette *The Satellite Charmer* (2020). By looking at how the shared theme of extractivism operates in these two texts, Tveit argues that while they differ in tone, both Lunde's and Diene's texts employ a bottom-up perspective on injustice, explore avenues of resistance, and portray experienced complicity and ambivalence in relation to natural resource extraction. Next, Ruth S. Wenske's chapter presents a hydrocolonial reading of the Norwegian speculative television series *Beforeigners* (2019), examining the thematic, visual, and setting-specific references to the ocean as central to the plot's unfolding. By contextualising these references within Norway's maritime history, Wenske argues that *Beforeigners* is characterised by a "hydrocolonial unconscious" that evokes various mythologies, both historical and folkloric.

In the last chapter of the section, Josefine Wälivaara focuses on borders of a more psychological sort, analysing the depictions of mental illness and their relations to space and time in Swedish science fiction film *Aniara* (2019). Wälivaara's analysis shows how the temporality of spaces becomes intrinsically connected to the mental states of the characters. Through this connection, the film avoids Othering mental illness and instead depicts distress, despair, and mental illness as intrinsic to what it is to be human.

The final section of the anthology turns to "Art, Games, and Beyond" fiction. Maria Ruotsalainen examines the intersections of gender and age in the gameplay and reception of Finnish game studio Housemarque's roguelike *Returnal* (2021). Ruotsalainen notes that even though age and gender in the game are mostly ignored in the critiques of the game, keeping in line with the traditional "masculine" ways of valuing games based on game mechanics, for many players, *Returnal's* representation of a middle-aged female protagonist proves important. Thus, the game and the players' reception of it both seem to resist the masculinist values inherent in game cultures. Oskari Rantala presents an overview of Finnish speculative fiction fandom through the examination of the history and debates around the Atorox Award, a prize annually awarded to the best Finnish speculative fiction short story published during the previous year. Rantala focuses on the aspects setting Finnish SFF fandom apart from other national fandoms, suggesting that many of these peculiar aspects can be traced back to the fandom's relatively young age, initial lack of commercial venues for genre material as well as decentralised structuring.

Finally, Caroline Elgh focuses on environmental imaginations in contemporary art, discussing the speculative in the work of two contemporary artists, Larissa Sansour and Johannes Heldén, who both have connections to the Nordic context. Influenced by the work of feminist science studies scholar Donna J. Haraway and the environmental humanist research of Kathryn Yussof and Jennifer Gabrys, Elgh approaches the work of the artists by a feminist visual analysis with a focus on "Chthulucene environmental imaginations." She argues that the artists' work builds – and contributes to the broader societal, global, and planetary building of – rich multispecies assemblages that, during the current ecological crisis, are essential for the survival of humans and nonhumans alike.

The anthology concludes with a thought-provoking coda, a collaborative, speculative and poetic conversation written by Finnish poet, researcher, and creative writer Aino-Kaisa Koistinen and Danish researcher and creative writer Line Henriksen. The text centres around two fictive readers from the future who read the collection at hand and discuss it between each other, unsure of what to make of it. In the spirit of found poetry/collage, the coda utilises textual material found in the anthology at hand and brings together poetry's techniques of estrangement with the estrangement of speculative fiction – as well as the register of scientific language (on the connections between speculative fiction, namely science fiction, and poetry, see Chu 2010). By beginning and ending the anthology with poetry, we wish to remind the readers that speculative fiction has its poetic roots and connections, especially so in the Nordic countries, where speculative imagination has its beginnings and strong traditional backgrounds in folk poetry and myths.

Note

1 As the chapters of the present anthology mainly revolve around literature – with a few exceptions, that is – we wanted to give a short overview on audiovisual fiction here. We nevertheless realise that there are many productions that remain unmentioned here.

References

Atwood, Margaret. 2011. *In Other Worlds: SF and the Human Imagination.* London: Virago.

Chu, Seo-Young. 2010. *Do Metaphors Dream of Literal Sleep. A Science-Fictional Theory of Representation.* Cambridge, Massachusetts: Harvard University Press.

Flieger, Verlyn. 2005. *Interrupted Music. The Making of Tolkien's Mythology.* Kent: Kent University Press.

Hellstrand, Ingvil, Aino-Kaisa Koistinen & Sara Orning. 2019. "Real Humans? Affective imaginaries of the Human and its Others in the Swedish TV-series *Äkta människor.*" *Nordic Journal of Migration Research* 9 (4): 515–532.

Koistinen, Aino-Kaisa & Helen Mäntymäki. 2020. "Affective Estrangement and Ecological Destruction: Mobilising Borders across Genres and Species in TV Crime Series *Fortitude.*" In *Transnational Crime Fiction: Mobility, Borders and Detection,* eds. Maarit Piipponen, Helen Mäntymäki & Marinella Rodi-Risberg, 261–277. Cham: Palgrave MacMillan.

Koistinen, Aino-Kaisa & Helen Mäntymäki. 2022. "Ympäristöuhkia ja tunnistamatonta vierautta: Affektiivinen ja ekologinen outouttaminen 'Nordic-SF-Noir'-televisiosarjassa *White Wall.*" *Kirjallisuudentutkimuksen aikakauslehti Avain* 19 (1): 50–63.

Korpua, Jyrki, Irma Hirsjärvi, Urpo Kovala & Tanja Välisalo. 2021. "Johdanto – fantasiasta." In *Fantasia - Lajit, ilmiö ja yhteiskunta*, eds. Jyrki Korpua, Irma Hirsjärvi, Urpo Kovala & Tanja Välisalo, 9–20. Jyväskylä: Nykykulttuuri.

Kosmorama. 2021. "New Nordic Magic." Issue #279. https://www.kosmorama.org /en/kosmorama/en/kosmorama-279-new-nordic-magic. Accessed 1 March 2024.

Kraatila, Elise. 2021. *The Crisis of Representation and Speculative Mimesis: Rethinking Relations between Fiction and Reality with 21st Century Fantasy Storytelling.* Tampere: Tampere University.

Le Guin, Ursula K. 2007. "The Critics, the Monsters, and the Fantasists." *The Wordsworth Circle* 38 (1/2): 83–87.

Polvinen, Merja. 2023. *Self-Reflective Fiction and 4E Cognition: An Enactive Approach to Literary Artifice.* New York: Routledge.

Roine, Hanna-Riikka. 2016. *Imaginative, Immersive, and Interactive Engagements: The Rhetoric of Worldbuilding in Contemporary Speculative Fiction.* Tampere: Tampere University Press.

Selling, Kim. 2004. "Understanding Speculative Fiction." *Metaphor* 3 (2004): 21–27.

Suoranta, Esko. 2023. *The Sky Above the Port Was the Color of Capitalism: Literary Affordance and Technonaturalist Speculative Fiction.* Helsinki: University of Helsinki.

Whittingham, Elizabeth. 2008. *The Evolution of Tolkien's Mythology. A Study of the History of Middle-earth.* Jefferson: McFarland & Co.

PART I
Strategies of Speculation

1

SPECULATIVE STRATEGIES IN STORIES ABOUT THE FUTURE OF FINNISH DEMOCRACY

Hanna-Riikka Roine

The future of democracy has been one of the enduring topics in speculative fiction. Imaginations range from the genre staples such as Ray Bradbury's *Fahrenheit 451* (1953), where a totalitarian future society censors literature by burning books, and Margaret Atwood's *The Handmaid's Tale* (1985), which depicts the theonomic state of Gilead, to the more recent ones like Malka Older's *Infomocracy* (2016), where an internet monopoly controls the network infrastructure for global micro-democracy. The most internationally renowned example of Finnish speculative fiction in this regard is probably Emmi Itäranta's *Teemestarin kirja* (2012; *Memory of Water,* trans. 2014), set in a future where fresh water is scarce and access to it is strictly guarded and limited by the armed forces. The capacity of speculative fiction to explore possible futures – especially threats and the ways in which societies might respond to them, as shown by the above examples – has lately drawn increased interest from both companies and governments. Companies such as Experimental.Design and SciFutures[1] have emerged to "help clients create forward-looking fiction to generate ideas and IP for progress or profit" (Merchant 2018) through what is referred to as "sci-fi prototyping," "futurecasting," or just "worldbuilding." In 2019, the French Army hired science fiction writers to imagine future threats to their "Red Team," but writers have been employed for this purpose at least since the Reagan administration in the United States enlisted the help of authors Larry Niven and Jerry Pournelle in establishing the Citizen's Advisory Council on National Space Policy (Liptak 2019).

Endeavours in such a scale have not yet been seen in Finland,[2] but the Finnish Innovation Fund Sitra has taken the initiative of trying them out as part of their projects. While Finland, along with other Nordic countries,

DOI: 10.4324/9781003561101-4

is often placed at the top of the world regarding not only the quality of its democratic institutions but also the happiness of its citizens,[3] various concerns remain both internally and externally. These include, for instance, the facilitation of a more direct citizen participation and the threat of possible hybrid operations by Finland's eastern neighbour, Russia, made even more urgent by the Ukrainian war. From 2018 to 2021, Sitra ran a project called "Kansanvallan peruskorjaus" ("Updating Democracy"). Its goal was to "strengthen Finland's position as a model democratic country with a capacity for renewal" and to rethink political decision-making as well as bring new perspectives into the discussion about the future of democracy in Finland.[4] In accordance with these goals, the project commissioned ten well-known fiction writers to imagine and play with the idea of Finnish democracy in 20 years' time. The resulting anthology of short stories, *2040: Tarinoita demokratian tulevaisuudesta* (*2040: Stories about the future of democracy*; from now on *2040*), came out from the publishing house Teos in late 2021.

With *2040*, Sitra joins companies and governmental agencies attempting to employ fiction for the purpose of drawing possible links to the future from the present on both individual and societal scales. All of them recognise the importance of speculative scenarios in the cultural imagination – for instance, in instituting the basis of a society or defining the role of technology in social change. While narrative, both as a strategy and as a form, is widely understood to play a crucial cultural role in this regard, speculation has mostly been left unexamined. In this chapter, I focus specifically on speculation, first laying out its elements, then looking at its relationship to social and technological imaginaries as well as to narrative. This way, I analyse different strategies the short stories in *2040* use to imagine and explore the future of Finnish democracy and discuss both the strengths and limitations of using written fiction in the attempts of "prototyping" or "future-casting" possible developments to come.

The ways in which the year 2040 in Finland is approached in the anthology give a good picture of the variety of speculative strategies. Roughly half of the stories can be said to fall under the generic umbrella of speculative fiction – following Marek Oziewicz (2017), all fiction within this broad category can be argued to share two qualities: interrogating normative notions about reality and offering no pretence of being factual or accurate. As rest of the stories do not clearly fit into the genre despite making use of speculative strategies, the anthology presents an interesting case study for testing the boundary between speculative fiction genre and future-oriented fiction more generally. Finally, the stories in *2040* showcase the ways in which speculative scenarios and imaginaries they both draw on and have the potential to shape are always bound to their social and cultural context. In this case, the context is the Nordic welfare state and especially the ways in which the role and functions of a democratic society are understood and discussed in Finland.

The Three Elements of Speculation as a Strategy

Previous accounts of both written fiction in general and science fiction in particular have emphasised their close engagement with the possible. For narrative theorist Hanna Meretoja, a crucial dimension of the ethics of storytelling is the fact that "narratives both expand and diminish our *sense of the possible*" (2018, 3; emphasis original). Fredric Jameson, in studying utopia as a socio-economic subgenre of science fiction, argues that it is not the representation of radical alternatives that would be inherent to utopia as a form; it is "rather simply the imperative to imagine them" (2005, 416). Although science fiction – and, more broadly, speculative fiction – have indeed been noted to require us to imagine alternatives and expansions, speculation itself has not received much focused attention, remaining ambiguous as a term (Oziewicz 2017). Within science fiction studies, it is usually either defined in opposition to extrapolation or used together with it as if they were interchangeable as terms (Landon 2014, 24), while outside them, most analyses focusing on readers' engagement with the possible give narrative the precedence over other strategies.

The core difference between narrative and speculation as strategies is that speculation can exist independently of the articulation of human experience – although in works of fiction, it almost invariably collaborates with different forms of storytelling. As a cognitive strategy, speculation serves to interpret information to arrive at possible conclusions within the limits of a certain scenario or premise (see Roine 2020, 9). Compared with predictions, forecasts, and prophecies, speculation is not about what *will or can reasonably be argued to happen*: it is about exploring what is *possible* (or showing something to be impossible). Defined this way, speculation is an umbrella term for all possibility-oriented strategies, making the attempts to separate speculative fiction from extrapolative fiction pointless. The latter figures in many of the classic definitions of science fiction, with the aim of distinguishing it from the genre of fantasy, such as in John W. Campbell's claim that to be "science fiction, not fantasy, an honest effort at prophetic extrapolation from the known must be made" (Eschbach 1964, 91). In my view, this distinction results from the historical line of science fiction research where extrapolation was used to suggest "the fidelity to known and possibly even to existing science and technology" (Landon 2014, 24). As I mentioned above, extrapolation and speculation have also been used somewhat interchangeably: in Robert A. Heinlein's influential discussions of science fiction in the 1950s, later published in *Turning Points: Essays on the Art of Science Fiction* (1977), both terms are grounded in adherence to the "scientific method" and function only in terms of plausibility (Landon 2014, 25).

To make the nature of speculation as an umbrella term clearer, I propose the following trichotomy of its elements: premise, thought experiment, and medium. By *premise* I mean the very starting point that limits and guides what will be explored as possible (or what will be shown to be impossible).[5] The possible and impossible are constructed within and in relation to the confines of the premise – in other words, they cannot simply be defined in terms of their congruence or incongruence with the states of affairs outside the premise. Premise may be understood as a model of sorts, which can concern a multitude of situations both individual and universal. In speculative fiction proper, these models often come across as worlds: as Brian McHale puts it, they are "scale-models" of reality that usually are, in some sense, systematically different from the ones inhabited by readers. To be effective, though, the models of any kind cannot be static structures, but must be dynamically worked through to develop possible consequences of the premise (McHale 2010, 21; Roine 2016, 47). This working through is what I call *thought experiment*, drawing from earlier science fiction studies.[6] The concrete "materials" for carrying this process out constitute the *medium*, such as a work of written fiction. In this, a work of written fiction is used as a means of both constructing and sharing the thought experiment based on the premise (as provided by the author) and as a means of accessing and making sense of it (as accomplished by readers).

While discussing speculation and extrapolation, Brooks Landon names them as the most important rhetorical strategies used by science fiction: "trying to imagine the future in terms of extrapolating from the present, in effect asking what might be 'if this goes on ...,' and trying to imagine conditions significantly different from those of the writer's reality by posing the question 'what if...?'" (2014, 23). Understanding speculation as a trichotomy of premise, thought experiment, and medium helps making the differences between the two rhetorical strategies even more concrete. Briefly put, in asking what might be "if this goes on ...," the premise is constructed to serve extension from the known to the unknown, whereas in asking "what if ...," the premise does not need to consist of things that are known or already valid for a certain situation. Both rhetorical strategies provide their own answer to the question of why speculative fiction is often said to require an "imaginative leap" of its reader (Roine 2016, 95). However, it is important to keep in mind that defining whether a premise and the following thought experiment are based on the rhetoric of extrapolation or speculation is always dependent on cultural, social, and historical contexts. This is something I wish to explore with my examples from Finnish written fiction using different speculative strategies.

In *2040*, quite a few of the stories choose the more extrapolative rhetoric as they approach the future of Finnish democracy. Harry Salmenniemi's short story "Kohtauksia: Manifesti" ("Scenes: A manifesto") presents an example of this by juxtaposing solemn political assertions about the importance of citizen participation with scenes of different people's lives. The manifesto-like fragment beginning the story states:[7] "Everyone wants to participate. Everyone with enough strength, voice, and resources, wants to participate, shape the world to their liking. That is why we need to dismantle the obstacles of participation" (*2040*, 115).[8] The fragment on the next page offers a glimpse into a life of a person who has lost their sense of being able to influence the world around them:

> You see that I am drinking tea. Of course I look distressed. I have tried to cover it up, but of course you can immediately see that I am in distress. It is impossible to hide. I look out my balcony window: a strip of asphalt, a tree, stones, a smoking figure, all my invention. I don't see any of them; all of them are equally fantasy.
>
> I am dreaming, sinking, listening to thoughts as if they were background music. ...
>
> Anyway the world spreads around me, goes on to every direction from here.
>
> *(2040, 116)*[9]

Later in the story, a fragment describes a man living a life where things just fit together, from his beard style to the apartment and lines of clothing, concluding that "[e]verything is about the style that puts the pieces into their right places" (*2040*, 144).[10] Fragment of a manifesto after this reminds readers: "It is never about the style only. It is never about the choices only. Usually it is about resources" (*2040*, 145).[11] All in all, Salmenniemi's story engages its readers to ask what happens when the lived realities of people do not correspond to the ideal state painted by the political speeches – in this case, about the need and possibilities to participate. Following the rhetorical strategies discussed by Landon, "Kohtauksia: Manifesti" asks what may be possible in the future if this goes on, if people's experiences continue to diverge not only from the formal expectations of their society but also from each other, resulting in the emergence of different "bubbles." Although the plausibility of extrapolative scenarios is usually discussed (especially in the science fiction studies) in terms of the centrality of science (Landon 2014, 23), in Salmenniemi's story, it hinges on sometimes chilling, other times harrowing juxtaposition of different discourses – or of different experiential worlds governed by divergent models by which people live (such as "My life is in my hands" or "We are at the mercy of the system"). In this, understanding the premise of the story as serving the extension from the known to the unknown requires that readers are familiar with the discourses, both the political and more everyday ones, as well as with the models or *imaginaries* underlying them. Next, I will look at these imaginaries in relation to speculation in more detail.

Speculation and Imaginaries: Premise and Thought Experiment

In reaching towards a realm of infinite possibilities, speculation bases its effectiveness on the creation of a manageable scenario (the premise) and the process of working towards its possible conclusions (the thought experiment).[12] Despite being rhetorically invested in asking "what if …," speculative premises are not detached from the known: one of the most powerful qualities of the stories in *2040* is the way in which they draw on current imaginaries when constructing a premise for their speculations on the future of Finnish democracy. The imaginary is the fundamental concept in philosopher and social critic Cornelius Castoriadis's thinking. For him, societies are never completed, but open-ended processes of creation and re-creation, which he calls "the instituting social imaginary" (2007, 72). In other words, social imaginary is a process through which a society posits its own existence as a society, making and defining itself. After Castoriadis, quite a few scholars have used the concept of imaginary to show how cultural meaning systems have the power to not only shape our beliefs and values but also affect our reality in general. Sociologist Jens Beckert (2016), for instance, has argued that the development of market economy and imaginaries of future go hand in hand, while Elisabetta Ferrari (2020, 121) defines the term of technological imaginary as a set of practice-based beliefs, individual and collective, implicit and explicit, about the role of technology in social life and social change. For her part, Meretoja (2018, 21) outlines narrative imaginary as including the ways in which individuals and communities actively engage with, reinterpret, and reimagine their myths, stories, and imageries. In what follows, I look at two examples of the ways in which contemporary social and technological imaginaries intertwine with the narrative ones in speculative strategies of *2040*.

In Juhani Karila's short story, "Milloin robotit tuhotaan" ("When will the robots be destroyed"), an ambitious technology company Töyrä Systems secretly replaces all inhabitants of the city of Tampere with robots. In the press briefing, the journalists find the stunt and its awe-inspiring implications about the rapid technological progress in robotics completely uninteresting, asking only after the company's dating app. The only journalist interested in the Tampere experiment enquires whether the robots have developed romantic relationships with each other. After the press briefing it suddenly turns out that some of the robots have not followed the company's plan to return to storage but have escaped to meet the Finnish prime minister and ask for civil rights. The prime minister then explains to them that because they are machines, they cannot get such rights, and that it would be best if they were destroyed. Roosa Töyrä, the representative of Töyrä Systems, tries to argue that the robots are the greatest innovation since the Internet, but the prime minister is not convinced:

> The Prime Minister said that the robots were undeniably funny gadgets. But they were also a military threat. If they wanted to, they would undoubtedly be able to take over Finland or the whole world. ... If the robots did not get their civil rights by fair means, they would take them by force. And that wouldn't be the end of it. It was therefore wise to turn these jacks-in-the-boxes into scrap iron now when they were still docile.
> ...
> The Prime Minister said that yeah, we will probably lose a technical revolution or two with the robots, but what's the hurry? The sun was shining, and there was enough juice for everyone. Almost everyone at least.
>
> *(2040, 68–69)*[13]

With its nihilistic representation of the politicians and the press, Karila's story resembles *Don't Look Up* (2021, dir. Adam Kay), the Netflix hit film where astronomers' warnings about the approaching comet fall on deaf ears. The black humour of "Milloin robotit tuhotaan" relies on its reimagination of the culturally dominant narrative of sentient robots: instead of relying on violence and subjugating humankind, the robots are gentle and caring and have changed their names into Grass, Butterfly, Wind, Dog, and Carrot Cake (*2040*, 68).[14] The tragic decision to destroy the robots, then, is shown to be based on the imaginary of the role technology serves in society, simplified as entertainment (dating apps, seeing robots as "funny gadgets"). In this sense, the thought experiment in Karila's story concerns not so much expanding our sense of the possible in terms of future technology but exploring how it is currently conceived within Finnish society.

Markus Leikola's story "Alastalon striimissä" ("In Alastalo's stream") provides a different take on reinterpreting a cultural narrative. It adapts the Finnish modernist classic, Volter Kilpi's *Alastalon salissa* (1933, *In Alastalo's Parlour*), where a group of wealthy men living in the Archipelago Sea of Finland assemble in the Alastalo parlour to decide whether to invest in building a sailing vessel. The novel is (in)famous for its 70-page passage where one of the men, Härkäniemi, chooses a pipe for himself, all the while reflecting on the qualities of other participants in the meeting. In Leikola's adaptation, Härkäniemi muses on the choice of an avatar in the waiting room of a virtual municipal board meeting, commenting on other politicians:

> so Härkäniemi actually was slightly relieved, maybe even more than slightly, when they thought that if they now gave this avatar a miss, then

Bukhila was sure to grab it and it would suit Pihla well indeed, perhaps that scallywag would even be so content with the character that she would refrain from her futile nagging when it was time to make the decisions.

(2040, 81)[15,16]

Leikola's adaptation thus uses a literary passage, rather well known in Finland, to speculate on the state of Finnish democracy in 2040. It seems that different gadgets and props (such as pipes and avatars) may change, but their role in the intercommunication between people making the decisions persists along with certain social structures of meetings and institutions. The belief in the persistence and stability of such structures may even be one of the instituting imaginaries of Finnish society.

Looking at the premises of both Karila's and Leikola's stories illustrates the importance of cultural and social imaginaries in creating effective speculations, engaging readers to consider what they are doing in the present, in the sense of both concrete acts and acts of meaning-making. Both stories can be called playful in their approach – "Milloin robotit tuhotaan" for its satirical tone, "Alastalon striimissä" for its dialogue with Kilpi's novel – and described to offer no pretence of being factual or accurate. They focus on inviting us to explore, for instance, our current imaginaries of technology by, to paraphrase Jameson, making it imperative that we imagine the alternatives while simultaneously making the constructedness[17] of their thought experiments clear. In this, fiction, for example Karila's and Leikola's stories, does not serve the purpose of "solidifying" the future in a manner that more "firmative speculations," represented by risk instruments such as insurance, annuities, and stock options, seek to do (uncertain commons, 2013). Instead, they remain open. Despite such open-endedness, I would argue that the ways in which the alliance between present imaginaries and various speculative scenarios is realised in written fiction can affect our understanding of the spectrum of the possible. This is a purpose that speculation, as an instrument, is suited to, and next, I will look at its instrumentality side by side with narrative in *2040*.

Speculation and Narrative: Instruments and Emotions

In both research and more generally, the power of speculation as an instrument is often seen subordinate to that of narrative: for example, emphasising that our "struggle against the climate crisis" (a story prompt itself!) is ultimately about stories. The instrumental view of narratives is clearly one of the main motivators behind quite a few contemporary projects with the goal of broadening our understanding of where we, as a civilization, are going.[18] A representative example of such ambitions is the Centre for Science and Imagination at the Arizona State University with their six anthologies,[19] three of which are based on the Everything Change Climate Fiction Contest and the larger Imagination and Climate Futures Initiative. The editors of the second volume, Angie Dell and Joey Eschrich, argue that both the contest and the initiative "operate on the belief that emotionally resonant stories are the most powerful tool we have" (2018, loc. 114) and that such stories broaden readers' experience of reality to encompass other lives, other minds. In a similar vein, the Sitra officials Petri Tuomi-Nikula and Antti Kivelä provide a background for *2040* with their conviction that unlike "more traditional future scenarios," written fiction can "genuinely surprise us, strike a chord with us, or inspire us to action" (*2040*, 8).

The appeal to emotion and ability to capture human experience have often been argued to be the unique capacity of narrative. As prominently claimed by cognitive narratologist Monika Fludernik, "there can ... be narratives without plot, but there cannot be any narratives without a human (anthropomorphic) experiencer of some sort at some narrative level" (1996, 13). In its temporal, sequential, and selective form, narrative creates order in our seemingly chaotic environment through allowing us to "make meaning out of raw experiences ... to provide a means for travelling beyond the personal," as Amy Shuman (2005, 1) has suggested. In this purpose, narratives – particularly those of personal experience – are constantly put to various uses both by individuals and in the public sphere, including social media, journalism, and politics.[20] However, such a focus on the experiential can also prove a limitation. When it comes to scenarios imagined by stories in the anthologies such as *Everything Change* and *2040*, the emphasis on the "experiences of individual people coping with displacement, terror, loss, ennui, or glimmers of hope" (Dell and Eschrich 2018, loc. 114) easily eclipses the power of speculation in limiting and guiding what is explored as possible (or what will be shown to be impossible). Instead of putting our trust solely in the emotional resonance of stories, we should also take a critical approach to the premises on which fictions, attempting to make the possible accessible to us, are constructed and why.

In the 2017 book *Curated Stories*, sociologist Sujatha Fernandes urges us to do just that and traces the process by which development that contributed to "telling one's story" became linked to discourses of participation, empowerment, and social capital during the 1990s (2017, 31). Fernandes is particularly critical of the ways in which many purposefully curated story formulae – such as macro-framings and epic narratives – can deny the expression of the experiences of the people using them (2017, 165–166). What I find most interesting about Fernandes's critique of curated stories, though, is the call for "new kinds of organisings" that would open spaces for different kinds of tropes, subjectivities, storylines, and narratives, or "we will be constrained to stories that conform to what is acceptable in the narrow vision of the mainstream" (2017, 170). In *2040*, Marisha Rasi-Koskinen's story "Toinen asukas" ("The other occupant") concretises this idea with its protagonist M.H. Saari, a writer whose stories have always relied on their imagination. However, the dogma of "individuality democracy" which has taken over Finland by 2040 has made writing almost impossible for Saari:

> Their problems started when all sorts of art based on imagination or sympathetic understanding of someone else's life was first morally condemned and then forbidden. You are the expert of your own life, was one of the slogans. Every true story is important, was another. Only the blind should talk about blindness, was the third and the sharpest one. ... The only honest, safe, and just way to write interestingly was to live interestingly. To get experiences. To be interesting. If the artists could not do it, experts by experience were hired to replace them.
>
> *(2040, 21)*[21]

Rasi-Koskinen's story thus combines M.H. Saari's experience of being lost in the new world celebrating "individuality" with the extrapolative premise built on the question of what might be possible in the future if contemporary, well-meaning discussions of "story ownership" and the trend of valuing experts by experience go to their extreme. In my view, if we want to analyse the ways in which stories in *2040* are curated to give form to the possible states of Finnish democracy in 20 years' time, we must focus not only on that which resonates with us emotionally but also on their potential to make us reflect on what is imagined and explored as acceptable and conceivable. In other words, we must consider the "organisings" that give rise to those stories.

Compared to the collections published by the Centre for Science and Imagination, *2040* leaves the overall premise for the anthology vague and more open-ended.[22] The opening of Saara Turunen's auto-fictional story "Suomalainen demokratia vuonna 2040" (Finnish democracy in 2040) makes this quite clear: "I get a phone call. I am asked if I would like to write something about Finnish democracy in 2040. ... Democracy is a big word, I ponder. ... I guess it perhaps means that people can vote and thus use their power" (*2040*, 169).[23] While Turunen's story follows the thought processes of the writer, ending with a list of hypothetical questions about the year 2040 ("Would our big neighbouring country be as unpredictable then as it is now? ... Whose songs would be sung? ... Would we be here, this species of ours?" *2040*, 191–192),[24] Emmi Itäranta's story "Maailman iho" ("The world's skin") takes up an approach that relies on concretising the speculative premise as a world model. Most of the story follows Kaisla, a composer who has retreated to an isolated cottage in the great outdoors to finish her composition that has been commissioned to the opening ceremony of the Parliament of Sustainability, comprising "representatives of nature" in 2043. The story also includes two fictional news stories from the Finnish Broadcasting Company YLE, detailing the beginnings of the Parliament of Sustainability from the citizen's initiative and its approval to the trial stage in the Finnish Parliament.

While at the cottage, Kaisla first discovers a deep hole that mysteriously appears in the middle of a path to the outhouse. She then decides to record the sounds within the hole, discovering that the resulting recording has a peculiar regularity to it: "Repetition, almost like an intentional rhythm and frequency that rises and falls. It is more complicated than a simple wave, like a letter, or many letters, syllables after one another" (2040, 289).[25] Later, listening to the repeating sound patterns with her ex-spouse Laura, who she has invited to the cottage, Kaisla likens the patterns to watching a theatre performance in a language one does not understand: "the sounds do not feel at all random. They have an intention, a direction. It sounds like music. It is humming. For a moment, it sings as a choir, before it narrows again into a one voice. How did they sing before the words had been invented? I-ho, i-ho, i-ho" (2040, 297).[26] Kaisla muses to Laura that perhaps the earth has something to say to humans, that perhaps the microbes and everything else living within it want to tell that they are in danger. Finally, she encounters a soil-black, strange being on the cottage yard in the early hours of a morning:

> The touch is cool and slightly damp, like the wall of the hole where she put the censors. It feels alive. The being stands still and holds her hand. … It does not have eyes, but it looks at her. Like a shadow, or a reflection in a mirror. Something made in her image.
>
> The understanding comes quickly: no. But something whose image she was shaped to be.
>
> *(2040, 302–303)*[27]

After the encounter, Kaisla fully learns to understand the music of the earth. She weaves its words within the composition she is making, to let others hear what the earth is saying, how everything in the world is intertwined: "She hears how they twist together, are more than *me* or *us*, are of the same matter as human bones and short human lives, are the light that ties everything into one" (2040, 306; emphases original).[28] Similar to Rasi-Koskinen's story focusing our attention to the possible dangers of "story ownership," Itäranta's story concretises two abstract ideas in weaving together speculation and narrative as strategies. "Maailman iho" concretises, first, the idea of the voice of nature and, second, the idea of representative democracy. These two ideas – and strategies of speculation and narrative – come together as Kaisla, after making sense of her experiences of meeting the being whose image she is made in, effectively acts as a representative of nature. She relays the message from the earth to the humans, an idea amplified in the story by the news stories discussing the Parliament of Sustainability.

The effectiveness of "Maailman iho" is not merely rooted in its emotional resonance as readers follow, for instance, Kaisla's experiences at the cottage. Furthermore, the story shows that speculation is not only about opening the future up as a "design space" (see Eschrich and Miller 2018, loc. 157). The "organisings" that include creating a premise and working it through concern, to my mind, the present as much as the realm of possible. As Ursula K. Le Guin's (1976) famous characterisation of science fiction suggests, the purpose of fictional thought experiments is "not to predict the future ... but to describe reality, the present world." This means neither limiting fiction making use of speculative strategies to the "displaced reflection of contemporary reality," as McHale (2010, 23) notes critically of Le Guin's characterisation, nor seeing it as a form of firmative speculation that focuses on what should *be done now* to solidify the possibilities to make most of them. Instead, our ability to reflect upon the ways in which certain general principles outlined by a premise can be concretised is important to the present moment for a different reason: it can help us to think about the ways in which the "now" may connect with possible. This, consequently, endows speculative fiction with its ability of "allowing us to think of the world *as otherwise as it currently is*" (McHale 2010, 23; emphasis original) – or, perhaps, allowing us to reflect on the ways in which the world is as it is.

Conclusions

In this chapter I have argued that the value of future-oriented fiction making use of different speculative strategies lies neither in instructing us what to do nor in emotionally embroidering possible threats or templates for a better future. Instead, through offering no pretence of being factual and thus exposing their constructedness, these fictions offer readers a critical distance to examine the imaginaries, assumptions, and aspirations of the present – to explore the ways in which the now might connect with the possible. This way, they can alert readers to the aspects of their current reality that usually elude their awareness and make different abstract ideas underlying, for instance, Finnish democracy and its institutions, more accessible to them.

Laying out the trichotomy of premise, thought experiment, and medium offered a way to consider speculation not only from the perspective of the socially and culturally situated imaginaries but also in relation to the boundaries of speculative fiction genre as well as speculation and extrapolation as rhetorical strategies. While the speculative strategy of developing the premise and the assumptions underlying it in and by means of a thought experiment was something that all stories in *2040* had in common, certain interesting differences emerged between the stories I analysed.

Salmenniemi's "Kohtauksia: Manifesti" collides different narrative models by which people live to evoke a thought experiment of what may follow if people's realities continue to diverge from each other, while "Toinen asukas" by Rasi-Koskinen uses a similarly extrapolative premise to create a rather dystopian future Finland where the idea of story ownership is concretised in the structures and laws of the individuality democracy. Leikola's "Alastalon striimissä" reimagines a well-known passage from the classic of Finnish modernist fiction to speculate on the structures and institutions of decision-making (including technologies and props), whereas Karila's "Milloin robotit tuhotaan" concretises the prevalent technological imaginaries through the fate met by the extremely advanced robots when they do not conform to the role that has been set aside for them in the society. Turunen's "Suomalainen demokratia vuonna 2040" attempts to make the idea of representative democracy more accessible through the description of the writer's own thought process on the matter, while "Maailman iho" by Itäranta intertwines the experiences of a composer encountering the embodiment of earth with the idea of the "representatives of nature" being included in the Finnish parliament.

In other words, stories by Rasi-Koskinen, Karila, and Itäranta all concretise the abstract ideas or imaginaries underlying their speculations as a fictional world, using the strategy of narrative to guide readers to make sense of the experiences of the characters (a writer, robots, a composer) living in these worlds. For their part, Salmenniemi, Leikola, and Turunen rely on different strategies in making the ideas accessible: Salmenniemi on the level of juxtaposing divergent discourses and experiential worlds with each other, Leikola by evoking the comparison between his story and Kilpi's novel, and Turunen through literalising the development of her own thinking on what democracy, being such a "big word," means. As a result, one of the strengths of *2040* is the sheer diversity of the stories and speculative strategies contained in it, but it can also prove a challenge to the reader as all strategies require different interpretative engagement. Still, the anthology demonstrates the importance of speculative scenarios in drawing the possible to the present and has the potential to hand its readers tools to understand various "organisings" the stories draw on, as well as shape.

Acknowledgements

Hanna-Riikka Roine wrote this chapter in the context of her postdoctoral project, "Drawing the Possible into the Present: Entanglements of Human and Computer in Speculation," funded by the Academy of Finland (grant no. 333768).

Notes

1 For more information, see the websites of ExperimentalDesign (https://experimental.design/) and SciFutures (https://www.scifutures.com/).

2 The closest larger-scale examples in Finland are undoubtedly the future scenarios Finnish government officials commissioned from philosopher Pekka Himanen and his company, concerning the prosperity of Finnish culture in the 2010s (*Kukoistuksen käsikirjoitus*, 2010) and the model for sustainable growth (*Kestävän kasvun malli: Globaali näkökulma*, 2020). Himanen's reports are not fiction, though, but rather examples of more traditional future scenarios. Furthermore, they received plenty of negative attention due to their high cost as well as the opacity of the process where Himanen was appointed as the writer of the reports.

3 As of March 2023, the World Happiness Report has named Finland as the happiest nation in the world six times in a row. The six key variables used to explain life evaluations in the happiness rankings are GDP per capita, social support, healthy life expectancy, freedom, generosity, and corruption.

4 For more information, see the website of the project: https://www.sitra.fi/en/topics/updating-democracy.

5 The premise can be likened with Darko Suvin's idea of the novum, an imaginative framework alternative to the author's empirical environment, often summarised in the form of a question beginning with "what if" or "imagine if" (1979, 63).

6 As an example of earlier research, Gwyneth Jones has argued that science fiction should be seen as a form of thought experiment, where "the consequences of some or other nova are worked through" (1999, 4). This means that it is the scientific method, the logical working through of a particular premise, not the scientific accuracy, that is important to science fiction (see Roberts 2000, 10).

7 All translations from Finnish into English are by the author of this chapter.

8 Kaikki haluavat osallistua. Kaikki, joilla vain on voimia, ääntä ja resursseja, tahtovat osallistua, muokata maailmaa mieleisekseen. Siksi on purettava osallistumisen esteitä.

9 Näette että juon teetä. Tietenkin näytän hädänalaiselta. Olen yrittänyt peittää sitä, mutta tietenkin minusta näkee heti, että minulla on hätä. Sitä ei voi salata. Katselen parvekkeen ikkunasta: kaistale asfalttia, puu, kivet, tupakoiva hahmo, minun keksintöäni kaikki. En näe niistä mitään; kaikki ne ovat samanarvoista kuvitelmaa. Olen unessa, vajoan, kuuntelen ajatuksia kuin taustamusiikkia. … Kuitenkin maailma leviää ympärilläni, jatkuu tästä kaikkiin suuntiin.

10 Kaikessa on kysymys tyylistä, joka asettaa palaset oikeille sijoilleen.

11 Koskaan ei ole kysymys pelkästä tyylistä. Koskaan ei ole kysymys pelkistä valinnoista. Yleensä on kysymys resursseista.

12 Due to the length of this chapter, I do not go into further detail about the third element, medium. Looking at speculative scenarios realised through different media (e.g. digital games, television series, films) and comparing would be interesting as a topic of further investigation.

13 Pääministerin mielestä robotit olivat kieltämättä vekkuleita kapineita. Mutta ne olivat myös sotilaallinen uhka. Epäilemättä ne pystyisivät halutessaan valloittamaan Suomen tai koko maailman. … Jos robotit eivät saisi kansalaisoikeuksia suosiolla, ne ottaisivat ne väkisin. Eikä se siihen jäisi. Kannatti tehdä vieteriukkoista romurautaa nyt, kun ne vielä olivat säyseitä. … Pääministeri sanoi, että joo, robottien mukana ehkä menetettäisiin tekninen vallankumous tai pari, mutta mikäs kiire tässä oli. Aurinko paistoi, ja kaikille oli mehua. Tai ainakin melkein kaikille.

14 Ruoho, Perhonen, Tuuli, Koira ja Porkkanakakku.
15 A small note on translation concerning both Leikola's "Alastalon striimissä" and Marisha Rasi-Koskinen's "Toinen asukas" quoted in the next section: despite Härkäniemi being clearly male in the original novel, neither of these stories clearly expresses the gender of their protagonist, as in Finnish the third-person singular "hän" is gender-neutral and can mean "she," "he," or "them." I have therefore decided to translate "hän" as "them."
16 joten Härkäniemi tunsi itse asiassa pientä huojennusta, jopa pientä vähän suurempaakin, kun hän ajatteli että jos hän nyt jättäisi tämän avatarin väliin, niin Bukhila sen varmasti nappaisi ja Pihlalle se hyvin sopisikin, olisipa tuo hyväkäs kenties jopa hahmoonsa sen verran tyytyväinen, että herkeäisi räksyt-tämästä joutavia sitten kun on päätöksenteon aika.
17 Making the constructedness clear is something that science fiction scholarship has emphasised for a long time, as summarised by Merja Polvinen in the description of science fiction as a genre that "depends on making fictions out of meta-phors – on embedding metaphor in a fictional reality and letting it grow" (2018, 67–68); Polvinen adds that the "genre not only literalizes metaphors in this way, but also ... structures of narrative" (2018, 68).
18 In the field of speculative fiction, there is also a growing number of literary move-ments that focus on opening future scenarios in a more instrumental manner: one of these is solarpunk, which the writer Andrew Dana Hudson sees impor-tant in moving "from simple speculation towards meaningful action" (2015).
19 The anthologies include three *Everything Change* anthologies (published in 2016, 2018, and 2020) on climate futures, *The Weight of Light* (2019) on solar futures, *Visions, Ventures, Escape Velocities* (2017) on space futures, and *Sickness, Systems, Solidarity* (2022) on the tangled relationships between pan-demics and games.
20 For more on the various uses of narrative especially in the public sphere, see the results of the *Dangers of Narrative* project in Mäkelä et al. (2021).
21 Hänen vaikeutensa alkoivat siinä vaiheessa, kun kaikenlainen kuvitteluun tai muiden elämään eläytymiseen perustuva taide ensin tuomittiin moraalisesti ja sitten kiellettiin. Olet itse paras asiantuntijasi, oli yksi tunnuslauseista. Jokainen tositarina on tärkeä, oli toinen. Vain sokea puhukoon sokeudesta, kuului kol-mas ja kärkevin. ... Ainoa rehellinen, turvallinen ja oikeudenmukainen keino kirjoittaa kiinnostavasti oli elää kiinnostavasti. Hankkia kokemuksia. Olla kiinnostava. Jos taiteilijat eivät siihen kyenneet, heidän tilalleen palkattiin kokemusasiantuntijoita.
22 For instance, the editors of *The Weight of Light,* an anthology on solar futures published by the centre, lay out the overall premise as follows: "What would a world powered entirely by solar energy look like?" (Eschrich & Miller 2018, loc. 64). A bit further on they add a narrative prompt to the premise: "what it will be like ... to live in the photon societies of the future?" (ibid.)
23 Saan puhelun. Minulta kysytään, haluaisinko kirjoittaa jotakin suomalaisesta demokratiasta vuonna 2040. ... Demokratia on iso sana, minä mietin. ... Kai jollakin tavalla sitä, että ihmiset voivat äänestää ja siten käyttää valtaa.
24 Olisiko suuri naapurimaamme yhtä arvaamaton kuin nykyään? ... Kenen lauluja laulettaisiin? ... Olisimmeko me täällä, tämä meidän lajimme?
25 Toistoa, kuin tarkoituksellista rytmiä ja taajuutta, joka nousee ja laskee. Se on mutkikkaampi kuin yksinkertainen aalto, kuin kirjain, kuin monta kirjainta, tavuja toistensa jäljessä.
26 äänet eivät tunnu lainkaan sattumanvaraisilta. Niissä on rytmi, niissä on aiko-mus, suunta. Se kuulostaa musiikilta. Se hymisee. Se laulaa hetken kuorona, ennen kuin kapenee taas yhdeksi ääneksi. Miten laulettiin, kun sanoja ei vielä

ollut keksitty? I-ho, i-ho, i-ho. [A note on translation: *iho* means "skin" in Finnish.]

27 Kosketus on viileä ja hieman kostea, kuin kuopan seinämä, johon hän asetti sensorit. Se tuntuu elävältä. Olento seisoo paikoillaan ja pitelee häntä kädestä ... Sillä ei ole silmiä, mutta se katsoo häntä. Kuin varjo, tai heijastus peilissä. Jokin hänen kuvakseen tehty. Ymmärrys tulee äkisti: ei. Vaan jokin, minkä kuvaksi hänet on muovattu.

28 Hän kuulee, miten ne punoutuvat toisiinsa, ovat enemmän kuin *minä* tai *me*, ovat samaa ainetta kuin ihmisten luut ja lyhyet elämät, ovat sitä valoa, joka kuroo kaiken yhdeksi.

References

2040: Tarinoita demokratian tulevaisuudesta. 2021. Helsinki: Teos & Sitra.

Beckert, Jens. 2016. *Imagined Futures: Fictional Expectations and Capitalist Dynamics*. Cambridge: Harvard UP.

Castoriadis, Cornelius. 2007. *Figures of the Thinkable*. Trans. Helen Arnold. Stanford: Stanford UP.

Dell, Angie & Joey Eschrich (eds.). 2018. *Everything Change: An Anthology of Climate Fiction, Volume II*. Kindle edition. Tucson: University of Arizona. Center for Science and the Imagination.

Eschrich, Joey & Clark A. Miller (eds.). 2018. *The Weight of Light: A Collection of Solar Futures*. Kindle edition. Tucson: University of Arizona. Center for Science and the Imagination.

Eshbach, Lloyd Arthur. 1964. *Of Worlds Beyond*. Chicago: Advent:Publishers.

Fernandes, Sujatha. 2017. *Curated Stories: The Uses and Misuses of Storytelling*. Oxford: Oxford UP.

Ferrari, Elisabetta. 2020. "Technocracy Meets Populism: The Dominant Technological Imaginary of the Silicon Valley." *Communication, Culture and Critique* 13: 121–124.

Fludernik, Monika. 1996. *Towards a 'Natural' Narratology*. London: Routledge.

Heinlein, Robert A. 1977. *Turning Points: Essays on the Art of Science Fiction*, ed. Damon Knight. New York: Harper & Row.

Hudson, Andrew Dana. 2015. "On the Political Dimensions of Solarpunk." Medium .com. https://medium.com/solarpunks/on-the-political-dimensions-of-solarpunk -c5a7b4bf8df4. Accessed 1 March 2024.

Jameson, Fredric. 2005. *Archaeologies of the Future: The Desire Called Utopia and Other Science Fictions*. London: Verso.

Jones, Gwyneth. 1999. *Deconstructing the Starships: Science, Fiction, and Reality*. Liverpool: Liverpool UP.

Landon, Brooks. 2014. "Extrapolation and Speculation." In *The Oxford Handbook of Science Fiction*, ed. Rob Latham, 23–34. Oxford: Oxford UP.

Le Guin, Ursula K. 1976/1969. *Left Hand of Darkness*. New York: Ace Books.

Liptak, Andrew. 2019. "The French Army is Hiring Science Fiction Writers to Imagine Future Threats." *The Verge*, 24 July 2019. https://www.theverge.com /2019/7/24/20708432/france-military-science-fiction-writers-red-team. Accessed 1 March 2024.

Mäkelä, Maria, Samuli Björninen, Laura Karttunen, Matias Nurminen, Juha Raipola & Tytti Rantanen. 2021. "Dangers of Narrative: A Critical Approach to Narratives of Personal Experience in Contemporary Story Economy." *Narrative* 28 (2): 139–159.

Meretoja, Hanna. 2018. *The Ethics of Storytelling: Narrative Hermeneutics, History and the Possible*. Oxford: Oxford UP.

McHale, Brian. 2010. "Science Fiction, or, the Most Typical Genre in World Literature." In *Genre and Interpretation*, eds. Pirjo Lyytikäinen, Tintti Klapuri & Minna Maijala, 11–27. Helsinki: Helsinki UP.

Merchant, Brian. 2018. "Nike and Boeing Are Paying Sci-Fi Writers to Predict Their Futures." *One Zero*, 28 November 2018. https://onezero.medium.com/nike-and-boeing-are-paying-sci-fi-writers-to-predict-their-futures-fdc4b6165fa4. Accessed 1 March 2024.

Oziewicz, Marek. 2017. "Speculative Fiction." *Oxford Research Encyclopedia of Literature,* 29 March 2017. https://doi.org/10.1093/acrefore/9780190201098.013.78. Accessed 1 March 2024.

Polvinen, Merja. 2018. "Sense-Making and Wonder: An Enactive Approach to Narrative Form in Speculative Fiction." In *The Edinburgh Companion to Contemporary Narrative Theories*, eds. Robyn Warhol & Zara Dinnen, 67–80. Edinburgh: Edinburgh UP.

Roberts, Adam. 2000. *Science Fiction*. London: Routledge.

Roine, Hanna-Riikka. 2016. *Imaginative, Immersive and Interactive Engagements: The Rhetoric of Worldbuilding in Contemporary Speculation Fiction*. PhD dissertation. Tampere: Tampere University.

Roine, Hanna-Riikka. 2020. "On Speculation as a Strategy" (Prefatory essay). *Fafnir – Nordic Journal for Science Fiction and Fantasy Research* 2: 8–15.

Shuman, Amy. 2005. *Other People's Stories: Entitlement Claims and the Critique of Empathy*. Urbana: Illinois UP.

Suvin, Darko. 1979. *Metamorphoses of Science Fiction: On the Poetics and History of a Literary Genre*. New Haven, CT: Yale UP.

uncertain commons. 2013. *Speculate This!* Durham: Duke UP.

2

AT THE INTERSECTION OF EXPERIMENTAL AND SPECULATIVE

Three Novels by Jaakko Yli-Juonikas

Laura Piippo

This chapter discusses three short Finnish novels by Jaakko Yli-Juonikas: *Valvoja* ("the Watcher," 2009), *Uneksija* ("The Dreamer," 2011), and *Kyyhkysinetti* ("the Dove Seal," 2015), and their relation to postmodernism, history, and genre hybridity. The first novel focuses on the successful historic attempt to break the world record in staying awake, which took place in Kotka, Finland, in the 1960s. The second novel is set in the circle of infamous sleeping preachers, or trance-preachers, who emerged in Finland during the politically and culturally turbulent era of the 1930s. The third novel revolves around the characters and events of the notorious Tattarisuo body part mystery that took place in Helsinki in the 1920s.

All these novels combine elements of realism and historical fact, events and personae, unnatural narratives and other experimental techniques, and a sense of suspense, horror, or surrealism, thus creating an interesting vein in Finnish speculative fiction (see also Juha Raipola's chapter in this volume). Previously, these works have mostly been addressed in the context of experimental or avant-garde literature (Piippo 2020; Nieminen 2020), but the analysis and contextualisation in this chapter illustrate the merit of these works also in the field of speculative fiction. According to Linda Hutcheon (1988, 89), "[w]hat the postmodern writing of both history and literature has taught us is that both history and fiction are discourses, that both constitute systems of signification by which we make sense of the past." The works above are examined, namely, as alternative or speculative histories blending fact and fiction, and drawing from literary tradition as well as the lesser-treaded paths and outskirts of Finnish history. In the light of this analysis, the connection between literary experiments of the contemporary

DOI: 10.4324/9781003561101-5

avant-garde and speculative genre fiction is still very much present in the Finnish context.

Yli-Juonikas's works are independent and distinctive entities and differ from each other in many respects. However, there are also many commonalities between them. So far, two collections of short stories, *Uudet uhkakuvat* ("New Threats," 2003) and *Yö on viisain* ("The Night Is the Wisest," 2018), and several novels from Yli-Juonikas have been published. Of these, four, *Uneksija* (2009), *Valvoja* (2011), *Vanhan merimiehen tarina* ("The Rime of the Ancient Mariner," 2014), and *Kyyhkysinetti* (2015), are shorter in form. The prize-winning and nominated novels,[1] *Jatkosota-extra* ("The Continuation War Extra," 2017), *Neuromaani* (2012), and *Tuhatkaunokin tuho* ("The Destruction of Daisy," 2024), are more extensive and maximalist. *Yö on viisain* includes both short stories and the first chapter of the upcoming six-part novel series. The following parts of the series are the novels *Tahdon murskatappio* ("The Crush Defeat of the Will," 2019), *Mitä uudet Galgalim-silmäni näkivätkään* ("What Did My New Galgalim-Eyes See," 2020), and *Jääasema Kooma* ("Ice Station Coma," 2021), as well as the vanity press volume *Teppo joutuu lahtiin* ("Teppo Gets Slaughtered," 2022).

Yli-Juonikas's works are published by three Finnish publishing houses, Sammakko, Otava, and Siltala, out of which the first is a somewhat smaller enterprise, the second is one of the largest ones in Finland, and the last has recently been profiled as the publisher of experimental literature, both original works and translations. In addition to these, Yli-Juonikas is one of the authors of the procedural collective novel *Ihmiskokeita* ("Human Experiments," 2016). He has also published several short stories and essays in cultural journals and various anthologies, sometimes including real or fictional counterparts to critiques or commentaries on his works. Yli-Juonikas is also known as a literary critic and translator. Jaakko Yli-Juonikas is indeed one of the most acclaimed and prolific writers of Finnish contemporary prose. His works, most prominently *Neuromaani*, have attracted academic attention (mostly in Finnish) (Haapala 2011; Kyllönen 2016; Kurikka 2017; Björninen 2017, 2022; Piippo 2016, 2018a, 2018b, 2019a, 2019b, 2020, 2021) and have also been a subject of several master's theses. Yli-Juonikas's works are yet to be translated, although there have been signs of interest for such a project.

In this chapter, I discuss three short novels by Jaakko Yli-Juonikas regarding their poetics and presumed genre hybridity. I aim to construct a cohesive analysis of the poetics of these novels, especially in terms of Genettean transtextuality and unnatural elements. In what follows, I discuss the relationship between postmodernism, avant garde, and speculative fiction and then move on to examine how the three novels by Yli-Juonikas respond to these genres. Finally, I summarise my analysis and these discussions by proposing the novels to be regarded as speculative historical fiction that locates the unnatural in both narrative and discourse.

Valvoja, Uneksija, Kyyhkysinetti

The language of Yli-Juonikas's works is characterised by combining materials from very different sources. The text is full of wordplay, or puns, "small-scale verbal creativity based on ambiguity" (Niemi, Joensuu & Ikonen 2018[2], 122). According to Marko Niemi, Juri Joensuu, and Teemu Ikonen (122), the category of wordplay can also be extended to "anagrams, letter transitions, language errors, palindromes, portmanteaus, spoonerisms, and neologisms." All of these, especially the latter three, can be found in Yli-Juonikas's prose works, often enhancing the thematic connections and connotations of these works. The logic of the portmanteau also expands into a metaphor on a sentence level. In *Valvoja,* "the local paper's journalists turned yellow and fell from the tree." Developed further, this logic also becomes an interpretive framework: even the most mundane content is often tinted with new, unexpected, gloomy, or disturbing shades.

The same logic is at work on the level of the story as well. Days often turn abruptly into nights, wakefulness into dreams, states of consciousness into others, and internal into external. The themes of Yli-Juonikas's works repeatedly feature murder, deception, religion, science, pseudoscience, paranormality, the lowly, paranoia, conspiracies, mental illness, violence, and anything in danger of being cleaned up or stacked away. The fictional and literary range of these works is wide. There is a lot of experimentation and exploration of different structures of a novel. It concerns the text layout, typography, and narration, as well as the reader's expectations, which are often being tested. Although the character gallery of the works is quite rich and versatile, the reader is usually not primarily directed to attach to or focus on them, which is not uncommon in the literary tradition of the avantgarde. I will now proceed to examine the novels at hand more closely.

Valvoja examines an elongated attempt to stay awake. It is built on a similar actual historical case, which took place in Finland in the 1960s. The novel takes the reader to the city of Hamina in February 1964. Toimi Silvo, who works in the port and considers himself an ordinary and simple man who just likes to stay awake, faces a big challenge: he plans to set a world record for staying awake and thus gain exposure for the city. Finally, he, indeed, takes the world record in his name. He walks around in the snowy Hamina to stay awake or rather to prevent himself from falling asleep. The press is following his record attempt and reporting on it in a rather unreliable manner.

During his walks, Toimi encounters Helise Leivo, who works as a secretary at the port offices. The two fall in love, but unfortunately Helise falls into a coma, creating a thematic counterpart for Toimi's wake state. The novel, with its language ripe with old-fashioned or archaic vocabulary, is divided into 16 chapters. The first 14 of these are named after the dates of Toimi's attempt, and the last two are unnamed. In the last chapters, as the narration takes a rather surrealist than mimetic turn, it seems that Toimi's and Helise's minds and states blend into each other, and they float by each other in a scene that is set on a boundary of sorts, resembling the surface of the water. It also seems that this won't be their last encounter:

> At the edge of the opening in the ice, they come against each other. One is just waking up from a deep sleep, the other is falling into a light sleep, just half a metre below the surface. They glide past each other with a smile. They are still going to meet. A date has been arranged for the weekend.
> They say: Are you asleep?
> I woke up, they say.[3]
>
> *(Valvoja, 191)*

Yli-Juonikas's *Uneksija* again draws inspiration from a real person, the sleep preacher Eino Teräs [Steel], who toured post-Civil War Finland and performed in front of crowds. In the novel, Eino does not hear his own ceremonies, during which also the narration switches to reciting the events of his repeated nightmares, where he is a little girl with her neck in the noose of the cruel executioner Jussila. The third storyline of the novel follows Saara, a large country girl, around whose hut a series of strange threats and visions appear. Many of these are familiar to the reader from Eino's dreams, and whereas Eino's wake state and dreams are separated from each other by distinctly locating them in separate chapters, in Saara's perception – and also in the third-person narration focalised through her – these two states of consciousness blend into each other. Eventually, Eino and Saara fall in love, prepare for marriage, and plan to move to the United States, as so many others in Finland did during the decade in question. Saara's presence seems to calm Eino and dissolve his nightmares, but Saara's secret visions do not disappear, on the contrary. In the end, it seems that strange otherworldly powers are talking to her through her wake visions and guiding her towards a destiny that might alter the state of reality and is somehow connected to her and Eino's yet-unborn child:

> The clear summer evening over the city hardens the rusted steel of the sun. When Saara fries the fish in the pan, the fish sings: The child of the resurrection will be born and shall come to you! The truth no longer needs crutches to support it! It is a sight of great joy. On the same evening, the third outburst of spores occurs, securing and sealing the initial impetus for new life. When the Father Sun and Mother Moon meet, the Star Child

begins. The universe around them rejoices. The man of steel who gave his all falls asleep in the naked arms of his bride and dreams of America.[4]

(Uneksija, *190–191*)

Uneksija borrows a lot of its discourse from the self-help and sex education literature of the earlier decades of the twentieth century, which explains, for example, "spores" and other uncommon or outdated expressions. The novel can be perceived as an unexpected romance, a collection of local historical oddities, a mystery, or all of these at once.

Kyyhkysinetti builds around the so-called Tattarisuo Case in 1930, where body parts were dug from open graves in the Malmi Cemetery, located in rural northern Helsinki. The parts were then dumped into the Tattarisuo spring by a black magic convent in hopes of gaining a treasure from the magical spring or to gain other, unforeseen powers. A passer-by found some of the body parts in the vicinity of the spring, and for a short time, the press extensively covered the suspected mass murder until the true nature of the matter came to light. The members of the convent, five simple local people in many ways let down by the society, were led on by a man whom they believed to be a powerful witch.[5] Half of them, including their leader, were later convicted for mutilating the dead bodies. The main storyline of the novel follows the life of Rauha Rautio, a dwarfed girl who is a fictive member of the Tattarisuo convent, the first place in her life where she encounters friendship and care.

The novel weaves a vivid picture of the scenery, speech, and mental landscape of the early twentieth century in the Finnish rural areas and developing communities where magical beliefs, pseudoscience, and everyday observations mix with each other. It is both a representation and an elaboration of the textual and discursive reality surrounding and constituting the minds of the protagonists. *Kyyhkysinetti* contains pseudo-facsimiles of the spells on the pages of the *Black Bible* with the novel's characters' marginalia scribbled on them. These pages can be found in the Finnish National Archive, but they are not directly related to the case of Tattarisuo. There are also a lot of quotations from other occult or pseudo-scientific literature of the time. *Kyyhkysinetti* combines the characteristic account of the protagonist Rauha Rautio's extremely passive narration, which she delivers in the third person with a story world ripe with sudden violence, occultism, and secret information. Each of these elements of the narrative is, in a way, equally violent and terrifying and at the same time fascinating. In the second to last chapter of the novel, focalisation suddenly switches, and the narration shows the otherworldly spectators of the scene:

He pulls a piece of paper from his chest pocket and begins to smear it with his bloody forefinger. A lanky young man and his mother squat on the ground and kill two still-living birds. For a ritual to work as expected, at least one pigeon must be buried alive in the ground. The adjutant, the woman in green, and her dwarf comrade are staring at their leader as if waiting for his instructions. The leader straightens his back, raises the mauled creature above his head, and says as solemnly as he can without his dentures, "Justice and truth for all we seek with an insurmountable force!"

The father of reason and mother nature are deeply moved by the sincerity of the coven. A few raindrops fall from the darkening sky. One cannot help but marvel at the inexhaustibility and ingenuity that *homo stultus* shows in their efforts to impress us.[6]

(Kyyhkysinetti, 235–236)

All three novels feature both the intense multifaceted intertextuality and the ontological "flickering" between "this world and the world next door" (McHale 1987, 75) often connected with postmodernism. As Linda Hutcheon argues, "[t]he textual incorporation of these intertextual past(s) as a constitutive structural element of postmodernist fiction functions as a formal marking of historicity – both literary and 'worldly'" (1988, 4). Mixing up different textual material is in general rather common in postmodernist fiction (McHale 1987, 202–203). Gérard Genette (1997, 1) defines this phenomenon as transtextuality, and states that "the subject of poetics is transtextuality, or the textual transcendence of the text," which they roughly define as "all that sets the text in a relationship, whether obvious or concealed, with other texts." According to Genette, transtextuality is divided into five subtypes, namely, intertextuality, paratextuality, architextuality, metatextuality, and hypertextuality (which is also known as hypotextuality). Intertextuality can take the form of quotation, plagiarism, or allusion and is defined as a "relationship of copresence between two texts or among several texts" (Genette 1997, 1).

Valvoja, Uneksija, Kyyhkysinetti, and other Yli-Juonikas's works include several intertextual references and allusions. Eino Teräs's dreams centre around a sinister scene, where he transforms into a little girl who is about to be cruelly hanged by a cruel judge. These paragraphs seem to be built around permutations of the last paragraph (excepting the epilogue) of Cormac McCarthy's *Blood Meridian or the Evening Redness in the West* (1985):

And they are dancing, the board floor slamming under the jackboots and the fiddlers grinning hideously over their canted pieces. Towering over them all is the judge and he is naked dancing, his small feet lively and quick and now in double-time and bowing to the ladies, huge and pale and hairless, like an enormous infant. He never sleeps, he says. He says he'll never die. He bows to the fiddlers and sashays backward and throws back his head and laughs deep in his throat and he is a great favourite, the judge. He wafts his hat and the lunar dome of his skull passes palely under the lamps and he swings about and takes possession of one of the fiddles and he pirouettes and makes a pass, two passes, dancing and fiddling at once. His feet are light and nimble. He never sleeps. He says that he will never die. He dances in light and shadow and he is a great favourite. He never sleeps, the judge. He is dancing, dancing. He says that he will never die.

Uneksija's version of the same scene reads as follows, creating a case of Genettean intertextuality, namely an allusion:

A man dances in the middle of screaming, dancing harlots. An old man. Saara would recognize him at any time. Executioner Jussila leads other dancers with his dance. He has painted a red mark on his forehead. He has a red bow tie around his neck. When he raises his hand in the air, the harlots do the same. Executioner Jussila dances while the others sleep. He never sleeps and he never dies. Amid the raucous music, screaming birds, mutilated bodies, and bare bloody breasts, Jussila dances, and laughs. He laughs at Saara with red teeth. The city is in ruins, fires rage in every direction and reach the trees and bushes of the park at any moment, but the executioner Jussila does not stop dancing. His limbs move faster than anyone else. It's amazing how an old man can move his limbs at such a fast pace.[7]

(Uneksija, *142–143*)

In Genettean terms, these permutations can also be seen as hypertexts to McCarthy's hypotext, although this term is mostly reserved for the permutations of a complete work of fiction. This transtextual connection is not necessarily available to the reader if they are not familiar with McCarthy's original paragraph. The relation between the different versions is an apt example of the general poetics of Yli-Juonikas's novels. *Blood Meridian* does not serve as a metaphorical background for Yli-Juonikas's works, nor does it offer the reader interpretive tools for analysis of their characters, themes, or imagery. These transtextual relations do, however, open new textual spaces and room for interpretations, and allow the – in this case eerie and terrifying – affects and affections of the former literary works to blend in with the ones of the newer novels, thus following the logic of excess (see Piippo 2019a). These relations are excessive also in the sense that recognising them is not always necessary for proceeding with Yli-Juonikas's novel or perceiving it as coherent and whole. Some of *Valvoja*'s intertextual references employ ekphrasis – the written description of a work of art – especially regarding audiovisual texts. As pointed out by Iina Nieminen (2020), the last chapter of *Valvoja* digresses from the main location of the novel to a leprosy hospital in Iran and describes the audiovisual narration and frames from a documentary short film *The House Is Black (Khaneh siah ast)* (1963) by Forough Farrokhzad. The novel also contains, as Nieminen notes, a synopsis of a Finnish film *Sensuela* (1973) by Teuvo Tulio, embedded into the narration of the novel as mere observations and memories of the protagonist:

> Toimi thinks of summer. Bustle at the harbor dock. A beautiful black-haired girl in overalls pushes a cart loaded with empty crates. A young welder will help him. … The girl is the daughter of a rich Sámi reindeer king. At one time she moved south with a German photographer. In the war, the photographer's plane was shot down in Lapland, and the girl rescued him. They fell in love and ran south. Soon the paths of the lovers parted, the girl, disgraced and angry, left the photographer. To secure her livelihood she was forced to get miserable jobs. … Her roommate engaged in prostitution and tried to lure her into the same industry.[8]
>
> *(Valvoja, 32–33).*

These intertextual passages are often serious in mood, which distances them from satirical tropes and brings them closer to pastiche, occasionally to more humorous parody (see Genette 1997, 27). The relationship between these passages in the novel and their hypotext is the same in nature as the one described above regarding *Blood Meridian*.

The main character and protagonist of *Kyyhkysinetti*, Rauha Rautio, already appears in *Uneksija* as a minor character. It is also mentioned that she is herself a charismatic speaker, not just an awestruck member of the audience. This reference, which can easily be overlooked, casts a different light on Rauha's character. It seems that she is not the mere bystander or onlooker of the events unfolding in front of her, but an active participant and practitioner of the occult arts. Next, I shall proceed to elaborate on the literary genres, which are most prominently at play in these three novels: experimental or avant-garde tradition, postmodern literature, and speculative fiction, alternate histories.

Experimental, Postmodern, Speculative

Hybridity and genre hybrids are an inherent part of speculative fiction also in the Nordics. Kristina Malmio and Kaisa Kurikka (2020, 5) argue that "the distinct mixture of global and local spatial relations in a certain territory, and the in-betweenness of the region, is what constitutes Nordic literature," which in this case seems to enhance focus on the hybrid textual landscapes of Yli-Juonikas's fiction. Following Jan Baetens, Marina Grishakova (2013, n.p.) even proceeds to suggest that hybridity "has become something like a catchword in contemporary literary and cultural studies." They also argue that "[n]ew hybrid genres and media modify the ways we see old, presumably homogeneous and non-hybrid phenomena. From this perspective, 'hybridity' is a stimulus and a sign of a perceptual and epistemological shift rather than of passing fashion" (ibid.).

The genres or traditions that are most often mentioned in connection to these novels are experimental literature or avant-garde and postmodernism. Later in this chapter, I will also suggest the genre of speculative historical fiction as an alternative for describing these works. Avant-garde and postmodernism share a long and often discussed past (McHale 2012). Their common ground can be found in some literary devices and what might be called "the unnatural." Jan Alber, Henrik Skov Nielsen, and Brian Richardson (2012, 352) state that

> [t]he category of the unnatural cuts across many existing subgenres – late modernism, avant-garde, nouveau roman, *écriture féminine,* magical realism, theatre of the absurd, postmodernism, but also genres that contain conventionalized manifestations of the unnatural – and invites us to identify and theorise strategies and concerns that are common to all.

As Brian Richardson (2017, 204) has pointed out, literary fiction, in general, has not concerned itself with solely mimetic pursuits, but tested the waters in other ways as well: "Since the late 1950s, we have seen extreme acts of antirealist narration, contradictory chronologies, variable kinds of emplotment, multiple endings, radically fragmented and conjoined characters, impossible narrative spaces, transgressions of the idea of narrative itself, and reconfigurations of the material book." It is also worth noting that realism as a periodic term or a style of narration does not represent the majority in the whole history of narrative fiction. The literary experiments mentioned above by Richardson have also been theorised through the concept of the unnatural, as opposed to the "natural" of, for instance, everyday exchanges (see Fludernik 1996).

One of the "conventionalized manifestations of the unnatural" is without a question the genre of speculative fiction. As Irmtraub Huber (2014, 71) notes, "the fantastic showcases the two competing literary stances of the mimetic and the marvellous, laying bare the mechanisms of production and reception which in other genres and modes often remain latent and hidden. Thus, fantastic hesitation exaggerates and exploits qualities which are in principle shared by all literary texts." This makes speculative fiction one of the key spaces for literature to examine not only the marvellous but also its own *'literaturnost':* the precisely literary quality of language use that distinguishes the poetic from the ordinary. Speculation also seems to be highly contagious. As Brian Attebery (2013, 3) suggests, speculative fiction "spills over into other genres, such as fantasy and historical fiction; it freely exchanges techniques and ideas with nonfictional forms such as scientific popularizations and utopian tracts." Derek Thiess elaborates this notion even further. Thiess (2014, 9) states that speculative fiction as a genre "engages many other forms of cultural production, not only literary texts but popular and scientific ones as well. As such, it tends to defy simple generic categorizations." In this regard, speculative fiction seems to generate or suggest hybridity. If we follow this line of thought and apply it to Yli-Juonikas's works, what kind of hybrids or vessels of the unnatural these novels are?

Brian McHale has famously named science fiction "postmodernism's non-canonized or 'low art' double" (1987, 59), for in many respects they share the same literary traits. Since the 1980s, however, the postmodern novel has taken a leap from the marginals of literature towards the mainstream, for so many of its central themes and devices have become mundane and a part of our everyday lives. Avant-garde genre fiction, like postmodernist literature, is often "concerned with the creation of new worlds and exploration of ontological arenas, particularly through devices of allegory, displacement, and incoherence" (Bray, Gibbons & McHale 2012, 6). Elena Gomel (2012, 393–394) argues that postmodernism has become the household name and staple of contemporary literature, which diminishes its revolutionary perspectives. They also state that while many works and genres are defined through their relationship with time, postmodernism is mostly concerned with space. Postmodernist (genre) fictions often patch the lack of time with inflation of narrative time, which then produces extremely long or even maximalist works or series of works. *Valvoja*, *Uneksija*, and *Kyyhkysinetti*, however, contradict this trend. They are rather short and compact, at least when compared to the author's maximalist or excessive (see Piippo 2019a, 2020) works, such as *Neuromaani* or *Jatkosota-extra*. These novels are, however, also interested in questions of time, since they are very specifically set in a certain historical moment. One possible answer for navigating this twofold dilemma could be found in the genre of alternate history.

Michael Butter (2009, 50) makes a differentiation between the genres of alternate history and speculative fiction or, more precisely, science fiction. They argue that "alternate history should be regarded as a genre of its own whose various forms and functions are best understood when compared with the different forms of contemporary historical fiction." Karen Hellekson (2009, 453) states that "[t]he alternate history asks questions about time, linearity, determinism, and the implicit link between past and present. It considers the individual's role in making history, and it foregrounds the constructed-ness and narrativity of history." Kathleen Singles (2013, 1) also points out that alternate history has evidently "achieved a degree of respect among readers outside of a specialised fan base." This as well as the connection between postmodernism and historical metafiction (see Hutcheon 1988) draws the genre towards the mainstream of fiction.

All three novels can be placed in their historical settings, and they all set out to explore the discursive mental imagery and worlds floating around – or set on paper – at the said time. *Valvoja*, *Uneksija*, and *Kyyhkysinetti* do not pinpoint and change a certain historical moment or event, but rather explore the literary resources and discourses connected to a certain historical location and period. Therefore, I regard these novels as speculative historical fiction rather than alternate histories. Put like this, speculative fiction that employs various experimental literary devices seems to reconnect with its revolutionary avant-garde past by denouncing the traits so heavily overworked in postmodernist (or at times post-postmodernist) fiction: irony and self-reflexivity. Postmodernism seems to be, indeed, more drawn to parody and pastiche, whereas avant-garde genre works more often aim to reconstruct history by creating new literary spaces (Bray, Gibbons & McHale 2012, 6). As Gomel writes:

> Revolution, then, becomes an object of nostalgia, an echo of the traumatic past rather than a vision of the utopian future. It is here that genre fiction comes into its own. In comparison to the literary mainstream, genre fiction is uniquely equipped to cultivate a poetics of nostalgia, invoking historical time through fictional space. Rather than deconstructing past forms, popular literature reconstructs them. Not in the modality of parody or pastiche, as has been theorised for postmodernism in general, but as alternative spaces, narrative heterotopias, in which history can be (re)-confronted, if only as a ghost.
>
> *(2012, 394)*

Elise Kraatila identifies the crisis of representation as the most durable and resistant legacy of postmodernism (2021, 69–70). This legacy has been discussed in terms of reconstruction, and the current forms of speculative fiction are also very much related to reconstructive practices (Huber 2014; Polvinen 2021; Kraatila 2021). The reconstruction of previous literary forms and textual spaces in the novels of Yli-Juonikas is, however, slightly different from what has been named "reconstructive fantasies" by Irmtraub Huber (2014, see also Polvinen 2021, 287). Huber stresses that "[r]econstructive literature addresses the perceived isolation of the individual, reaching out to establish connections both with others and with the realities we live in" (2014, 49–50). They explicitly affirm the idea of re-negotiating the inherent ontological instability of postmodernism to regain the ability to communicate with one another (8–10, 55–61). Polvinen follows this line of thought and proceeds to argue that these kinds of reconstructive fantasies afford the reader to enact not "just the world represented in the text, but instead … an abstract cognitive space where artifice, figuration, and narrative structure are also part of the environment" (2021, 401). This notion seems to resonate more with the poetics of *Valvoja*, *Uneksija*, and *Kyyhkysinetti*. They present themselves first and foremost as fictional literary artefacts, which is also typical of experimental literature.

Experimental literature often questions the dominant structures and forms of the current literary field. It poses the very ontological question of its own '*literaturnost*': is this literature or could it be (Bray, Gibbons & McHale 2012)? These kinds of questions are also at the heart of the broad genre of speculative fiction. As Hanna-Riikka Roine (2016, 14) writes:

> work at hand must not only involve a speculative premise but also address it or work it through in a processual manner. The premise (or the idea, often summarised in the form of a question beginning with "what if" or "imagine if") is not always, or even in most cases, immediately apparent to the user, as the crucial part of both the rhetoric and the aesthetics of the speculative practice is to engage the users into addressing it, working it through.
>
> It is precisely this call – what if, imagine if – that also lies in the heart of many experimental works of fiction.

In the case of Yli-Juonikas, however, the call often seems to be formulated differently: just "imagine." What the reader is asked to imagine in the case of the novels analysed here is the possible mental landscape of the time and the feel of its language, discourse, narrative positioning, and the literary resources available to the characters in the storyworlds they inhabit. After that, the reader is invited to imagine if the paranormal, unnatural, or magical in connection to the event is real and accurate. Imagine if one could actually stay awake for several weeks and thus breach the limits of one's consciousness (see Nieminen 2020), if the dreams of the sleep preachers did predict or formulate reality, or if the ancient and otherworldly powers called upon by the lowly members of the convent of *Kyyhkysinetti* were watching over us. Experimental or avant-garde literature tends to place the unnatural on the level of the text: narration, language, typesetting, et cetera, whereas speculative fiction favours impossible worlds, narratives, or events, even though the different literary techniques and poetics have an important part in this as well (see Roine 2016, 46–47). The novels of Jaakko Yli-Juonikas seem to combine these two aspects explicitly, thus creating unique poetics and permutations of the speculative histories.

Conclusions

In this chapter, I have discussed three short novels by Jaakko Yli-Juonikas regarding their presumed genre hybridity, with focus on the poetics of these novels. This discussion has pointed out different kinds of literary devices and poetics at play in the novels and highlighted their literary character that is largely based on different forms of intertextuality and unnatural elements. The three novels draw up mental landscapes characterised by different literary resources, sometimes already forgotten in the present-day context. Speculation in these novels is attached both to the level of the story and to how it is created, namely, its literariness. This presents these novels first and foremost as literary artistic works, but does not, however, diminish their speculative qualities – quite on the contrary. *Valvoja*, *Uneksija*, and *Kyyhkysinetti* all invite the reader to consider the mental landscape of the novels' protagonists, which is created through different borrowed historical settings, events, and phenomena, but most prominently different literary works of the time. Creating the novels' atmosphere like this allows the reader to encounter the otherworldly or unnatural events as a possible or plausible part of the novel's reality. In the light of this analysis, the connection between literary experiments of the contemporary avant-garde and speculative genre fiction in the Finnish context is alive and well and continues to produce new and unexpected offspring.

Notes

1 *Neuromaani* received the Jarkko Laine Prize in 2013 and was nominated for the Runeberg Prize the same year. *Jatkosota-extra* was nominated for the Finlandia Prize in 2017. *Uneksija* received the Kalevi Jäntti Prize in 2011.
2 All translations from Finnish originals are by the author of this chapter.
3 In the original passage it is unclear which character utters which line. Therefore, I have used gender-neutral pronouns in this particular translation even though the characters in the original novels are gendered. In other references to the novels by Yli-Juonikas, the pronouns are used according to the original text. Finnish original: Avannon reunalla he tulevat toisiaan vastaan. Toinen heräilee juuri syvästä unesta, toinen on vaipumassa kevyeen uneen, vain puoli metriä pinnan alle. He liukuvat hymyillen toistensa ohi. He aikovat vielä tavata. Viikonlopuksi on sovittu treffit.
   Hän sanoo: Nukutko sinä?
   Minä heräsin, hän sanoo.
4 Kuulas kesäilta kaupungin yllä karkaisee auringon ruostuneen teräksen. Kun Saara paistaa kaloja pannulla, kalat laulavat: Herätyksen lapsi on syntyvä ja saapuva teidän luoksenne! Totuus ei enää tarvitse tueksensa kainalosauvoja! Se on suuren ilon näky. Samana iltana tapahtuu vielä kolmas itiöpurkaus, joka varmistaa ja sinetöi uuden elämän alkusysäyksen. Kun Isä Aurinko ja Äiti Kuu kohtaavat, saa alkunsa Tähtilapsi. Maailmankaikkio heidän ympärillään riemuitsee. Kaikkensa antanut teräsmies nukahtaa morsiamensa alastomaan syliin ja näkee unta Amerikasta.
5 In the Finnish context, especially in early and pre-modern times, all practitioners of witchcraft are and were referred to as witches (see Lahti 2016).
6 Hän vetää povitaskusta paperinpalan ja rupeaa tuhrimaan sitä verisellä etusormella. Hontelo nuorukainen ja hänen äitinsä kyykistelevät maassa ja runnovat kahta vielä elävää lintua hengiltä. Jotta rituaali toimisi odotetulla tavalla, on vähintään yksi kyyhky haudattava maahan elävältä. Adjutantti, vihreänuttuinen

nainen ja tämän kääpiökasvuinen toveri tuijottavat johtajaansa, kuin odottaen tämän ohjeita. Johtaja suoristaa selkänsä, kohottaa raatelemansa luontokappaleen päänsä yläpuolelle ja lausuu niin juhlallisesti kuin ilman tekohampaita pystyy: "Oikeutta ja totuutta etsimme kaikille ylitse pääsemättömällä voimalla!" Järjen isää ja luontoäitiä noitapiiriläisten vilpittömyys liikuttaa sydänjuuria myöten. Tummenevalta taivaalta putoaa muutama sadepisara. Ei voi kuin hämmästellä sitä uupumattomuutta ja kekseliäisyyttä, jota *homo stultus* osoittaa pyrkiessään tekemään meihin edullisen vaikutuksen.

7   "Kiljuvien tanssivien porttojen keskellä tanssii mies. Vanha mies. Saara tunnistaisi hänet milloin tahansa. Pyöveli Jussila johtaa tanssillaan muita tanssijoita. Hän on maalannut otsaansa punaisen merkin. Hänen kaulassaan on punainen kissanrusetti. Kun hän nostaa kätensä ilmaan, portot tekevät samoin. Pyöveli Jussila tanssii kun muut nukkuvat. Hän ei nuku koskaan eikä hän kuole koskaan. Riehakkaan musiikin, kirkuvien lintujen, silvottujen ruumiiden ja paljaiden veristen rintojen keskellä tanssii ja nauraa pyöveli Jussila. Hän nauraa Saaralle punaisin hampain. Kaupunki on raunioina, tulipalot raivoavat joka suunnassa ja tavoittavat puiston puut ja pensaistot hetkenä minä hyvänsä, mutta pyöveli Jussila ei lopeta tanssia. Hänen raajansa liikkuvat nopeammin kuin kellään muulla. Ihmeellistä, miten vanha mies voi riuhtoa raajojaan noin nopeaan tahtiin."

8   "Toimi ajattelee kesää. Kuhinaa sataman telakalla. Kaunis mustatukkainen haal-
.   arityttö työntää kärryä, johon on lastattu tyhjiä sälelaatikoita. Nuori hitsaajamies tulee auttamaan häntä. ... Tyttö on rikkaan saamelaisen porokuninkaan tytär. Aikoinaan hän muutti etelään saksalaisen valokuvaajan kanssa. Sodassa valokuvaajan lentokone ammuttiin alas Lapissa, tyttö pelasti hänet. He rakastivat ja karkasivat etelään. Pian rakastavaisten tiet erosivat, tyttö häipyi valokuvaajan luota häväistynä ja vihaisena. Henkensä pitimiksi hänen oli pakko hankkia kurjia töitä.... Hänen asuintoverinsa harjoitti prostituutiota ja yritti houkutella häntä samalle alalle...."

References

Alber, Jan, Henrık Skov Nielsen & Brian Richardson. 2012. "Unnatural Voices, Minds, and Narration." In *The Routledge Companion to Experimental Literature*, eds. Joe Bray, Alison Gibbons & Brian McHale, 351–367. London & New York: Routledge.

Attebery, Brian. 2013. "Science Fictional Parabolas: Jazz, Geometry, and Generation Starships." In *Parabolas of Science Fiction*, eds. Brian Attebery & Veronica Hollinger. Middletown: Wesleyan UP.

Björninen, Samuli. 2017. "Realismia aivotieteen ajassa – Jaakko Yli-Juonikkaan *Neuromaani* ja psykologisen realismin kirjallinen perinne." *Niin & näin* 2/2017: 45–50.

Björninen, Samuli. 2022. "Romaani pakenevan elämän jäljillä: Jaakko Yli-Juonikkaan Neuromaanin realismista." In *Kertomus Postmodernismin Jälkeen*, ed. Samuli Björninen, 169–194. Helsinki: SKS.

Bray, Joe, Alison Gibbons & Brian McHale. 2012. "Introduction." In *The Routledge Companion to Experimental Literature*, eds. Joe Bray, Alison Gibbons & Brian McHale, 1–18. London & New York: Routledge.

Butter, Michael. 2009. *The Epitome of Evil: Hitler in American Fiction, 1939–2002*. New York: Palgrave MacMillan.

Fludernık, Monika. 1996. *Towards a 'Natural' Narratology*. London: Routledge.

Genette, Gérard, et al. 1997. *Palimpsests: Literature in the Second Degree*. Lincoln: University of Nebraska Press.

Gomel, Elana. 2012. "'Rotting time': Genre Fiction and the Avant-garde." In *The Routledge Companion to Experimental Literature*, eds. Joe Bray, Alison Gibbons & Brian McHale, 393–406. London & New York: Routledge.

Grishakova, Marina. 2013. "Complexity, Hybridity, and Comparative Literature." CLCWeb: *Comparative Literature and Culture*, 15 July 2013: np.

Haapala, Vesa. 2011. "Strömungen der finnischen Gegenwartsliteratur." In *Finnland – Geschichte, Kultur und Gesellschaft*, ed. Hartmut E. H. Lenk. Landau: Verlag Empirische Pädagogik.

Hellekson, Karen. 2009. "Alternate History." In *The Routledge Companion to Science Fiction*, eds. Mark Bould, Andrew M. Butler, Adam Roberts & Sherryl Vint, 453. London: Routledge.

Huber, Irmtraub. 2014. *Literature after Postmodernism: Reconstructive Fantasies.* New York: Palgrave Macmillan.

Hutcheon, Linda. 1988. *A Poetics of Postmodernity: History, Theory, Fiction.* Oxford: Routledge.

Kraatila, Elise. 2021. *The Crisis of Representation and Speculative Mimesis: Rethinking Relations Between Fiction and Reality with 21st-century Fantasy Storytelling.* Tampere: Tampere University.

Kurikka, Kaisa. 2017. "Kokeellinen romaani, kokeileva lukija: Jaakko Yli-Juonikkaan *Neuromaani.*" In *Maamme romaani: esseitä kirjallisuuden vuosikymmenistä*, eds. Jussi Ojajärvi & Nina Työlahti, 311–325. Jyväskylä: Nykykulttuuri.

Kyllönen, Vesa. 2016. "Maksimalistinen aivokartta: Metafyysinen salapoliisikertomus Jaakko Yli-Juonikkaan Neuromaanin tiedollisena työkaluna." *Kirjallisuudentutkimuksen aikakauslehti Avain* 1/2016: 24–38.

Lahti, Emmi. 2016. *Tietäjiä, Taikojia, Hautausmaita: Taikuus Suomessa 1700-luvun Jälkipuoliskolla.* Jyväskylä: University of Jyväskylä.

Malmio, Kristina & Kaisa Kurikka. 2020. "Introduction: Storied Spaces of Contemporary Nordic Literature." In *Contemporary Nordic Literature and Spatiality*, eds. Kristina Malmio & Kaisa Kurikka. Cham: Palgrave MacMillan.

McCarthy, Cormac. 1985. *Blood Meridian or The Evening Redness in the West.* New York: Random House.

McHale, Brian. 1987. *Postmodernist Fiction.* New York: Methuen.

Niemi, Marko, Juri Joensuu & Teemu Ikonen. 2018. "Menetelmällisen kirjoittajan perussanasto." In *Menetelmällisen kirjallisuuden antologia*, ed. Teemu Ikonen. Helsinki: Post-Oulipo ry. & MKS.

Nieminen, Iina. 2020. *Niillä rajoilla: outous ja piilotajunta Jaakko Yli-Juonikkaan romaanissa Valvoja.* Master's Thesis in Finnish Literature. Helsinki: University of Helsinki.

Piippo, Laura. 2016. "'650 sivua tiivistettyä hulluutta on liikaa': Jaakko Yli-Juonikkaan Neuromaani (2012) elämystalouden karstana ja polttoaineena." In *Elämykset kulttuurina ja kulttuuri elämyksinä: kulttuurintutkimuksen näkökulmia elämystalouteen*, eds. Sanna Karkulehto, Tuuli Lähdesmäki & Juhana Venäläinen, 347–371. Jyväskylä: Jyväskylä UP.

Piippo, Laura. 2018a. "Aperitiffin perintö: esimerkkinä Jaakko Yli-Juonikkaan *Neuromaani.*" In *Avoin Aperitiff: kirjoituksia Kari Aronpuron kollaasiromaanista Aperitiff – avoin kaupunki*, eds. Mikko Keskinen, Juri Joensuu, Laura Piippo & Anna Helle, 165–185. Tampere: Tampere UP.

Piippo, Laura. 2018b. "The Brain in Our Hands: The Materiality of Reading *Neuromaani.*" In *Reading Today*, eds. Heta Pyrhönen & Janna Kantola, 45–56. London: UCL Press.

Piippo, Laura. 2019a. "Ylenpalttisuutta ja äärimmäisyyskokemuksia. Jaakko Yli-Juonikkaan *Neuromaani* 2000-luvun eksessiromaanina." In *Muistikirja ja matkalaukku. 2000-luvun suomalaisen romaanin muotoja ja merkityksiä*, eds. Elina Arminen & Markku Lehtimäki, 211–240. Helsinki: SKS.

Piippo, Laura. 2019b. "Ääni on meissä, joka olemme, kun meitä ei ole – Skitsofrenian muotoja *Neuromaanissa*." In *Hulluus ja kulttuurinen mielenterveystutkimus*, eds. Saara Jäntti, Kirsi Heimonen, Sari Kuuva & Annastiina Mäkilä, 305–328. Jyväskylä: Jyväskylä UP.

Piippo, Laura. 2020. *Operatiivinen vainoharha normaalitieteen aikakaudella: Jaakko Yli-Juonikkaan Neuromaanin kokeellinen poetiikka*. Jyväskylä UP.

Piippo, Laura. 2021. "Dissident Poetics, Experimental Excess: Jaakko Yli-Juonikas' Finnish Novel Neuromaani." In *Humanities, Provocateur: Towards a Contemporary Political Aesthetics*, ed. Brinda Bose, 111–125. Delhi: Bloomsbury Publishing India.

Polvinen, Merja. 2021. "The Dark Inside the Prologue: Enactive Cognition and Eerie Ontology in Catherynne M. Valente's Radiance." *Style* 55 (3): 385–405.

Richardson, Brian. 2017. "Introduction: Experimental Literature and Narrative Theory." *Frontiers of Narrative Studies* 3 (2): 203–205.

Roine, Hanna-Riikka. 2016. *Imaginative, Immersive and Interactive Engagements. The Rhetoric of Worldbuilding in Contemporary Speculative Fiction*. Tampere: Tampere UP.

Singles, Kathleen. 2013. *Narrating Futures/Alternate History*. Berlin: De Gruyter, Inc.

Thiess, Derek. 2014. *Relativism, Alternate History, and the Forgetful Reader: Reading Science Fiction and Historiography*. Lexington Books.

Yli-Juonikas, Jaakko. 2009. *Valvoja*. Helsinki: Otava.

Yli-Juonikas, Jaakko. 2011. *Uneksija*. Helsinki: Otava.

Yli-Juonikas, Jaakko. 2015. *Kyyhkysinetti*. Helsinki: Otava.

3

THE MODERNITY THAT WAS YET TO COME

On Claës Lundin's Science-Fiction Novel *Oxygen och Aromasia: Bilder från år 2378*

Michael Godhe

Flying velocipedes, scent claviers, surviving on pills. These are some of the novelties in store for the readers of what has been heralded as the first Swedish science fiction novel: *Oxygen och Aromasia: Bilder från år 2378* (*Oxygene and Aromasia: Pictures from the Year 2378*). The novel was written by the cosmopolitan liberal writer and publicist Claës Lundin (1825–1908) and published in 1878. It was partly based on the German science-fiction writer and philosopher Kurd Laßwitz's (1848–1910) two novellas, "Bis zum Nullpunkt des Seins" ("To the Zero Point of Existence,", 1871) and "Gegen das Weltgesetz" ("Toward the Universal Law," 1874). The two novellas were published in *Bilder aus der Zukunft: Zwei Erzählungen aus dem vierundzwansigsten und neununddreißigsten Jahrhundert* ("Images of the Future: Two Stories from the Twenty-Fourth and the Thirty-Ninth Centuries," 1878).

This chapter discusses *Oxygen and Aromasia* by relating the novel to other works by Lundin and situating it in the socio-political and cultural context of nineteenth-century Sweden. In short stories, novels, essays, causeries, books on Stockholm inspired by the Parisian tableaux form, and other genres, Lundin *staged* modernity; that is, he placed science and technology as well as liberal reforms at the centre of society's journey into the future, aimed at an imagined ideal community of the bourgeoisie. Lundin discussed the impact of technology and science on human life and culture, with a great belief in the modern project and its flagship idea of progress. Communication and transportation technologies were especially connected to political liberalism and social reforms. Departing from *Critical Future Studies*, I'm interested in "the ways in which cultural texts not only *represent* the future, but also actively shape it by opening up or closing down

DOI: 10.4324/9781003561101-6

imaginative possibilities" (Godhe & Goode 2018, 151). What sort of people (Goode & Godhe 2017, 121) are supposed to live in the futural fictive landscape of Lundin? What kind of political economy is envisaged in *Oxygen och Aromasia*. By deconstructing the novel and emphasising the cracks in the narrative, I show that Lundin's expressed progressiveness in his other writing is more ambivalently narrated in this tale. At the same time, I ask questions concerning how the *text* in the novel as well as his other writings both widens the scope of possible futures and shuts down imaginative possibilities (cf. Goode & Godhe 2017).

Lundin borrowed especially the scientific and technological elements from both novellas by Laβwitz, but as Eric Johannesson (1984) points out, the episodes containing social, political, and cultural references to contemporary Sweden are Lundin's own invention. Lundin had also been inspired by the Paris World's Fair (Exposition Universelle) in 1878 (Ekström 1999, 28). In this chapter, I first discuss some of Lundin's work prior to *Oxygen och Aromasia*, followed by an analysis of the novel, read through the lens of Critical Future Studies. Subsequently, I discuss some of his works post *Oxygen och Aromasia*, ending with a conclusion.

Lundin's Works Prior to *Oxygen och Aromasia*

Throughout Lundin's writings from the early 1860s to the end of his life at the beginning of the twentieth century, he always returned to and showcased how technology and science will alter our lives. As I have discussed elsewhere (Godhe 2004), through shaping and creating a narrative room for an imagined community consisting of the bourgeoisie (cf. Stenport 2004, 88; Edoff 2016), Lundin was in some sense a popular science writer, even though popular science as a genre was still yet to be developed in Sweden (Kärnfelt 2000). Nevertheless, from the end of the 1850s and onwards, Lundin used different genres for interpreting technology's and science's role in economic, societal, and cultural development. In his writings, Lundin was almost obsessed with contrasting the old society and tradition versus the new changing society. A rural way of living was not an imaginative possibility in Lundin's writings, and he showcased a future where traditional ways of living were abandoned and opened up for the rising bourgeoisie as the ideal way of living. He was not the only one doing this, of course. During the nineteenth century, as Anders Ekström points out, it became common that science protocols were published in newspapers, with the scientific journey as a basic theme. Plenty of future prognoses in the shape of novels, travel stories, and newspaper reporting were published during the nineteenth century, where science's power to revolutionise societal change was emphasised and at the centre of the narratives. Museums, exhibitions, and an increasing number of public lectures contributed to the development of a popular science with pedagogic ambitions. The assumption that the world became intelligible through science also contained the notion that science should guide the public (Ekström 1999, 26–29. Cf. Beckman 1999, 214–220; Stenport 2004).

Not only were science protocols published in Swedish newspapers during the nineteenth century. There were also plenty of representations staging the imagined pending impact of science and technology on society and culture. Technology and science were presented in forms far from the hierarchical ideal that was more and more developing in popular science, for example, that popular science should not be left to amateurs but should be written by the scientist themselves (cf. Kärnfelt 2000; Godhe 2004). Especially in newspapers and magazines during the 1860s and 1870s, Lundin expressed his visions, or wishful thinking, of how science and technology inevitably would change and reshape our life sphere.

One of the genres Lundin used in the beginning of his career as a professional writer was "causeries" (kåserier, that is, a lighter version of the essay form). Lundin published a lot of causeries in *Ny Illustrerad Tidning* (*New Illustrated Paper*), a magazine known during the period 1865–1872 for a touch of laissez faire liberalism and church criticism as well for its cosmopolitan imprint (Johannesson 1970, 1980). Between 1866 and 1871, Lundin had the column "Omnibus" where he commented on news from Stockholm's "fashionable social and cultural life with urbanity, and in a conversational French tone" (Johannesson 1984, 320).[1] The mix of esprit and seriousness was inspired by the causerie writer Oscar Patrick Sturzen-Becker (1811–1869), who used the signature Orvar Odd (Johannesson 1984; Sylwan 1919; Kjellén 1985), and the French feuilleton concept where style dominated: of great importance was how the subject discussed in the causerie was treated and explored. The pun and a light and elegant non-academic style belong to the causerie and feuilleton style. A common requirement was that the feuilleton should be piquant (juicy), that is, to awaken an appetite or a curiosity for the subject (Johannesson 1984; Sylwan 1919).

Lundin transformed the causerie and feuilleton genres and commented not only on Stockholm's social life but also on the city's transformation. I have elsewhere (Godhe 2004) discussed Lundin's causeries at length. In this section I will give a few examples and summarise some of the most important conclusions regarding his anthropology and ontology, that is, his visions of how humankind and the world will be changed in the future by the pending modernity. The public for his one and only science fiction novel was with certainty well acquainted with his previous writings. Thus, I claim that there is a web of interpretation or interpretative communities, a contract between Lundin and his readers where the public has a generic competence for reading the causeries as well as *Oxygen och Aromasia*.

In the Omnibus causeries, Lundin invites his readers to guided tours with horse cabs (i.e. omnibuses), an early form of collective traffic common in larger cities during the nineteenth century, with the purpose of "quickly touch science, let industry be reviewed, not despise trade and shipping, but rather stay at art" (Lundin 1866:16, 126).[2] During the omnibus tours, Lundin shares his experiences from his travels on the continent, especially Paris, while he also comments on modern phenomena such as Banting's slimming cure (Lundin 1866:48, 382): "Let us make ourselves as slim as possible – that is the order of the day, slender, light, almost thin, somewhat transparent would not hurt. On the contrary, it is modern."[3] The tone is full of esprit, and he is tickling his bourgeois public by mocking their habits, while at the same time endorsing the pending modern life.

Even if Paris's and Copenhagen's street life was an ideal for Lundin (1880, 73), he is picturing Stockholm as a modern city for the readers of his Omnibus causeries. In 1868 (1868:43, 343), he wrote that what is modern one day is old the next day. If we should be struck by all wonderful technological novelties, we would be nothing but surprised day in and day out (Lundin 1868:43, 343). In another article from 1869, he claims that our time is distinguished by rapid development and that news travels from one continent to another within 24 hours. We are getting used to that, and it does not surprise us anymore: "We do not live today anymore but tomorrow" (Lundin 1869:8, 62).[4]

Technological innovations are discussed in a number of causeries, but chiefly it is innovations in communication technologies that caught Lundin's attention and interest, with "urban public transportation as a favourite vantage point for observation" (Stenport 2004, 88). He ponders the new bourgeoisie pastime, the bicycle, with fascination, and at the same time, he is quite ironic over the phenomenon (e.g. Lundin 1869:1, 7; 1869:8, 62f; 1869:13; 102; 1869:17, 136). The telegraph and increasingly faster transportation technologies such as the tram are discussed (e.g. Lundin 1867:37, 295; 1870:21, 167–168) – technological novelties shaping and contributing to the modern city public life much wanted by Lundin.

What kind of anthropology is expressed in Lundin's causeries? What sort of people are supposed to live in a modern society? What is the modern man replacing the premodern man (Goode & Godhe 2017; Godhe & Godhe 2018)? The causeries expressed a prospect about modern life and modernity, and judging by this and other of his non-fiction work, modernity for Lundin meant releasing our true nature and empowering us with freedom and a better and certainly more exciting life. The modern man is a city man, abandoning tradition. To the modern life the flaneur also belongs, according to Lundin, a phenomenon introduced in Sweden in the 1830s and 1840s, modelled after French models or archetypes and introduced by Swedish writers such as Carl Jonas Love Almqvist (1793–1866) and Sturzen-Becker och August Blanche (1811–1868) (Kjellén 1985, 9). In his usual style, Lundin was mocking the flaneurs: the main thing is that they are modern (Lundin 1867:30, 239), but in another sense they epitomise Lundin's anthropology. In a French context, the flaneur life and its literature were part of a rising bourgeoisie. The flaneur was perceived as a witty person with an ability to quickly comprehend a situation and make a fast analysis of it – he (it is always a male) is what you in contemporary jargon would call street-smart. This kind of person was primarily to be found in Paris with its quaysides, boulevards, and street life (Kjellén 1995, 10–14).

The concept of the flaneur spread rapidly from France to other countries in Europe, including Sweden. But if Sturzen-Becker's flaneur leads an idle life, living on interest rates and heritage, then Lundin's interpretation of the flaneur is somewhat different. Lundin's flaneur is a fast observer and interpreter of the changing urban landscape and street life, and of science and technology's role for the pending modern life since Lundin staged modernity. In the 1860s and 1870s, the streets in Stockholm were in fact in a bad shape, and a street-planning regulation for overcoming traffic congestion and sanitary inconveniences was implemented in 1867 (cf. Godhe 2004; Stenport 2004). Anyway, the role of the flaneur meant training observational skills, something that gave incitements to writing belles-lettres, and not least novels. But even businessmen, artists, actors, and rich young men strolled (Kjellén 1995, 10–16, 31).

For Lundin, the modern city life called for new demands on the citizens, and technology became a tool for making this new life as comfortable as possible. When scientists and artists are highly respected in society, that is proof that a society is highly cultivated, according to Lundin, "and this does not indeed rule out caring for material acquisition" (Lundin 1867:47, 374).[5]

In a sense, Lundin in his flaneur alter ego transformed the causerie and feuilleton genres into a kind of popular science journalism directed to a bourgeois public opening up for a bright modern future. At the same time, it was closing down other imaginative possibilities (Goode & Godhe 2017; Godhe & Goode 2018) not belonging to an emerging liberal capitalism with its pros and cons. Modernity was wishful thinking for Lundin. As Kjellén (1995, 172) points out, when Lundin returned from his stay in France in 1866, he found that Stockholm could not compare to Paris. Despite this, it is a swirling, turbulent, and modern Stockholm that greets the readers of Lundin's early causeries. It was urban life in its most idealised form that represented the good life, a good life advanced by the fruits of modern technology in the form of better communications and public transportations. With the help of technology and science, the modern man would or must appear, freeing himself from the burden of tradition, narrowmindedness, philistinism, and bigotry (cf. Lundin 1867:13, 103). And this made its imprints in the language used by the flaneur writers and other fiction writers (cf. Ekström 1994, 78).

It is the great modern city Stockholm with its freethinkers set against the conservative and underdeveloped countryside. Lundin occasionally evoked a sense of modernity close to Marshall Berman's classic characterisation of modernity as a state of mind grounded in material experiences:

> To be modern is to find ourselves in an environment that promises us adventure, power, joy, growth, transformation of ourselves and the world – and, at the same time, threatens to destroy everything we have, everything we know, everything we are.
>
> *(Berman 1982/1983, 15)*

In an article from 1872, Lundin described the street life of Stockholm with an "effervescent lust for life," on one hand, and as full of crimes, misery, and poverty, on the other hand, even if we also should see "science and art in its full bloom, present day ideas and future prognosis of the most beautiful kind, a diligence and ambition to free itself from the old and worthless to achieve the new and capable" (Lundin 1872:4, 27).[6]

This ambiguity was even more emphasised in Lundin's science-fiction novel *Oxygen och Aromasia*, where he described the futurescape of Stockholm with its advantages and pathologies. The novel is not a utopian representation of the future, as Anna Westerståhl Stenport points out (106): "Neither does it offer a straightforward denunciation of the capitalist practices of Lundin's Sweden."

Oxygen och Aromasia

Science fiction published in Sweden during the nineteenth century prior to Lundin's *Oxygen och Aromasia* was with few exceptions represented by translations of some of Jules Verne and Camille Flammarion's novels (see e.g. Godhe 2021).[7] Lundin's novel *Oxygen och Aromasia* (1878) has been counted as the first of its kind written by a Swedish writer (Nyblom 2001).

The plot is centred around three characters: Aromasia Doftman-Ozodes, Oxygen Warm-Blasius and the poet Apollonides. Aromasia's career is that of a concert pianist, and she also has a PhD in finance operation science ("finansoperationslära"). However, she is not an ordinary pianist since she plays a scent klavier ("ododion") and composes olfactory symphonies. Ordinary music is almost extinct since Wagner and his disciple's bombastic music have destroyed people's eardrums. In the beginning of the novel, Aromasia decides to run for parliament in Gothenburg, the new capital city of Scandinavia. Oxygen Warm-Blasius represents the new: he is an industrial weather manufacturer, which is a highly paid occupation in the year

2378. The third character, Apollonides, represents the past. In the nineteenth century, the poet would have been "an intolerable realist, but five hundred years later, he was regarded not only as an excessive idealist but also as an eager romanticist."[8] Apollonides yearns wistfully to the poetic age of steam power, and his opinions about men's and women's place in society are outdated (Lundin 1878, 6–14, 18–19, 26).

Apollonides is in love with Aromasia, but she and Oxygen are espoused. When Aromasia plays an old-fashioned piece titled "the Seasons" ("Årstiderna") during a concert, Oxygen suspects that she is under the influence of Apollonides. He decides to work against Aromasia's candidacy to the parliament since he "wants to fight against each and one belonging to the reversion pack" (Lundin 1878, 42).[9] Aromasia is indeed under the influence of Apollonides. She starts to hesitate in her modern perception à la 2378 of women's place and role in society and withdraws her candidature to the parliament. When Oxygen tries to win her heart back, he and the poet become bitter rivals. The plot revolves around this eternal triangle (Lundin 1878, 10–11, 42–43, 101 et passim).

When Apollonides dies in an accident, this symbolises a return to the way things were. Aromasia returns to her modern values and into politics. Oxygen fails to win her love back despite using a "will enforcer" ("viljetvingare"), and he is miserable when he realises that he cannot win her heart back even with the help of science. He escapes to a tunnel construction site where he has become chief engineer. The novel ends shortly after Oxygen regains his self-esteem (Lundin 1878, 218–243).

In *Oxygen och Aromasia*, people are living in large cities and the technology described is often communication and transportation technologies, as per usual in Lundin's writings. The most common public transport is air-bicycles. The sidewalks are paved with glass, and there are carriages and wagons propelled by "the force that has replaced electricity" (Lundin 1878, 3).[10] Aromasia lives in a 15-floor-house, and there are lots of galleries. The Swedish language has been replaced by a form of Scandinavian (Lundin 1878, 1–3).

Due to rapid scientific and technological progress, the weather as well as social contacts can be affected and manipulated. There is a fully developed public sphere, and the difference between employers and employees is almost dissolved. Every citizen owns stock; for example, Oxygen has shares in the weather company he is working for, a production-association. Ordinary wages do not exist anymore, but the co-workers have a share in the profits of the companies. After concerts, the audience gives Aromasia shares and stock obligations instead of flowers. Poverty is more or less extinct.

Social life and the political economy are imbued by technology and science. Most people have their meals in restaurants. Those who are in a hurry can be served universal-craft-extract-pills. The food is made by machines in laboratory-like kitchens run by engineers and chemists. In her spare time, Aromasia creates proto plasma, "the lowest organic form," a very common social pastime in the citizen's leisure time (Lundin 1878, 14–15, 20–25).[11]

In the evening assemblies, the equivalent of the bourgeois saloon in the nineteenth century, people are spending time with arithmetic games, mathematical needlecraft, reading, and short lectures. Another popular pastime is reading the *Last Hour News* (*Senaste Timmens Nyheter*), a paper changing its name to *News of the Next Week* (*Nästa Veckas Nyheter*) in competition with the newspaper *Tomorrow's News* (*Morgondagens Nyheter*) (Lundin 1878, 39–40, 43–47, 60–61, 187–188).

Technological development is more ambiguously described in *Oxygen och Aromasia* in comparison with Lundin's other writings. Democratisation thanks to technology is one of the good things. Every citizen can take part in news from all over the world and have access to parliament and people's assembly meetings. Voting procedures have been simplified, and a sort of tele-democracy has been implemented. Voting machines are installed in the parliament, and during election time, the citizens send their votes through a telephone-phonograph, which means that they can vote from home if they like. It is every citizen's, that is, every man and *woman* that has turned 20 years old, duty to vote; otherwise, they are charged with high fines (Lundin 1878, 10, 130, 136). So, this is also a future where suffragettes are not needed. As Anna Westerståhl Stenport (2004, 105) points out, Lundin's "views on gender equality are radical for a period that understood middle-class life stratified strictly according to gender" (cf. Ljungquist 2001). In this future, traditional ways of living are shut down as an imaginative possibility, while at the same time gender equality is opened up as a possible future thanks to a fully developed modernity (cf. Goode & Godhe 2017).

But despite gender equality and material prosperity, people in the year 2378 have not changed for the better from a spiritual and moral standpoint. In the evening assemblies, people are gossiping; in public spaces, people are doing the same things they have always been occupied with: discussing politics, discussing their neighbour's affairs, gossiping, et cetera: "The human race is moving forward in every way, but the human mind and the human heart are still the same." Envy, hate, and retaliation have not disappeared (Lundin 1878, 48, 72, 82–86).[12]

Technology also has a destructive potential. In the novel, a decade-long ongoing war between China and North America is discussed, as well as an older war between Russia and China that went on for decades. Later in the novel, a message arrives saying that China's air fleet has been defeated by North America's air defence. But the doomsday mechanisms of science and technology also concern the potential to change people. The educational institutions described in the novel are almost like laboratories aimed at brainwashing children. From the age of three, the children are lobotomised so they can begin solving scientific and ontological problems at the age of five. The design of the teaching is decided one-third by the children, one-third by the school, and one-third by the parents (Lundin 1878, 194–207).

By and large, *Oxygen och Aromasia* expresses a rather radical, if somewhat ambiguous, view on technology and science. Already in the "Omnibus" causeries, a Faustian view on development could be discerned. We have no time for admiring this or that, Lundin wrote in one of the causeries; we must create our own wonders: "We shall travel to the North Pole to do great things for science, we shall find out the lowest forms of organic life, we shall build steamways over the seas and rush forward, not spending time with unnecessary reflections" (Lundin 1868:43, 343).[13]

In *Oxygen och Aromasia*, the industrial weather maker Oxygen expresses a similar but even more radical view on development, targeted against Apollonides. Oxygen holds no brief for the old times. In anger and jealousy, he tells the poet that he is already obsolete: "In my opinion, it is the duty of most of us to boldly move forward, even if it is over those [old-fashioned] people's dead bodies. They are vermin in society" (Lundin 1878, 190).[14]

In the later part of the novel, Oxygen is considering suicide after he has lost Aromasia's love. Eventually, he pulls himself together and returns to the tunnel construction site where he works as an engineer after he left his work as an industrial weather maker. When the tunnel starts to crack, he destroys the mountain, stopping the tunnel construction. The other engineers admit that he is superior to them and obey his instructions. The thoughts of suicide disappears after his victory over nature: "I am not an ancient human either!" (Lundin 1878, 237–240).[15]

Maybe the character Apollonides represented everything Lundin seemed to dislike in his time – a comparison to most of what Lundin expressed in his other writing indicates this. Apollonides is stuck in the old (read: 1878), and he is writing poems such as "The Last Steam Train" ("*Det sista lokomotivet*"). The poet symbolises political as well as technological conservatism. Even if he writes about novelties in Lundin's times, they are old and obsolete in the novel's fictional time. Apollonides represents the realism that Lundin in some of his other writings expressed dislike for, while Oxygen represents bold vision and enterprises. There were too many doubters (realists) for the progressive liberal Lundin, and Apollonides is one example of how Lundin portrayed pessimists (cf. Lundin 1875, 1–5; Godhe 2004). Obstacles are there to be overcome. In *Från Stockholms synkrets* (*From the View of Stockholm*), Lundin let some realists express their doubts about implementing tram traffic in Stockholm. Since Stockholm is full of hills and slopes, it is impossible. A few years later, tram traffic is implemented in Stockholm, and the hills and slopes are no longer a problem. From being doubtful about the possibility of tram traffic, people now say: "We have hills indeed, but they can be bypassed, reduced, levelled" (Lundin 1874, 150–154).[16]

When the poet dies in a dreadful way at a rocket launch, it is also a symbol for how the old times are replaced by a new era. A scientist studying the dead poet's brain notices that it was old-fashioned and ancient: "They are pretty rare these days, and science should be happy to acquire a specimen" (Lundin 1878, 218–220).[17]

But Oxygen is also an extreme, going too far in his Faustian view of development. When Aromasia plays a piece concerning how the social question is solved by developing perfect machines, the smell from her scent clavier causes the concert hall to explode. Maybe this was a signal from Lundin that technocracy is not the sole solution to all problems in his time. Technological and scientific development must also contribute to social and political reforms (cf. Lundgren 1993). Perhaps Lundin also signalled that we must have a balance between emotions and science as Andreas Nyblom (2001) points out.

Oxygen's Faustian view on development is relaxed by the end of the novel. When he becomes the main protagonist in the narrative, Lundin certainly interpreted changes in his times, and he returned in his later writings to the engineers' role for progress (e.g. Lundin, *Nya Stockholm*, 118–121). At the time when the novel was written, the engineer enters the social, economic, and political scene and has a key role in ever more industrial contexts (Eriksson 1978). For example, in an essay on the engineer Johan Erik Cederblom (1844–1913), Nils Runeby points out that Cederblom saw the engineer's duty as being a negotiator between the capital and the worker. The engineer should lead work in such a way that the workers rise economically, ethically, and morally but at the same make the capital fruitful. Thereby the different social classes would join in striving for the common good, according to Cederblom (Runeby 1987).

In Claës Lundin's writings, the engineer is ascribed a similar function, as transcending class struggles and as creating spiritual and material progress. The engineer becomes an exponent for the progressive middle class Lundin aimed at. The public appeal in *Oxygen och Aromasia* is also reinforced by depicting a future world where every citizen in principle belongs to the middle-class and where the right to vote has been expanded. In this sense, Lundin staged a future congenial with the rising bourgeoisie's conception of the good life, closing down other imaginative counter-hegemonic ways of perceiving the future, despite the cracks in the novel (cf. Goode & Godhe 2017).

Lundin's Writings Post *Oxygen och Aromasia*: The New Era and Its Pathologies

If Lundin orchestrated modernity in his causeries and *Oxygen och Aromasia*, the tone changed somewhat in his later Stockholm tableaux. I will give a few examples here (for further exploration of Lundin's Stockholm tableaux, see Stenport 2004; Godhe 2004). In *Nya Stockholm (New Stockholm*, 1890), Lundin still embraces a progressive and liberal middle-class way of life, where the citizens also have compassion with the less fortunate in society. Apart from some spots still in need of hygienical improvement, Stockholm is represented as a nice and modern place to live in, not least due to technological development.

But even if Lundin's enthusiasm for changes and technological development is further accentuated in his depictions of Stockholm in the 1890s and onwards, there are also some undesired effects brought by development. The modern city brings new disorders and diseases, as Lundin writes in *Nya Stockholm* (131), and exercise is needed: "Neurosis, anaemia, fatigue and similar diseases must be countered."[18] During the latter part of the nineteenth century, it became fashionable to look upon the modern human as nervous and worried, and modern times was according to these ideas marked by nervousness and hence the normal modern condition was neurotic (see, e.g., Björck 1946, 50; Gustafsson 1996, 58–67).

There were also material problems such as scarcity of fresh air and water, and the solution according to Lundin (1896, 5–6) was improved transportation, enabling the citizens to go to places where they could rest and have a bath as well as clean air. The modern hectic life has its pathologies, but they could be solved by technologies such as the medical-mechanical institutes where officials, wholesale distributors, clerks, scientists, writers, and other people in need of exercise could go (Lundin 145–146). In this sense, technology is a necessity not only to further support societal development but also to counteract the unbalances and pathologies caused by it. After all, technology was closely related to the liberal progressive good life, changing our conceptions of time and space, and supporting the development of liberal democracy. In these times, humanity became free in an era not "so stern" but "undoubtedly more democratic" (Lundin 1867:26, 206).[19]

The development of communication and transportation technologies was associated with bourgeoisie cultural development where circulation, communication and exchange meant progress, enlightenment and new conceptions of time and space, as Runeby remarks: "Railways, steamships and the telegraph were constantly stressed as representing industrial progress" (Runeby 1987, 307. Cf. Schivelbusch 1986; Stenport 2004).

Conclusion

Ny Illustrerad Tidning, Oxygen och Aromasia, and Lundin's books on Stockholm had with certainty a stratified public, even if "he formulated and reflected the concerns of an expanding, comfortable, and educated bourgeoisie with cosmopolitan pretensions" (Stenport 2004, 88. Cf. Edoff 2016).

In the contemporary world of Claës Lundin, science and technology were put on display and interacting with the public in a very wide range of different media. In visual cultures, museums and exhibitions, public lectures and newspapers and magazines, and many other arenas and media, technological and scientific development were represented and interpreted. Lundin orchestrated modernity and placed science and technology on a market modelled after a liberal and progressive middle-class public. He was not alone in doing this. As Stenport points out (2004, 2), "arts and literature of the time brought forth a generation obsessed with the representation, production, and creation of Stockholm as a modern metropolis, most often in relation to Paris" (cf. Edoff 2016).

For Lundin, however, this was also a kind of a reform liberalism project. By depicting how science and technology would transform urban space and interpersonal relations, Lundin confirmed the self-image of the new upcoming hegemonic elite in nineteenth-century Sweden (cf. Ekström 1994, 204–232). He also prepared the bourgeoisie (and maybe also the common public) for how the good life could look like in a world with liberal democracy – as well as some of the pathologies the modern world would bring, especially in his articles and books post-*Oxygen och Aromasia,* as well as the novel itself. It was a future where the old world must give way to the new modern democratic society. In a sense, this was a utopia where the upper classes would fade away and the lower classes would rise from poverty and ignorance to be full members of the bourgeoisie through reforms, education, and the abolishment of old customs and traditions. He guided his intended public for the shape of things to come – if the right path was taken. This is a future where a new human is created – quick, street smart, on the move, dashing into the future – and there is no place for nostalgia or alternative visions of the future. It was an ideal for living, excluding any futures except those in favour of liberal capitalism.

Oxygen and Aromasia is an ambiguous novel. It is full of irony and criticism of bourgeois life, and for a reader today, much of the context is hidden in the depths of history. I have tried to reconstruct some of the context here as well as illustrate how the genres Lundin used work. Nonetheless, despite some criticism of laissez faire capitalism, it was endorsed. The flaneur and the engineer, as I interpret it, were ideals for Lundin (or his alter egos in the different genres he used). At the same time, Lundin was radical in his favour of gender equality, as illustrated by the character Aromasia. From a critical future studies perspective, Lundin staged and opened up for a future that is in many ways here already (i.e. if you live in the gentrified parts of the big cities and if you are well educated middle class with a high salary) – an ideal of living closing down other imaginative possibilities. The novel in some sense foresighted some of the pathologies that plague our times – poverty, a mass media apparatus spreading the news so fast that we in many ways can talk of the news of next week, et cetera. One cannot help thinking about some lines in the seminal novel *Brideshead Revisited*, when the main character Charles Ryder arrives in New York: "In that city there is neurosis in the air which the inhabitants mistake for energy" (Waugh 1945, 231). But if Evelyn Waugh's main protagonists, with some exception, loathed modernity and modern capitalism, there was no longing for a past in Lundin's writings. If there was neurosis in the air, technology and modern communication would help to solve these pathologies and transform it to energy.

But the modernity that Lundin had described up to the 1890s was yet to come, of course. In this sense, his writings gained a speculative dimension: Stockholm and Sweden as he would like it to be. Later in his life, he confessed that he had perceived Stockholm (and Sweden) as a backwater, and in the light of this, it is obvious that he was staging modernity in his earlier writings. In *Tidsbilder* (1895), he depicted a Stockholm in 1866 that differed very much from the Omnibus causeries and some of his other writings: it was a city where even the most exclusive streets were laid with cobblestone. The sewage was deficient, and the fire department was in a very bad shape. The law enforcement system was not good enough, and the street sanitation left a lot to be desired. There was not enough health care, and still there were four estates (the nobility, the priest, the burghers, the farmers), despite the implementation of the new representational reform in 1866: "The new era was on the rise, but we hardly believed in her"[20] (Lundin 1895, 182).

Acknowledgements

I want to thank Bruno Varenhorst Godhe, Jyrki Korpua, Magnus Rodell, and Marta Tveit for valuable comments on the text.

Notes

1 "mondäna sällskaps-och kulturliv med urbanitet och i en konverserande fransk ton."
2 "som hastigast beröra vetenskapen, låta industrien passera revy, alldeles icke förakta handel och sjöfart, men helst stanna vid konsten."
3 "Låtom oss göra oss så smala som möjligt – det är dagens lösen, smärta, smidiga, nästan tunna, en smula genomskinliga skadar icke. Det är tvärtom modernt."
4 "Vi lefva icke mera idag, utan i morgon."
5 "och detta behöfver sannerligen icke utesluta omsorgen för det materiella förvärfvet."
6 "brusande lefnadslustig"; "se vetenskap och konst i full blomning, nutidsidéer och framtidsutsigter af vackraste slag, en äflan och sträfvan att befria sig från det gamla och odugliga för att vinna det nya och dugliga."
7 There were also a few short stories written in Swedish by Finnish-Swedish writers such as Gabriel Ishan Hartman's "En dröm" ("A Dream", published in 1803, when the area of (future) Finland was part of Sweden), Zacharias Topelius's "Simeon Levis Resa i Finland" ("Simeon Levis's Travels in Finland," 1860) or Alba Ödegård's (pseudonym for Rosalba Cederman) "I Zululandet efter

sjuhundratjugofem år" ("In the Zulu Land After Seven Hundred and Twenty-Five Years," 1880).

8 "en odräglig realist, men femhundra år senare ansågs han icke blott för en omått-tlig idealist, utan också för en ifrig romantiker."

9 "vill kämpa mot hvar och en som tillhör återgångsflocken."

10 "af den kraft som utträngt elektriciteten."

11 "den lägsta organiska bildning."

12 "Människoslägtet går fram åt i alt, men människosinnet och människohjertat äro likväl altid de samma."

13 "Vi skola fara till nordpolen för att uträtta stora saker för vetenskaper, vi skola taga reda på det organiska lifvets enklaste former, vi skola bygga ång-vägar öfver sjöarne och rusa framåt, utan att taga upp tiden med öfverflödiga reflexioner."

14 "jag håller det helt enkelt för flertalets pligt att oförskräckt gå fram åt, äfven om det vore öfver de där människornas döda kroppar. De äro skadedjur i samhället."

15 "Jag är väl icke någon forntidsmänniska häller!"

16 "Visst ha vi backar, men de kunna kringgås, minskas, utjämnas."

17 "Sådane äro ganska sällsynta nu för tiden, och vetenskapen bör vara glad att komma öfver ett exemplar."

18 "Nevrosen, bleksoten, lefnadströttheten och öfriga sådana åkommor måste motarbetas."

19 "så sträng" utan "onekligen mycket mer demokratisk."

20 "Den nya tiden grydde, men vi trodde knappt på henne."

References

Beckman, Jenny. 1999. *Naturens palats: Nybyggnad, vetenskap och utställning vid Naturhistoriska riksmuseet 1866–1925*. Stockholm: Atlantis.

Berman, Marshall. 1983. *All That is Solid Melts into Air: The Experience of Modernity*. London & New York: Verso.

Björck, Staffan. 1946. *Heidenstam och sekelskiftets Sverige: Studier i hans nationella och sociala författarskap*. Stockholm: Bokförlaget Natur och Kultur.

Edoff, Erik. 2016. *Storstadens dagbok: Boulevardpressen och mediesystemet i det sena 1800-talets Stockholm*. Lund: Mediehistoriskt arkiv.

Ekström, Anders. 1994. *Den utställda världen: Stockholmsutställningen 1897 och 1800-talets världsutställningar*. Stockholm: Nordiska Museets förlag.

Ekström, Anders. 1999. "Förväntningshorisonter, ca 1870-1920." In *Vetenskapsbärarna: Naturvetenskapen i det svenska samhället, 1880–1950*, ed. Sven Widmalm, 23–36. Hedemora: Gidlunds Förlag.

Eriksson, Gunnar. 1978. *Kartläggarna: Naturvetenskapens tillväxt och tillämpningar i det industriella genombrottets Sverige 1870–1914*. Umeå: Acta Universitatis Umensis.

Godhe, Michael. 2004. "Att iscensätta det moderna: Stockholmsskildraren Claës Lundin som vetenskapsjournalist." In *Den mediala vetenskapen*, ed. Anders Ekström, 165–187. Hedemora: Nya Doxa.

Godhe, Michael. 2021. "Att lära sig framtidsberedskap: Om science fiction, didaktik och pedagogik." In *Moderna pedagogiska utopier*, eds. Anders Burman, Joakim Landahl & Daniel Lövheim, 143–161. Huddinge: Södertörn högskola.

Godhe, Michael & Luke Goode. 2018. "Critical Future Studies – A Thematic Introduction." *Culture Unbound: Journal of Current Cultural Research* 10 (2): 151–162.

Goode, Luke & Michael Godhe. 2017. "Beyond Capitalist Realism – Why We Need Critical Future Studies." *Culture Unbound: Journal of Current Cultural Research* 9 (1): 108–129.

Gustafsson, Torbjörn. 1996. *Själens biologi: Medicinen, kulturen och naturens ordning 1850–1920.* Stockholm/Stehag: Symposion.

Hartman, Gabriel Israel. 1803. "En dröm", *Åbo Tidning*, 1803:27, 06.04.1803 *Åbo Tidning* no 27 - Digitala samlingar - Nationalbiblioteket (kansalliskirjasto.fi).

Johannesson, Eric. 1970. *Ny Illustrerad Tidning 1865–1871: En press- och litteraturhistorisk studie.* Uppsala: Avdelningen för litteratursociologi vid Litteraturvetenskapliga institutionen.

Johannesson, Eric. 1980. *Den läsande familjen: Familjetidskriften i Sverige 1850– 1880.* Stockholm: Nordiska Museets förlag.

Johannesson, Eric. 1984. "Lundin, Claës Johan." *Svenskt biografiskt lexikon*, Band 24. Stockholm: Svenskt biografiskt lexikon.

Kärnfelt, Johan. 2000. *Mellan nytta och nöje: Ett bidrag till populärvetenskapens historia i Sverige.* Stockholm/Stehag: Symposion.

Kjellén, Alf. 1985. *Flanören och hans storstadsvärld: Synpunkter på ett litterärt motiv.* Stockholm: Almqvist & Wiksell International.

Ljungquist, Sarah. 2001. *Den litterära utopin och dystopin i Sverige 1734–1940.* Hedemora: Gidlunds Förlag.

Lundgren, Frans. 1993. *Oxygen och Aromasia: En radikal-oscariansk utopi*, unpublished seminar paper. Uppsala: Institutionen för idé- och lärdomshistoria.

Lundin, Claes. 1866–1870. "Omnibus", *Ny Illustrerad Tidning*, 1866:16; 1866:48; 1867:13; 1867:37; 1867:47; 1868:43; 1869:1, 7; 1869:8; 1869:13; 1869:8, 1869:17; 1870:21.

Lundin, Claës. 1872. "Stockholm från en högre synpunkt", *Ny Illustrerad Tidning*, 1872:4.

Lundin, Claës. 1878. *Oxygen och Aromasia: Bilder från år 2378.* Stockholm: Jos. Seligmann & C:is Förlag.

Lundin, Claës. 1880. *Från Stockholms synkrets: Spridda intryck.* Stockholm: Marcus.

Lundin, Claës. 1890. *Nya Stockholm.* Stockholm: Hugo Gebers Förlag.

Lundin, Claës. 1895. *Tidsbilder: Ur Stockholmslifvet.* Stockholm: J. Beckmans Förlag.

Nyblom, Andreas. 2001. "Samtiden fångades i litteraturen om framtiden." *Svenska Dagbladet*, 22.9 2001.

Ödegård, Alba (pseudonym for Rosalba Cederman). 1880. "I Zululandet efter sjuhundratjugofem år", *Åbo Underrättelser.*

Runeby, Nils. 1987. "Större fart. Framåt: Kring en ingenjörs föreställningsvärld." *I teknikens backspegel: Antologi i teknikhistoria*, ed. Bosse Sundin, 302–331. Stockholm: Carlssons.

Schivelbusch, Wolfgang. 1986. *The Railway Journey: The Industrialization of Time and Space in the 19th Century.* 1977; Berkeley: University of California Press.

Sylwan, Otto. 1919. *Oscar Patrick Sturzen-Becker: Hans levnad och författarskap.* Stockholm: Bonnier.

Stenport, Anna Westerståhl. 2004. *Making Space: Stockholm, Paris and the Urban Prose of Strindberg and His Contemporaries.* Berkeley: University of California.

Topelius, Zacharias. 1860. "Simeon Levis resa till Finland." *Helsingfors Tidningar*, 24 April 1860.

Waugh, Evelyn. 1945. *Brideshead Revisited: The Sacred and Profane Memories of Captain Charles Ryder.* Boston: Little, Brown and Company.

4

THE FIGURE IN THE MAGIC CARPET

Structuralism of Literary Fantastic on the Map of Northern Philology

Pekka Kuusisto

The question whether the writer Hugh Vereker has or has not hidden some secret figure in his work is one that the characters of "The Figure in the Carpet" share in its kind with a number of other Henry James's narrative casts. In its central motif of hidden figure, however, this story stands out for its metafictional aspects that highlight the structures of ambiguity of James's turn of the twentieth-century fiction more in general.[1] Thus, the narrator in his obsessive quest for truth on Vereker's figure is an aspiring literary critic in London, who with his and his colleagues' actions creates, as it were, a pattern of reading that eventually adapts into the critical history of not only this story particularly but even more forcefully perhaps of the most famous of James's ambiguous fictions, *The Turn of the Screw*, that was published two years later in 1898. Indeed, more than any of James's other works, the story of Bly created a critical field intensely divided upon the main lines of reading of its central enigma of interpretation – the question whether the ghosts the young governess sees are real or whether they are merely projections of her disturbed mind.[2] When read through the critical history of its famous follower story, however, in its narrative rhetoric, already "The Figure in the Carpet" introduces some of the basic images and motifs of ambiguity that surface decades later in the criticism of *The Turn of the Screw*. When the latter narrative finally in the high days of structuralism is taken for a paradigm of the literary fantastic by Tzvetan Todorov, his study creates a line of criticism that builds in James's house of fiction at Bly, an expansive system of generic forms of speculative fiction. Whereas James draws his famous image in illustration of the individual vision of each writer in residence out on the

DOI: 10.4324/9781003561101-7

world through various windows of the building, a floor plan shows better the genrefication of speculative fiction in structuralist poetics.[3]

Indeed, when put in focus of narrative ambiguity, Vereker's "figure in the carpet" opens James's image on to a more abstract level of many adjacent rooms and floors of a house of genres and critical schools. This house involves not only a synchronic plan but also a diachronic structure of historic floors, so to speak, of sorted (proto-)structuralists, formalists, and philologists both before and after Todorov, with some influential residents assigned their badged lodgings. Todorov's attack and subsequent retracing of words on Northrop Frye is a case in point. There is Vladimir Propp, too, having his issue with the Finnish school of folklorists, and many more, in indication that structural poetics derives from philology as "the forgotten origins of the modern humanities," as James Turner (2014) describes the field.

Tolkien is surely somewhere there as well. Obviously, he is an honorary member in the more recent sections of genre fantasy. But he seems to feel more at home on level of the ground stones such that he found from his beloved *Beowulf*.[4] The floor he is said to detest is the one of modern literary criticism, and yet his reading of *Beowulf*'s "structure" is still appreciated today, hinting that his thinking is not altogether at odds with structural linguistics at least, given his bearings in comparative philology, as it was for Ferdinand de Saussure.[5]

But Tolkien's mind is occupied more with the house of genres' location on the European linguistic map he divides between the lands of the southern and the northern myth. He prefers north-western and Baltic Sea traditions, but includes eventually the entire continent into his life-long work of mapping it onto what he calls the history of the Middle-earth. Prominent as the old English, Gothic, Scandinavian, and Finnish traditions are, this history concludes in "re-establishment of an effective Holy Roman Empire with its seat in Rome than anything that would be devised by a 'Nordic'" in its contemporary political associations.[6] Tolkien's map is, then, a fictional construction of a history of northern spirit with southern illumination which, while looked at from its western shores to where the enemies "mostly come" from the east, is, however, a complex one.[7] On the level of its philological scholarship, this map should come with markings not only on Oxford but on Saussure's Geneva, Herder's Königsberg, and Propps's St. Petersburg too, as sites where the tension of the historical versus structural schools is felt. Finally, if Beowulf is a "fusion-point of imagination"[8] of the Christian and pagan worlds, then Tolkien's Middle-earth has that function for schools for literary criticism, opened out in what follows through the structuralist poetics of the fantastic narrative. Every evil does not originate from the east for Tolkien either. Even if the modern literary criticism appears to do over the decades of formalisms and structuralisms, so does philology, much entwined therein, with its roots spreading all over the map of historical

Europe. Germanic philology and, following it, the east-central European literary criticism travel both westward for Tolkien. Whether or not the time of literary criticism is passing as Galin Tihanov has recently argued and Tolkien in his day maybe wished, announcements of a reinvigoration of philology, for one, have now been heard as well, indicating that the long defeat or victory, which way you may look at it, is not up just yet.[9]

A paradox in Tolkien's legacy in the closing of the circle of twentieth-century literature back to myth in his wake that Frye works up may nevertheless be that it has proceeded more along the structuralist, generic vein rather than in Tolkien's philology – albeit it is a philology with an evident structuralist sensibility.[10] No other writer of fantasy, science fiction, or horror since Tolkien has worked the way he does – by starting from a set of invented languages with their structures, history, and cultures and building the characters that speak (or are presented to) these languages and their stories on such a linguistic ground. His work, Tolkien emphasises, "is fundamentally linguistic in inspiration" (1995, 219). The "invention of languages," therefore, "is the foundation. The 'stories' were made rather to provide a world for the languages than the reverse" (219). He writes accordingly: "I began the construction of languages in early boyhood: I am primarily a scientific philologist. My interests were, and remain, largely scientific" (345). The tension of history and structure remains, then, unresolved in the history of the Middle-earth, too.

Figures and Modalities of Narrative Ambiguity in James

The carpet spreading on the floors of James's early modernist house of fiction shows a faint hue of colours and forms of the literary fantastic already in Hugh Vereker's room. At the centre of the carpet here is a figure ambiguous and evocative in many respects of its supposed pattern. Thus, in his moments of disillusion on the truth of Vereker's "general intention," the narrator feels the writer's figure is "hollow" (291) and ultimately "nothing" (307), if not "a bad joke" and "a monstrous *pose*" (286).[11] Yet in opposite moments of rapture, George Corvick's fiancée-to-be Gwendolen Erme quotes Corvick's two-word telegram from Bombay – "Eureka. Immense (296) – about Corvick having finally cracked Vereker's code supposedly – whereupon her swift cable in reply – "Angel, write" (298) – sets a course into nuptials more than mundane, of a promise of revelation into "knowledge" of "all gold and gems" that was "in all time, in all tongues, one of the most wonderful flowers of art" (300).

Such opposites of evaluation are appropriated from the narrator's shifting standpoint that records and sets the course of the plot to locate Vereker's hidden figure for James's story. Passing from one Vereker's student to the next, this obsessive undertaking soon replicates "the very string" that "my pearls are strung on" (289) in Vereker's image for his work's secret. While the source of the enterprise is initially Vereker himself, who puts the chain of interpretations in motion, through the first-person narrator, the task soon passes on to Corvick and Erme, and finally to latter's second husband, Drayton Deane.

Thus, having first been hired to step in to review Vereker's newest title by Corvick as Corvick himself "should have spoken of him" – to say what Corvick wants him to say about Vereker, of a "rare pleasure" and a sense of "something or the other" (274–275) – the narrator's review triggers Vereker in turn to confide a series of teasing suggestions of that "loveliest thing in the world" (285) that, he says, lies undetected in his work. The dynamic of the interpretive quest changes, however, along the narrator's account of it. The more he personally grows disillusioned on the prospect of ever finding Vereker's figure and eventually even of its reality, the more the reality of the vision is illuminated in Corvick's and Erme's mind, up until the narrator sees "the fury" of his "unappeased desire" to sink into Drayton Deane in promise of the narrator's eventual "consolation" and "revenge" of his futile attempts (315).

The contours of Vereker's figure are thus sounded from the narrator's perspective that moves from one contact to another as various characters get attached to its drawing. The result is an expansive pattern of images and forms of speech that seek to appropriate what is at issue. The heart of the figure opens out into a thread of Vereker's own firsthand auto-critical images that substitute one another in replication of the "string of pearls" at the head of it, highlighting perhaps the profoundly figurative sense of his initiative in the first place. As Vereker's eventual tease for the narrator to "give it up" suggests, his guiding lights are those of an artistic play – from a "little trick" and "exquisite scheme" (282) to "a bird in a cage, a bait on a hook, a piece of cheese in a mouse-trap" (283–284) and such – which leave his string of images unlocked and open for further readings that start to multiply into that "complex figure in a Persian carpet" (289) that is ultimately James's.

Whereas Vereker appropriates his secret in images that shift from the vehicle of his "every page and line and letter" (283) to their highest tenors of "the organ of life" (284), next in line of his readers, the narrator changes the approach from tropes to forms of speech. What the narrator in turn proposes is yet another figure in the carpet, sewn now in terms that seek to capture its focal point within an expansive modal system of speech. Is it "some idea about life, some sort of philosophy" or "a kind of esoteric message?" he asks, only to hear in reply that "it can't be described in cheap journalese" (283). But if not in esoterism or journalese, then, should its terms be sought rather in between, from literary criticism, as "something in the style or something in thought," "form," or "feeling" (284)?

Vereker refusing it, the challenge of interpretation is taken over next from the disillusioned narrator by Corvick and Erme, a young literary couple whose courtship takes James into tones of a latter-day marriage of philology and mercury of sorts. My reference to the Roman philosopher Martianus Capella's (1977) fifth-century planetary allegory of the seven liberal arts holds apparently more with the couple's expertise in literatures and languages – "quite incredibly literary – quite fantastically!" (293) as they are. But beyond the spheres of philological humanities, also those of what Capella's ancient allegorical tradition understands as a learned ascent to mathematics and metaphysics may reflect in their interpretive quest into "knowledge" (311 and elsewhere) up to certain esoteric realm that Vereker both hints at and plays down. Indeed, James's figuration of this gnoseological romance echoes the traditional pattern of ascent from the demonic to the divine – beginning from the "little demons of sublety" (283) of Vereker's description of literary critics and Erme's novel "Deep Down," and going up to the cable to her "angel" to communicate more of his revelation of Vereker's "one descent from the clouds" (315).

Reading "The Figure in the Carpet" through the famous critical history of *The Turn of the Screw*, we realise that James is putting in place an outline of modal ambiguity of his subsequent story already here. More precisely, at issue is an opening of a speculative space of interpretation of the central enigma into a spectrum of opposing modalities of appropriation of realism, on the one hand, and the supernatural mode, on the other hand. Published in the literary journal "*The Middle*", the narrator's article on Vereker's novel triggers a series of interpretations that mostly fall on one side or the other of a certain literary-aesthetical center of phrasing of the enigma. Thus, on the factual side of the literary speak of "style" and "form" (284), Vereker's figure takes the values of "journalese" of an everyday, mundane sense. But these tones soon give way to revelatory glimpses of a "temple of Vishnu" (297) and other sorted esoterica of Indo-European philology that add their colours on the Persian carpet. James has also left a key for readers curious of echoes of a gnostic epic in his storyline. Erme's Virgilian reference – "Vera incessu patuit dea," "in her step she was revealed a very goddess" (296)[12] – evokes a high poetic vision, if only to inflect its classical code into late nineteenth-century London literary circle intrigue.

Over its traditional vertical dimension and markers of "philosophy" (284), the Verekerian curriculum is, however, mainly built of literary notions of "anecdote" and "panegyric," and images of what still in James's day are understood as philological. The plot of finding Vereker's figure assumes thus also the mode of a philological romance in the sense of what "'love of learning" still carries with it in James's day as a comprehensive science of humanities.[13] Whereas Miss Erme stays home with her literature, Corvick's journey to India and Italian Rapallo opens out a world map that brings in items from the related lexicons of antiquarianism, archaeology, and comparative religion of oriental temples into reading of the sought-out figure.

At the centre of the passionate enterprise, Vereker the writer, before abruptly passing away like Corvick soon after, is the one whose cool temper is the most in tune, perhaps with the sign of times in arts and sciences. Whereas Corvick follows his intuition like "maniacs who embrace some bedlamitical theory of the cryptic character of Shakespeare" (291), Vereker's focus instead is fixed on "the order, the form, the texture" (282) of his work – or, in a word, on its structure. As with Saussure's image of the system of language as a game of chess (Saussure 1983, 87–88), Corvick is on track of Vereker's secret like "a chessplayer bent with a silent scowl, all the lamplit winter, over his board and his moves," behind him Erme, who "rested on his shoulder and hung upon" (292) those moves. While for these people, literature is "a game of skill" (292) overall, in Vereker's case, "the stake on the table was of different substance, and our roulette was the revolving mind, but we sat round the green board as intently as the grim gamblers at Monte Carlo" (296). Indeed, the scientific mind of the turn of the twentieth century finds structures in many instances – not only in language but also in the nature. James's ideas and images are on the wavelength of such modern notions. Thus, his narrative "gaps" that feed the readers' imagination with their "divine light cast on holy little virtualities" of the storyline, set by the writer with a "sacred primaeval joy,"[14] are inviting also as an articulation of the fabric of physical reality discussed in the natural sciences at the time.[15]

The "figure" that lures James's readers' imagination soon even more is the ghost of Peter Quint, the dead valet, seen standing on top of the Bly manor tower by the first-person narrator of *The Turn of the Screw*, the young governess (15).[16] Appropriately for a ghost story, James's design is now built more expressly on patterns of literary imagination. James analyses his working method in following "my young woman engaged in her labyrinth" as seeking a form between two traditions of the fairytale, the compact anecdote of "Cinderella" and "Blue-beard," on one hand, and the more exuberant "Arabian Nights," on the other. He has felt both embarrassed and delighted on those "more or less fantastic figures" (128) proposed in reactions on "this little firm fantasy – which I seem to see draw behind it today a train of associations – so numerous that I can but pick among them for reference" (126). James's opposition of the fairy tale classes – "the short and sharp and single" (124–125) Grimm's stories and "the long and the loose, the various, the endless" course of the "Arabian Nights" – serves for his formal purposes of putting his heroine into fictional labyrinth, but its cultural orientalism unravels further when placed on the philological map of folk tales that shows the universality of "Cinderella's" motifs, for instance.[17]

The first ten years proved but a beginning for one of the most intense of critical histories in modern literature. The first reviewers join the governess and tend to play down the narrative ambiguity in favour of Christian super-naturalism. They thus in many ways repeat the acts of interpretation under-taken first by James's characters. A reaction from the side of psychoanalytical criticism to such initial readings both reflects the course of the twentieth-century intellectual history and reveals the dynamic James designed for his tale, as naturalism was seeking to overtake supernaturalism, and vice versa, at times in this history of critical debate.

Remarkably, James repeats Vereker's gesture in his note on *The Turn of the Screw* as "a piece of ingenuity pure and simple, of cold artistic calcula-tion, an amusette to catch those not easily caught" (125),[18] acknowledging having put in motion as a writer a passionate quest to locate the truth on the figure of this tale, too.

For this aim, James conceives a poetic of chosen images that rehearses and renews his previous experiments in "The Figure in the Carpet." The ver-tical of the story is now set by a traditional Christian figuration of heavenly innocence of the children Flora and Miles, as against the depraved evil of the ghosts Quint and Miss Jessel. In a more pronounced manner than previ-ously, this central thematic axis makes also for a vertical of education and learning. The very image of the turning screw recalls the dialectic course of the hermeneutic spiral approaching its goal of wisdom and knowledge, whereas when seen from a reverse perspective, it illustrates the governess' duress in her ordeal in protecting her charges from damnation. Still, on days when ghosts are not confronted but are rather more successfully forgotten, the Bly's garden turns into a memory theatre, where the first steps into arts and sciences are taken in a playful manner. These are days when the chil-dren, who had

> shown me from the first a facility for everything, a general faculty which, taking a fresh start, achieved remarkable flights. They got their little tasks as if they loved them; they indulged, from the mere exuberance of the gift, in the most unimposed little miracles of memory. They not only popped out at me as tigers and as Romans, but as Shakespeareans, astronomers and navigators. (37)

Geography is taught in Bly, too, in a lesson conducted in the manner of a play in which "the lake was the Sea of Azof" (28).

Together with the labyrinth where James places the governess, these are traditional images and models of cultural knowledge reflected in philosophy and semiotics. They are taken up, for example, when Diderot's colleague D'Alembert conceives the design of the famous encyclopaedic dictionary of the Age of Reason. "The general system of the sciences and the arts is a sort of labyrinth," D'Alembert writes, "a tortuous road which the intellect enters without quite knowing what direction to take." For a better view, the philosopher should take "a vantage point, so to speak, high above this vast labyrinth, whence he can perceive the principal sciences and the arts simultaneously" (1963, 47). The result is an image of the tree of sciences as "a kind of world map which is to show the principal countries, their position and their mutual dependence, the road that leads directly from one to the other" (47–48). More recently, Umberto Eco (2014) has taken up D'Alembert's lead in conceiving a history of semiotic models of cultural knowledge with its successive orders. Starting with the bestiaries and histories of wonders of the classical and early medieval world that take cumulation of information for true knowledge at face value, the late medieval tree of knowledge with its more refined scholastic logic of the world, the world map of encyclopaedists of the eighteenth century with its novel sensibility of modern science, and finally the postmodern open network or Deleuzian rhizome, this is a history that reflects the growing challenge of processing the increasing cultural information and the crisis this induces for the orders of knowledge.

Still, such are but few in the immense wealth of images that supply the rhetoric of cultural knowledge in traditions of arts and literature. Eco's (1989, 87) notion of epistemological metaphor and Frye's (1957, 365) anagogic symbol are reminders that such a rhetoric is as often at work in shorter literary forms as it is in the novel or epic. With *The Turn of the Screw*, however, James wires up his trap from its more formal testing ground of "The Figure in the Carpet" into a full-fledged narrative of literary fantastic. While both are first-person stories, the changing narrative perspective turns the setting of literary imagination over. What in the first case is a quest story moving on a metafictional level around and out from Vereker the writer's work is in the second a quest closing into a fictional world placed within a layered narrative frame. This resetting results in tightening of the thematic field of the short story into an intensely drawn world of narrative modalities of the novella with its contrary lines of interpretation of the central narrative enigma. Whereas the search for Vereker's secret proceeds along more traditional philological tones, that of Bly has proven inviting for a structuralist approach.

James in Todorov's Poetics of the Fantastic

Tightened indeed as if by a turning screw, the closure of the setting with its opposing spiral threads of reading makes James's novella a famous interpretive hotbed. It appears as if James had set Bly's clockwork to reveal its machinery a bit only after some 70 years of scrutiny. To be sure, flashes of an unresolved ambiguity are seen in its glass covering earlier too, but only momentarily before fading away quickly. Not before Todorov's theory of the fantastic was such a narrative structure opened and explained.

The result of letting James's ghosts out of their confines and putting them under the cool eye of structuralism is, however, curious. For the "pure fantastic," Todorov's primary object is but a ghostly, vanishing line, too, drawn in the middle to demarcate a system of genres that runs from the uncanny on its left side to the marvellous on its right. It is a line conceived more for its dividing central position in the system (uncanny | fantastic-uncanny | fantastic-marvelous | marvelous) rather than observed in history – a theoretical genre, the literary historical instances of which are of secondary importance. Eventually, Todorov's structural approach on this genre is but one chapter for the sake of the general theory of literature and culture.

In the more empirical sense Todorov bequeaths for his commentators, one paradox concerns the number of narratives that fulfill the conditions he outlines for the fantastic narrative. Perhaps not even *The Turn of the Screw* is pure enough a structure of unresolved ambiguity, while some other titles have been suggested since then. But as the map of the fictional world of Bly is projected on to a map of genres, also the question of contours and limits of the genre system becomes acute, opening a speculative space at both ends of the linear map.

The "pure uncanny," Todorov starts the line of reflection on his system, is delimited only towards the fantastic (via "fantastic-uncanny"), whereas on its other side "it dissolves into the general field of literature" (1975, 46) through novels such as Dostoyevsky's. If with the uncanny the map of genres keeps still within literary limits, this limit is crossed with the marvellous, which "as an anthropological phenomenon, exceeds the context of a study limited to literary aspects" (57) and concerns "the total exploration of universal reality."[19] A small step for the implied reader, but a giant leap for the real one, the crossing of the borders of the map of genres introduces new questions for structural theory of the fantastic.

Neil Cornwell (1990, 39) joins in this interesting history of Todorov's reception by adding several new genres and subcategories to the original system of four, ending up in dividing his map in two subsequent sets otherwise "too long for most printed pages." Cornwell not only illustrates the expansion in the diagram's supernatural end with the intriguing category of "mythology etc." but also creates a speculative continuum on the natural side with forms of realism and documentary writing (Table 4.1).

Cornwell writes how his category of non-fiction "would shade off, to the far left, into journalism, history and, in a general sense, scientific literature," whereas "[m]ythology, on the right, may shade off into theology and other forms of cosmogony (or the irrefutable absurd?)" (39). The expansion of the linear diagram leads to a sense of absurd with writers of pseudo-science such as Erich von Däniken and Immanuel Velikovski, who signal a bending of the diagram into a circular map (214).

TABLE 4.1 Neil Cornwell (1990, 39).

1.	Non-fiction	Faction	Realism	Uncanny Realism	Fantstic uncanny	PF
2.	PF	Fantastic marvellous	Marvellous		Mythology etc.	

These genre maps are congenial of speculative fiction's theory but also in its history. Edgar Allan Poe is a prime example of an early innovator in the field, who takes advantage of its uncharted possibilities of generic diversity in his stories of the fantastic, horror, science fiction, and detective fiction.[20] Poe's method of structural possibilities of narrative kinds works out in fiction what Saussure later outlined of language as a system of permutations.[21] In literary theory, the useful tool of the genre map often impacts its own dynamic to the result that, as Alastair Fowler puts it, "[t]he idea of a map of literature may be taken to imply a comprehensiveness of view. We are entitled to assume that if time allowed, all literature could in principle be located on the white spaces of the map" (1982, 249).

Todorov already hints on turning of the linear genre system into a circular map. This happens with the problem of Kafka. On the one hand, implying the coincidence of the opposite categories of the natural and the supernatural, Kafka's fiction appears to surpass the positivist metaphysics of science-based conception of reality of the nineteenth-century with fantastic literature as its "bad consciousness" (1975, 168). On the other, it thus indicates a twentieth-century "generalized fantastic" with its sensibilities of fantasticalness of everyday reality and literature as such. While a traditional fantastic narrative starts out from a natural world to develop into a climax of a possibly supernatural element, a contrary movement of adaptation from the supernatural to the natural characterises Kafka's narratives (171). Furthermore, such a structure is like "the best science fiction texts" which "are organized analogously" (172).

Christine Brooke-Rose (1981, 84) proposes a turning of the linear map into a circle in coincidence of the genres of uncanny realism and the marvellous in postmodern science fiction (Vonnegut, McElroy) and the French nouveaux romans (1981, 67). In her generic circle, science fiction does not have a separate section of its own but is rather a collision product of what in Todorov's paradigm are still taken as exclusive terms (Figure 4.1).

Apparently unaware of Brooke-Rose, but likewise reflecting directly on Todorov's linear map, Albert Wendland (1985, 57) draws a circular diagram, too, with a more detailed and substantial articulation of three different forms of science fiction (Figure 4.2).

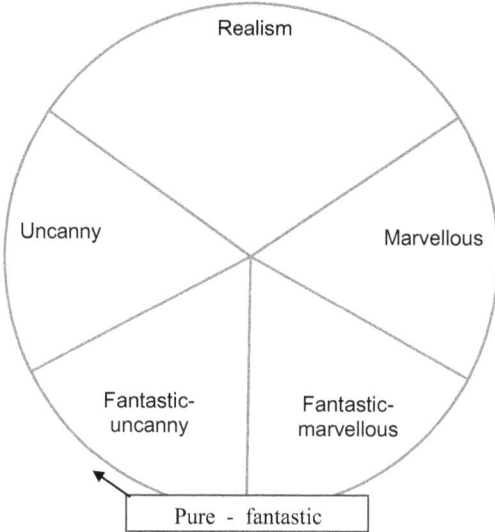

FIGURE 4.1   Christine Brooke-Rose (1981, 84).

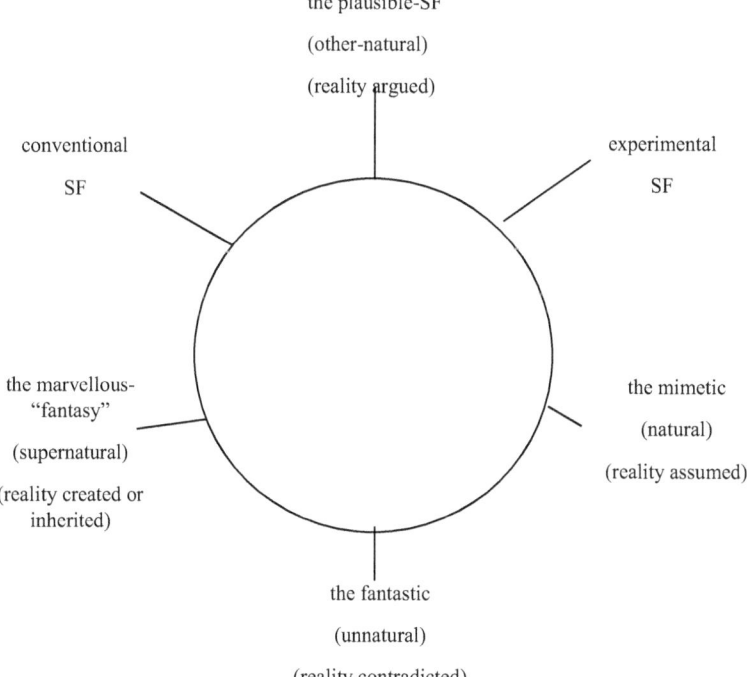

FIGURE 4.2   Albert Wendland (1985, 57).

Such diagrams implicate a surfacing of the circle of knowledge, the primary traditional model of cultural knowledge, in the wake of James's fictions of narrative ambiguity.[22] This results from a double logic of Todorov's poetics – the inverse relation between the evasive, fantastic limit between two adjacent genres, the uncanny and the marvellous, and the expansive system that such an unattainable work of generic definition of the fantastic feeds around it. In this sense, the pure fantastic has a function of a mathematical limit constantly approached but never quite reached in theoretical clarification. The closing curve creates also an opposite value of expansion of the function: a dynamic structuration that turns the system into an encyclopaedia of genres.[23]

Todorov's approach testifies to Claudio Guillén's observation how in "the European tradition, poetic theory, far from being simply critical or descriptive, has tended to propose and establish genuine examples of intellectual order" (1971, 377) that can be followed from Aristotle's system of the sciences through the tradition of the liberal arts (380).

It is evident by now why the definition of the fantastic narrative postulates a deductive grammar of a universal order of not only literature but, implicitly, also of sciences of culture and nature in their whole. Todorov accordingly applies Mendeleev's periodic table of the chemical elements for a paradigm for his literary purposes.[24] If Frye's *Anatomy* remains for Todorov a "little like those pre-Linnaean classifications of living organisms which readily constructed a category of all animals which scratch themselves" (1975, 19), Roberto Barbolini acutely detects in young Todorov the "Linnaeus of the literary fantastic."[25]

From Philology to Structuralism and Back Again

Although modern literary theories make their way from the early twentieth century on, the philological tradition was still dominating literary studies especially in French universities by the time of the rise of structuralism in 1960s. Todorov's parsing of the fantasy studies of the past brings out interesting points of connection of early structuralism to its philological roots.

Todorov's 14-page dissection of the *Anatomy* speaks accordingly of Frye's stature but especially, I think, of a certain genealogical line of philology in the structural analysis Todorov seeks to disavow:

[T]he author of *Anatomy of Criticism* rather puts one in mind of those dialect-lexicographers of the nineteenth century who combed remote villages for rare or unknown words. No matter how many thousands of words are collected, one does not thereby discover the principles – of the functioning of a language – for language is not a stockpile of words but a mechanism.

(Todorov 1975, 19)

Apparently for Todorov at this point, *Anatomy* (with its working title of "Structural Poetics," as we now know) resembles his own approach in a manner of a remote relative, whose illogical antiques require a prompt retort before recognition.[26] Sixteen years later, however, Todorov retraces his assessment with the result of recognising in Frye closer traits of resemblance: "In 1970 I devoted the first chapter of *The Fantastic* – to a 'structuralist' critique of Frye. I criticize Frye for not being internal enough or systematic enough. The debate now seems to me to be situated between two variants of 'structuralism'" (Todorov 1987, 93).

At issue is Todorov's transition from literary studies to cultural theory. Putting his structuralist bearings into frame of strategies of textual interpretation from Patristic exegesis to philology, Todorov starts retracing his structuralist years back to philology, by noting how "philology and structural analysis simply carry out different parts" in interpretation (Todorov 1973/1983, 168) and how both "philology and poetics provide the reader with tools" of textual analysis (Todorov 2008, 92).

If the French structuralist are after describing "a linguistic mechanism" of the narrative, Frye's *Anatomy* aims then to "catalog the most persistent metaphors in the Western tradition" and classify "the favorite plots of two thousand years of European history." To illustrate the difference, Todorov applies the opposition of the dictionary and the encyclopaedia discussed in the semiotics of language at the time. Whereas dictionary model purports to dissect the semantic of the word into primary, indivisible nuclei of meaning, encyclopaedia records the potentially infinite cultural archive of meaning of the word in its various uses (Cf. Eco 1984, 2014). Thus, Frye with his circular images "writes an encyclopaedia" in Giambattista Vico's tradition, while the French "produce a dictionary" in a relation that is eventually complementary rather than contradictory (Todorov 1984, 92–93).

Todorov's turn to culture studies parallels with the lineage of his roots in the "pioneer structural analyst of narrative" Propp. Surprisingly, Todorov does not discuss the scholar of the fairy tale, but a theorist of the genre who "employed analogies with botany and zoology" (Todorov 1975, 5), indicating nevertheless his significant debt also to the Russian Formalists.[27] Indeed, Boris Tomashevsky (and Vladimir Soloveyv before him) conceive Todorov's nucleus of narrative ambiguity of the literary fantastic already in 1925:

  It is curious that in sophisticated literary media influenced by a demand for realistic motivation, fantasies are usually open to a double interpretation. They may be accepted both as real events and as fantasies. [Solovyev's words] contain a satisfactorily precise formulation of the techniques of the fantastic narrative viewed from the norm of realistic motivation. The tales of Hoffmann, the novels of Mrs. Radcliffe, etc., use the technique.

Sleep, delirium, optical or other illusions, and so on, are the usual motifs that permit the possibility of double interpretation.

(Tomashevsky 1965, 83–84)

Todorov includes Tomashevsky's chapter on literary thematic in his edition of the Russian Formalists' text in 1965 for the French readers (Todorov 1965, 262–307) but forgets to cite it in his study of the fantastic (cf. Todorov 1975, 4–5).

Invocations of a "return to philology" have been heard in past decades' literary studies (cf., e.g., Lönnroth 2017). One road of return has been going through Tolkien's Middle-earth for quite some time, leading to the tradition behind the structuralist moment of the speculative fiction studies. Also Propp, along with the Formalists, was schooled in nineteenth-century philology with its Russian offset of the historical poetics (cf. Kliger & Maslov 2016, 1–16 and passim). Like Todorov's later, Propp's initiative was to introduce a better order in the philological archive of the folktales of the world, from its condition, he argued, left by previous generations of collectors, and especially of the Finnish historical-geographical school. Building on the work of Julius (1835–1888) and his son Kaarle Krohn (1863–1933), Antti J. Aarne's (1867–1925) typological index (1910) – with its further editions by Stith Tompson in 1928/1961 (Aarne 1961) and Hans-Jörg Uther in 2004 – was a standard reference work and a core material in Propp's 1928 study on the *Morphology of the Folktale* (cf. Propp 1984, 72 and passim.)

The Krohn family history also includes writers of speculative fiction Aino Kallas (1878–1956, e.g., in *The Wolf's Bride: A Tale from Estonia* [*Sudenmorsian,* 1928] and Leena Krohn (1947–, *Collected Fiction,* 2015). Leena Krohn represents a contemporary writer of both philological and structuralist aspects and distinctive international thematic in her work. Already her titles such as *Tainaron* (1985), *Gold of Ophir* (*Oofirin kultaa,* 1987), *Umbra* (1990), *Tribar* (1993), *Pereat Mundus* (1998), *Datura* (2001), and *Hotel Sapiens* (2013) seem to be in search for a commentator of their linguistic bend. Likewise, her narrative blending of the fantastic with science fiction and horror, often rounded out with essayistic writing, should be intriguing for a reader dedicated to find a proper place on the map of genres for them. To highlight such entwining paths of reading, her recent collection of autobiographical sketches and essays, takes us down in the family tree to her great-grandfather Leopold August Krohn, who was "interested in occultism" (Krohn 2021, 145) as was his son, Leopold Wilhelm, Leena Krohn's grandfather. Paranormal experiences and their reflection by rationalist scepsis make a prominent thread also in the carpet of Leena Krohn's writings, among so many others.

The Krohn genealogy illustrates further the Finnish geographic-historical school's background in the comparative Indo-European studies. Like

Vladimir Propp's, the Krohn family was initially part of nineteenth-century St. Petersburg's German colony.[28] With its history of national identity construction, the *Kalevala* is then an early exception in the Finno-Ugrists' fieldwork, collecting and comparative research of similarities of related languages and cultures as a structuralism-in-the-making of its day.[29]

Notes

1 The ambiguous stories central in James studies are "The Lesson of the Master" (1888), "The Figure in the Carpet" (1896), *The Turn of the Screw* (1898) and *The Sacred Fount* (1901); cf. Rimmon (1977).

2 On the reception of *The Turn of the Screw*, cf. James (1969, 1999).

3 "The house of fiction has – not one window, but a million – every one of which has been pierced – in its vast front, by the need of the individual vision" (James 1986, 290–291).

4 Tolkien (1990, 7–8).

5 Cf. Shippey (2003, 1–28), Tolkien (1990, 28ff.); Saussure opens his famous lecture course of 1906–1911 on general linguistics with a historical survey of the field, putting on note how, at the outset, "linguistic structure is not the central concern of philology," for "philology seeks primarily to establish, interpret and comment upon texts. This main preoccupation leads to a concern with literary history, customs, institutions, etc." (Saussure 1983, 1). He then follows the formation of comparative philology in the nineteenth century, when "it was discovered that languages could be compared with one another" (2). The modern, structural linguistics that he is conceiving must finally take for its aim "to delimit and define linguistics itself" and be therefore "carefully distinguished from ethnography and prehistory" and "anthropology" (6) to the effect that it becomes evident that philology "is clearly separate from linguistics" (7) as a science.

6 Tolkien (1995, 376).

7 Ibid. (212).

8 Tolkien (1990, 19).

9 Cf. Tihanov (2019).

10 On the essential place of philology in Tolkien's work, cf. Shippey (2003).

11 References to "The Figure in the Carpet" are to James (1964, 273–315).

12 Referring to *Aeneid*, I, 405; translation in Virgil (1967, 290–291).

13 "1. Love of learning and literature; the branch of knowledge that deals with the historical, linguistic, interpretative, and critical aspects of literature; literary or classical scholarship" ("Philology, n."), *OED*.

14 Henry James in his *Notebooks*, qtd. in Blanchot (1982, 84). Blanchot continues: "(W)e know the dangerous, almost pathological attraction, which the possible – that ghostly, unreal existence of what might have been, of those presences we are always waiting for – exerted on James, and which perhaps only art enabled him to explore and exorcise" (84).

15 Strother B. Purdy argues accordingly that "Contemporary writers have begun to explore the hole in the fabric that Henry James found. Others, in other ways, found it too, of course – Niels Bohr and Albert Einstein, J. Robert Oppenheimer and Edward Teller, the physicists … who destroyed what we now look back on as if it were the safe certainty of eighteenth-century Deism or medieval Catholicism, the Euclidean universe of up-down, left-right, and explorable surfaces" (Purdy 1977, 3).

16 References to *The Turn of the Screw* are to James (1999).

17 Cf. Nos. 510–511 in Aarne & Thompson (1961).

18 James (1999, 123–129).

19 Pierre Mabille, *The Mirror of the Marvelous*, qtd. in Todorov (1975, 57).

20 "One of my chief aims has been the widest diversity of subject, thought, & especially tone & manner of handling. Were all my tales now before me in a large volume – the merit which would principally arrest my attention would be the wide diversity and variety. I do not consider any of my stories better than another. There is a vast variety of kinds and, in degree of value, these kinds vary – but each tale is equally good of its kind" (Poe 2004, 684–685).

21 "*In the language itself, there are only differences.* Even more important than that is the fact that, although in general a difference presupposes positive terms between which the difference holds, in a language there are only differences, *and no positive terms*" (Saussure 1983, 118)

22 Cf. Kuusisto (2009).

23 This point was taken up by Italo Calvino in an early occasion of a symposium dedicated to Todorov's theory of fantastic in 1970: "This study of Todorov is very accurate on one meaning of fantasy and full of suggestions with regard to other meanings, aiming at some possible general classification. If we wish to compile an exhaustive atlas of imaginative literature, we will have to start with a grammar of what Todorov calls 'wonder' at the level of the earliest combinatorial operations of signs in the primitive myths and fables, and of the symbolic requirements of the unconscious – as indeed at the level of the intellectual games of all times and all cultures" (Calvino 2004, 134).

24 "It is therefore necessary to deduce all the possible combinations from the categories chosen. ... as in Mendeleev's system one could describe the properties of elements not yet discovered, similarly we shall describe here the properties of genres – and therefore of works – still to come" (Todorov 1975, 14).

25 Barbolini (1984, 209).

26 On Frye's working title, cf. Ayre (1989, 252) and on Frye's connection to early structuralism, see, e.g., Salusinszky (2006, 20–21).

27 Cf. De Berg and Zbinden (2020, 244).

28 Cf. Forrester (2012, xxii); Autio (2005).

29 Cf. Honko (1993, 43ff.).

References

Aarne, Antti. 1961. *The Types of the Folktale. A Classification and Bibliography. Antti Aarne's Verzeichnis der Märchentypen (FF Communications No. 3).* Trans. and enlarged by Stith Thompson. Second Revision. Helsinki: Suomalainen tiedeakakatemia.

Autio, Veli-Matti. 2005. "Krohn. suku." Kansallisbiografia-verkkojulkaisu. Studia Biographica 4. Helsinki: Suomalaisen Kirjallisuuden Seura, 1997–. Accessed 25 September 2023.

Ayre, John. 1989. *Northrop Frye. A Biography.* Toronto: Random House.

Barbolini, Roberto. 1984. *La chimera e il terrore: saggi sul gotico, l'avventura e l'enigma.* Milano: Jaca Book.

Blanchot, Maurice. 1982. *The Sirens' Song.* Ed. Gabriel Josipovici. Trans. Sacha Rabinovitch. Sussex: The Harvester Press.

Brooke-Rose, Christine. 1981. *A Rhetoric of the Unreal: Studies in Narrative and Structure, Especially of the Fantastic.* Cambridge: Cambridge UP.

Calvino, Italo. 2004/1970. "Definitions of Territory: Fantasy." In *Fantastic literature. A Critical Reader*, ed. David Sandner, 133–134. Westport: Praeger.

Cornwell, Neil. 1990. *The Literary Fantastic: from Gothic to Postmodernism*. New York: Harvester Wheatsheaf.

D'Alembert, Jean Le Rond. 1963. *Preliminary Discourse to the Encyclopedia of Diderot*. Trans. Richard N. Schwab with the collaboration of Walter E. Rex. Indianapolis: The Bobbs-Merrill.

De Berg, Henk & Karine Zbinden. 2020. "Interview with Tzvetan Todorov." In *Tzvetan Todorov. Thinker and Humanist*, eds. Hank De Berg & Karine Zbinden, 236–258. Rochester: Camden House.

Eco, Umberto. 1984. "Metaphor, Dictionary, and Encyclopedia." *New Literary History* 15 (1984): 255–271.

Eco, Umberto. 1989. *The Open Work*. Trans. Anna Cancogni. Cambridge: Harvard UP.

Eco, Umberto. 2014. *From the Tree to the Labyrinth: Historical Studies on the Sign and Interpretation*. Trans. Anthony Oldcorn. Cambridge: Harvard UP.

Forrester, Sibelan. 2012. "Preface. Vladimir Propp and the Russian Folktale." In Vladimir Propp: *The Russian Folktale*, ed. and trans. Sibelan Forrester, xiii–xxvi. Detroit: Wayne State UP.

Fowler, Alastair. 1982. *Kinds of Literature: An Introduction to the Theory of Genres and Modes*. Cambridge: Harvard UP.

Frye, Northrop. 1957. *Anatomy of Criticism: Four Essays*. Princeton: Princeton UP.

Guillén, Claudio. 1971. *Literature as System: Essays Toward the Theory of Literary History*. Princeton: Princeton UP.

Honko, Lauri. 1993. "Oral Poetry: The Comparative Approach." In *The Great Bear. A Thematic Anthology of Oral Poetry in the Finno-Ugrian Languages*, eds. Lauri Honko, Senni Timonen & Michael Branch, 43–62. Poems trans. Keith Bosley. Oxford: Oxford UP.

James, Henry. 1964. *The Complete Tales of Henry James*. Edited by Edel, Leon. Vol. 9. London: Rupert Hart-Davis.

James, Henry. 1969. *A Casebook on Henry James's "The Turn of the Screw."* Ed. Gerald Willen. Second Edition. New York: Thomas Y. Crowell Company.

James, Henry. 1986. *The Art of Criticism: Henry James on the Theory and the Practice of Fiction*. Eds. William Veeder & Susan M. Griffin. Chicago: The University of Chicago Press.

James, Henry. 1999. *The Turn of the Screw: Authoritative Text, Contexts, Criticism*. 2nd edition. Eds. Deborah Esch & Jonathan Warren. New York: Norton.

Kliger, Ilya & Boris Maslov. 2016. "Introducing Historical Poetics. History, Experience, Form." In Klieger, Ilya & Maslov, Boris: *Persistent Forms: Explorations in Historical Poetics*. New York: Fordham University Press, 1–36.

Krohn, Leena 2021. *Mitä en koskaan oppinut*. Helsinki Teos.

Kuusisto, Pekka. 2009. "Gregory Benford's Against Infinity and the Literary, Historical and Geometric Formation of the Encyclopedic Circle of Knowledge." In *Science Fiction and the Two Cultures. Essays on Bridging the Gap Between the Sciences and the Humanities*, eds. Gary Westfahl & George Slusser, 140–159. Jefferson: McFarland.

Lönnroth, Harry. 2017. *Philology Matters! Essays on the Art of Reading Slowly*. Leiden: Brill.

Martianus Capella. 1977. *The Marriage of Philology and Mercury, Vols 1–2*. Trans. William Harris, Richard Johnson & E. L. Burge. New York: Columbia UP.

Oxford English Dictionary. "Philology, n.". https://www.oed.com/view/Entry/142464?redirectedFrom=philology&amp. Accessed 1 March 2024.

Poe, Edgar Allan. 2004. *The Selected Writings of Edgar Allan Poe*. A Norton Critical Edition. Ed. G. R. Thompson. New York: Norton.

Propp, Vladimir. 1984. *Theory and History of Folklore*. Trans. Martin Y. Ariadna, Richard P. Martin et al. Minneapolis: University of Minnesota Press.

Purdy, Strother B. 1977. *The Hole in the Fabric: Science, Contemporary Literature, and Henry James*. Pittsburgh: University of Pittsburgh Press.

Rimmon, Slomith. 1977. *The Concept of Ambiguity - The Example of James*. Chicago: The University of of Chicago Press.

Salusinszky, Imre. 2006. "Northrop Frye." In *Modern North American Criticism and Theory. A Critical Guide*, ed. Julien Wolfreys, 19–25. Edinburgh: Edinburgh UP.

Saussure, Ferdinand de. 1983. *Course in General Linguistics*. London: Duckworth.

Shippey, Tom. 2003. *The Road to Middle-Earth. How Tolkien Created a New Mythology*. Revised and Expanded Edition. Boston: Houghton Mifflin.

Tihanov, Galin. 2019. *The Birth and Death of Literary Theory. Regimes of Relevance in Russia and Beyond*. Stanford: Stanford UP.

Todorov, Tzvetan. 1965. *Théorie de la littérature: textes des formalistes russes*. Paris: Éditions du Seuil.

Todorov, Tzvetan. 1975. *The Fantastic: A Structural Approach to a Literary Genre*. Trans. Richard Howard. Ithaca: Cornell UP.

Todorov, Tzvetan. 1983. *Symbolism and Interpretation*. Trans. Catherine Porter. London: Routledge.

Todorov, Tzvetan. 1987/1984. *Literature and Its Theorists. A Personal View of Twentieth-Century Criticism*. Trans. Catherine Porter. Ithaca: Cornell UP.

Todorov, Tzvetan. 2008. *Duties and Delights. The Life of a Go-Between. Interviews with Catherine Portevin*. Trans. Gila Walker. London: Seagull Books.

Tolkien, J. R. R. 1990. *Monsters and the Critics, and Other Essays*. Ed. Christopher Tolkien. London: Harper Collins Publishers.

Tolkien, J. R. R. 1995. *The Letters of J.R.R. Tolkien*. Ed. Humphrey Carpenter, with the assistance of Christopher Tolkien. London: Harper Collins Publishers.

Tomashevsky, Boris. 1965. "Thematics." In Boris Tomashevsky: *Russian Formalist Criticism. Four Essays*. Trans. Lee T. Lemon & Marion J. Reis, 61–95. Lincoln: University of Nebraska Press.

Turner, James. 2014. *Philology. The Forgotten Origins of the Modern Humanities*. Princeton: Princeton UP.

Virgil. 1967. *In Two Volumes. 1, Eclogues; Georgics; Aeneid I-VI*. Trans. H. Rushton Fairclough. London: Heinemann.

Wendland, Albert. 1985. *Science, Myth, and the Fictional Creation of Alien Worlds*. Ann Arbor: UMI Research Press.

PART II

Uncanny and Ecological Impulses

5

THE UNCANNY IN TOVE JANSSON'S SHORT STORIES

Motifs of the Sublime and the Horror

Jyrki Korpua

Tove Jansson (1914–2001) had a talent for *the uncanny,* something strangely familiar, but at the same time unsettling, eerie and mysterious (see, e.g., Royle 2003, vii). We can see a glimpse of that in the terrible and gloomy short story "The Dark" ("Mörkret"), from the autobiographical collection *Sculptor's Daughter* (*Bildhuggarens dotter,* 1968):

> Behind the Russian church there is an abyss. The moss and the rubbish are slippery and jagged old tins glitter at the bottom. For hundreds of years they have piled up higher and higher against a long dark red house without windows. The red house crawls round the rock and it is very significant that it has no windows. Behind the house is the harbour, a silent harbour with no boats in it. The little wooden door in the rock below the church is always locked. Hold your breath when you run past it, I told you Poyu. Otherwise Putrefaction will come out and catch you.
>
> *(Jansson 2013, 9)*

The uncanny, here, is broadly understood as an experience that utilises literary motifs such as the sublime and the horror and is therefore structured by these motifs. My focus here is, firstly, to achieve a better understanding of Tove Jansson's short story style. Secondly, this chapter is also written as a contribution to studies of the uncanny, which is a concept not often connected with literary works of Tove Jansson.

Tove Jansson, internationally mostly known as the creator of the Moomin stories, was a multidisciplinary artist, children's and youth author, novelist, short story writer, comics artist and cartoonist, illustrator, painter, and sculptor. In Jansson's literary work, we see a wide variety of styles that can

DOI: 10.4324/9781003561101-9

be simplistically labelled as "fantastic," "adventurous," "prosaic," or "psychological." Jansson's use of variable genres is also evident: she wrote, for example, children's books, adult novels, self-portraying memoirs, and horror stories. This genre hybridity[1] can also be seen in Jansson's texts addressed to adult audiences, such as the collections analysed for this chapter, *Travelling Light*, *Letters from Klara*, *Bulevarden och andra texter*, *The Listener*, and *Art in Nature*. These are all short story collections where weird, fantastic realism meets sophisticated and intimate psychological fiction. I have chosen five short stories from five different collections because of the ways in which they intertwine the motifs of sublime and horror with a realistic narrative. These short stories are read as prime examples of the uncanny in Jansson's fiction.

Jansson was not a horror author, but she produced many literary works that include horrific elements. They in fact wrote in a letter to publisher Åke Runnquist in 1965 of a love for horror fiction (Jansson 2014b, 469).[2] Jansson's fantasy fiction, the Moomin books, is known for its distinctive blend of humour, sentimentality, lyricism, but also darker intrusions (Stableford 2005, 222). On the one hand, it should be noted that Jansson's Moomin books include horror elements, which are a vital part of the stories, whether seen in the form of catastrophes, unfamiliar monsters, or an existentialist search for identity (Ylönen 2014, 16; see Takahashi 1996, Rehal-Johansson 2006, Buckland 2007, Laajarinne 2009). Jansson felt that experiences of horror and fear should be included in children's fiction (Jansson 2017b, 201–205; see Aejmelaeus 1994, 55–56). On the other hand, Jansson's prose addressed to adult audiences includes the sublime and the horror as affects and motifs, the latter meaning repeated patterns in particular stories. In Jansson's short stories, these motifs and affects are repeated to point towards the larger theme of uncanniness, an experience of obscurity and outsiderism.

This chapter focuses on different kinds of uncanny in Tove Jansson's fiction. I argue that there are at least two distinct kinds of uncanny experiences that Jansson uses in fiction. There are clear horror motifs that can be unveiled. First, I analyse the outsider motif and the doppelgänger (double) motif. Secondly, I analyse the motif of the haunted house. These motifs and elements are analysed mainly from five short stories by Jansson: "Summer Child" ("Sommarbarnet") from the collection *Travelling Light* (*Resa med lättbagage*, 1972, hereafter TL), "Emmelina" from *Letters from Klara* (*Brev från Klara*, 1991, hereafter LK), "Cliché" ("Kliche," 1935) published in the posthumous collection *Bulevarden och andra texter* (2017, hereafter B), "Black-White" ("Svart-vitt") from the collection *The Listener* (*Lyssnerskan*, 1971, hereafter L), and "The Doll's House" ("Dockskåpet") from the collection *Art in Nature* (*Dockskåpet och andra berättelser*, 1978, hereafter AN). The Doppelgänger motif can be also found in other short stories by Jansson, such as "The Other" ("Den andra," 1971), "The Locomotive" ("Lokomotiv," 1978), and "The Woman Who Borrowed Memories" ("Kvinnen som lånade minnen," 1987).

I acknowledge that there are two kinds of uncanny motifs in Jansson's fiction. The first kind is a clear uncanny occurrence, which could also be seen as an intertextual reference, for example when Jansson dedicates a short story to a well-known horror author and deliberately uses elements of the chosen genre. I label this kind of uncanny experience as *intrusive*, as a reference to "intrusive fantasy" from Farah Mendlesohn's genre theory (2008, xxiii). The uncanny occurrences create an experience of amazement or horror. The second kind is more indefinite, unclear, and almost aleatoric, which I call *liminal uncanny* as reference to "liminal fantasy" from Mendlesohn's genre theory (2008, xxiii). There is the transliminal moment, the point when the story could cross the threshold into the uncanny, but usually it chooses not to do so. Still, elements of the uncanny leak through the portal. Even though the story could be read as (semi)realistic prose, the reader can experience the uncanny. In my close reading of the texts, I found that Jansson uses both the intrusive and liminal kinds of the uncanny.

The Uncanny: The Sublime and the Horror

The uncanny, here, is understood extensively as something weird and mysterious that is at the same time familiar and unfamiliar, as a reference to Freud's *das Heimliche* and *das Unheimliche* (see Freud 1989, 339–341). As Nicholas Royle (2003, 1) discusses, the uncanny "involves feelings of uncertainty, in particular regarding the reality of who one is and what is being experienced. … The uncanny is the crisis of the proper: it entails a critical disturbance of what is proper." Royle (2003, 1) also acknowledges that the uncanny is not "simply an experience of strangeness or alienation … [but] specifically, it is a peculiar commingling of the familiar and unfamiliar." The term has been used philosophically as well as in psychoanalytic writing "to indicate a disturbing, vacuous area" (Jackson 1981, 63). The term was first identified in Ernst Jentsch's essay "Zur Psychologiedes unheimlichen" ("On the Psychology of the Uncanny," 1906). However, the term was popularised by Sigmund Freud in his essay "Das Unheimliche" ("The Uncanny," 1919), where he expanded Jentsch's views and added many new perspectives to the term in his case study of E.T.A. Hoffman's horror short story "Der Sandman" ("The Sandman," 1817).

The uncanny in literature could manifest as, for example, motifs and elements of the sublime and the horror. Sublime, here, is seen as Edmund Burke saw it, as an aesthetic experience when a person fears something which is larger, greater, and more powerful than herself/himself. Burke wrote that "[n]o passion so effectively robs the mind of all its powers of actioning and reasoning as *fear*" (Burke 1834, 38). We are experiencing the sublime, when in our ordinary and familiar life, a door to something unfamiliar, other, or possibly supernatural opens (Lyytikäinen 2000, 11). In Jansson's fiction, for example, when the main character in "The Other" sees his doppelgänger for the first time: "Suddenly, and with dreadful clarity, he saw himself. Not in a mirror. He actually stood beside himself for an instant and though quietly, there stands a skinny, timid, stoop-shouldered fellow buying cheese and milk and a piece of ham" (Jansson 2014a, 70). The scene itself is depicting ordinary life, but seeing your own doppelgänger is a sublime, perhaps supernatural, and clearly uncanny experience.

Sublime is closely connected with horror, but the specification and identification of experiences is always difficult. When writing on the "weird tale," S.T. Joshi (1990, 2) points out that works in the field have caused "irremediable confusion of terms such as horror, terror, the supernatural, fantasy, the fantastic, ghost story, Gothic fiction, and others." Generally, horror fiction is fiction of fear. In his seminal text *Supernatural Horror in Literature*, H.P. Lovecraft, the master of supernatural horror, wrote, following Burke's reasoning, that "[t]he oldest and strongest emotion of mankind is fear, and the oldest and strongest kind of fear is fear of the unknown" (Lovecraft 1973, 12). As Jason Colavito (2008, 3) writes, "horror stories are a way of understanding and ultimately transcending the limits of mind, knowledge, and science through fear." Colavito argues that "[t]he emotion of horror is a combination of fear and revulsion, and it is related closely to terror, a feeling of fear and anxiety" (Colavito 2008, 13). For their part, Manuel Aguirre emphasises the uncanny, unfamiliar, side of horror: "the awful, awesome, numinous presence in its dark aspect: with a world of order touched by the non-natural – whether this be 'unnatural', 'supernatural', or … 'contranatural'" (Aguirre 1990, 84). The sublime questions the power of a human subject (Alanko & Korhonen 2000, 9). Therefore, it also challenges the subject of the text, as we can see from Tove Jansson's fiction, where main characters battle with their own identities and are on the verge of losing their own personas. Next, I will demonstrate how this uncanny problem with the self can be seen functioning in Jansson's fiction.

Problems with the Self: Uncanny Outsiders and the Doppelgänger

Tove Jansson's fiction is full of characters who have problems with their own identities. There are those who do not know who they are, those whose sense of reality has become altered, and those who battle with their own self or have problems placing themselves in the society and society's norms and regulations (see Jones 1984, 155; for a larger context to this, see Sandbacka 2018, 23). Their actions have elements which could be interpreted as mental health problems. Bernard McElroy (1989, 95) points out that "madness can also fascinate, for it is a foreign and frightening way of life, a form of knowledge, of alien knowledge certainly, but knowledge nonetheless." It is an uncanny element.

Many of Jansson's characters are outsiders. They are strange, unfamiliar, and uncanny. For example, "Summer Child," a short story from the collection *Travelling Light* (*Resa med lättbagage*, 1972) tells us about a weird, "thin, gloomy child of eleven" (TL, 35). He is spending the summer with a family previously unknown to him, and the family becomes somewhat troubled with the boy. His appearance is somewhat uncanny: "a suspicious piercing stare that was anything but childlike" (TL, 35). The boy, Elis, himself resembles uncanny child characters like the horrifying anti-Christ figure Damien from the horror movie *The Omen* (1976, directed by Richard Donner). There is nothing supernatural about Elis, but his actions are unfamiliar and create the same kind of strangeness as those more horrific characters. In addition to his staring gaze and weird behaviour, he also speaks fatalistically about nuclear war and the end of the world and is obsessed with capitalism and money. Other people were "all a little afraid of him" (TL, 44).[3] In modern horror fiction, children are often seen as uncanny horror motifs, and society can be hostile when threatened by its own offspring (see Aguirre 1990, 214). Then again, "Summer Child" only has some liminal uncanny qualities which are repaired in the end. The short story ends when Elis is (kind of) accepted as a part of the family. The ending, where the father of the family brings a bird skeleton to Elis to play with, closes the story cycle. The uncanny short story ends in experiences of comfort and relief, which could be interpreted as catharsis.

Lena Kåreland (1996, 50), in their psychoanalytic reading, sees elements of familiar and unfamiliar and attributes of outsiders also in the Moomin books. In the picture book *The Dangerous Journey* (*Den farliga resan*, 1977), a human character Susanna travels to Moominvalley and is seen there as an outsider, an unfamiliar intruder.[4] Kåreland compares Susanna to Lewis Carroll's Alice in *Alice in Wonderland*. They are both outsiders to the fantasy world, observers who are offensively realistic compared to their environment. Reality is subjective and depends on the point of view. We can see the uncanny working in both directions; a realistic character can be seen as an intrusion in a fantastic story, as well an element of fantasy or horror could be seen as an intrusion in a realistic story, as our examples show.

The subjectivity of truth is questioned also in the short story "Emmelina." In the centre of the story, there is a strange 19-year-old woman, Emmelina, who has served as a lady's companion for an old miss spinster in an apartment building. Now the spinster has died, and Emmelina lives alone in an apartment. The main character of the story, David, becomes infatuated with the young lady although other people in the building see Emmelina as a quite frightening person. A housemaid describes how Emmelina "sends shivers down my spine" (LK, 86). For the reader, however, it is never quite specified what makes Emmelina such a frightening character inside the story world. We might just assume that it is her unfamiliar and weird behaviour.

Altogether, Emmelina's uncanniness as a character is made visible in many ways. The first time David sees her at night coming down a staircase step by step with a burning candle in her hand, he describes her as "ethereally and mysteriously beautiful" (LK, 87). She is like a character from a classical horror romance, beautiful but remote and perilous. Her cold-bloodedness becomes clear in a scene where Emmelina and David see a large bird cage filled with canary birds. One of the birds is being plucked and tormented by the other birds. David feels sorry for the miserable bird, but Emmelina "opened the cage, caught the bird quick as a wink and broke its neck" (LK, 95). Afterwards, Inger, the owner of the birds, is terrified by Emmelina, although her action could be seen as a mercy killing. In the story, the narrator tells us that David both respects and is fond of Emmelina, but still, "somewhere there was a little fear, the kind you feel for things that are alien and different, unpredictable" (LK, 102). David was no longer able to "hold on to the image of the girl with the candle. The unreachable had somehow grown even more distant (LK, 102). At the end of the story, Emmelina tells David that "it's getting late for me and I have to go" (LK, 102). In a strange and surprising ending, Emmelina disappears from the house without a note and leaves David aching for her return. He is left in limbo, a state of uncertainty. The story itself, even without any supernatural elements, reminds the reader of a romantic fairy tale where the girl of dreams is just an image, a fairy daydream or just a flight of fancy.

Emmelina is maybe just a hopeless fantasy for David, a classic example of unrequited love, but in a short story "Cliché," Jansson uses a classical doppelgänger horror motif.[5] These, compared to the liminal uncanny in "Emmelina" or "Summer Child," are clear examples of the intrusive uncanny. Use of the doppelgänger or alter ego motif was popularised in the nineteenth-century literature. On the one hand, Julia Briggs (2000, 123) calls doppelgänger one of many types of supernatural visitations common to Gothic ghost stories. Aguirre, on the other hand, combines the double motif with Victorian horror, emphasising that the double cannot be severed from its original. Aguirre differentiates it from Gothic horror, writing

> that the difference with the Gothic haunter is a simple one: then it was bonded to a house, a castle, a family; not, to an individual; then it was circumscribed to a specific locale, now it stalks the world; then it was purely a being from the Other side, now it is *also* part of a human individual: his shadow, his reflection, his mechanical parody.
>
> *(Aguirre 1990, 131)*

Jansson's "Cliché" is a story of a murder and its background. A self-conscious murderer has met a woman whom he thinks is his evil twin, and because of that, he later harasses, and eventually murders, her. The murderer explains to the narrator, with whom he spends a New Year's Eve, that the victim had become his Mr. Hyde and his doppelgänger. There are references to both *Strange Case of Dr Jekyll and Mr Hyde* (1886) by Robert Louis Stevenson and "William Wilson" (1839) by Edgar Allan Poe in the text, both famous doppelgänger horror stories. For the reader it becomes evident that the murderer has mistaken a love interest and affection for persecution or harassment. The murderer confesses his crime to the narrator in an innocent, innocuous way. The murderer states that he killed her in self-defence, and even after that, he happily proposes a toast for a new year (B, 31). In the end of the story, the reader, as well as the narrator character, is left with an uncanny sensation. The story leaves its reader in a state of shock and wonder.

Problems with the Reality: The Haunted Houses

American imagistic poet H.D. (Hilda Doolittle) famously wrote that "we are all haunted houses" (Royle 2003, 1). Human characters can (and have been) metaphorically and allegorically compared to houses. For H.D., we are not just (allegorically) houses, but more psychologically "haunted" as such. Domestic milieu, a house more precisely, has been closely connected to the human experience of mind and soul, and this kind of interpretation is also possible in Jansson's fiction. Therefore, my next examples of uncanny from Jansson's fiction focus on haunted houses, which are common uncanny motifs specifically in horror fiction. However, in Jansson's fiction, it is not necessarily the houses that are haunted, but the occupants of the houses. This is quite different from Gothic horror. Aguirre points out that the

> Gothic castle is "alive with a power that perplexes its inhabitants or visitors. It tends to have irregular, asymmetric shape; its geometry is uncanny, whether because of an actual distortion of the whole or because a part of it remains unknown. ... The haunted house is by definition a not-home, an *unheimlich* centre.
>
> *(Aguirre 1990, 92)*

Although Jansson's haunted houses may not be alive, they are still uncanny (das Unheimliche) and geometrically interesting.

Jansson's "Black-White" is influenced by classical horror and mystery stories. It is in fact dedicated to American writer and artist Edward Gorey, who is famous for his surrealistic, macabre, dark, (neo-)Gothic art style, although Gorey himself classified his works as "literary nonsense" (see Dery

2018, 14), a genre made famous by Lewis Carroll, who then again could be seen as an inspiration for Tove Jansson's work.

"Black-White" is a macabre short story where the main character, an unnamed illustrator, gets a commission to illustrate a horror anthology and decides to go to an abandoned villa to work on the project. The short story concentrates on the spaces, the houses, that the main character occupies and more importantly on the psychological breakdown – a mental collapse – that the character suffers. The ending of the story follows the narrative logic of horror stories, such as short stories by Edgar Allan Poe, and the description of the abandoned Faster's Villa in the story follows the narrative style of classical ghost stories of haunted houses. Yet in this case, it is perhaps the main character that becomes "haunted" – by his own mind obsessed by the black-and-white horror paintings, his own illustrations.

There is a clear juxtaposition of spaces, a dichotomy of light and darkness, white and black, which is central for the story. At the beginning of the story, the narrator tells that the main character lives with his wife, Stella, an interior designer. They live in a house designed and drawn by Stella herself. Their home is a house that is "an enormous openwork of glass and unpainted wood" (Jansson 2014a, 40).

> When dusk entered their rooms, it was met with low, veiled lighting, while the glass wall reflected the night but held it at a distance. They stepped out onto the terrace, and   hidden spotlights came on in the bushes. The darkness crept away, and they stood side by side, throwing no shadows, and he thought, This is perfect. Nothing can change.
>
> *(L, 40)*

The starting point of the story seems to be, in a way, idyllic. Then again, it is idyllic only on the surface, since it is revealed to the reader that the main character has terrible back pains and in fact cannot work in his own house. The milieu of their home seems more fitting for Stella than for her husband.

When the main character gets the commission to illustrate a horror story anthology with 15 large whole-page black-and-white illustrations, he decides to leave his homely house of light and glass. He says to his wife that, in his illustrations, he will "use black as a dominant element. I'm going to do darkness" (L, 42). There, psychologically, the man leaves behind the white, idyllic light and steps into the world of black and darkness – to a chthonic, daemonic depth.

The main character travels to Faster's Villa, the second house and central space in the story. The villa is certainly a different kind of milieu than their homely house. It can be compared to Gothic castles or geometrically to the haunted houses of Victorian horror. The villa is located on top of the hill. A road there is surrounded by a tall spruce fence. And "the house clung tightly to the hill at an impossible angle, just below the crown, and the house, the fence, the fir trees, all seemed to be holding themselves upright with a terrible effort" (L, 45). But the illustrator sees it as a beautiful space that has been forgotten on its own. Yet he still "felt his darkness drawing closer" (L, 45).

For the next few days, the man works diligently on his illustrations. Although he finds the text of horror anthology itself banal, and not at all horrifying, he draws passionately, almost in a frenzy. Ultimately, the man does not illustrate the anthology, but begins drawing pictures, which he describes as

> pieces of reality or unreality carved at random from a long and ineluctable course of events – the darkness I draw continues on endlessly. I cut across it with narrow and dangerous shafts of light. ... I am not illustrating any longer. I'm making my own pictures, and they follow no text.
>
> *(L, 47)*

The man becomes obsessed with the house, in a way haunted by his illustration work and the house itself. He starts by depicting the house, thinking that he must draw the house as long as it is there (L, 49). He ends up drawing many more than the ordered 15 illustrations, but they all portray the house. Unstable and troubled, all alone in a house which he is obsessed with, the man longs for his wife and describes her lyrically – but also quite strangely – as "white as blank paper, as white as innocent challenge of the empty surface, and now she alone gives off light, Stella, my star" (L, 49).

The man reflects his inner mental instability to his surrounding space. He feels the house leaning, possibly collapsing. This is a clear reference that the house has become metaphorically connected to his mind. He finds it hard to remember his wife's eyes; he is losing his memory of that idyllic past. He just works for days, nights, and weeks and no longer cares about the outcome. When he finishes a drawing, he just sets it aside and starts a new one.

In the horrifying, uncanny ending of the short story, the man draws

> a terrifying room without doors, bulging with tension, the white walls shadowed with imperceptibly tiny cracks. He let them run on and widen. He drew them all. He saw that the window wall's enormous sheet of glass was on the point of bursting from the pressure from within, and he began drawing it as fast as he could, and at the same time he saw the cleft that opened in the floor and it was black. He worked faster and faster, but before his pen could reach the darkness the room he was drawing turned and crashed outwards to its ruin.
>
> *(L, 51)*

The ending could be interpreted as a clear descent into a chthonic darkness. On the whole, overwhelming darkness is a recurring theme in Jansson's fiction. Darkness is seen as offensive, aggressive, and horrifying. In "The Dark," from *The Sculptor's Daughter*, a large grey faceless character creeps over the docks and islands. Darkness is uncanny; it is unfamiliar, frightening, and intrusive. We can also sense this feeling of overwhelming fear in the Moomin books, when the reader for the first time encounters the horrific characters of The Groke and The Lady of the Cold, who both favour the night and are both bringers of ultimate coldness (see Korhonen 2011).

Like in "Black-White," a tone of spatial horror is evident also in the short story "The Doll's House." There, a retired artisan and upholsterer Alexander nearly alienates his partner Erik by turning their house into a studio for the stunning creation of the large-scale doll's house. Alexander puts all his ability, effort, and time on building the doll's house, and it fully consumes his imagination. Like the illustrator in "Black-White," Alexander in "The Doll's House" loses himself to the project and becomes obsessed with it. The project seems to be consuming Alexander; he declares that he wants to build a house for him and Erik. Yet the house cannot be a real house without working electricity, since Alexander wants the house to glow, to live from the inside.

Therefore, Alexander cannot finish the project on his own, and he ends up persuading an electrician called Boy to work on the project with him. This results in a kind of a "love triangle," since Boy also becomes obsessed with the doll's house. In the end of the story, all of this escalates in a strange way. When Alexander is out buying cigarettes, Boy manages to finalise the electric work for the house, getting the lights to revolve in different colours, and is overwhelmed by the achievement:

> "We did it!" Boy shouted, laughing out loud. "Alexander and me! We made it work. We've topped off the house and the beacon's working just the way it should. Well? What do you think of our house?"
>
> "It's not yours," said Erik very softly.
>
> "Oh yes it is," Boy said. "It sure is! You'd better believe it is! Come and look from the other side. Come look at the way the lights reflect in the bedroom mirrors!" When Erik didn't move, he took him by the arm.
>
> *(AN, 79–80)*

When excited, Boy pushes Erik to look closer, something finally snaps in Erik's head. Erik takes a drill from the workbench and hits Boy on the ear with it. Boy tries to flee from Erik's attack, but it is not possible, so Boy hides behind the Doll's house:

> "Turn it [the light] off so I can see you, or I'll smash the whole tower to pieces!"

He took one step toward Boy and said, "Shall I smash you or the tower?" By now he was shaking so hard he could barely stand. "Shall I smash you to pieces? Is it you I shall smash?"

"No," Boy said. "Not me." ...

When the light came on, he put the drill handle back on the workbench. Boy put his fingers carefully to his ear and looked at his hand. "Blood," he said. "It's running down on my collar."

(AN, 80–81)

Erik and Boy are still collecting themselves after the attack when Alexander comes back from the shop. Alexander can see that Boy is bleeding from the attack, but weirdly he is more concerned with the doll's house:

"What have you done?" [Alexander asked.]

"I don't know," Erik said. "But I saved our tower. It's all in one piece."

Slowly, Alexander opened a pack of cigarettes, took one out and lit it. "It actually rotates," he said. "You know your stuff, Boy. Now the whole thing's perfect. No one's ever built such a house as Erik's and mine."

(AN, 80–81)

In the above excerpt, we can see that although the scene itself turns into a more tranquil ending, the uncanny nature of the story remains. The doll's house occupies Alexander's mind, and he does not care what has happened before he arrives as long as the house itself is functioning and "perfect." The reader is still lingering in a state of uncertainty. The story ends, and we remain uncertain of the outcome. The liminal uncanny element of the attack is pushed back over "the threshold," it seems to be forgotten or ignored, and the characters of the text seem to be satisfied by the outcome. But for the reader, the text remains weird, strange, and uncanny.

Conclusion: The Uncanny in Tove Jansson's Fiction

Tove Jansson uses uncanny elements in their short stories: they make these stories interesting. Horror and uncanny were their literary passions. This becomes obvious when closely reading their works like I have done in this chapter. Jansson, as I argued in the beginning, "loves horror" (Jansson 2014b, 469). Jansson's legacy as a speculative fiction writer is wider and more impressive than just their work as an author for the Moomins. Uncanny elements in Jansson's stories, and Jansson's production of strange or weird texts, were well ahead of their time in terms of today's ideas of speculative fiction. Jansson produced genre hybrid texts of uncanny twists and psychological accuracy, which is still breathtakingly up to date in the twenty-first century.

Juhani Niemi points out that illustrator, cartoonist, writer, and artist characters in Jansson's texts "are all characterised by the fact that they do not know what they are striving after". They have "lost touch with shared reality which would unite them with the world experienced by others" (Niemi 1996, 30). I would claim that the main characters know what they are striving after, but the goal itself has become unfamiliar and even insane. The main characters in short stories like "Black-White" or "The Doll's House" have all lost their touch with reality and stepped into a quasi-reality of the uncanny world.

In Jansson's short stories, motifs of the sublime and horror create uncanny experiences for the reader, since on many occasions we do not exactly know what we are reading. Texts invoke questions that are not answered or are not plainly answered. For example, why is the character of Emmelina seen as frightening inside the story world? What makes people uneasy around Elis in "Summer Child"? What really happens in "The Doll's House" or "Black-White"? Are we witnessing mental breakdowns or just reading on the experience of being an artist? The uncanny, whether it is intrusive or liminal, is clearly there.

As readers, we are left with the experience of unsettling and strange sensations. Of course, it must also be acknowledged that open endings and open questions are common in the medium (and a genre standard) of short stories.

The power of the uncanny experience is the strength of Jansson's short stories. Texts can be interpreted in many ways. The uncanny, here, is based on the fact that we cannot say for sure whether these are instances of insanity or depictions of horror. These stories could be read either as inner cognitive experiences of characters in the stories and instances of psychological problems or simply as depictions of unfamiliar horror. It is left for the reader to decide.

Acknowledgements

Jyrki Korpua wrote this chapter when working in the global Tove Jansson project, funded by Kone Foundation and led by Doctor Jussi Ojajärvi. I would like to thank the Tove Jansson research group for valuable comments on the manuscript.

Notes

1 For genre hybridity in Nordic speculative fiction, see also Piippo's and Raipola's chapters in this book.
2 At the time, Jansson was working on illustrations for Lewis Carroll's *Alice in Wonderland*. She wanted to make it a pure horror book and emphasised in their letter (2014b, 469) Carroll's work as horror fiction.

3 In the original text, the phrasing is a bit gentler: meaning more precisely *almost a little afraid of him.*
4 Another clear example of an outsider character in Moomin books is Ninny, the invisible character in the short story "The Invisible Child" ("Det ösynlika barnet," 1962).
5 We should also note that when Jansson wrote the story in 1935, "cliché" was known as a term used by printers and artists in their discourse to refer to a cast plate or block print that could reproduce images. Jansson clearly uses this double meaning in a doppelgänger story. For the meaning of the term and Edgar Allan Poe's influence on Jansson's work, see Sirke Happonen's essay on the subject (2017, 251–253).

References

Aejmelaeus, Salme. 1994. *Kun lyhdyt syttyvät. Tove Jansson ja muumimaailma.* Saarijärvi: Suomen Nuorisokirjallisuuden Instituutti.
Aguirre, Manuel. 1990. *The Closed Space. Horror Literature and Western Symbolism.* Manchester: Manchester UP.
Alanko, Outi & Kuisma Korhonen. 2000. "Lukijalle." In *Subliimi, groteski, ironia.* In *Kirjallisuudentutkijain seuran vuosikirja 52 1999*, eds. Outi Alanko & Kuisma Korhonen, 8–10. Helsinki: SKS.
Briggs, Julia. 2000. "The Ghost Story." In *A Companion to the Gothic*, ed. David Punter, 122–131. Oxford: Blackwell Publishers Ltd.
Buckland, Corinne. 2007. "Tove Jansson and Humble Sublime." In *Tove Jansson Rediscovered*, eds. Kate McLoughlin & Malin Lindström Brock, 28–40. Newcastle: Cambridge Scholars Publishers.
Burke, Edmund. 1834. *The Works of the Right Hon. Edmund Burke, Vol. 1.* London: Holsdworth and Ball.
Colavito, Jason. 2008. *Knowing Fear. Science, Knowledge and the Development of the Horror Genre.* Jefferson: McFarland.
Dery, Mark. 2018. *Born to be Posthumous: The Eccentric Life and Mysterious Genius of Edward Gorey.* London: Hachette.
Freud, Sigmund. 1989. "The Uncanny." In *Sigmund Freud: Art and Literature*, ed. Albert Dickson, 335–376. Harmondsworth: Penguin Books.
Happonen, Sirke. 2017. "Efterord." In Tove Jansson: *Bulevarden och andra texter*, ed. Sirke Happonen, 237–268. Helsingfors: Förlaget M Oy Ab.
Jackson, Rosemary. 1981. *Fantasy. The Literature of Subversion.* London & New York: Methuen.
Jansson, Tove. 1968. *Bildhuggarens dotter.* Stockholm: Albert Bonniers Förlag.
Jansson, Tove. 1978. *Dockskåpet och andra berättelser.* Helsingfors: Schildts.
Jansson, Tove. 1987. *Resa med lättbagage.* Uddevalla: Holger Schildtsförlag.
Jansson, Tove. 1991. *Brev från Klara.* Falun: Schildts.
Jansson, Tove. 2010. *Travelling Light.* (TL). Trans. Silvester Mazzarella. London: Sort of Books.
Jansson, Tove. 2012/1978. *Art in Nature.* (AN). Trans. Thomas Teal. London: Sort of Books.
Jansson, Tove. 2013/1968. *Sculptor's Daughter. A Childhood Memoir.* Trans. Kingsley Hart. London: Sort of Books.
Jansson, Tove. 2014a/1971. *The Listener.* (L). Trans. Thomas Teal. London: Sort of Books.
Jansson, Tove. 2014b. *Kirjeitä Tove Janssonilta.* Eds. Boel Westin & Helen Svensson. Trans. Jaana Nikula & Tuula Kojo. Helsinki: Schildts & Söderströms.

Jansson, Tove. 2017a/1991. *Letters from Klara. And Other Stories.* (LK). Trans. Thomas Teal. London: Sort of Books.

Jansson, Tove. 2017b/1971. *Lyssnerskan.* Malmö: Modernista.

Jansson, Tove. 2017c. *Bulevarden och andra texter.* Ed. Sirke Happonen. Helsingfors: Förlaget M Oy Ab.

Jones, W. Glynn. 1984. *Tove Jansson.* Boston: Twayne Publishers.

Joshi, S. T. 1990. *The Weird Tale.* Holicong: Wildside Press.

Kåreland, Lena. 1996. "Todellisuutta uhkaavat lastenkirjasankarittaret. Vaarallinen matka ja Liisan seikkailut ihmemaassa psykoanalyyttisestä näkökulmasta." In *Muumien taikaa. Tutkimusretkiä Tove Janssonin maailmaan. The Magic of the Moomins. Exploring Tove Jansson's World,* ed. Virpi Kurhela, 47–61. Helsinki: BTJ.

Korhonen, Kuisma. 2011. "Muumipeikko ja mörkö." In Kuisma Korhonen: *Lukijoiden yhteisö. Ystävyydestä, kansanmurhista, itkevistä kivistä,* 112–132. Helsinki: Avain.

Laajarinne, Jukka. 2009. *Muumit ja olemisen arvoitus.* 2nd edition. Jyväskylä: Atena.

Lovecraft, H. P. 1973. *Supernatural Horror in Literature.* New York: Dover Publication, Inc.

Lyytikäinen, Pirjo. 2000. "Äärettömiä olioita. Subliimi ja groteski Leena Krohnin tuotannossa." In *Subliimi, groteski, ironia. Kirjallisuudentutkijain seuran vuosikirja 52 1999,* eds. Outi Alanko & Kuisma Korhonen, 11–34. Helsinki: SKS.

Mendlesohn, Farah. 2008. *Rhetorics of Fantasy.* Middletown: Wesleyan UP.

McElroy, Bernard. 1989. *Fiction of the Modern Grotesque.* London: The Macmillan Press Ltd.

Niemi, Juhani. 1996. "From Moomins to a Party Game. Journey into Tove Jansson's World." In *Muumien taikaa. Tutkimusretkiä Tove Janssonin maailmaan. The Magic of the Moomins. Exploring Tove Jansson's World,* ed. Virpi Kurhela, 25–34. Helsinki: BTJ.

Rehal-Johansson, Agneta. 2006. *Den lömska barnboksförfattaren: Tove Jansson och muminverkets metamorfoser.* Göteborg: Makadam.

Royle, Nicholas. 2003. *The Uncanny: An Introduction.* Manchester: Manchester UP.

Sandbacka, Kasimir. 2018. "Myöhäismoderni melankolia Tove Janssonin novelleissa 'Aikakäsite' ja 'Lokomotiivi'." *Avain – Kirjallisuudentutkimuksen aikakauslehti* 4/2018: 22–37.

Stableford, Brian. 2005. *The A to Z of Fantasy Literature.* Plymouth: The Scarecrow Press, Inc.

Takahashi, Shizuo. 1996. "Persoonallisuudenkukka. Vieraantuminen ja vapautuminen muumitarinoissa." In *Muumien taikaa. Tutkimusretkiä Tove Janssonin maailmaan. The Magic of the Moomins. Exploring Tove Jansson's World,* ed. Virpi Kurhela, 73–81. Helsinki: BTJ.

Thomson, Philip. 1972. *The Grotesque.* London: Methuen.

Ylönen, Susanne. 2014. "'Meidän maailmamme möröt ovat sisäpuolella': muuminologian vaikutus lastenkirjallisuuden eksistentiaalisten kauhujen arvottamiseen." In *Lastenkirja. Nyt,* ed. Marleena Mustola, 217–240. Helsinki: Suomalaisen Kirjallisuuden Seura.

6

WELCOME TO THE UNCANNY VALLEY

Speculations on the Posthuman Condition in Contemporary Danish Fiction

Sophie Wennerscheid

In recent years, a great many Danish novels have been published that portray a dramatically changing world. These are speculative narratives about humans and the "more-than-human world" (Abram 1996, 24) in which humans are enmeshed. In *Ecology Without Nature*, the environmental philosopher Timothy Morton underlines the idea of interrelatedness by suggesting that "[t]here is no such 'thing' as the environment, since, being involved in it already, we are not separate from it" (Morton 2007, 163). This all-encompassing relatedness is what Morton calls "the Mesh." As within this mesh there is no longer any human supremacy, in this chapter I propose to speak of human–nonhuman entanglements out of human control. A related term denoting these specific entanglements is "posthuman"; to be understood as a condition in which clear-cut separations between animate and inanimate, organic and inorganic, life and death, are questioned, and any privileges founded on anthropocentric dominance rejected (Wolfe 2010).

To depict the peculiarity of the posthuman condition, many of the novels in question make use of the concept of the uncanny, strengthening the idea of insecurity and distress. The world is no longer seen and described as a world of objects over which humans can rule, but as "a world of forces and agencies that are strange, other and often deeply disturbing when viewed from an anthropocentric standpoint" (Henriksen & Radomska 2015, 113).

In my view, two interrelated societal changes account for why uncontrollability as such looms large in contemporary Danish literature: proceeding rapid technological development, on the one hand, and increased awareness of the environmental crisis, on the other. Dissipated in millions of bits and bytes, the world has become more and more abstract and unfathomable. Every single moment we encounter something, the effect of which we

DOI: 10.4324/9781003561101-10

feel but whose specific cause we cannot grasp. Technological developments, instead of making our lives more predictable and manageable, have created a spectral layer to existence. Consequently, the digital uncanny (Ravetto-Biagioli 2019) proliferates. At the same time, the climate crisis is experienced as something that humans, in particular those in the Western world, have brought about and are no longer in control of. Exploited for centuries, the biosphere, animated and hostile, seems to fight back. As a result, the feeling of the ecological uncanny (Morton 2010; Gosh 2016) spreads. With its strong interest in technological innovation and its likewise strong environmental concern, Denmark represents the specific ambivalence of the modern society in which progress and destruction go hand in hand. It is this ambivalence that contemporary Danish fiction addresses by means of speculative narratives.

The aim of this chapter is to examine how contemporary Danish novels and short stories, which I classify as speculative fiction, deploy speculation as a means of opening up for unknown dimensions of reality beyond the anthropocentric horizon and how they portray uncanny intimacies between human and more-than-human worlds that arise when the anthropocentric point of view is abandoned. More specifically, I will examine the 'uncanny valley' as a metaphorical or concrete place where the current environmental crisis is felt, disorienting the novels' characters and exposing them to the feeling of being stuck, overpowered, or invaded by unknown forces.

My examination proceeds in five steps. First, I will briefly unpack the concept of the uncanny. Then, I will outline the genre of speculative fiction for the purpose of this chapter and in relation to the philosophical movement of speculative realism. Although the literary works to be analysed pursue a new approach to the speculative genre, they nevertheless draw on previous notions of the speculative that can be found in Danish literary history, as well as in modern Danish science fiction. To make these connections clear, I will briefly delineate these traditions. From there, I will examine the representation of uncanny human and more-than-human relationships in the novels and short stories by Ursula Scavenius, Jonas Eika, and Olga Ravn, which I consider representative of contemporary Danish speculative fiction authors.

The Uncanny

The uncanny is a concept[1] used to describe encounters with something that has previously been familiar, as for instance a doll, but suddenly seems alive and therefore exceeds the framework of understanding the world and gives us the "flickering sense of something supernatural" (Royle 2003, 1). As a psychological and philosophical concept, the uncanny has a long tradition in Western cultural history, but only recently it has attracted attention in a broader environmental context.

The notion of the uncanny was introduced by psychoanalyst Ernst Jentsch, who in 1906 defined the uncanny as a product of intellectual uncertainty. It arises when one cannot tell exactly whether a thing is alive or not. This uncertainty means loss of control and inability to resist an "attack by hostile powers" (Jentsch 1906, 205).[2] To illustrate his point, Jentsch refers to E.T.A. Hoffmann's fantastic short story "Der Sandmann" (1816), where the mechanical doll Olimpia drives the young Nathanael insane because he mistakes the lifelike doll for a real woman.

In 1919, Sigmund Freud elaborates on Jentsch's understanding of the uncanny by arguing that horror does not arise from uncertainty, but from confrontation with something that should have remained private and hidden, a secret within the family, but instead "has come to light" (Freud 1955, 225). Predicted on the idea of discomfort in encountering something that lies hidden inside us, Freud's concept of the uncanny is basically a border phenomenon. It questions the boundary between present and past, between known and unknown, living and dead.

This very idea is also at the centre of a short text by the roboticist Masahiro Mori. In this text, first published in Japanese in 1970 and later disseminated in English under the title "The Uncanny Valley" (2012), Mori argues that humans have a certain affinity for inanimate objects, for example robots, that look humanlike. Indeed, Mori states, humans react more positively to robots the more similar they are to us. However, this happens only up to a certain point. When a robot that is so human-like that it is mistaken for a human suddenly becomes recognisable as nonhuman, we react with horror. The sudden decline of our affinity for the humanoid object is termed the valley of the eeriness phenomenon, in short, the uncanny valley.

In this chapter I will draw on the concept of the uncanny valley to describe a creeping sense of unease that arises when the nonhuman biosphere shows humans its hitherto unknown face. With this, I tie in with Morton's use of the uncanny.

Morton speaks of "environmental creepiness" (Morton 2010, 54) to describe the sense of helplessness humans feel when becoming aware of their entanglement with the biosphere. It returns every time we experience our being in the world as "a vast, sprawling mesh of interconnection without a definite centre or edge." In the same context, Morton refers to this feeling as "radical intimacy" with other beings (Morton 2010, 8).

A similar thought is put forward by Amitav Ghosh, who emphasises that our repressed entanglements with the biosphere return in uncanny experiences with "non-human interlocutors" (Gosh 2016, 30). According to Ghosh, the fact that the proximity between humans and the biosphere has been concealed for such a long time is due to the negative effects of modernity and even more so of modern literature. While pre-modern literature was inspired by the idea of animated nature, the modern realist novel tried "to erase every archaic reminder of Man's kinship with the non-human" (70). What we thus are in need of today, Ghosh argues, are novels that again open "a doorway into what we might call a 'spirit world' – a universe animated by non-human voices" (73).

This idea of a doorway into the more-than-human world corresponds with the wave of new speculative fiction that is indebted to the philosophy of speculative realism. It is, as the leading figure of speculative realism, Graham Harman, emphasises, not "a dull commonsense realism" (Harman 2010, 2) that the new speculative writers seek to explore, but a realism characterised by uncanny forces.

Speculative Fiction, Speculative Realism, and Speculative Futurism

The term "speculative fiction" was introduced by the American author Robert A. Heinlein to characterise science fiction texts that extrapolate from scientific facts but are not at odds with the scientifically possible (Heinlein 1977). Literary motifs such as unicorns or speaking nonhuman actants therefore have no place in Heinlein's literary universe.

In contrast to Heinlein, writer and editor Judith Merril deliberately included fantastic elements in her genre definition, representing speculative fiction as "a special sort of contemporary writing which makes use of fantastic or inventive elements to comment on, or speculate about, society, humanity, life, the cosmos, reality" (Merril 1967, 3). The literary scholar Marek Oziewicz points out that Merril's understanding of speculative fiction as "a cluster of non-mimetic genres striving for social change" (Oziewicz 2017, n.p.) was a precursor to a new trend in speculative fiction that took off in 2000. However, despite his strong interest in non-mimetic texts critical of an empirical concept of reality, Oziewicz does not pay any attention to texts that seek to go beyond the horizon of human experience by exploring the uncanny posthuman dimensions of reality.

In my opinion, however, it is precisely the posthumanist approach that challenges normative and anthropocentrically limited notions of reality and foregrounds a more-than-human world. Instead of considering the world as something objectively given, ready to be explored by a human subject, both contemporary speculative fiction and the philosophical movement of speculative realism pay special attention to the long-ignored proximity of more-than-human forces and humans' entanglement with it.

Speculative realism was first proposed as a term at a philosophy workshop of the same name, held at Goldsmiths College, University of London in 2007. The workshop brought together theorists who were in critical opposition to Immanuel Kant's epistemological reservations about the possibility of recognising reality beyond human experience. Whereas Kant emphasised the limits of speculative reason, the speculative philosophers gathered at the workshop deemed it necessary to explore the aspects of "real reality," "das Ding an sich," that are unknowable according to Kant. Since "the real reality" cannot be reached through science, it is considered uncontrollable and strange. In his introduction to speculative realism, Levi Bryant explains: "One of the key features of the Speculative Turn is precisely that the move toward realism is not a move towards the stuffy limitations of common sense, but quite often a turn towards the downright bizarre" (Bryant 2011, 7). Or as Graham Harman pointedly puts it: it is "a darker form of 'weird realism'" speculative realism is interested in (2010, 2).

With the term "weird," Harman refers to the American author H.P. Lovecraft, best known for literary texts that, according to Lovecraft himself, are characterised by a "certain atmosphere of breathless and unexplainable dread of outer, unknown forces" (Lovecraft 2004, 84), against which humans are helpless. Meeting these forces, the human self falls into an abyss of nothingness and experiences itself as utterly insignificant. This experience is described as cosmic horror or cosmic fear.

However, if we want to make the case for speculation as a means of opening up for unknown dimensions of reality, on the one hand, and for unknown futures scenarios, on the other hand, we shouldn't put too much emphasis on dread and horror. Not to own the future might evoke the feeling of wandering through an uncanny valley, but it also provides images of possible futures that might be less gloomy, maybe even luminous.

This might become clearer when we take a look at very early meanings of speculation. In Latin, *speculari* means to look, to spy, and in the New Testament the apostle Paul brings the word into the context of *speculum*, or in Greece ἐσόπτρου, a mirror. In his first letter to the Corinthians, he emphasises that after death people will see God face to face, whereas now we can only see the truth in or through a dark mirror, "a mirror dimly" (I Cor 13,12, English Standard Version 2016), as in a riddle.

Both aspects, the confrontation with a dark present and the hope for a better future where the limitations of human perception are transcended, play an important role in contemporary fiction concerned with the more-than-human world. To stress this aspect of speculation as going beyond the surface of the present and to open for unknown futures and strange realities, I propose to talk about speculative futuring. However, before diving deeper into speculative future narratives, a brief look at possible historical antecedents to this kind of fiction is appropriate.

Historical Antecedents

The Nordic countries have a long tradition of speculative poetry that thematises humans' encounters with human-like supernatural beings such as elves, dwarves, hulders, and mermaids, on the one hand, and with nonhuman beings on other planets, on the other. The latter can be seen, for example, in the satirical novel *Niels Klim's Underground Travels* (orig. in Latin, *Nicolai Klimii Iter Subterraneum*, 1741) by the Norwegian-Danish author Ludvig Holberg, depicting the utopian society Potu from an earthling's point of view.

While the last-named tradition has its root in the age of Enlightenment, the first originates from mediaeval texts and folklore (Kvideland 1991) and received a strong revival in the Romantic era. In this context, the idea of an animated and speaking nature gets intertwined with nature philosophy's attempt to reveal nature's hidden meaning. For instance, Danish-Norwegian philosopher of nature Henrik Steffens was well acquainted with F.W.J. Schelling's speculative nature philosophy and muses on a nature pervaded by spiritual forces (Wennerscheid 2021).

Influenced and inspired by both folkloristic tales and technological developments of his time, the Danish author of Romanticism H.C. Andersen was concerned with the impact of new technologies on nature. In his late fairy tale, *The Wood Nymph: A Tale from the 1867 Paris Exposition* (1868), for instance, he tells the story of a wood nymph who praises the human-made technological wonders at the World Fair Exhibition in Paris, but soon perishes in the "plant-suffocating city air" (Andersen 2006, 398). Likewise, in his travelogue *In Sweden* (*I Sverrig*, 1851), Andersen portrays modernity as fascinating and frightening at the same time. When the narrator visits a huge waterfall and the evolving industry around, he learns about an uncanny figure called Bloodless who symbolises industrialisation.

Another key figure of Danish literature with a strong interest in the uncanny is Karen Blixen. In particular in *Seven Gothic Tales* (*Syv Fantastiske Fortællinger*, 1934), Blixen makes excessive use of it (Kastbjerg 2013). Drawing on the tradition of romantic storytelling, her story "The Monkey" ("Aben") is a good example. Central to the story is the relation between the Prioress of a venerable cloister and her little monkey, with whom she has a strange bond. In accordance with Nordic mediaeval ballads and folkloristic tales about shapeshifting (Raudvere 2022), she every autumn exchanges her identity with this mysterious animal. Accordingly, "The Monkey" has recently been read as an example of Nordic EcoGothic (Mortensen 2019).

While contemporary speculative fiction from Denmark draws on this tradition of uncanny narratives, the relation to texts that display more typical traits of science fiction, as for example advanced science and technology, space travel and exploration, and encounters with extra-terrestrials (Latham 2014), is vague. However, there are a few connection points. In the 1950s American science fiction author Ray Bradbury became popular in Denmark. According to science fiction scholar Niels Dalsgaard, Bradbury's stories appealed to the Danish audience because of their "strong reservations about technological progress," but at the same time also due to their romantic representations of the wonders of space travel (Dalgaard 2010, 234). With these stories, Bradbury had a strong impact on Danish science fiction author Niels E. Nielsen, who shared Bradbury's technological pessimism.

In the 1960s, pessimism briefly gave way to enthusiasm for technology, and mainstream fiction writers started to make use of science fiction elements. Anders Bodelsen, for instance, published the novel *The Freezing Point* (*Frysepunktet*, 1969), a speculation on the promise of immortality, and avant-gardist author Svend Åge Madsen tried out the science fiction genre as well. Likewise, Jens Smærup Sørensen "occasionally used space travel in stories of loneliness and human estrangement" (Dalgaard 2010, 236), and Dorit Willumsen with her novel *Programmed for Love* (*Programmeret til kærlighed,* 1981) on the robot Bianca focused on humans' alienation from nature and gave Danish science fiction a feminist twist.

Contemporary Danish Speculative Fiction

When we now turn to contemporary Danish fiction that deals with the dissolution of the boundaries between humans and nonhumans, and thus with humans living under posthuman conditions, we might see to what extent some traits of the traditions outlined reappear. While the large number of the texts in question makes it impossible to elaborate on their specific characteristics, a rough distinction can be made between two trends. On the one hand, there are texts that portray increasing technologisation and digitalisation as the cause of our current crises and the insecurities that accompany them. Examples are Jeppe Krogsgaard Christensen's *April 2026* (2017), Theis Ørntoft's *Solar* (2018), Svend Åge Madsens *Fremtidsspejl* (2020, "The Mirror of the Future"), Kristian Byskov's *Græsset* (2020, "The Grass") and Viggo Bjerring's *Verdenshjertet* (2021, "The Heart of the World"), all of which concern new media, technology, or artificial intelligence that frightens people by depriving them of their autonomy.

On the other hand, there are weird eco-fictions that tell of a world that is affected by environmental problems people can no longer cope with. Examples include Kristian Byskov's post-apocalyptic novel *Mitose* (2013, 'Mitosis'), in which a monstrous toad plays an important role; Charlotte Weitze's novel *Den afskyelige* (2016, "The Abominable Snowman"), in which climate crisis is associated with the mythological figure of the Abominable Snowman; and Dennis Gade Kofod's novel *Nancy* (2015), which tells a story about underground creatures trying to reclaim the isle of Bornholm from humans who have despised nature for too long. In all these novels, nature is portrayed as a violent and sinister force, of which humans become increasingly afraid.

While all of these texts deal with the digital, the technological, or the ecological uncanny in one way or another, in the following I will focus on books in which the uncanny technosphere and the uncanny biosphere are addressed at the same time: Ursula Scavenius's collection of short stories *Fjer* (2015, "Feathers") and *The Dolls* (*Dukkerne*, 2020); Jonas Eika's *After the Sun* (*Efter solen*, 2018), likewise a collection of short stories; and Olga Ravn's short novel *The Employees* (*De ansatte*, 2018). What makes these books special is not only that they bring together aspects of the digital, the technological, and the environmental uncanny but also that they do so in a literary language that makes the boundaries of reality shimmer and open a doorway into a posthuman world "animated by non-human voices" (Gosh 2016, 73). However, this world does not exist here and now but is connected, as Ursula Le Guin formulates it, "to the unverifiable past and the unpredictable future" (Le Guin 1989, 45).

In a Mirror Dimly

The idea of unfathomable time is crucial in Scavenius's, Eika's, and Ravn's fiction. In their books, time cannot be fitted into the ordinary directional order but is, as in a dream, meandering back and forth, beyond the rules of causality and plausibility. Since this fictional time is experienced in disjointed moments, the language used to represent it makes excessive use of arbitrary images and sensory metaphors that evoke the feeling of insecurity, distress, and eeriness.

In all three stories of Ursula Scavenius's 2015 debut book *Fjer* ("Feathers"), there is a nightmarish atmosphere with surrealist undertones that opens up glimpses of an unreliable future, viewed from a threatened but still anthropocentric point of view. The first story, "Majinski," is set in the outskirts of Sofia, Bulgaria, and starts with an unsettling flashback that brings the readers back to the "January of the Dogs." "The first time I met Peter Majinsky, he threw a cabbage head at an old dog, and it died" (Scavenius 2015, 11). This act of killing a dog appears necessary because the many free running and loudly barking dogs seem to pose a serious threat to the city dwellers.

Since there is no functioning societal order that secures the well-being of people, everyone is left to their own devices. When people seek help from others, this results in disaster. This becomes evident when the title character Majinski asks the first-person narrator Alexander to take care of Majinski's daughter Lucia, who looks like a wolf. When Alexander goes out into the night to find Lucia, the scene is transformed into a werewolf tale, which both gestures towards Nordic ballads of shapeshifters (Raudvere 2022) and to surrealist fiction that brings the unconscious to the surface. "It was eleven o'clock when I went out. ... Now the dogs were satisfied for a time and lay like long, limp watch-wisher in a row along the street. Time stood still when the animals slept. I think I felt eternity in me, and an unspeakable fear" (Scavenius 2015, 14). When we read this passage in the light of speculative futuring as referred to above, the apostle Paul's hope for better has vanished. Behind the mirror of the present there is only darkness.

The same goes for "Luna seconda," a story about a moon that has given birth to another moon, causing the water to rise. Most people and animals are already dead; only some have survived, among them Anker and Sabina who face their end in horror. From the beginning of the story, there is an atmosphere of unease and destruction. "They drive aimlessly along the roads past sick people and animals, past two donkey foals huddled together inside a barbed wire fence, past a dead calf stuck under a fallen wall, and past cars swimming in the valley" (41). Although the story does not elaborate on the motif of the valley, it is no coincidence that the story is set in a place where people are particularly vulnerable to rising water levels.

The bleak atmosphere is reinforced by an ambivalent representation of sensory impressions. A cow roars; otherwise everything seems mute. The water is pitch black, but there is a pink glow in the sky. It smells of seaweed and decay. The forces of the biosphere, against which people are powerless, are reflected in Sabina's delusions. She "feels something that feels like little wings on her tongue, and she spits and spits, but the sensation of wings on her tongue stays on her throat all the way home" (49). As in the dog story "Majinski," the gloomy and uncanny atmosphere comes from humans that feel threatened by animals which suddenly are recognised as being alive in another way than expected. While in modern society humans tend to treat animals as inanimate, as for example seen in the large-scale meat industry, the human characters in Scavenius's stories in a flash see the animals' 'soul' and agency and therefore experience them as uncanny. Furthermore, the characters seem to realise how irreconcilable humans' treatment of nonhumans is if they do in fact have 'soul' and are suffering from humans destroying their habitat.

With reference to Morton and Ghosh, the atmosphere of Scavenius's stories can be described as an atmosphere of the environmental uncanny. As Morton has argued for, this kind of eeriness emerges when people are unable to master nature because they are enmeshed in it. This enmeshment becomes obvious when, as is the case in "Luna seconda," the rising sea level erases the urban coordinate system and turns everything into dark and muddy waters where birds are the last survivors. Sabina's "steps lead nowhere, and she wades like in a dream" (47).

The representation of humanity on the verge of disintegration also dominates Scavenius's second book, *The Dolls*. This becomes particularly clear in the title story, "The Dolls," in which we meet a family living in a ruined city ruled by an unspecified "Machine." The first thing we hear about in the story is an eerie violin music that sounds like "chicken bones scraping against teeth" (Scavenius 2021, 7). The first-person narrator Agnes will remind the reader of this sound throughout the story. There is no way out. The sound invades the family's home as do swarms of clothes moths and some owlet moths. As the music gets louder, the moths grow bigger. Soon, one of them is as big as a kitten. "I imagine it inside my mouth and it makes my stomach turn" (30).

As the story progresses, it becomes clear that Agnes's family is involved in some kind of murdering migrant children to use their hair to set it on doll heads. While Agnes's sister has withdrawn from this work by living in the cellar, Agnes follows her father's instructions to produce the lifelike dolls. As Agnes becomes more and more aware of her being involved in processes of destruction, she notices uncanny changes in the biosphere: "The vegetables have all grown together; a carrot and a beet are tangled up, a courgette is intertwined with a cabbage head and the potatoes have fused with the Jerusalem artichokes" (42).

Finally, the looming apocalypse takes the form of the great machine, sometimes portrayed as a kind of factory, at other times as a kind of gigantic excavator. At the end of the story, the machine takes up more and more space and finally destroys the family's house. While the walls of the house collapse, Agnes receives a strange package through the chimney. She unwraps it and sees "a pre-cut chicken, with a brown face nestled between the drumsticks. A child with black hair. The child's mouth is agape, and staring out at me from behind the cellophane is a pair of terrified eyes" (88). Looking at the child's eyes, Agnes is confronted with her own complicity in social and environmental crimes.

To sum up, the humans in Scavenius's stories have lost their humanity but do not gain anything else in return. When it comes down to it, they cling to their anthropocentric view and perceive the nonhuman other, be it a barking dog, a butterfly, a doll, or a machine, as an uncanny mirror of their own moral failure. Therefore, the posthuman condition they live in is experienced as nothing but a nightmare.

Jonas Eika's *After the Sun* is somewhat different. Here, from the first to the last of the total of five stories, we can see a certain opening towards a posthuman future that contains some luminous, even utopian moments.

Ghosts from the Future

Jonas Eika's award-winning book *After the Sun* is a blend of science fiction, eco-fiction, and social criticism. Experiences of the uncanny play a major role but creep into the stories almost unnoticed. The opening story, "Alvin," is a good example of how effective this storytelling technique is. "Alvin" tells of an "extremely fictional flight" (11) to Copenhagen. On board the plane is a feverish young man, the story's first-person narrator, who is about to meet

Alvin, an IT administrator of a bank. However, arriving in Copenhagen, the narrator learns that the bank no longer exists; it has collapsed for reasons unknown. The scene is described matter-of-factly, but evokes a grotesque and disturbing atmosphere, subtly linked to the climate crisis. "Three or four servers protruded between the floorboards and whiteboards; funny, I thought, since the floors had just been elevated in expectation of rising sea levels" (13).

When shortly afterwards the protagonist meets Alvin, things and relations become even more unstable. Alvin looks somewhat unreal and trades in derivatives, or rather, as he points out, in the future. "Forget about the forces of the free market, my friend," Alvin explains. "Commodity prices no longer refer to any value, past or present – they're just ghosts from the future" (18). If a value is no longer tied to something concrete, but merely a speculative quantity, a ghost from the future, something dead before it is even born, then chronological time has broken down. "Collapse into the present. Zero time," as the British writer Nick Land (2011, 391) puts it in his aphoristic text "No Future," in which he discusses the accelerating dimensions of capitalism.

The narrator experiences the collapse of time when he one day takes a shower, and Alvin gives him a massage with a strange shampoo that makes the skin pulse. Only the places that Alvin omits to massage feel numb, "like dark matter contracting into itself. ... For maybe ten seconds, I was in a funnel of time, seeing only myself at the other end. It was very lonely" (Eika 2021, 27). The feeling of loneliness in a dark tunnel of time is reminiscent of Lovecraft's idea of cosmic horror. However, it is not "outer, unknown forces" (Lovecraft 2004, 84) that threaten the protagonist but forces that are brought about by his own imaginations. As in a dream the uncanny images appear and disappear. When, at the end of the story, the ghostlike Alvin vanishes into thin air, it is as if he had just been a dream, an unreliable speculation on the future.

The question of what is real and what is not is also central to the story "Rachel, Nevada." In this story, an extradiegetic narrator gives account of an old man, Antonio, who wanders in the endless valleys of the desert, where at one point he makes the acquaintance of the "Sender," a two-metre-high object emitting a strange but fascinating sound. In the beginning the Sender appears "like an object meant to travel through the world oblivious to whatever matter it encountered," but three years later, it is "overgrown with a greenish-white fungus that had fused with its surface, making it spongy and porous" (Eika 2021, 61). Antonio perceives the object as breathy and feels a strong attraction to it. The same goes for plants and animals. They all creep up to the Sender and coalesce with it.

The proximity between the technological object and the animals arouses Antonio's desire to be part of their "radical intimacy" (Morton 2010, 8). To get, quite literally, on the same wavelength with the Sender, he implements a three-centimetre piece of it into his own windpipe. When, after this very painful operation, he succeeds in producing a tone in tune with the Sender, his whole being transforms. He turns into "pure vibration" and his "organs oscillate so that a formless life gushed forth" (Eika 2021, 77). By radically transcending his humanity and connecting his breath with the Sender, indeed with the whole nonhuman world, the animals accept Antonio as one of them: "The birds landed on his shoulders, lizards leaped from the antelopes to his chest and pressed their bellies against him" (77). At the end of the story, however, doubts arise as to whether this almost paradisiacal human-machine-animal entanglement is real. After a few more strange incidents, Antonio suddenly awakes "full of fear" (79) and heads home, where he collapses.

However, the utopian potential that flashes in the story is carried on in other stories of Eika's collection. Ultimately, it is up to everyone to engage with what is beyond the human horizon. Either you shake the future speculations and "images out of [your] head" (80), as Antonio does, or you dare to follow the call into the unknown that can be heard at the very end of the last story, "Bad Mexican Dog.". Against the backdrop of a changing world where the light "stretches its tentacles down and draws out the contours of the things" (152), we read the very last sentence of the book: "Come, let's go inland" (154). The reader learns neither who is speaking here nor what exactly the call to go inland means. What will await us in the interior? What lies beyond the limits of what we see here and now? We do not know. The only thing we know is that we are supposed to move and to give the future a chance. That is exactly what happens at the end of Olga Ravn's science fiction novel *The Employees*. However, here it is not humans who venture out into an unknown valley on an unknown planet, but human-made humanoids.

Welcome to the Unknown Valley

Olga Ravn's novel *The Employees* is a novel that makes the reader feel trapped in the uncanny valley of ontological uncertainty. We are on board the Six-Thousand Ship, an uninviting workplace in the future where the titular employees work. We learn about these employees through a series of more than 100 fragmentary statements that make up the content of the novel. The reader is left in the dark about the identity of the senders; it might be humans or human-made humanoids. Also, the setting is disconcerting because the statements, as a very brief preface informs the reader, are the result of a questioning carried out by an anonymous committee investigating the impact of strange objects on the morale of the workers.

The objects in question were brought to the ship from the planet New Discovery and seem to arouse strange feelings in the employees. As a result, the previously dominant mentality of efficiency and utility cracks and gives way to new, more ambivalent emotions. The mysterious objects arouse the feeling of uncertainty because they cannot be placed in the coordinate system humans are used to working with. They look like large stones but seem to be alive. Also, they have a certain resemblance both to animals and to plants. They emit scents and produce an indeterminate sound. They pulsate. Most of the employees who encounter the objects are attracted to them and want to touch them. Others are more sceptical because the objects challenge the conventional notion of things as separate entities. One employee explains: "Sometimes I'm not sure if they're all one or three separate ones. Three individual units attuned to each other. I've seen intimacy between them. It frightens me. I hate it" (Ravn 2021, 14).

Although this entanglement of the objects is experienced as unsettling and uncanny, it also helps to connect with deeper layers of existence. In Ravn's novel, this can be seen in the objects' capacity to awaken good memories, often memories associated with nature. In statement 011, the speaker refers to the objects' scent and explains: "At the base of this fragrance is soil and oakmoss, incense, and the smell of an insect captured in amber. A brown scent" (20). Indulging in reminiscences, the crew members who identify as humans whisper to each other: "Remember when it rained at the beach, how when we paddled out, the sea was warmer than the rain? Remember bananas with cream topping?" (84).

As the story unfolds, the spaceship's board of directors loses control over the employees and their sensual memories. Therefore, they decide to destroy the ship's human employees and to reprogramme the human-like robots. When faced with their imminent end, however, the pilots steer the spaceship to the planet New Discovery, which seems to have an all-encompassing, liberating power. "Above the planet, the stars, whispering as if with a single voice, a name that pertains to us all" (125). Indeed, one of the employees, as if enlivened by a great peace of mind, starts chanting a kind of mantra: "I believe in the future. I think you need to imagine your future and then live in it" (126).

I propose to see this mantra as a posthuman speculation on a future that transcends time and space. After the termination has been carried out and all the humans on board the spaceship are dead, the surviving posthumans set out to "go out in the valley" (135). This is highly interesting because the valley referred to is no longer an uncanny valley. Instead, it is a valley full of hope and peace. Located on the planet New Discovery, it bears a strong resemblance to a valley in the garden of Eden before the "Fall of Man," in other words, a garden before anthropogenic destruction: "Slender, green blades peeping out of the wet earth. It rains nearly every day in the valley; a cold and persistent rain. The earth is darkened by it. The earth, I lie down on it" (135).

In the last entry of the novel, we read that the remaining posthumans will stay in the valley, consisting of fertile soil that not only makes flowers and trees flourish but also pushes "various objects to the surface, where they now lie scattered about in the moist earth" (136). With this scene, the novel portrays speculative growth quite differently than the protagonist Alvin does in Eika's story, namely not in the sense of a certain profit, but as an undefined hope for a life in harmony with nature.

Conclusion

The aim of this chapter has been to examine how contemporary Danish novels and short stories, which I classify as speculative fiction, represent the uncanny intimacy of humans' relationship with the more-than-human world. In the two collections of short stories by Ursula Scavenius, *Feathers* and *The Dolls*, we have seen that the uncanny atmosphere of the stories is associated with a biosphere out of human control. When the nonhuman world comes close, or even intrudes the human body, humans recognise their social and environmental failures that ultimately put humanity at risk.

In *After the Sun*, Jonas Eika leads his reader one step further into the realm of uncanny speculations, with a utopian twist. While in "Alvin" the speculation on future is represented as a play where nothing is real, in "Rachel, Nevada" the protagonist's desire to merge with a technological object, the Sender, turns out to be a challenging and uncanny experience, but also a very liberating one. Antonio gives up on his body's integrity and opens for the sensual power of the Sender. Here, the human–nonhuman entanglement reveals its utopian potential.

Likewise, the indefinable objects in Ravn's *The Employees* are first experienced as uncanny. They do not fit into the established order that has been set up to guarantee trouble-free and effective work processes in which feelings, wishes, hopes, and memories of past happiness would interfere. However, the power of the nonhuman objects seems to be so strong that the human-made order collapses, as did the bank in Eika's "Alvin." The very moment the employees give up their supposedly fixed identity as either human or humanoid being and instead engage in radical intimacy with the nonhuman objects, they experience themselves and the world in a radically new way. Suddenly, speculations on a better future might become true.

In conclusion, we can note that all examples of contemporary Danish speculative fiction give us an idea of what happens when we encounter what has been hidden for a long time, namely the hidden face of the biosphere we are entangled with: we, humankind, experience unease because we seem to be trapped in a kind of uncanny valley where the borders between human and nonhuman is about to disappear. However, as we accept the idea of a future without these kind of borders as something positive, all the stories explored end with an outlook at a possible world of tomorrow, an "unknown valley" that resembles an environmental paradise before humans fall.

Notes

1 On the concept, see also the previous chapter by Jyrki Korpua in this book.
2 All translations are by the author unless stated otherwise.

References

Abram, David. 1996. *The Spell of the Sensuous: Perception and Language in a More-than-Human World*. New York: Pantheon Books.

Andersen, H. C. 2006. *Fairy Tales*. Trans. Tiina Nunnally. New York: Penguin Books.

Bryant, Levi, Nick Srnicek & Graham Harman. 2011. "Towards a Speculative Philosophy." In *The Speculative Turn: Continental Materialism and Realism*, ed. Levi Bryant et al., 1–18. Melbourne: re.press.

Dalgaard, Niels. 2010. "Afterword. An Extremely Short History of the Danish Science Fiction Short Story." In *Sky City. New Science Fiction Stories by Danish Authors*, ed. Carl Eddy Skovvgaard, 232–241. Copenhagen: Science Fiction Cirklen.

Eika, Jonas. 2021. *After the Sun*. Trans. Sherilyn Nicolette Hellberg. London: Lolli Editions.

Freud, Sigmund. 1955. "The Uncanny." In *The Standard Edition of the Complete Psychological Works of Sigmund Freud*, XVII, 218–252. Trans. James Strachey. London: Hogarth.

Gosh, Amitav. 2016. *The Great Derangement: Climate Change and the Unthinkable*. Chicago: University of Chicago Press.

Harman, Graham. 2010. *Towards Speculative Realism. Essay and Lectures*. Winchester: Zero Books.

Heinlein, Robert A. 1977/1952. "Pandora's Box." In *Turning Points: Essays on the Art of Science Fiction*, ed. Damon Knight, 238–258. New York: Harper & Row.

Henriksen, Line & Marietta Radomska. 2015. "Missing Links and Non/Human Queerings: An Introduction." *Somatechnics* 5 (2): 113–119.

Jentsch, Ernst. 1906. "On the Psychology of the Uncanny." *Psychiatrisch-Neurologische Wochenschrift* 22: 195–198 & 23: 203–205.

Kastbjerg, Kirstine. 2013. "The Aesthetics of Surface: The Danish Gothic 1820–2000." In *Gothic Topographies: Language, Nation Building and 'Race'*, ed. Matti Savolainen & P. M. Mehtonen, 153–167. Farnham: Routledge.

Kvideland, Reimund & Henning K. Sehmsdorf (eds.). 1991. *Scandinavian folk Belief and Legend*. Oslo: Norwegian University Press.

Land, Nick. 2011. "No Future." In *Fanged Noumena. Collected Writings 1987–2007*, ed. Robin Mackey and Roy Brassier, 391–399. Falmouth: Sequence Press.

Latham, Rob (ed.). 2014. *The Oxford Handbook of Science Fiction*. Oxford: Oxford University Press.

Le Guin, Ursula K. 1989/1980. "Some Thoughts on Narrative." In *Dancing at the Edge of the World: Thoughts on Words, Women, Places*, 37–45. New York: Grove Press.

Lovecraft, H. P. 2004. "Supernatural Horror in Literature." In *Collected Essays*, Vol 2, ed. S. T. Joshi, 82–135. New York: Hippocampus Press.

Merril, Judith. 1967. "Introduction." In *SF: The Best of the Best*, 1–7 New York: Dell.

Mori, Masahiro. 2012. "The Uncanny Valley." *IEEE Robotics & Automation Magazine*, 98–100.

Mortensen, Peter. 2019. "'Monkey-Advice and Monkey-Help': Isak Dinesen's EcoGothic." *Gothic Nature Journal* 1 (1): 202–225.

Morton, Timothy. 2007. *Ecology without Nature: Rethinking Environmental Aesthetics*. Cambridge: Harvard UP.

Morton, Timothy. 2010. *The Ecological Thought*. Harvard: Cambridge UP.

Oziewicz, Marek. 2017. "Speculative Fiction." In *Oxford Research Encyclopedia of Literature,* ed. Paula Rabinowitz. New York: Oxford UP.

Raudvere, Catharina. 2022. "Transforming, Transgressing and Terrorizing. Some Werewolves and their Antagonists in Swedish Ballads." *Religionsvidenskabeligt tidsskrift* 74: 726–742.

Ravetto-Biagioli, Kriss. 2019. *Digital Uncanny*. New York: Oxford University Press.

Ravn, Olga. 2021. *The Employees: A Workplace Novel of the 22nd Century*. Trans. Martin Aitken. London: Lolli Editions.

Royle, Nicholas. 2003. *The Uncanny*. Manchester: Manchester UP.

Scavenius, Ursula. 2015. *Fjer*. Copenhagen: Basilisk.

Scavenius, Ursula. 2021. *The Dolls*. Trans. Jennifer Russell. London: Lolli Editions.

Wennerscheid, Sophie. 2021. "Die unheimlichen Kräfte der Natur in,spekulativen Seinserzählungen' von der Romantik bis zur Gegenwart." In *Form- und Bewegungskräfte,* ed. Frank Fehrenbach et al., 333–352. Berlin & New York: De Gruyter.

Wolfe, Cary. 2010. *What is Posthumanism?* Minneapolis: University of Minnesota Press.

7

THE STRANGE ECOLOGIES OF THE NORTH

Finnish Weird as an Environmental Genre

Juha Raipola

In the early 2010s, Finnish author Johanna Sinisalo (2011) introduced the term *Finnish Weird* (*suomikumma* in Finnish) as a broad marketing concept for the local output of speculative fiction and hypothesised that it might very well become "the next Nordic literary phenomenon, concept and cultural export product" and develop into a success story akin to the international fame of Nordic crime fiction. Sinisalo argued Finnish Weird to be a hybrid genre where certain "non-realistic elements" and different genres such as science fiction, horror, fantasy, folklore, myths, and mundane mimetic fiction are used in order to "reflect, analyse and to try and deconstruct certain – often societal – problems and issues." During the last decade, Sinisalo's expectations have largely become a reality as Finnish Weird has become a well-rooted cultural phenomenon in both the local and global cultural soil. Speculative fiction has grown from a marginal position to a notable part of the Finnish literary landscape, and Finnish Weird has been established as a recognisable concept often used in the international marketing of speculative novels originating from Finland.

Sinisalo's call for the appreciation of Finnish Weird may also be seen as part of a larger cultural renaissance of weird fiction during the last two decades. In the Anglophone world, the New Weird movement started in 2003, and in the following years, it was associated with authors such as Jeff VanderMeer, China Miéville, Steph Swainston, K.J. Bishop, Thomas Ligotti, Felix Gilman, and Michael Cisco. From early on, one of Sinisalo's primary examples of Finnish weird writers, Leena Krohn, was also linked to the wider New Weird movement. New Weird is a hybrid literary genre that joins together elements from fantasy, horror, and science fiction. While it tends to share some commonalities with the older tradition of weird fiction

DOI: 10.4324/9781003561101-11

by authors such as H.P. Lovecraft, it typically avoids the overt antihuman-ism of its early twentieth–century predecessors. Benjamin J. Robertson (2018, 24–30) has distinguished New Weird from the earlier weird fiction in three respects. First, whereas the weird was typically generically slip-pery due to the lack of development in clear genre markers, authors of the New Weird tend to consciously draw on different generic structures and conventions. Second, the politics of the New Weird tends to espouse its unfathomable monsters rather than treating them as mere sources of hor-ror. Third, while weird stories are often set in the "primary world" mostly resembling the reader's consensus reality, the New Weird characteristically makes use of secondary worlds with often indiscernible relationships to the real world.

Although Finnish Weird may be seen as a local outgrowth of the New Weird, there are also some distinct differences between the two. The term "Finnish Weird" is often used without much acknowledgement of the impor-tance of horror as a key component in the tradition of weird writing, and the term is sometimes employed either as a broad marketing term for Finnish speculative fiction in general or as a rather inexact term for genre hybrids that feature non-mimetic elements. There are also some differences in the explicit intentions behind the use of subversive elements in each genre (Roine & Samola 2018, 185). While writers of New Weird have been outspoken in their goal to "subvert the romanticised ideas about place found in traditional fantasy" (VanderMeer, xvi), proponents of Finnish Weird have usually been more adamant in challenging the conventions of realist writing that have dominated the Finnish literary canon. Authors such as Sinisalo have per-ceived the Finnish expectations of literary realism as restricting and have treated "weird" genre hybrids as a useful method of introducing speculative fiction that contains fantastic and science fictional elements to the reading audience.

One of the strongest common features of both Finnish Weird and the New Weird movement in general is their close affinity to environmental themes. In an increasing number of recent readings, the New Weird has been strongly linked to the recent "nonhuman turn"[1] in environmental theory, while philosophers such as Timothy Morton (2016) and Graham Harman (2012) have also encouraged their audiences to view the world through a "weird" lens. In the epoch of the Anthropocene (Crutzen 2002), where human influence on the Earth's environment has become globally signifi-cant and undeniably noticeable, humans and nonhumans seem to co-exist through visible interconnections across micro- and macro-scales. Emerging acknowledgement of such connections is often accompanied by a simultane-ous sense of estrangement and fascination – an affective experience typically associated with the weird (Turnbull 2021). Authors such as VanderMeer and Miéville have also explicitly been trying to employ the New Weird and its strange storyworlds as an aesthetic portal into this increasingly weird-looking and ultimately unrepresentable ecological reality.

A similar attraction to environmental questions defines many of the key works of the Finnish Weird. Authors such as Sinisalo and Krohn have been rather outspoken in their critical awareness of planetary boundaries and global environmental issues of the Anthropocene. In their fiction, such ecological subject matters are often explored through various literary devices that explore the ambiguous border zones between human and nonhuman. In the following, I will delve deeper into these particular modes of ecological awareness in Finnish Weird with a comparative lens on the wider tradition of New Weird writing. With such an approach, my aim is to approach Finnish Weird both as a distinctive literary phenomenon in the field of Nordic speculative fiction and as a unique form of speculative environmental fiction.[2]

Birth of a Genre

The birth of the Finnish Weird as a genre is often associated with Leena Krohn's novella *Tainaron: Mail from Another City* (*Tainaron: Postia toisesta kaupungista*, 1985). *Tainaron* was a nominee for the prestigious Finlandia prize[3] in 1985 and is commonly regarded as Krohn's breakthrough work that introduced her distinctive writing style to the larger literary audience in Finland. At the time, the Finnish literary landscape was still very much dominated by expectations of mimetic verisimilitude, and Krohn's strange fictional travelogue set in the imaginary city of Tainaron was a unique literary phenomenon that garnered her some deserved attention. Later, the English translation of the novella happened to be published during the peak interest in the emerging New Weird movement in the Anglophone world. The translation was received with great enthusiasm by Jeff VanderMeer, who was quick to associate Krohn's writing with his own interest in the (new) weird fiction. In 2008, Jeff and Ann VanderMeer included excerpts from *Tainaron* in their edited collection *The New Weird*, and *Tainaron* was promptly considered as one of the classics of the newly found genre.

Before the publication of *Tainaron*, Krohn had already established herself as a pioneer of environmentally oriented (non-mimetic) fiction in Finland. Environmental themes were an essential element in almost all her early works in the 1970s. Toni Lahtinen and Markku Lehtimäki (2011) consider Krohn's debut work *Vihreä vallankumous* ("The Green Revolution," 1970) to be the first environmentally themed children's book in Finnish. The book was illustrated by Leena's sister Inari Krohn, and it featured a plot of children fighting against politicians and their plan to turn a walled-off park in its natural state into a parking lot. In *Ihmisen vaatteissa* ("In Human Clothes," 1976), Krohn had already established some of the weird building blocks of her later fiction. The book's target audience was described as everyone that is "still not fully grown," meaning that it was intended for both children and adults with child-like curiosity in the imaginative and fantastic. Its main plot features a pelican living in disguise among humans due to the loss of the species' natural habitat, with only the book's child protagonist being able to see him as a bird. The story explores the uncertain borders between fantasy and reality as well as between human and nonhuman, and such themes would later become the hallmark of Krohn's fiction.

Despite the existence of some "weird" elements already in Krohn's earlier works, the proper weird turn in Finnish literature is strongly associated with the publishing of Krohn's *Tainaron,* an epistolary novella with philosophical overtones that also pertain to environmental themes. With its lyrical and metaphorical portrayals of the faraway city of Tainaron, the book meditates on the questions of life, death, identity, and perpetual change. Tainaron's namesake city is known in Greek mythology as the entrance to the underworld, but in Krohn's book, Tainaron is also a city of partly anthropomorphised insects whose strange local habits are perceived by the unnamed human narrator with both intrigue and shock. With their letters to a non-responding receiver, the reader is offered a glimpse into the impersonal workings of the nonhuman world of life at a microscale. *Tainaron* is a travelogue into this alien, otherworldly landscape, where the mysteries of the nonhuman world often blend into mysteries of life in general. While the most obvious formal characteristic of *Tainaron* is its epistolary structure, it may also be noted that it utilises the conventions of travel writing to construct its fictional world. The mysterious cityscape of insects is thus explored from a foreign visitor's point of view: the local customs, scenery, and "people" are contrasted to the culture at "home" – which, in this case, is the human world at its usual scale. The habits of the insects are described from an outsider's perspective, through which many of the local customs are deemed mysterious or strange. Sometimes the narrator is even outright frightened by the outer appearances and habits of the local inhabitants.

New Weird is generally described as a genre that tends to focus both on physically weird and on aesthetically grotesque characters and foreign and disorienting urban spaces (Weinstock 2016, 185–186), and *Tainaron* seems to encapsulate both tendencies. In *Tainaron*, the physical environment and the human imagination are also profoundly intertwined: the fictional world of the work can be seen at once as a portrayal of the nonhuman natural world and as an extension of the narrator's psyche. The epigraph of the work, "You Are Not in a Place; the Place Is in You," is a quote from the German mystic Angelus Silesius, and it functions as a suggestion that the novella is deeply invested in the exploration of the limits between the mental and the physical world. Same kinds of themes are probed through the fictional inhabitants of the world, who typically show both human and insect characteristics. While the insect figures are clearly based on existing natural species, their strange physical features and odd habits are also associated with questions pertaining to mysteries of human experience and life in general. They are also situated in a strange border zone between anthropomorphised, "humanlike" characters and "realistically" portrayed animals whose experiences remain impenetrable to us: the insects live in a largely humanlike city environment and are able to speak, yet their habits are observed from an outsider's point of view with no access to the intentions behind their strange behaviour.

With this estranging effect, *Tainaron* invites its reader to ponder on questions of life beyond the control of supposedly autonomous human subjects. Besides describing Tainaron as her most extensive meditation on the "philosophy of life," Krohn (1989) herself has labelled the work as "a book of changes."[4] In the novella, the problems of identity and change are indeed typically on the forefront. For example, the Virgil-like local guide for the human narrator, Longhorn, describes the innermost characteristics of Tainaron in a manner that alienates the fictional world from our common human experience: "Tainaron is not a place, as you perhaps think. It is an event which no one measures. It is no use to anyone trying to make maps" (Krohn 2004, 125). Whereas human life is built on supposedly stable identities, both the city of Tainaron and its inhabitants are described as constantly changing creatures. This is also the reason for the narrators' alienation from the surrounding city shaped by irresistible forces – the weird cityscape brings forth the unnerving idea that human existence is based on similarly impersonal and "nonhuman" forces as the ones demonstrated in the life of Tainaron.

The Weird North and Weird Scales

The inclusion of *Tainaron* in the classics of the New Weird by VanderMeers in 2008 may be speculated to have been a central influence behind Sinisalo's 2011 call for the endorsement of Finnish Weird. She has also mentioned Jalmari Helander's action horror film *Rare Exports* (2010) – a strange origin story of Santa Claus set in the Finnish Lapland – to have been a key influence in her struggles to find a common denominator for some quintessential works of Finnish speculative fiction (Sinisalo 2014). Sinisalo's own works may also be included as crucial contributions to the emerging canon of the Finnish Weird.

In Sinisalo's fiction, environmental themes are more of a rule than an exception. For example, Sinisalo's debut novel *Not Before Sundown (Ennen päivänlaskua ei voi*, 2003, translated also as *Troll – A Love Story* for the US market) employs its weird love story between a man and a troll as a commentary on the loss of an ecological habitat of nonhuman animals. With its pseudoscientific characterisations of the fictional species of trolls, the narrative also touches on questions of anthropocentrism and growing human impact upon the planet. Sometimes Sinisalo's own environmental concerns tend to also overshadow the thinking of her characters. For instance, in *Renaten tarina* ("Renate's Story," 2018), the protagonist observes environmental problems of the Earth from the estranged point of view of the resource austerity of Moon colonisers. The novel itself is a satirical portrayal of a society of Nazis living on the Moon, set in the same fictional universe as Timo Vuorensola's comic science fiction film *Iron Sky* (2012), which was based on Sinisalo's script.

One of the typical features of Finnish Weird regarding environmental themes is their characteristically Finnish or northern setting. In *Not Before Sundown*, for example, the events are set in Sinisalo's hometown Tampere and its nearby forests. Usually, however, the local events are also somehow connected to the destiny of the entire Earth's biosphere. For example, in Sinisalo's *Birdbrain* (*Linnunaivot*, 2008), the initial starting point for the story is a touristy ski centre in the Finnish Lapland, but the main part of the plot centres on the trekking experiences of a Finnish couple in the wilderness of New Zealand and Tasmania. With this kind of a global viewpoint, the northern protagonists of the narrative may be interpreted as environmental colonisers, who have contaminated the southern wilderness with their actions. Functioning as a synecdoche of the entirety of the human species, they also demonstrate the progressively uneasy relationship between humans as colonisers of the entire planet and Earth's biosphere in the current time of planetary crisis. Through a weird twist, *Birdbrain* showcases the inseparability of human actions from their nonhuman environment (Raipola & Lahtinen 2020). In the Tasmanian wilderness, the nonhuman environment starts to gain increasingly disturbing qualities, as its deep entanglement with the human protagonists begins to become more and more obvious.

In contrast to Robertson's (2018, 24–30) notion of secondary worlds being a clear marker of the New Weird genre, the environmentally oriented works of Finnish Weird are characteristically set in a world that closely resembles our own quotidian reality or a "weird," speculative future version of it. In Sinisalo's novels, the setting is often a rather mundane modern-day world set apart from the actual world by the intrusion of a handful of fantastic or speculative elements such as the imaginary species of trolls in *Not Before Sundown*. In *Blood of Angels* (*Enkelten verta*, 2011), the most obvious fantastic feature is a strange portal that provides the protagonist access into a pristine wilderness where dead organisms from the local flora and fauna seem to be well off and thriving. The novel is set in a near-future Finland – more precisely in an imaginary rural location near the Tampere region – where a beekeeper is struggling with a global problem of "Colony Collapse Disorder (CCD)." Extrapolating on the real problem of a decline in global honeybee populations, the novel portrays a world where CCD has appeared as the near-catastrophic end point of the disappearance of bees and its ecosystemic consequences. Outside of Finland, the disappearance of pollinators has already had some major effects on the availability of basic food products. The plot focuses upon the experiences of the beekeeper in his grievance of both a tragic death of his son and his own beehives, which seem to now also suffer from CCD, although it has not previously been observed in Finland.

Building on different mythological traditions connecting bees with the afterlife, *Blood of Angels* employs its strange vision of the afterlife as a method of discussing the human impact on the environment. The Elysium-like "other side" is hinted to exist more in the manner of a parallel universe than as a hallucinatory vision and to be inhabited by both human and non-human forms of life that have ceased to physically exist on the local land-scape. The dysfunctional over-generational relationships between the main character and both his father and son also bear a metaphoric resemblance to a bee colony – the colony preserves its existence despite and due to the suf-fering and death of its individual members.

In Krohn's novels since the late 1990s, as well, the events may typically be interpreted as being set in present-day or near-future Finland. Still, some purposefully odd and vague details of their storyworlds also contribute to them being interpreted as satirical portrayals of our contemporary society in a very general sense. In both *Unelmakuolema* ("Dream Death," 2004) and *Mehiläispaviljonki* ("The Bee Pavillion," 2006), for example, the events are set in a dystopian neoliberal city that is clearly reminiscent of Krohn's hometown Helsinki. In the highly commercialised future setting of the nov-els, services such as assisted suicide with the entertainment of your liking are freely available and marketed as "rational" consumer choices. In Krohn's works, generally, neoliberal notions of instrumental rationality are often satirised and parodied as well as contrasted with another kind of rational-ity – the mysterious and uncontrollable forces of nature that create order out of chaos. In *Hotel Sapiens* (2013), the eventual outcome of the neoliberalist mode of rationalism is portrayed as a vast-scale environmental disaster that has swept out much of the life on Earth. Here, the local post-apocalyptic setting is a strange technological safehouse, Hotel Sapiens, where mysterious posthuman intelligences are studying the remnants of humanity as specimens of a past life form. In Hotel Sapiens, the purported rationality of humans is contrasted with dreams, visions, speculation, and imaginary fantasies of the hotel dwellers that seem to define our species much more strongly than calculative reasoning for optimal choices (Raipola 2017). References to a more recognisable mode of life – including places reminiscent of Finland – are depicted as memories of the characters and as a past almost forgotten.

The relationship between local and global is, of course, a key problem of the Anthropocene, where humans as a species are acting as a force of nature and local human actions are affecting the natural processes of the entire planet.[5] In our current understanding of vast-scale environmental issues, even seemingly inconsequential human actions and decisions of everyday life may bear global ecological consequences when rehearsed daily by massive groups of people. However, issues of scale in the ongoing ecological crisis are not limited to such easily understandable dynamics as the relationship between human individuals in Finland and the global impact of their actions. The embracement of weird as an aesthetic strategy for expressing Anthropocene anxieties has to do with this general "crisis of scale and agency" (Clark 2015, 139) in the new modes of thinking required for the current ecological situation. The new situation of global ecological threats forces one to constantly change one's perspective on different levels of scale such as the microbial or viral, the individual human, the local environment, the global society, and the planetary system. The New Weird has been hailed as fiction that tries to overcome this crisis by moving beyond it and embracing the monstrous unknowability of different nonhuman scales in the Anthropocene (Ulstein 2021).

Both Sinisalo's and Krohn's works are involved in probing the question of scale from a weird viewpoint. In Sinisalo's fiction, the intimate relationship between humans and nonhumans is typically explored with explicit references to different species and human entanglement with them. In *Blood of Angels,* for example, the interconnections between humans and nonhumans are represented through a focus on the food industry and its complex links with ecosystems and different individual species and individual organisms within them. In a similar fashion, the structure of a bee colony is employed as an image of order within nonhuman natural systems. In *Birdbrain,* the overwhelming and ultimately threatening number of mutual relationships between humans and nonhumans at different scales starts to become ominously apparent in the heart of the Tasmanian jungle. As the initial realism of the story starts to make way for increasingly grotesque details and inexplicable fusions between different entities, the intimidating proximity of nonhuman others in the Anthropocene becomes menacingly obvious.

In Krohn's novels, the issues of scale are more clearly tied to the entire poetics of her whole oeuvre. While Krohn's works are commonly categorised as novels, their unique form and philosophical themes often bring them closer to a collection of narrative essays. They typically consist of an assortment of short story-like episodes, which are connected through a loose plotline. Depending on the number of narrative links between the chapters, they could therefore usually be called either episodic novels or short story cycles. Since the reader's attention generally gets guided towards the philosophical and ethical dilemmas represented in the different chapters, the overall plot seems to lose its importance. More significance is given to recurring literary images and philosophical dilemmas that expose how ambiguous and uncertain human interpretations of reality often are. Even the traditional limits of a novelistic narrative often become unsettled, as the characters and narrative situations keep reappearing in Krohn's different works. Remarkably, this distinctive narrative technique is also related to questions of scale, which is a central theme of Krohn's fiction.

The theme of moving up and down through different spatial and temporal scales is emblematic of Krohn's fiction. In general, this produces an estranging effect, where the epistemic limits of human cognition are brought to the fore. There is a definite epistemic disjunction between different levels of scale, and this is the starting point for both horror and awe: enough jumps from one level to another, and one loses sense of their human identity. For example, in the opening chapter of *Hotel Sapiens*, the narrator likens human species to an aquatic animal called Physalia physalis or Portuguese man o' war:

> It is a zooid, at once an autonomous animal and a whole society, one and a hundred thousand. Watch how this empire churns, contracts and expands, how it swims by coral reefs and shipwrecks flowering with seaweed, lulled by slow tides, and how its giant shadow slides past the ruins of ancient cities. …
>
> Humankind looked like seven billion individuals, but if only had you inspected this species a little more closely. It was one and the same creature. On terra firma we jointly constituted a similar medusa-like monster. Or if you had to pick a single organism, any fleshly person from here at Hotel Sapiens, for instance, anyone, this one here, for example, who we see holding a pen. Is that really one? His body, his vehicle, his temporary apartment, who is called by his name as if that was himself there, is a nation of billions of creatures. And his mind – it includes numerous different wills, numerous selves, alternating, contesting each other.
>
> *(Krohn 2013, 9, trans. by the author)*

The very beginning of the novel thus describes an image of a strange colonial organism made up of specialised individual animals. Eventually, the image is complemented with a straightforward comparison to humankind, which is depicted as a similar kind of collective entity, "one and the same creature." Then, the narrator moves down to the scale of the human body, which is, once again, depicted as a collection of numerous entities. Finally, the examination is directed towards the human mind, from where, of course, the narrator finds a similar structure.

For a discussion about the Anthropocene, the most interesting feature of these kinds of jumps between different scales lies between the individual and human species as whole. In her essays, Krohn has often toyed with the idea of a shared consciousness of the entire humanity, and the same principle seems to apply to her fiction. While the idea might at first glance seem like a celebratory mystification of human abilities, a humanistic vision at the global scale, the effect is usually somewhat horrific. Being part of a larger creature, a "medusa-like monster," emphasises the limited human ability to know and to control this larger form of human existence. The species-being operates under no centralised control, and nobody can be entirely sure where this larger collective is headed. This kind of vision of humanity undoes different progressive grand narratives of humanity and modernity, which provide individuals with meaning in the "larger scheme" and suggests that we all operate just as unknowingly as different cells in our bodies or individual zooids making up the body of the colonial animal. In *Hotel Sapiens*, for example, humanity is portrayed as a self-destructive species that has unknowingly brought itself to the brink of extinction in a post-apocalyptic setting.

Questions of Genre

Due to its hybrid formal characteristics, weird fiction is a genre that tends to generally avoid exact definitions and easily discernible genre-specific features. In the case of the early tradition of weird fiction, the development of modern genre categories such as fantasy, horror, and science fiction was still in progress during the publication of the stories. For the early writers of the pulp magazine *Weird Tales,* the common term for their fiction was thus drawn from the title of the magazine, and in later commentary, the term has also been extended to cover earlier fiction with similar elements. Despite the lack of clear genre markers, there are some common features that are typically associated with the weird. Central among them is H.P. Lovecraft's idea of weird fiction as narratives of cosmic horror. One of the strongest common features among weird fiction thus seems to be the "weird" and uncomfortable realisation of human insignificance in the universe. Typically, this realisation tends to be associated with an affective response that may itself be called "weird." For example, Mark Fisher (2016, 5–6) suggests that one should see the weird both as an affect and as a mode and notes that the weird is strongly associated with a sense of *wrongness* – a conviction that something does not belong. It may be contrasted to a similar affect of the *unheimlich,* which is about the strange within the familiar. The weird conjoins two or more things that do not belong together, and as such, it brings to the familiar something which ordinarily lies beyond it. Unlike the unheimlich, the weird cannot be reductively interpreted, translated, or returned (Luckhurst 2017, 1052). According to Fisher, the weird may also be compared to the *eerie,* which is "constituted by a *failure of absence* or a *failure of presence*" (2016, 46, italics in the original). In practice, however, the affective repertoire of the genre of weird fiction may be somewhat broader, and Gry Ulstein (2021, 30) has suggested that "categories like the sublime, cosmic horror, the uncanny, the eerie, the grotesque, and other, similar categories interested in the unknown and the strange" can all be thought of as key forms or affects of the weird.

The New Weird, on the other hand, may be understood as contemporary fiction that draws on the generic features and common affects of the weird. In ecocritical considerations, it is often suggested that the New Weird employs the common affects of the weird to consider the ecological reality of the Anthropocene. Rather than focusing on the mere horror at the loss of human individuality and agency, the New Weird is understood to offer an "expanded set of literary resources through which to think the nonhuman and to think beyond some of the paradoxes that thought presents" (Marshall 2016, 634). Besides exposing human insignificance, New Weird tends to thematise the breakdown of the modern idea of human separateness from the nonhuman and to undermine the sovereignty of the human subject. These kinds of definitions may, however, demarcate the scope of the New Weird too closely to a limited number of authors invested in such environmental considerations. Even in New Weird, the defining common feature of the narratives is still their "weird" affect – a certain feeling of "wrongness," of that which does not belong.

Sinisalo's idea of using Finnish Weird as a marketing term or a "brand" for genre-bending Finnish speculative fiction, on the other hand, has resulted in the term "weird" being used more broadly than in the New Weird movement. In Sinisalo's account, weirdness typically relates more to questions of genre hybridisation than to the affective experience of the "weird." Being "weird" in the Finnish context does not necessarily account to similar feelings of awe and horror as in the New Weird. Weird is something out of ordinary that makes one re-evaluate their thinking, but it is not necessarily connected to any particular affective experience.

Still, at least authors like Krohn and Sinisalo are also consciously employing the affective side of the "weird" in their poetics to address questions of the human role within the wider environment. For Sinisalo, this is connected to a wider literary strategy of using elements from different (popular) genres as the basic building blocks of her fiction. In Sinisalo's novels, the narratives are typically imbued with self-reflexive combinations of various genres and text-types. As a rule, the novels draw on extensive references to Finnish folklore, general mythology, world literature, and encyclopaedic texts. They feature quotations and pseudo-quotations from fictional and factual literature, from blog posts, from online encyclopaedias, and from practically all other kinds of textual sources. This kind of plurality of genres, text-types, and source materials seems to emphasise the role of fiction in tackling the environmental questions discussed within its pages. It blurs the hard distinction between facts and fantasy and employs fiction as a strategy for managing the cognitive difficulty of dealing with the different scales of the Anthropocene.

For Krohn, the inclusion of her works among the genre categories of Finnish and New Weird is somewhat more incidental. In contrast to Sinisalo, who was already a well-known figure in the Finnish science fiction fandom before the publication of her debut novel, Krohn has never been intimately associated with the generic traditions of fantasy or science fiction. Before VanderMeers's adoption of Krohn into the New Weird movement, Krohn's fiction was generally likened to modernist and postmodernist "literary" fantasists in the tradition of Franz Kafka, Jorge Luis Borges, and Italo Calvino (see, e.g., Tarkka 1990; Majander 1995). For her, the genre marker of Finnish Weird is thus not a self-appointed starting point of her fiction, but rather one way of categorising her works that do not easily fall into any clear-cut genre. The affective experiences associated with Krohn's fiction, however, are typically very closely in tune with the weird in general – her novels are invested in exploring both the cosmic awe and the cosmic horror related to the alien scales of contemporary ecological thinking.

Krohn's fiction is also generally riddled with paradoxes that also relate to the question of genre in her books. Her books characteristically feature "impossible objects" that require the observer to constantly shift one's interpretation or viewpoint of the perceived object.

Similarly, the form of her works typically forces their readers to perform similar interpretational gymnastics. With a massive number of suggestions for competing reading strategies, Krohn's stories actively resist categorisation into any single genre or final interpretation (Raipola 2015). With different kinds of intertextual strategies such as nonexplicit references and allusions to a numerous amount of literary works, her fiction thus features a poetics that parallels the central themes of her works, such as ambiguous and competing interpretations of reality, and self-organisation and emergence in both human and nonhuman systems across different scales. Rather than simply celebrating these features, however, the weird narratives often paint them with a shade of menacing presence of the nonhuman.

For both Sinisalo and Krohn, the hybrid generic form of their works is thus intimately connected to their weird exploration of the human entanglement with the nonhuman. With an emphasis on generic indefinability and various techniques of intertextuality, their fiction seeks to transcend boundaries between the known and the unknown and to unveil the epistemological, ontological, and ethical weirdness of life in the time of environmental issues on the planetary scale.

Conclusion

Ecological questions of human relationship with the nonhuman have been an essential part in the formation of the genre of Finnish Weird. Two of the most recognisable names associated with the genre, Sinisalo and Krohn, have both been explicit in their interest in the emerging environmental problems of the last decades, and with their own idiosyncratic ways, both have also incorporated these issues into their works. Besides them, there are also a couple of other authors of Finnish Weird worth mentioning in connection to the aestheticisation of the Anthropocene.

First, Tiina Raevaara's surrealist fiction is often linked to environmental themes. In her debut novel *Eräänä päivänä tyhjä taivas* ("One Day, an Empty Sky," 2008), for example, Raevaara explores the question of human and non-human with a fever-dreamish narrative about a girl reconnecting with her unwelcoming male family members – dad and 19 brothers – in a world after nuclear war. The house of her father is a strangely nightmarish location that resembles an anthill abandoned by its queen: everyone is still following their menacingly instinctual and unconscious habits, but without any clear reason for their continued existence. The narrative builds towards a climax at the end, where the father finally turns into a literal war machine, representing an allegory of environmental doom. In recent years, Raevaara has extended her generic repertoire towards more straightforward horror and thrillers.

Another author with a decided interest in the weird aesthetics is Maarit Verronen, whose long publishing career since the 1990s makes her one of the pioneers of Finnish speculative fiction. Sarianna Kankkunen, in her analyses of Verronen's fiction, has pointed out how her novels often investigate questions of scale through the experiences of monomaniac protagonists. With individuals on monomaniacal quests, Verronen's works thus "present a critique of what is considered sane or reasonable" (Kankkunen 2021, 162) in the Anthropocene epoch. In her employment of such protagonists as searchers for nonhuman scales of life, Verronen defends the role of rationalist and scientific pursuits in contemporary environmental thinking (Kankkunen 2021, 2022).

In this chapter, the focus has been on writers who have been particularly vocal about their own investment in the ongoing environmental anxieties and can be argued to have employed weird writing as a platform for probing the theme. For a more comprehensive analysis of the environmental poetics of Finnish Weird, one would also need to consider authors without such an overt interest in environmental themes. For example, such authors as Pasi Ilmari Jääskeläinen or Jyrki Vainonen have often been associated with the Finnish Weird, but their works are not usually read as expressions of a particular environmental vision. Jääskeläinen's playful usage of genre-bending to engage in metafictional storytelling may still be rather confidently categorised as weird in the Finnish context. The same goes for the surrealist, dreamlike settings of Jyrki Vainonen's novels. The extension of analysis to such authors would, however, change the focus of the study from the Finnish Weird as a genre of environmental fiction to a more general investigation of place and environment in the genre.

Some further consideration could be also given to the role of "monsters" in Finnish Weird, which seem to clearly deviate from the Anglophone tradition of weird writing. In Sinisalo's *Blood of Angels*, for example, there are hardly any horror elements in the story – the tragedy of the story is mostly a realistic one. If there are some sort of weird Anthropocene monsters lurking in Sinisalo's novel, they are not that much associated with the main speculative elements of the story but are rather a result of the actual science-backed ecological complexity discussed within the narrative. In fact, the weird speculative element of the novel, the parallel universe of pristine wilderness, elicits its affective weirdness from the fact that it is not monstrous enough – its paradisiacal vision of all life thriving does not match with the now-common knowledge of planetary ecological mess created by the human species. It would thus be enlightening to further problematise the role of monsters as the main environmental device of New Weird fiction. Such an approach would, however, require a more comprehensive comparative analysis of Finnish Weird with its international counterpart.

Even without such further probing, it is rather safe to say that Finnish Weird as an environmental genre might be understood as a strange Nordic cousin of the New Weird in general. Its Finnish taste of weirdness is often imbued with vast amounts of literary references and a close connection to the actual world and its ecological anxieties. With such an approach, it tries its best to tackle the many scales of the Anthropocene and its nonhuman weirdness.

Notes

1 The term refers to different contemporary philosophies (such as ANT, affect theory, animal studies, new materialisms, and speculative realism) that seek to emphasise the agency of the nonhuman world and to explore human coevolution, coexistence, and collaboration with the nonhuman (Grusin 2015). It is also tied to the proliferation of terms such as "more-than-human" and "other-than-human" that seek to reconceptualise the complex relationalities between humans and nonhumans. Such conceptualisations have also been critiqued for their lingering anthropocentrism: Katherine N. Hayles (2017, 30), for example, has proposed the distinction between *cognisers* versus *noncognisers* as an alternative to replace human/nonhuman.
2 By "environmental fiction," I aim to denote the broad category of fictional texts that are concerned with environmental degradation and humans' changing relationship to the natural world. While the term may be seen as paradoxical, this includes works that are invested in dismantling the anthropocentric tendency to separate human subjects from their environment. This kind of relocation of the human in a wider web of connections may, for its part, be termed "ecological," as it is based on an interest in the relationships between living organisms, including humans, and their physical environment.
3 The Finlandia prize is awarded by the Finnish Book Foundation and is considered the most important literary prize in the nation. The prize was first awarded in 1984. Today, Finlandia prizes are awarded in three categories: fiction (novels), non-fiction, and children's and youth literature.

4 Translated by the author.
5 However, the grand narrative of the Anthropocene as a story of collective human impact and responsibility tends to evade any questions of the unequal role of different social and ethnic groups, genders, social classes, or societies in the production of global-scale ecological change. For the narratological problem of *Anthropos* as the protagonist of the Anthropocene narrative, see Raipola (2020).

References

Clark, Timothy. 2015. *Ecocriticism on the Edge: The Anthropocene as a Threshold Concept.* London: Bloomsbury Academic.

Crutzen, Paul J. 2002. "Geology of Mankind." *Nature* 415: 23.

Fisher, Mark. 2016. *The Weird and the Eerie.* London: Repeater.

Grusin, Richard. 2015. "Introduction." In *The Nonhuman Turn,* ed. Richard Grusin, vii–xxx. Minneapolis: University of Minnesota Press.

Harman, Graham. 2012. *Weird Realism: Lovecraft and Philosophy.* Winchester: Zero Books.

Hayles, Katherine N. 2017. *Unthought. The Power of the Cognitive Nonconscious.* Chicago, London: The University of Chicago Press.

Kankkunen, Sarianna. 2021. "Maarit Verronen's Monomaniacs of the Anthropocene. Scaling the Nonhuman in Contemporary Finnish Fiction." In *Narrating Nonhuman Spaces,* eds. Marco Caracciolo, Marlene Karlsson Marcussen & David Rodriguez, 151–165. New York: Routledge.

Kankkunen, Sarianna. 2022. *Harassing Habitats. Experiences Space in Finnish Contemporary Fiction, a Study on Maarit Verronen.* Helsinki: University of Helsinki.

Krohn, Leena. 1989. *Rapina: ja muita papereita.* Porvoo, Helsinki, Juva: WSOY.

Krohn, Leena. 2004. *Tainaron: Mail from Another City.* Trans. Hildi Hawkins. Canton, Ohio: Prime Books.

Krohn, Leena. 2013. *Hotel Sapiens. Irrationaalisia kertomuksia.* Helsinki: Teos.

Lahtinen, Toni & Markku Lehtimäki. 2011. "'Kaikki korttelin lapset, kissat ja koirat - yhtkää!': Vihreä vallankumous ympäristömanifestina." In *Tapion tarhoista turkistarhoille. Luonto suomalaisessa lasten- ja nuortenkirjallisuudessa,* eds. Maria Laakso, Toni Lahtinen & Päivi Heikkilä-Halttunen, 181–193. Helsinki: SKS.

Luckhurst, Roger. 2017. "The Weird: A Dis/Orientation." *Weird Fiction,* a special issue of *Textual Practice* 31 (6): 1041–1061.

Majander, Antti. 1995, April 14. "Läheisyys ja poissaolo hallitsevat Leena Krohnin ihmisiä: Kasvottoman kauhun vanavedessä." *Helsingin Sanomat.*

Marshall, Kate. 2016. "The Old Weird." *Modernism/Modernity* 23 (3): 631–649.

Morton, Timothy. 2016. *Dark Ecology: For a Logic of Future Coexistence.* New York: Columbia UP.

Raipola, Juha. 2015. *Ihmisen rajoilla: Epävarma tulevaisuus ja ei-inhimilliset toimijuudet Leena Krohnin Pereat munduksessa.* Acta Universitatis Tamperensis 2056. Tampere: Tampere UP.

Raipola, Juha. 2017. "Miksi *Hotel Sapiens* on olemassa? Leena Krohnin romaani postapokalyptisen fiktion lajikonventioiden valossa." In *Pakkovaltiosta ekodystopiaan: Kotimainen nykydystopia,* eds. Saija Isomaa & Toni Lahtinen, 88–105. Joutsen/Svanen, Erikoisjulkaisuja 2. Helsinki: Helsingin yliopisto.

Raipola, Juha. 2020. "Unnarratable Matter: Emergence, Narrative, and Material Ecocriticism." In *Reconfiguring Human, Nonhuman and Posthuman in Literature and Culture,* eds. Sanna Karkulehto, Aino-Kaisa Koistinen & Essi Varis, 263–280. London: Routledge.

Raipola, Juha & Toni Lahtinen. 2020. "Colonized Environments: The Weird Ecology of Johanna Sinisalo's Birdbrain." In *New Perspectives on Dystopian Fiction in Literature and Other Media,* eds. Saija Isomaa, Jyrki Korpua & Jouni Teittinen, 227–242. Newcastle upon Tyne: Cambridge Scholars Publishing.

Robertson, Benjamin J. 2018. *None of This Is Normal: The Fiction of Jeff VanderMeer.* Minneapolis: University of Minnesota Press.

Roine, Hanna-Riikka & Hanna Samola. 2018. "Johanna Sinisalo: The Genre and the New Weird." In *Lingua Cosmica: Science Fiction from Around the World,* ed. Dale Knickerbocker, 183–201. Urbana: University of Illinois Press.

Sinisalo, Johanna. 2011. "Weird and Proud of it." https://www.booksfromfinland.fi /2011/09/weird-and-proud-of-it/. Accessed 1 March 2024.

Sinisalo, Johanna. 2014. "Rare Exports." In *Finnish Weird,* eds. Toni Jerrman & J. Robert Tupasela, 3–4. Helsinki: Helsinki Science Fiction Society.

Tarkka, Pekka. 1990, November 23. "Ajattelun ja fantasian rikas leikki: Leena Krohn Jorge Luis Borgesin ja Italo Calvinon kentällä." *Helsingin Sanomat.*

Turnbull, Jonathon. 2021. "Weird." *Environmental Humanities* 13 (1): 275–280.

Ulstein, Gry. 2021. *Weird Fiction in a Warming World: A Reading Strategy for the Anthropocene.* Gent: Universiteit Gent.

VanderMeer, Jeff. 2008. "The New Weird: 'It's Alive?'" In *The New Weird,* eds. Ann Vandermeer & Jeff Vandermeer, ix–xvii. San Francisco: Tachyon Publications.

Weinstock, Jeffrey Andrew. 2016. "The New Weird." In *New Directions in Popular Fiction. Genre, Distribution, Reproduction,* ed. Ken Gelder, 177–200. London: Palgrave & Macmillan.

8

REFERENCES TO THE PRIMARY WORLD IN FINNISH CLIMATE FICTION

Claudia Nierste

Climate fiction has seen a rise in popularity in recent years, also in Finland. However, this popularity has not come without criticism. Toni Lahtinen (2017; Laurinolli 2019), a Finnish scholar specialising in Finnish literature and ecocriticism, considers the genre's tendency towards didacticism a possible sign of a new political current and an impoverishment of reading habits. The didacticism, they argue, is evident from the epilogues that some authors add to their novels. These epilogues often directly reference the supposed readers' reality and seem designed to influence their understanding of the text by proving its scientific validity. But how strong is the didactic influence in the narrative texts themselves? What references to the supposed readers' reality does Finnish climate fiction utilise in its narrative texts, and what functions do they serve? This chapter intends to examine these questions by analysing four novels of Finnish climate fiction: *Herääminen* (2000, H) and *Sarasvatin hiekkaa* (2005, SH – translated as *The Sands of Sarasvati*, 2013) by Risto Isomäki as well as *Teemestarin kirja* (2012, TK – translated as *Memory of Water*, 2014) and *Kudottujen kujien kaupunki* (2015, K3 – translated as *The City of Woven Streets* and *The Weaver*, both 2016) by Emmi Itäranta.[1]

Climate fiction – defined by Matthew Schneider-Mayerson (2018, 473–474, 481–482) as literature centring the relationship between humanity and nature amidst the effects of climate change – is a diverse field of works employing both fantastic and non-fantastic storytelling (Nikkanen 2017). Naturally, the four novels analysed in this chapter cannot represent Finnish climate fiction as a whole. They do, however, provide an illustrative example of two conceptually different kinds of Finnish climate fiction. While

DOI: 10.4324/9781003561101-12

Herääminen and *Sarasvatin hiekkaa* both depict the struggles of international research teams to uncover and prevent a looming global catastrophe – with *Herääminen* even including the involvement of extraterrestrials – *Teemestarin kirja* focuses on the personal story of a young woman in post-apocalyptic Lapland who defends the last source of freshwater from a military regime. Similarly, *Kudottujen kujien kaupunki* tells the story of a young woman living on an isolated island plagued by regular flooding who stands up to an authoritarian government by harnessing the power of her dreams.[2] The novels' narratives differ not only on a surface-level but also in their eco-philosophical undercurrent. While Isomäki favours a more superficial understanding of environmentalism and the relationship between humanity and nonhuman nature in which problems can be solved with technology, Itäranta's analysis of ownership and power dynamics tends more towards deep ecology (cf. Otto 2012, 46–48; Meretoja 2018, 201). Isomäki's epilogues also represent the trend of didacticism by way of overt references to the supposed readers' world mentioned by Lahtinen, to which Itäranta, who dispenses with such devices, forms a clear contrast. Finally, both Isomäki and Itäranta have received international attention, and Itäranta even wrote both novels simultaneously in Finnish and English (Teos 2021). They can therefore be considered high-profile representatives of Finnish climate fiction that shape its reputation both in Finland and abroad.

As Elise Kraatila (2021, 19–24) observes, it is especially fantastic worlds that consciously draw the readers' attention to their separation from reality and their nature as artificial constructs. They therefore consider fantastic fiction to be uniquely suited to reflecting on the methods and devices of storytelling in general and to addressing the ongoing crisis of representation, understood by Kraatila (2021, 18) as a "general loss of faith [prevalent in contemporary Western art] in the notion that art can faithfully reflect any reality outside itself," with the underlying doubt that there is "any solid and singular reality" to be reflected in the first place. Following this line of thinking, I would argue that climate fiction provides an interesting case study in this regard as it deals at its core with the fragility and complexity of our own world and environment (Raipola 2019), often revealing its stability and coherence as an illusion and a narrative created by and for humans. It should therefore be interesting to see how the four novels examined here make use of this potential.

Theoretical Framework

To begin with, it should be established how this chapter understands the fantastic. According to Kathryn Hume (1984, xi–xii, 3), the fundamental problem of defining literary fantasy[3] is based on a Western tradition of thought that evaluates literature according to how well it depicts reality and presupposes a mimetic motivation for all literary creation. This assumption, they argue, leads to a disregard for fantastic features in the established canon as well as the stereotyping of fantasy as a marginal phenomenon. Herein, Hume (1984, 8–17, 19–25) sees the origin of many exclusionary definitions, such as those proposed by Tzvetan Todorov (1992, 26–33), J. R.R. Tolkien (1989, 51–63), and Rosemary Jackson (1981, 175–176), who conceive of the fantastic as a separate literary form. Hume, however, denies that the essential impulse of literary creation is a mimetic one and that fantasy is a peripheral phenomenon. Instead, they propose an inclusive definition of the fantastic not as a genre in its own right or a literary form, but as an impulse. All literature, according to them, is ultimately the product of two impulses: the mimetic impulse to describe the world in such a way that others might share in one's experiences and the fantastic impulse to modify what is given. Fantasy, in this framework, is therefore "any departure from consensus reality, an impulse native to literature and manifested in innumerable variations, from monster to metaphor" (Hume 1984, 21). This notion of fantasy as an integral part of world literature and storytelling is echoed by Kraatila's (2021, 23–24, 232) recent doctoral dissertation that examines contemporary fantasy in its historical context as a response to the ongoing crisis of representation.

Hume's definition is particularly useful for this analysis both because Itäranta's and Isomäki's novels combine mimetic and fantastic storytelling, and because the analysis examines their usage of techniques from both literary traditions. However, Hume's proposed idea of a consensus reality is not understood here as universal. Instead, the analysis of the four novels conducted in this chapter assumes a more specific consensus between the author and the supposed readers that is heavily influenced by the cultural background of the Nordic context. The epilogues of Isomäki's novels especially hint at this specificity, as they seem to represent the author's effort to ensure the readers share the same consensus with them.

Hume's idea of a departure from consensus reality also lends itself to the analytical tool employed later in this chapter, namely the sliding scale between a primary and a secondary world. The term "primary world" is used here to designate the world the supposed readers inhabit and, therefore, the world that is used as a reference for the mimetic portions of the storytelling by way of a culturally imbued consensus. In contrast, a "secondary world" is a fantastic world that is consciously set apart from this primary world (see Faber 2018, 216). Finally, the term "story world" refers to all fictional worlds regardless of their mimetic or fantastic elements. It is defined by David Herman (2009, 106) as "the world invoked implicitly as well as explicitly by the narrative." The term thus encompasses both the worlds of Isomäki's novels, which tend towards factuality and accuracy in service of a didactic impulse, and Itäranta's more fantastical worlds. According to Marie-Laure Ryan (2014, 33), story worlds are also dynamic models that change via the reader's imagination as the plot progresses. This participation of the reader in the construction of the story world is essential, as many of its elements are only implicitly hinted at or not mentioned at all (Faber 2018, 217). For example, in *Teemestarin kirja*, the state of the international transportation system is not explicitly explained. However, the fact that even great distances are covered by train suggests that passenger flights are no longer available.

In line with Ryan's emphasis on dynamic processes, it should be noted that despite its name, the term "worldbuilding" is not used in this chapter to designate the ontologically orientated building of an altogether separated world. Instead, it refers to a twofold category as suggested by Hanna-Riikka Roine: while Roine (2016, 17–19) does not oppose the post-Tolkienian understanding of worldbuilding, they do propose a distinction between the understanding of worlds as ontological constructs centred around the authority of an author-creator and as processes in which active engagement of readers, speculative thought-experiments, and the communication of abstract ideas play a central part. When understood in this sense, worldbuilding does not presuppose a strict separation between the fictional and the world of the supposed readers, but invites a crossing of interworldly borders. This chapter aims to proceed accordingly by not only describing the building blocks of story worlds but also examining the way they communicate information and shape the readers' interaction with the text.

The Analytical Scale

The novels discussed in this chapter do not lend themselves easily to a comparative analysis of their story worlds. The explicit references within the narrative to climate change in its scientific and historical dimensions speak to a greater mimetic impulse towards accuracy and factuality in *Sarasvatin hiekkaa* and *Herääminen*, whereas the story worlds of *Teemestarin kirja* and *Kudottujen kujien kaupunki* contain significantly more fantastic elements. An additional factor is the influence of their position within the field of genre on the readers' interaction with their story worlds (Till 2010, 73–75), with Isomäki's novels representing a more science fictional and Itäranta's novels – to a varying degree – a more fantastic tradition by comparison. At the same time, they are subject to a global shift in speculative writing described and dated by Marek Oziewicz (2017, 16–19) as having begun around the early 2000s that foregoes the separation into distinctive genres in favour of the broader category of speculative fiction. *Teemestarin kirja*, for example, cannot be called a secondary world in the classic sense, which like many worlds of what Farah Mendlesohn (2008, 83) calls immersive fantasy presents a self-contained entity where the fantastic constitutes the norm for both the protagonist and the supposed reader without explanation or explicit ties to the primary world. Even for *Kudottujen kujien kaupunki* with its scarce explicit references to the primary world, Itäranta has foregone world maps and other instruments that are used to create the illusion of a self-contained fictional world (Ekman 2013, 14–15). To account for this heterogeneity, the analytical tools employed here will draw from several sources. Central among them is the analytical framework developed by Mark J.P. Wolf (2012) that draws on both the concept of subcreation and elements of the possible worlds theory.

According to Wolf (2012, 24–25), the term "subcreation" was coined by Tolkien in the 1947 essay "On Fairy-Stories" to designate a process in which elements from the primary world are combined in unprecedented ways to create new entities for a story world. These entities, they argue, then replace an assumed standard adopted from the primary world – a "rare and terrible blue moon" (Tolkien 1989, 25), after all, would not be a surprise if not for the prior expectation that the moon would appear in its usual colour. Consequently, this expectation shows that a story world initially has the same standards as the primary world and that these standards persist in the reader's mind unless the text gives explicit or implicit hints to the contrary. In the narratological theory of possible worlds, this is called the principle of minimal deviation (Herbert et al. 2017, 55) and is discussed by Ryan (1991, 51) as the principle of minimal departure. As Wolf (2012, 27–28) notes, the more hints towards deviation the text gives, the more standards from the primary world are replaced and the further the story world departs from consensus reality. Different story worlds can therefore be ranked on a scale that reflects the occurrence of entities formed by subcreation within them and thus their departure from said consensus.

The scale proposed by Wolf has two ends: it starts with a story world that almost completely coincides with the primary world and ends with a secondary world that has only little in common with it. Between these two points, different worlds from autobiography to historical novel and science fiction adventure to high fantasy epic can be placed as depicted in Figure 8.1 according to Wolf.

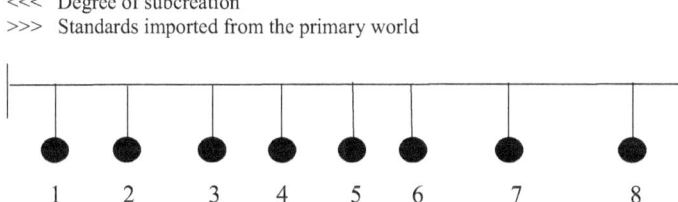

FIGURE 8.1   The analytical scale. Graphic by the author. Rekeyd by the editor.

Wolf (2012, 28) notes that the story worlds on the left side of the scale are often designed to appear typical for certain settings in the primary world and evoke corresponding associations in the audience. However, even on the far right side, authors still make use of deliberate or unconscious borrowings from the primary world.

To facilitate a more detailed analysis, the similarities or deviations that determine a given world's position on the scale are divided into four categories according to Wolf (2012, 35–36): nominal, cultural, natural, and ontological. Nominal deviations occur when new names are given to existing concepts of the primary world. This may only be a change of name, but usually implies changes in the cultural domain as well: an example from *Teemestarin kirja* is the autumn festival *kuukekri* "moon kekri" (TK, 218). Here, the name already indicates that the *kekri* festival familiar to Finnish readers[4] has been changed in a material way. Cultural similarities or deviations refer to anything created by humans (or other species), be it physical objects, technologies, customs, institutions, or ideas and concepts. The natural category includes entities belonging to nonhuman nature, such as meteorological phenomena, landscapes, and other species. Finally, the fourth of Wolf's categories refers to the ontological parameters of the world, such as its physical laws.

According to Wolf (2012, 35), the four categories are interdependent and can be arranged in a hierarchy. Changes in the ontological parameters of the world, for instance, usually entail changes in the natural category, which in turn have consequences for the cultural and finally the nominal category. When ranking a story world on the scale, deviations in categories that have consequences for other categories should therefore carry greater weight. Even with numerous small deviations in the nominal or cultural category, for example, a story world necessarily places further towards the left end of the scale than a story world exhibiting serious changes to the laws of physics. It should be noted that the separation of these categories and their interaction with one another follows the logic of speculative worldbuilding as a culturally biassed thought experiment and makes no claim to scientific or universal applicability.

This heterogenous framework of analytical tools is particularly suited to the study of fictional worlds that are conceptually located between the mimetic and the fantastic due to its core concept of a gradual shift in their departure from a supposed consensus reality. The gradual scale also fits well with Kraatila's (2021, 19–22, 39) and Roine's (2016, 33–34) discussions of fantastical worldbuilding as a communicative act that rejects the one-directional, imitative relationship between supposedly self-contained worlds of fiction and external reality in favour of a more interactive theorisation about reality where authors and readers can alternate between and experience both worlds simultaneously. Accordingly, the analysis conducted here is not concerned with absolute placements on the scale. Rather, the four story worlds are analysed in relation to each other, and the distance between them does not reflect statistical measurements.

The (Post)apocalyptic Worlds of Itäranta and Isomäki: An Overview

On the comparative scale, *Sarasvatin hiekkaa* takes the position at the far left end with the smallest departure from the primary world, followed by *Herääminen, Teemestarin kirja,* and finally *Kudottujen kujien kaupunki* (Figure 8.2).

The story worlds of Isomäki's novels show less significant deviations from the primary world in the nominal, cultural, natural, and ontological category than those of Itäranta's novels. *Kudottujen kujien kaupunki* is the only one out of the four story worlds that includes deviations in the ontological category.

The factors that determine the above positioning of the story worlds shall now be discussed in detail. In the interest of a uniform basis of evaluation, an equivalent place in the primary world serves as a comparative value when judging similarities and deviations. If possible, a distinction is made between unusual things, on the one hand, and non-existent or impossible things, on the other hand. Bowing and sitting in a kneeling position, characteristic of the tea ceremonies in *Teemestarin kirja*, for example, might be unusual both in the geographical setting of the novel, a village in Northern Finland, and for supposed readers with a Nordic cultural background. Outside of this context, however, these behaviours are consistent with the consensus reality of a large portion of humanity. The extraterrestrials as they are depicted in *Herääminen*, on the other hand, fall into the realm of the impossible. If precise places of comparison for a story world's setting can be found at all, this in itself speaks for a closer connection to the primary world. Since such a place does not exist for *Kudottujen kujien kaupunki*, the general physical parameters of the primary world and the Nordic cultural context serve as a basis for comparison. Another point to consider are elements that are subject to rapid change over time, such as technology. In *Herääminen*, which is set in 2038 and 2039, mobile video calls are widespread. This does not

<<<   Degree of subcreation
>>>   Standards imported from the primary world

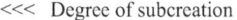

FIGURE 8.2   The relative positions of *Sarasvatin hiekkaa, Herääminen, Teemestarin kirja* and *Kudottujen kujien kaupunki* on the analytical scale. Graphic by the author. Rekeyed by the editor.

represent a deviation from the primary world in the year 2022. However, in 2000, the year of publication, this technology was not common. In order to do justice to the time in which the novels were published, the basis for comparison in the primary world is dated to the year of publication.

The minor deviations in the nominal, cultural, and natural category in *Sarasvatin hiekkaa* are mostly found in the epilogue, which describes the world after the great tidal wave. The transition from the part of the novel that shows minimal deviations from the primary world to the post-apocalyptic state is seamless: the post-apocalyptic world is described in the same style as the world before the tidal wave. This creates a powerful contrast between familiar descriptions of spruce trees, red deer, and grey seals (SH, 300), on the one hand, and the global scale of destruction, on the other. In the nominal category, Isomäki uses familiar terms and linguistic patterns to establish new designations and meanings. The term "geyser" refers not only to a fountain of hot water but in the new world also to eruptions of radioactive steam from submerged nuclear power plants (SH, 306). The new body of water formed by the flooding of Europe is called the *Gulf of Europe* (*Euroopanlahti*; SH, 299), referring to seas from the primary world such as the Gulf of Bothnia (*Pohjanlahti*). Among the few deviations in the cultural category is the fact that the dialogue of all characters, regardless of their background, consists of standardised written Finnish.

Herääminen includes deviations from the primary world within the nominal, cultural, and natural category. However, almost all of these deviations are explained using concepts familiar to the supposed readers. The story world's extreme changes in climate, for instance, are presented as extrapolations of global trends at the time of the novel's publication. A more severe case is the appearance of extraterrestrials, which brings about further deviations, be it genetically optimised super-plants (H, 240–241), the planned epidemics of AIDS and Ebola (H, 228–232), or the disappearance of the moon (H, 284). However, the behaviour of these aliens is explained using analogies to human customs such as hunting for population control (H, 223–227) or the difference in species between humans and ants (H, 224). Changes in climate also cause deviations in the cultural category. This manifests itself in an altered geopolitical situation and has implications for currency and brand names. For example, as a result of Russia's geopolitical dominance, the exchange rate of the ruble is more than 60 euros (H, 21). Finally, Isomäki adopts historical events from the primary world but reinterprets them considerably. As in *Sarasvatin hiekkaa*, the dialogue for all characters is written in standardised Finnish.

Teemestarin kirja shows clear deviations in the nominal, cultural, and natural category but maintains its connection to the primary world through purposeful references. In the nominal category, Itäranta combines familiar elements into neologisms such as *blazefly* (*roihukärpänen*; TK, 11; cf.

tulikärpänen "firefly") and *water guard* (*vesivalvoja*; TK, 22; cf. *uimaval-voja* "lifeguard"). Moreover, *Teemestarin kirja* explicitly draws attention to the cultural dependency of conceptualisations:

> I knew this stood for the ice that had sometimes been called eternal ice, until it became clear that it wasn't eternal after all. Near the end of the past-world era the globe had warmed and seas had risen faster than any-one could have anticipated.
>
> *(Itäranta 2014, 64–65)*[5,6]

In the cultural category, Itäranta's novel mixes Baltic Finnic traditions like the harvest festival *kekri* (TK, 42, 110) and the *lament-women* (*itkijänaiset*; TK, 120) with Far Eastern customs such as the tea ceremony (TK, 39) and acupuncture (TK, 128). As is the case in *Herääminen*, these cultural devia-tions might be attributed to the geopolitical consequences of climate change. In *Teemestarin kirja*, however, the reasons for the post-apocalyptic state of the story world are only hinted at, as the characters themselves have little information about them. Their ignorance about their own past and the ref-erences to the primary world that give readers an accessibility point to the story world are combined in the mentioning of TDK cassettes and CDs. To the main characters, they constitute mysterious remnants of a bygone era (TK, 52–53). Many deviations in the natural category are also recognisably tied to the primary world, for instance, through names such as *Alvinvaara* (TK, 12; cf. the mountain *Ounasvaara* in Northern Finland) and *Ladoga Bay* (*Laatokanlahti*; TK, 85; cf. *Pohjanlahti* "Gulf of Bothnia"), or through indications of how much the story world differs from a state in the past and thus the present of the readers. Winters in the area of present-day Lapland, for example, are no longer cold, but the main character, Noria, reads about the cold in old books (TK, 9, 45). As in Isomäki's novels, the story world of *Teemestarin kirja* shows no deviations in the ontological category, and all characters speak in standardised written Finnish.

The story world of *Kudottujen kujien kaupunki* represents a novelty on the scale. Although it also contains deviations in the nominal, cultural, and natural category, the decisive factor for placing the story world to the right end is the fact that its physical reality can be influenced through the power of thought. For example, the main character, Eliana, increases the density of the air to such an extent that an attacker is physically repelled by it (K3, 305). This represents a clear break with the physical laws of the primary world and thus a deviation in the ontological category. Deviations in the other categories are difficult to assess, since no concrete place of comparison in the primary world can be identified. Itäranta remains largely nonspecific in the descriptions of their story world: the economic system of the island is only hinted at, and its inhabitants wear simple clothes without distinctive features and eat plain foods. Some more distinctive references to the primary world remain, however. On the one hand, many of the named plants and herbs have a counterpart in the primary world – most conspicuous here is the name *passion flower* (*kärsimyskukka*; K3, 12), referring directly to Christianity – and, on the other hand, many neologisms represent a recombination of familiar concepts, such as the *singing jellyfish* (*laulumeduusat*; K3, 13; cf. *laulujoutsen* "whooper swan," lit. "singing swan") or the white *bone corals* (*luukorallit*; K3, 29). In the case of these white corals, no direct reference is made to the primary world. However, an indirect association is possible: in the House of the Stained (*Tahrattujen Talo*), Eliana is forced to dive for red corals, which have largely disappeared from the sea. White corals, on the other hand, are in abundance (K3, 213–215). In the primary world, corals are one of the species most affected by climate change, and ocean warming is causing their increased bleaching and death (Wille 2020).

The Functions of References to the Primary World: Four Examples

After evaluating the story worlds in their entirety, I will now analyse exemplary scenes from each of the four novels to discuss how references to the primary world can be used in fictional worldbuilding. In the following two scenes from *Sarasvatin hiekkaa*, references to the primary world are used to demonstrate the scale of both the narrative itself and that of single events. In the first scene, the narrator supplements the immediate setting of the plot – Sergei taking a flight to India – with a variety of references to the primary world.

> That upper **fjord**, extending from **north-east** to **south-west**, was clearly the **Gulf of Kutch**. And that lower **gulf** stretching from north to south, nearly splitting the **state** of **Gujarat** in two, had to be the **Gulf of Cambay** – or, in **Indian**, the **Gulf of Khambhat**, his actual destination. So the slightly larger **city** at the north-east end of the gulf was probably **Baroda**, and the city on its eastern **shore** was **Surat**.
>
> *(SH, 51; translation and emphasis by C.N.)*[7]

The precise references that later include a mention of Mahatma Gandhi as well as Sergei's reflections on the geological origin of certain landscape formations support the effort to create a story world that strongly resembles the primary world. However, this is not their only function. They also place Sergei and Amrita's portion of the plot in a larger regional context that supports the novel's thematic arc. The discovery of the ruins off the coast of India does not constitute a minor curiosity – even though it is treated as such at the beginning of the novel (SH, 10). Instead, it has far-reaching

consequences for the prevailing interpretation of Indian history, the relationship between East and West, and ultimately the fate of the entire world.

In the last part of the novel, on the other hand, a small-scale setting serves
to make an apocalyptic catastrophe tangible. After reporting on the large-
scale flooding of Northern Russia, Denmark, and the Netherlands as well
as the collapse of the Gulf Stream, the narrator directs the reader's attention
first to Northern Germany, then to the city of Hamburg, and finally to a
single street:

> A couple of hours later, they were driving through the streets of **Hamburg,**
> which lay submerged ten meters deep under water. The water was clear,
> they could see all the way to the bottom. They could see the streets, the
> cars parked along them, the lampposts, the broken windows of the vari-
> ous shops and department stores and sidewalk cafés, and the shards of
> glass sticking out of the window frames. ... Amrita turned the rudder to
> the left and the bow of the Oannes turned into the **Bahnhofstrasse** [*sic*].
>
> *(SH, 306–307)*[8]

This reference to a specific place in the primary world shows the effects of
the catastrophe on a palpable scale. It also parallels Sergei and Amrita's earlier diving trips among the ruins of the underwater city off the coast of India
(SH, 80–86), which was itself devastated by a tidal wave long ago. This
constellation reflects the cycle motif of the novel and the warning expressed
by several characters (SH, 33–34, 107) that natural disasters are not a phenomenon of the past.

Another example from *Sarasvatin hiekkaa* shows how abstract concepts
and processes can be made more comprehensible by referring to familiar
places from the primary world. In the following scene, polar explorer Susan
Cheng is talking to a journalist with no experience in the Arctic. Isomäki
uses the reference to melting snow in Finland and Sweden in the spring, a
sight familiar to readers with a Nordic cultural background, to illustrate a
physical process on the Greenland glacier.

> This accelerates the warming and, in the worst case, the surface of the
> ice eventually forms a completely uniform, almost pitch-black layer. The
> kind that covers **roadside snowbanks in Finland and Sweden,** for exam-
> ple, in late spring, when most of the winter snow has already melted and
> the sooty particles from the melted snow form a black layer on top of the
> remaining snow.
>
> *(SH, 144)*[9]

References to the primary world can also give clues to the historical background of the story world, be it geographically, politically, or culturally. In

the following scene from *Teemestarin kirja*, the narration uses modified references to well-known cities of the primary world to give the reader points of orientation in the story world. This is particularly important because Itäranta does not use additional material such as a world map or a timeline to communicate this information.

> "How would you feel about living in one of the cities?" asked my mother. "In a place like **New Piterburg**, or **Mos Qua**, or even as far as **Xinjing**?"
>
> *(Itäranta 2014, 46)[10]*

All three cities mentioned here are recognisable as references to Russian and Chinese cities of the primary world: *New Piterburg* (*Uusi Pietari*) brings to mind St. Petersburg (*Pietari*), *Mos Qua* appears to be a sinicised form of Moscow, and *Xinjing* may refer to either 新 靖 (*Xīnjìng*) or 新 景 (*Xīnjǐng*) in contemporary China. Noria's mother considers these cities to be secure places of residence – rather than cities west or south of Finland – which suggests that the areas where Russia and China are located in the primary world are still habitable in this post-apocalyptic story world. Moreover, the name change to *Mos Qua* implies that the influence of the culture associated with the China of our present primary world has extended further west in the past of the story world. The order these cities appear within the sentence and the expression "as far as" (*asti*) at the end hint at the distance between them and Noria's village: *New Piterburg* and *Mos Qua* appear to be closer to the village than *Xinjing*. In the names of the cities themselves, the narration maintains a careful balance between references to the primary world and fictional concepts: *New Piterburg* and *Mos Qua* may be fictional names as such, but the supposed readers are familiar with the concept of naming new cities after old ones (e.g., New York), as well as toponyms having different spellings in different languages (e.g., Moscow and Moskova).

This technique of hinting at past developments within the story world by using modified references to the primary world is not limited to the more fantastic world of *Teemestarin kirja*. Similar elements can be found in the story world of *Herääminen*. An example is the following scene in which six heads of state are introduced with references to the primary world that hint at the political situation of the story world:

> Gabrielle de Wit, **Secretary General of the remaining EU**. Arto Niemenkylä, **Prime Minister of the Nordic Union**. Vladimir Cherenkov, **President of Russia**. Akiko Nakamoto, **Prime Minister of China-Japan**. Jose Anderson, **President of the American Union**. And Mariama Mbuju, **Prime Minister of the Federation of Southern Africa**.
>
> *(H, 128)[11]*

As with *Mos Qua* in *Teemestarin kirja*, the narrator uses modified references to the primary world to illuminate major political developments in the past of the story world. The expression "remaining EU" (*tynkä-EU*, lit. "stump EU," possibly referencing a common designation for the Federal Republic of Yugoslavia in Finland in the 1990s; see Närhi 1995) combines a reference to the familiar institution from the primary world with an evocative word that clearly communicates the same institution's drastic loss of power in the story world.

Finally, in the story world of *Kudottujen kujien kaupunki*, several references to the primary world serve a symbolic function. The fictional places depicted within the story world draw on associative cultural and literary images of the primary world. This is especially true for the main setting of the novel: an isolated island in the middle of the sea, constantly threatened by floods, with a population oppressed by the totalitarian *Council*. The sea surrounding the island plays a central role both in the spatial design of the setting and in a thematic sense. It naturally separates the islanders from the people on the mainland, but over the course of the story, it becomes clear that this isolation is not as self-evident as it seems. Ships travel between the island and the mainland, and in the past, people from the island were allowed to pursue their education on the continent (K3, 151). Here, the narrator uses a topographically manifested boundary familiar from the primary world. In its strictness, however, this boundary ultimately refers primarily to the atmospheric setting (*gestimmter Raum*, cf. Haupt 2004, 78) of the narrative and not to physical reality. The isolation of the island is manufactured by humans and can be broken. Furthermore, the sea in itself is a fragile and constantly changing ecosystem that the islanders depend on for clothing, nourishment, and even light. This source of life is threatened by the pollution that originates from the factories producing tattoo ink (K3, 276) and is ultimately linked to the *Council*'s oppressive rule utilising the dream-suppressing effect of these tattoos (K3, 154). Towards the end of the novel, then, it is at first glance the sea that destroys the island:

> The ink districts are leaking sediment into the sea, making people sick. The **island lies in the middle of the sea**, getting smaller and smaller. On the horizon, a **big wave** is approaching.
>
> *(K3, 323)*[12]

However, in an earlier scene, the narrator explicitly mentions the prisoners in the *House of the Stained* and that the island is ultimately collapsing under the weight of their dreams (K3, 57). The main character, Eliana, imagines herself standing on a rock in the sea and whipping up its waves into a destructive storm (K3, 224–225). Thus, the sea – a familiar and highly associative part of the primary world – becomes a symbol for the indomitable power of dreams.

Conclusion

Overall, the novels presented in this chapter demonstrate that the story worlds of Finnish climate fiction have a complex relationship to the primary world and thereby to the supposed readers' reality. The primary world serves both as a source of explicit and implicit references and as a foil against which the story worlds are contrasted. Their general proximity to the primary world can be evaluated on a comparative scale,[13] with *Sarasvatin hiekkaa* placing closest to and *Kudottujen kujien kaupunki* furthest from the primary world. References to the primary world within the texts fulfil a variety of functions. They can be used to demonstrate the scale of both the narrative itself and that of single events, to illustrate abstract concepts and processes, to give clues regarding the historical background of the story world, and to imbue fictional places within the story world with symbolic meaning, to name only a few possibilities. Even explicit references to the primary world should not be seen as detractions from fictionality or literary quality, but rather as tools for shaping story worlds that can be used to communicate, for example, ecopolitical themes effectively.

Although Isomäki and Itäranta differ in how they construct their story worlds, in the eco-political messages of their texts, and in the way these texts interact with their readers, there is no clear-cut difference in the way they utilise references to the primary world. In the speculative story world of *Teemestarin kirja*, Itäranta uses at times precise references to present-day Finland, and there are fantastical elements to be found in Isomäki's more mimetic story worlds.

Taking into consideration their categorisation on the book market, it could be argued that the dichotomies created by genre expectations contribute to obscuring the nuances and diversity of methods used in speculative worldbuilding. However, just as the term speculative fiction has been employed to extenuate the separation into genres in favour of an overarching classification of fantastic texts, the same can be achieved in the study of worldbuilding. As Roine (2016, 33–34) suggests, the focus should not be on ontological aspects and strict divisions, but rather on an awareness of fluid transitions and the possibility of multiple worlds existing simultaneously. Climate fiction is particularly suited for this purpose because of its inherent preoccupation with the fragility of what we believe to be our reality. Increased research in this area would not only broaden the understanding of worldbuilding and readers' interactions with fictional worlds but also provide authors with new tools and thus possibly even counteract the didactic tendencies criticised by Lahtinen (2017).

Notes

1 Editor's note: Unlike most chapters in this book, in this chapter, the source texts are referred to by their original (Finnish) titles and not by their English translations. This is due to the article's focus on textual origins and translation.

2 It should be noted that the topic of climate change itself is not explicitly addressed in *Kudottujen kujien kaupunki*. Aspects of what has come to define the genre of climate fiction are instead found in the novel's discussion of human endeavours to exploit the surrounding ecosystem, the consequences of the resulting damage, and the dependence of humankind on physical nature.

3 Although Hume talks about "fantasy," it is clear from their usage of the term that they are referring to fantastic literature in general.

4 *Kekri* is an old Finnish labour and harvest festival that until the beginning of the twentieth century marked the end of the harvesting season and the time of the cattle market (Hänninen 2010). Interestingly, Itäranta (2014, 39) drops this explicit reference to Finnish culture in the English-language version of *Teemestarin kirja* in favour of the term *Moonfeast*.

5 Tiesin, että se kuvasi jäätä, jota oli joskus kutsuttu ikijääksi, kunnes kävi ilmi, ettei se ollutkaan ikuista. Entismaailman ajan lopulla maapallo oli lämmennyt ja merenpinnat nousseet nopeammin kuin kukaan oli osannut ennustaa (Itäranta 2012, 68).

6 The examples and quotes in this paragraph are from the English-language version of the novel written by Itäranta.

7 Tuo ylempi, lounaasta koilliseen kurkottava vuono oli selvästikin Kutchin lahti. Ja tuon alemman, lähes pohjois eteläsuuntaisen lahden, joka jakoi koko Gujaratin osavaltion melkein kahtia, täytyi olla Cambaynlahti – tai intialaisittain sanottuna Khambhatinlahti, siis hänen varsinainen määränpäänsä. Tuo lahden koillispäässä sijaitseva vähän isompi kaupunki oli varmaankin siis Baroda ja tuo lahden itärannalla oleva kaupunki Surat (Isomäki 2005, 51).

8 Pari tuntia myöhemmin he ajoivat kymmenen metrin paksuisen vesikerroksen peittämiä Hampurin katuja pitkin. Vesi oli kirkasta, he näkivät selvästi pohjaan asti. He erottivat kadut, niiden varsille pysäköidyt autot, lyhtypylväät, erilaisten kauppojen ja tavaratalojen ja katukahviloiden rikkinäiset ikkunat ja ikkunanpielistä pistävät lasin sirpaleet. ... Amrita käänsi peräsintä vasemmalle ja Oanneksen keula kääntyi Bahnhofstrasselle [*sic*] (Isomäki 2005, 306–307).

9 Tämä kiihdyttää lämpenemistä ja pahimmassa tapauksessa jään pinnalle muodostuu lopulta aivan yhtenäinen, melkein pikimusta kerros. Sellainen, kuin mikä peittää esimerkiksi Suomen ja Ruotsin tienvarsien lumipenkkoja loppukeväällä, kun suurin osa talven lumesta on jo sulanut ja kaikki sulaneen lumen sisältämät nokihiukkaset ovat mustana kerroksena jäljellä olevan lumen päällä (Isomäki 2005, 144).

10 "Miltä sinusta tuntuisi asua jossain kaupungeista?" äiti kysyi. "Vaikkapa Uudessa Pietarissa, tai Mos Quassa, tai Xinjingissä asti?" (Itäranta 2012, 50).

11 Gabrielle de Wit, tynkä-EU:n pääsihteeri. Arto Niemenkylä, Pohjolan Unionin pääministeri. Vladimir Cherenkov, Venäjän presidentti. Akiko Nakamoto, Kiina-Japanin pääministeri. Jose Anderson, Amerikan Unionin presidentti. Sekä Mariama Mbuju, Eteläisen Afrikan liittovaltion pääministeri (Isomaki 2000, 128).

12 Mustekortteleista valuu mereen sakkaa, joka tekee ihmiset sairaiksi. Saari erottuu meressä yhä pienempänä. Horisontissa lähestyy suuri aalto (Itäranta 2015, 323).
13 The scale developed over the course of this short chapter should be understood as a preliminary tool that proved useful for the comparison of the four story worlds in question, but would naturally have to be developed further.

References

Ekman, Stefan. 2013. *Here Be Dragons. Exploring Fantasy Maps and Settings.* Middletown: Wesleyan UP.

Faber, Sarah. 2018. "Flights of Fancy, Secondary Worlds and Blank Slates: Relations between the Fantastic and the Real." In *Exploring the Fantastic. Gender, Ideology, and Popular Culture*, eds. Ina Batzke, Eric C. Erbacher, Linda M. Heß & Corinna Lenhardt, 213–237. Bielefeld: transcript publishing.

Hänninen, Anneli. 2010. "Kekri ja pyhäinpäivä." *Kotimaisten kielten keskus.* https://www.kotus.fi/nyt/kolumnit_artikkelit_ja_esitelmat/tiesitko_taman_(2004_2014)/kekri_ja_pyhainpaiva. Accessed 1 March 2024.

Haupt, Birgit. 2004. "Zur Analyse des Raums." In *Einführung in die Erzähltextanalyse*, ed. Peter Wenzel, 69–87. Trier: Wissenschaftlicher Verlag Trier.

Herbert, Anna, Vanessa Leck, Diana Opitz & Janek Sturm. 2017. "Possible-Worlds-Theory und Film." *Paradigma. Studienbeiträge zu Literatur und Film* 1/2017: 54–59.

Herman, David. 2009. *Basic Elements of Narrative.* Malden: Wiley-Blackwell.

Hume, Kathryn. 1984. *Fantasy and Mimesis. Responses to Reality in Western Literature.* New York: Methuen.

Isomäki, Risto. 2000. *Herääminen.* (H.) Helsinki: Tammi.

Isomäki, Risto. 2005. *Sarasvatin hiekkaa.* (SH.) Helsinki: Tammi.

Itäranta, Emmi. 2012. *Teemestarin kirja.* (TK.) Helsinki: Teos.

Itäranta, Emmi. 2014. *Memory of Water.* New York: HarperVoyager.

Itäranta, Emmi. 2015. *Kudottujen kujien kaupunki.* (K3.) Helsinki: Teos.

Jackson, Rosemary. 1981. *Fantasy: The Literature of Subversion.* London et al.: Methuen.

Kraatila, Elise. 2021. *The Crisis of Representation and Speculative Mimesis. Rethinking Relations between Fiction and Reality with 21st-century Fantasy Storytelling.* Tampere University Dissertations 496. Tampere: Tampere UP.

Lahtinen, Toni. 2017. "Ilmastokirjallisuus, nyt!" *Alusta!.* https://alusta.uta.fi/2017/12/11/ilmastokirjallisuus-nyt. Accessed 1 March 2024.

Laurinolli, Heikki. 2019. "Ilmastokirjallisuus kasvoi räjähdysmäisesti." Tampere University. https://www.tuni.fi/fi/ajankohtaista/ilmastokirjallisuus-kasvoi-rajahdysmaisesti. Accessed 1 March 2024.

Mendlesohn, Farah. 2008. *Rhetorics of Fantasy.* Middletown: Wesleyan UP.

Meretoja, Hanna. 2018. "Vesi, tarinankerronta ja todellisuuden hahmottaminen Jeanette Wintersonin Majakan-vartijassa ja Emmi Itärannan Teemestarin kirjassa." In *Veteen kirjoitettu. Veden merkitykset kirjallisuudessa*, eds. Markku Lehtimäki, Hanna Meretoja & Arja Rosenholm, 186–210. Suomalaisen Kirjallisuuden Seuran toimituksia 1441. Helsinki: SKS.

Närhi, Eeva Maria. 1995. "Erikoisia erisnimiä ja erisnimiä yleisnimissä." *Kielikello* 3/1995. https://www.kielikello.fi/-/erikoisia-erisnimia-ja-erisnimia-yleisnimissa. Accessed 1 March 2024.

Nikkanen, Hanna. 2017. "Fiktion lämpötila nousee." *Image.* https://www.apu.fi/artikkelit/suomalainen-kaunokirjallisuus-elaa-ekologisten-kriisien-kuvaamisen-aikaa-joka-tuntuu. Accessed 1 March 2024.

Otto, Eric C. 2012. *Green Speculations. Science Fiction and Transformative Environmentalism.* Columbus: Ohio State UP.

Oziewicz, Marek. 2017. "Speculative Fiction." *Oxford Research Encyclopedia of Literature.* https://oxfordre.com/literature/view/10.1093/acrefore /9780190201098.001.0001/acrefore-9780190201098-e-78. Accessed 1 March 2024.

Raipola, Juha 2019. "What is Speculative Climate Fiction?" *Fafnir* 2/2019. http:// journal.finfar.org/fafnir-2-2019. Accessed 1 March 2024.

Roine, Hanna-Riikka. 2016. *Imaginative, Immersive and Interactive Engagements. The Rhetoric of Worldbuilding in Contemporary Speculative Fiction.* Acta Universitatis Tamperensis 2197. Tampere: Tampere UP.

Ryan, Marie-Laure. 1991. *Possible Worlds, Artificial Intelligence, and Narrative Theory.* Bloomington: Indiana UP.

Ryan, Marie-Laure. 2014. "Introduction." In *Storyworlds across Media: Towards a Media-conscious Narratology*, eds. Marie-Laure Ryan & Jan-Noel Thon, 1–21. Lincoln: University of Nebraska Press.

Schneider-Mayerson, Matthew. 2018. "The Influence of Climate Fiction. An Empirical Survey of Readers." *Environmental Humanities* 10/2: 473–500. http:// read.dukeupress.edu/environmental-humanities/article-pdf/10/2/473/555850 /473smayerson.pdf. Accessed 1 March 2024.

Teos. 2021. "Emmi Itäranta." http://www.teos.fi/kirjailijat/emmi-it%C3%A4ranta .html. Accessed March 1, 2024.

Till, Dietmar. 2010. "Konvention und Gattung." In *Handbuch Gattungstheorie*, ed. Rüdiger Zymner, 73–75. Stuttgart: Metzler.

Todorov, Tzvetan. 1992. *Einführung in die fantastische Literatur.* Aus dem Französischen von Karin Kersten, Senta Metz und Carolin Neubaur. Frankfurt a. M.: Fischer.

Tolkien, J. R. R. 1989/1947. *Tree and Leaf. Including the Poem "Mythopoeia".* Boston: Houghton Mifflin.

Wille, Joachim. 2020. "Sterben die Korallen, sterben die Küsten." *Klimareporter.* https://www.klimareporter.de/erdsystem/sterben-die-korallen-sterben-die -kuesten. Accessed 1 March 2024.

Wolf, Mark J. P. 2012. *Building Imaginary Worlds. The Theory and History of Subcreation.* New York: Routledge.

PART III
Border Crossings

9

REDREAMING EUROPE

The Historical Past and the Speculative Present in Jani Saxell's *Europe* Series

Kasimir Sandbacka

This chapter explores the tension between a historical past and a speculative present in Finnish author Jani Saxell's sprawling *Europe* series, which to date consists of three[1] volumes: *Unenpäästäjä Florian* (2010, "Florian the Dream Deliverer", hereafter UF), *Sotilasrajan unet* (2014, "Dreams of the Military Frontier", hereafter SU), and *Tuomiopäivän karavaani* (2017, "Doomsday Caravan", hereafter TK). Saxell is a diverse writer and journalist who has published, among other things, short stories, novels, and a travelogue of the alternative scene in the United States. His award-winning[2] *Europe* series is a critical exploration of the ethos and praxis of the European project, but also indicates a desire to rethink the past, present, and future beyond what is conventionally possible. As an alternative present-day (ca. 2010–2016) Europe that features psionics, cybernetics, ghosts, and demigods, the series's story world is far from realistic. The series could be considered science fiction or fantasy or placed under the umbrella category of speculative fiction. Nonetheless, the series's account of history is mostly realistic, and despite the supernatural and futuristic elements, even its present-day story world remains quite familiar. The series thus navigates the boundaries between speculative, historical, and mainstream fiction; this chapter discusses it in the broader context of ontologically pluralistic literature after postmodernism. The chapter examines how intersubjective dreaming in the series allegorically implies a historically determined European political unconscious that has both utopian and dystopian dimensions as well as how shared dreams enable intersubjective communication and understanding of history.

It has been suggested that during the twenty-first century, Western culture has entered a new period, metamodernism, defined as a structure of feeling that oscillates between modern commitment and postmodern detachment

DOI: 10.4324/9781003561101-14

(Vermeulen & van den Akker 2010). In this chapter, I will analyse Saxell's *Europe* series as exemplifying emerging metamodernism in contemporary Finnish fiction. European ideals and utopia have been recurring themes in twenty-first century Finnish novels, such as Marjo Niemi's *Ihmissyöjän ystävyys* (2012, "The Friendship of a Cannibal"), Emma Puikkonen's *Eurooppalaiset unet* (2016, "European Dreams"), and Riikka Pulkkinen's *Paras mahdollinen maailma* (2016, "The Best of Possible Worlds") that are not entirely realistic but move between different realities and dreamlike states (see Sandbacka 2021). Saxell's *Europe* series is one of the most substantial and ambitious demonstrations of this renewed interest in European utopianism in ontologically pluralistic Finnish literature – literature that is certainly aware of the postmodern condition, but whose ethos is not one of scepticism, relativism, suspension of meaning, or disruption of master narratives, but rather the search for a reconstructive stance in the contemporary, unstable reality.

I begin by discussing a shift in the ontological and epistemological accents of literature at the change of the millennium and how the speculative elements of fiction are central to this shift. I then explore Saxell's series's ontological differences from actual reality and its fluctuation between a utopian and an anti-utopian stance. Moreover, I consider how the extensive realistic historical narration is in juxtaposition to the speculative present and produces an epistemological backflow from the story world to the actual world. Finally, I propose that intersubjective dreaming represents a form of metamodern in-betweenness that contributes to the reconstruction of historicity, depth, and authenticity after an era of postmodern deconstruction.

From Slipstream to Other Slippery Ontologies

According to van den Akker (2017, 21), the metamodern historical moment has brought about a new "regime of historicity." The previous, postmodern, regime was aligned with Francis Fukuyama's (1992) notion of the "end of history": with the fall of the Communist bloc, history, as the development of societies, had come to its teleological conclusion, the dominance of liberal democracy and capitalism. Cold War suspicions and "capitalist triumphalism" after 1989 fostered a thoroughly anti-utopian political culture in the late twentieth century (Levitas 2014, 7). Whereas this postmodern era was wary of utopias as inherently totalitarian constructions, history, utopian figurations, and the imagining of possible futures are returning in metamodern culture (Vermeulen & van den Akker 2015, 55, 57; Gibbons 2021, 138). Epistemologically, metamodernism adopts a strategy of "informed naivete" that proceeds "as if" history would result in the moral and political progress of humanity – while realising that no such "natural but unknown goal" can be reached or even exists (Vermeulen & van den Akker 2010). Ontologically, metamodernism can be described by *metaxy*, a sense of in-betweenness, an oscillation between opposite poles, such as sense and senselessness, construction and deconstruction, irony and sincerity (Akker & Vermeulen 2017, 10–11).

In dialogue with the theory of metamodernism, Irmtraud Huber and Wolfgang Funk have suggested that the emerging poetics of the twenty-first century is best defined as literature of reconstruction. They maintain that contemporary literature does not abandon the sceptic, deconstructionist impulses of postmodernism but searches for ways in which fiction enables intersubjective communication and meaning (Huber & Funk 2017, 153). One such way is metareference, a textual strategy that foregrounds the fictionality of the text by introducing epistemological or ontological ambiguity. Unlike postmodernism, however, literature of reconstruction does not deploy ambiguity to undermine but to explore the possibility of communication. Huber and Funk see metareference as the formal correlate of the irrepresentability of authenticity. The authentic is immediate and without composition – but once communicated, it is given a mediated form and is no longer the thing itself. Yet instead of a deconstructive void beyond the surface of the text, reconstructive fiction can offer the glimpse of "a depth that is full of meaning and relevance, even if it may not be directly accessed" (Huber & Funk 2017, 152, 155–156). Huber suggests that literature has moved on from its preoccupation with ontology and epistemology to pragmatic and ethical questions regarding communication. Although reconstructive literature is aware of the postmodern caveats to truth and reality, it nonetheless explores the possibility to convey meaning in this unstable world, instead of "continually interrogating the text's relation to reality" (Huber 2014, 15, 40).

Indeed, a shift of focus seems to be taking place in ontologically pluralistic literature in recent decades. In a 1989 essay, cyberpunk author Bruce Sterling coined the term "slipstream" to describe an emerging genre of fiction that captures the strange feeling of living in the late twentieth century. He aligns slipstream with a postmodern sensibility that is sceptical of our ability to make sense of the world. Slipstream contains "fantastic elements which are not clear cut 'departures from known reality,' but ontologically part of the whole mess" (Sterling 1989). In a follow-up essay, he describes slipstream as a nonrealistic genre that gratifies a postmodern sensibility. It is "post-ideological" fiction for a "post-ideological epoch," at home in postmodern cultural circumstances of subjectivity and fragmentation, rather than trying to empower the reader to escape them. As such, it lacks the extrapolative intention of science fiction. Instead of using the intellectual tools of science, slipstream is based on cultural studies, from which it has adopted an attitude of ironic distance (Sterling 2011, 7–10). Paweł Frelik criticises Sterling's account as an attempt to legitimise science fiction by conflating it with mainstream fiction. Nevertheless, he notes that whereas McHale (1992) considered cyberpunk as the "end product" of the inter-relation between science fiction and postmodernism, slipstream has over-taken cyberpunk as the literary "boundary discourse" that most intensely "combine[s] the energies" of science fiction and postmodernism[3] (Frelik 2011, 33, 41–42). What is more, Frelik (2011, 41) suggests that slipstream and other boundary discourses between science fiction and mainstream fic-tion "reflect the twilight of the prescriptive Suvinian paradigm," that is, the assessment of science fiction through what Darko Suvin (2016a, 15) defines as its central feature: cognitive estrangement.

However, recent analyses of contemporary fiction suggest that this Suvianian dusk might be a dawn, of sorts. In the introduction to the *Style* special issue on uncertain ontologies in twenty-first-century literature, Lieven Ameel and Marco Caracciolo propose that ontological uncertainty is a significant concept in understanding contemporary fiction. Unlike post-modernism, this uncertainty does not primarily "evoke detachment or self-referential playfulness, but it tends to take on direct real-world relevance." To describe this engagement with the real, they maintain that contempo-rary literature features "earnest ontologies" (Ameel & Caracciolo 2021, 314–316). In the afterword to the same issue, McHale reflects on the dif-ferences between the ontological instability of postmodernist fiction and that of twenty-first-century mainstream fiction. He concurs with Ameel and Caracciolo (2021, 316) that twenty-first-century literature features a certain sincerity uncommon in postmodernism: it sets up alternate realities to "*ear-nest* ends," inviting readers to consider specific aspects of actual reality. He suggests that this return from the fictional to the actual reality is, in fact, a form of cognitive estrangement. Accordingly, post-postmodernism could be described as the "science-fictionalization of mainstream literary fiction" (McHale 2021, 455–457, 459–460).

In Sterling and McHale, then, we have different accounts of ontologically pluralistic border discourses before and after the turn of the millennium. Although both accounts describe literature that features alternate realities and ontological departures from the actual world, there are also consid-erable differences. Whereas slipstream ironically displays messy ontologies without the extrapolative impulse of science fiction, twenty-first-century lit-erature features earnest ontologies flickering between this world and another and deploys cognitive estrangement to make sense of the actual reality. Moreover, slipstream is post-ideological[4]: it holds no stake (or presumes not to hold) in the "totalizing, world-solving" (Sterling 2011, 8) narratives of the twentieth century; it is thus a manifestation of the postmodern scepticism towards the master narratives of modernity. Conversely, Suvin's (2016a, 25) concept of cognitive estrangement has very much to do with world-solving narratives, namely utopianism.

What is the significance of the discrepancies between the literature described by Sterling and the one by McHale? Are they writing about unrelated bodies of fiction, say, popular and literary, or have they interpreted some of its features in opposite ways? Or has ontologically pluralistic literature somehow changed during the twenty-first century? In fact, McHale contemplates whether the metaphors he developed "for ontological instability that once seemed to apply to postmodernist fiction are no longer adequate to contemporary fiction" and "now seem too binary to capture the complex layering of alternative and actual realities in fictions of earnest ontology" (McHale 2021, 458). McHale is here referring to his seminal theorisation in *Postmodern Fiction* (1987). One of his central arguments is that the dominant of modernist fiction is epistemological, and the dominant of postmodernist fiction is ontological. This is to say, postmodernism foregrounds ontological questions (McHale 2003/1987, 10). McHale illustrates his point by describing science fiction "postmodernism's non canonised 'low art' double" and "*the* ontological genre *par excellence*" (McHale 2003/1987, 59). However, as Fredric Jameson (2007, xiv) points out, Suvin's cognitive estrangement, which McHale now endorses, defines science fiction predominantly in terms of an *epistemological* function.

That McHale maintains the dominant of science fiction is ontological, but later defines the genre through its epistemological function seems somewhat contradictory. Yet his original analysis of postmodernism in terms of dominants is not all that binary to begin with: "Intractable epistemological uncertainty becomes at a certain point ontological plurality or instability: push epistemological questions far enough and they 'tip over' into ontological questions. By the same token, push ontological questions far enough and they tip over into epistemological questions – the sequence is not linear and unidirectional, but bidirectional and reversible" (McHale 2003/1987, 11). In a sense, then, McHale (2021, 458) returns to this idea of "tipping over" as he comments on the ontological "flickering, oscillation, iridescence, opalescence" and "resonance" of twenty-first century literature, a "toggling back and forth between" worlds.

I suggest that it is not only a toggling between worlds that characterises twenty-first century literature, but a toggling between epistemological and ontological dominants, in other words, a metamodernist oscillation between modernism and postmodernism (see Vermeulen & van den Akker 2010). It makes use of postmodernist "techniques and tropes" to "surpass the postmodern" and contains a utopian impulse that was mostly absent in postmodernism (Vermeulen & van den Akker 2015, 62). Ultimately, the oscillation between epistemology and ontology activates ethical questions of intersubjective communication and responsibility.

Utopian Oscillations

The *Europe* series's primary ontological departure from actual reality is introduced in the very first sentence of *Unenpäästäjä Florian*: "Europe was slowly running out of dreams"[5] (UF 9). The continent is suffering from "dream-loss" (UF 9), a strange ailment that deprives its victims of the ability to dream. The cause of the condition and the reason for its geographical focus are unknown, and theories abound. Scientific hypotheses include the sensory overload caused by work stress and multimedia overconsumption as well as speculations relating to the Charcot–Wilbrand syndrome, a form of dream-loss caused by brain damage. The more metaphysically inclined conjecture that the victims may have become separated from their astral bodies or that God may have abandoned humanity. The series's main protagonist, Romanian Roma Florian Timár, retains a privileged vantage point to the phenomena. As an infant, he was subjected to radiation experiments by the Romanian secret police Securitate's operation "Fortune teller" (2010, UF 133), targeting especially Roma children. As a result, Florian developed supernatural abilities that allow him to witness and affect the dreams of others. As an adult, he makes his living in Helsinki as a "dream releaser," a therapist of sorts, who helps people suffering from dream-loss to dream again.

Progressively, the series evolves from a detective story with some supernatural elements into a fanciful epic about the past, present, and future of Europe. As the story progresses, the historical and political scope of the events becomes ever greater, as does the ontological gap between the actual reality and the story world. The supernatural abilities represented in *Unenpäästäjä Florian* are relatively subtle and revolve around Florian's and a few others' ability to induce dreams in others. *Sotilasrajan unet* introduces a number "mutants" (SU 81) who have similar abilities as Florian – and beyond. By the end of *Tuomiopäivän karavaani*, some of the protagonists and antagonists possess superhero-like powers: for instance, one can fly and control weather, others can read minds, and one even has spirit foxes do his bidding. Throughout the series, the protagonists are guided by visitations from demigodlike entities called "the holies" (TK 503), particularly Sarah the Black, the patron saint of the Roma. Technology, too, has advanced beyond the limits of present-day reality: from *Sotilasrajan unet* onwards, the novels' story world, while set in the 2010s, features, among other things, flying cars, sense-television, psychic amplifiers, invisibility-granting stealth suits, and combat exoskeletons. The origins of these advancements are mostly overlooked or, at best, insubstantially explained. At the same time, even at its most fantastic, the story world remains mostly recognisable, as the novels never methodically investigate the social and political implications of the supernatural or technological differences from the actual world. The series thus resembles slipstream in that it does not focus on scientific extrapolation (see Sterling 2011, 7); its key interest is not to give an intellectual answer to how society would change if people lost their ability to dream and some developed psychic powers. All in all, dream-loss and the other speculative elements of the series fall short of the hegemonic quality of the novum, defined by Suvin (2011, 73, 75) as typically a "single interruption" from the empirical norm that "determines the whole narrative logic" of the work of fiction.

The function of dream-loss in the series can, then, better be described as a politico-ethical intensification of a contemporary European sensibility rather than an empirical extrapolation of it. During a nocturnal visitation, Sarah the Black, the series's personification of benevolence, relates the cause of dream-loss to Angelica, another Roma with supersensory abilities: "The dream-loss was a symptom, a warning. Of the waning of imagination, of the ability to empathise with other people" (UF, 200). Because dreams, as phenomenological events and as literary devices, are significant vessels of utopian anticipation (see Levitas 2011, 138), the decline of the ability to dream also signals the subsidence of the social imagination, namely of utopian thinking. The connection between dreams, dream releasing, and utopia is indicated already in *Unenpäästäjä Florian*:

> There were no shared daydreams, no time to build, no romantic utopias. Naïve, perhaps, but necessary amid the realism of missile tests and surveillance flights. ... The offerings of Cinema Florian were private starry skies, the dead unburied and walking, or potent lust.
>
> *(UF 193)*

Utopias as shared daydreams are contrasted with the realistic threat of nuclear catastrophe as well as with the private fantasies Florian evokes in the dream release sessions with his customers.

This juxtaposition encapsulates a central concern of both Florian's character and the entire *Europe* series: the struggle between utopianism and anti-utopianism. The main agents in this conflict are the "Bless-Cursed," a group of social outcasts and mutants headed by Florian, and the "Army of the Dispossessed," a clandestine militant organisation led by Florian's son, Flavius, "The Nightmare Prime Minister" (TK, 577) of Europe. However, rather than being champions of either utopianism or anti-utopianism, both the Bless-Cursed and the Army of the Dispossessed are torn between these poles. The Army is divided between the "*fundis*," who endorse a utopian plan called the "exodus of the liberated peoples," and the cynical "*realos*," who are content with "teaching the world a lesson and becoming filthy rich in the process" (TK, 211–212).

While this may eventually change in the fourth part of the series, so far, the novels never systematically describe the utopian programme of the exodus, or the "doomsday caravan" (TK 92), as it is resentfully called by Florian. Instead, the reader is provided with clues and fragments of the plan, most of them haphazardly delivered to Florian by Daniela, Flavius's mother and member of the Army of the Dispossessed. According to Daniela, the Army has established a base of operations in the Gobi Desert on the border between Mongolia and China. While Europe barricades its borders against immigration, dislocated and disenfranchised peoples from all over the world are drawn to this desert community: refugees fleeing war and oppression in Northern Africa and the Middle East, but also the unemployed youth of Southern Europe as well as the Eastern European 50-somethings declared obsolete. What the *fundis* hope to create is a "new, secular religion: humankindness, a planetary doctrine of salvation" (TK 90). The army plans to build an irrigation system in the desert and reintroduce extinct species with the technology in their "yurts, mechanised Noah's Arks" (TK 211), which are implied to be protective bio-domes that allow the army to continue building even if "Europe and the whole world destroy themselves" (TK 211). The ultimate plan is even more ambitious: to colonise "Mars, the Asteroid Belt, and the moons of Jupiter" (TK 211), to prepare a "caravan of yurts, the free people's exodus to other stars. As shown to them by the spirit of the future" (SU 527). In short, they are conceiving a "new humanity" (SU 527). Hence, the name "Army of the Dispossessed" ("osattomien armeija" in Finnish) alludes to Ursula K. Le Guin's utopian classic *The Dispossessed* (1974, translated into Finnish as *Osattomien planeetta*, 1979), in which an anarcho-socialist utopia has been established on another planet after an exodus from the home world. Undoubtedly, the army's over-the-top plans are radically divorced from present actualities and possibilities and would have little use as a utopian blueprint for any foreseeable future.

The home of the Bless-Cursed is a curious counterpart to the desert stronghold of the Army of the Dispossessed. It is a former school building in Räksylä, an imaginary municipality somewhere in southern Finland. Like the army's base in Mongolia, Räksylä attracts mutants, outsiders, and misfits from all over the world. Even though the school building is protected by a supernatural mist called the *magla* (Serbo-Croatian for fog), which confuses unwanted guests and makes the site invisible to satellites and aerial photography, the arriving Bless-Cursed have no trouble finding it. Together, the outcasts of Räksylä renovate the decrepit building and form a small, utopian commune, where their special abilities and idiosyncrasies are accepted, welcomed even, and where they are protected from persecution by the outside world. Yet countering this utopian withdrawal is a sense of an approaching confrontation with the Army of the Dispossessed: "That. Which. Is. About. To. Come." (SU 140). In other words, the inhabitants know that Räksylä is only a temporary haven.

Hence, whereas the exodus of the liberated peoples is ultimately too grandiose a plan to be feasible, the utopian enclave of Räksylä is, on the contrary, too limited both spatially and temporally to claim any universal relevance. These utopian visions on two different scales seem to contain their own anti-utopian refutation. The *Europe* series is not entirely utopian or anti-utopian, but wavers between these poles, refusing to succumb to apathy, but also retreating from complete naivete, as is emblematic of metamodernism (Vermeulen & van den Akker 2010; Akker & Vermeulen 2017, 11). To better understand the utopian sentiment of Saxell's *Europe* series, its fanciful present and extravagant visions of the future must be balanced with the gravity of its approach to history. It is through its relationship with the past that the series's story world emits "backwash" (see McHale 2021, 459) to the actual reality of the reader and foregrounds a utopian impulse.

Epistemological Backwash and Metamodern Historicity

The *Europe* series features an excess of history. Whereas *Unenpäästäjä Florian* still explores the history of Communist Romania to a relatively moderate extent, the following parts offer an almost encyclopaedic account of history of the Balkans. Included in the beginning of *Sotilasrajan unet* is a map of the so-called Military Frontier, a fortified borderland spanning the Balkan peninsula between the Holy Roman and the Ottoman Empires in 1512. Sections titled "Sarajevo, the 550-year delirium" begin with the establishment of the city of Sarajevo during the fifteenth century; follow its development into a melting pot of Christian, Islamic, and Jewish cultures under Ottoman, Habsburg, and Yugoslav rule; and end with the city's siege by the Bosnian Serb forces in 1992. Further sections titled "The Military Frontier Dreams" explore the history of the Balkans as a political and cultural borderland between the Christian and Islamic cultural spheres.

Consequently, a curious contradiction builds up throughout the series: the more painstakingly the reader becomes informed about the historical intricacies of the Balkans, the further the present of the story world ontologically recedes from the actual world. There does not seem to be any specific point of historical bifurcation, back to which the divergences of past, present, and, speculatively, future events could be traced. Rather, it seems that the diverging ontology of the *Europe* series enables an allegorical exploration of the historically constructed mindset of Europe. The oneiric titles of the historical sections of *Sotilasrajan unet*, "Sarajevo, the 550-year delirium" and "The Military Frontier Dreams," infer that the novel's exploration of the past is also an exposition of the European cultural and political unconscious: "The Military Frontier sleeps. Beneath the cerebral cortex, beyond custom, rationality, and morals. ... The Military Frontier, *Militärgrenze*, *Vojna Krajina* is nobody, nothing – and still in all of them. In all of us" (SU

245). The conflict-ridden history of the Balkans is represented as a collective dream, and as centuries pass, the Frontier evolves from a geographic place into a psychological space: "The Military Frontier had become a nocturnal land, a topsy-turvy land, the collective unconscious" (SU 290).

In the beginning of *Tuomiopäivän karavaani*, the reader is reminded that Florian is the father of Flavius, "the prime minister of the secret realm living in the collective unconscious and nightside of Europe" (TK 11) – suggesting a historical cross-generational genealogy of the European unconscious. The "secret realm" exists on two ontological levels in the story world. First, it represents the underground organisation of the Army of the Dispossessed, which plans both the utopian exodus to the Gobi Desert, and eventually to other planets, and the terrorist attacks on Europe that are supposed to deter the European powers from interfering with Flavius's plan. Second, the secret realm exists in the collective unconscious of a Europe deprived of dreams. The implication is that the secret state has been brought about by Europe's loss of its ability to dream, that is, its utopian impulse. The beginning of the collapse of the Soviet bloc in 1989 is also a watershed year in the *Europe* series: a moment of wasted utopian potential unable to hold on to "the rapture that followed the fall of the Berlin Wall, the ideals of joint responsibility, friendship between nations, and free movement" (TK 30–31). It is the year the Ceausescu regime fell, and the year Flavius was conceived by Florian and Daniela. Unbeknownst to Florian, who thinks Daniela had an abortion, the child was born the next year in Sarajevo, where Daniela worked at the Romanian embassy. Flavius thus becomes the surreptitious embodiment of both Florian's disconnection from his past and, with time, of the resentment caused by Europe's disconnection from its own ideals.

The deadliest manifestation of this disconnection was the Yugoslav Wars, which the West was unable to prevent despite ample evidence of the troubling trajectory of the Balkans during the 1980s (see Glaurdić 2011, 303). It sets the foundation for Flavius's bitter hatred – but also for his utopian desire. Saxell's series recounts the atrocities of the Bosnian War (1992–1995) in detail. *Sotilasrajan unet* describes the events leading to the Srebrenica massacre (1995) and its aftermath. The Dutch UN forces' failure to stop the murder of thousands of Bosnian Muslim men becomes emblematic of Western Europe's impotence facing the violence in the Balkans, culminating with disarmed, starved, drunk UN peacekeepers roaming the woods of Srebrenica with Serb soldiers and hunting dogs in search of Muslim refugees. *Tuomiopäivän karavaani* focuses on the siege of Sarajevo (1992–1996), which Flavius lived through as a child. Not only does he witness the death of his little sister, Mujesira, in a grenade barrage, but he also must use his psionic powers to convince his mother, Daniela, that nothing remains to be done for the girl lying still inside her baby sling in Sarajevo's infamous Sniper Alley: "*Suddenly, the coldest of considerations. Stemming from her son's hand. Flavius fears that mommy will go away, too. The boy's powers scan the nearby streets, insist that Mujesira will only lie still. Until Judgement Day and the resurrection of bodies"* (TK 149, emphasis in original). Though distraught, Daniela eventually heeds the suggestion of her three-year-old son and does not return to Mujesira. Soon after, Flavius wonders about her sister's life in Paradise and asks what happens if one dies there. Daniela answers: "The angels wake you up. Don't worry, the angels wake you. And there's no more sickness, evil, profiteering, self-regard. No more queuing, scurrying, nights in the bomb shelter." To which Flavius replies: "Is there such a land?" (TK 151). The tragic death of his sister is the formative trauma that sets Flavius on a quest for a better world.

As a counter-image to the 1990s dystopian dissolution of the federation, the *Europe* series suggests that the Federal People's Republic of Yugoslavia was, in its post-Second World War nascent years, a utopian attempt to mitigate the ethnic and religious tensions in the Balkans: "After a horrible war and the darkness of nationalist zeal, the Balkans would be a pioneer, on its way towards socialism with a human face and the equality of all nationalities" (SU 316). The series captures the utopian hope and tolerance that emerged after the war.

> Sarajevo was filled to the brim with refugees. … A spacious apartment, three rooms and a kitchen, could fit three families. And there was to be no segregation in the name of *brotherhood and unity*. Residents of one room made the sign of the cross their way, others in the second room another way, and the ones in the third room bowed towards Mecca.
>
> *(SU 187)*

Extensive projects of social betterment, such as "literacy courses and sexual education," were implemented, and as "the Latin alphabet and suffrage proliferated, typhus, syphilis, and tuberculosis would be driven to the bitter pages of a toxicological manual called history" (SU 188). The Muslim delegates of the Women's Antifascist Front of Bosnia encourage gender equality, political participation, and abandonment of the niqab. "The war had perhaps taken the Balkans back to the 19th century or the mediaeval eternity of the Military Frontier. Yet women were now striding to catch up with a hundred years of human progress" (SU 188).

This emerging utopianism is at odds with the malicious collective unconsciousness of Europe: "The Military Frontier could not believe its ears. Just like that, basic human urges were dismissed, shoved in a closet for the moths to feed on. Like a uniform never to be worn again" (SU 316). Indeed, the utopian potential of the post-war years was undone by the Yugoslavian ruling elites during the 1960s and 1970s (Suvin 2016b, 265). *Sotilasrajan unet* outlines the failures and collapse of Yugoslav utopianism with its increasing paranoia, nationalism, and oppression – which ultimately lead to the catastrophe of the Yugoslav wars. The potential and failure of the Yugolavian project sets by its example the utopian and dystopian poles of Flavius's historical understanding and of his revolt against the political mindset of contemporary Europe. The Army of the Dispossessed adopts as its rallying cry no other than "brotherhood and unity" (TK 90), the slogan of the Communist Party of Yugoslavia.

Accordingly, a central ideological "backwash" from the story world to the actual world is Yugoslavia as a prefiguration of the European project. This is not to be taken literally to mean that Yugoslavia would be a historical scale model of the European Union or that Europe is heading for war. Rather, what Saxell's novels express is the concern that the European Union has lost sight of its motto "united in diversity," quite reminiscent of that of Yugoslavia. Daniela tells Florian that their son had high hopes for the European Union:

> You probably won't believe this, but there was a time when your son Flavius was excited about the Balkans' path to the EU. As a grammar school idealist when he still could pretend that the Hague sought justice. Some good things did come out of the membership aspirations: nationalist hardliners were put on planes to Holland, new laws protecting minorities were put forward.
>
> *(TK 233)*

Daniela doubts the future of the European project due to the standstill of EU expansion as well as the upsurge of nationalist populism:

> The Union ... has made it clear on many occasions that Bosnians and Serbs are at the bottom of the pile and forever under observation. And what would we even be doing there, anymore? In the same "community of values" with Gert Wilders, Viktor Orbán, and Marine Le Pen.
>
> *(TK 233)*

Despite its ontological departures from actual reality, Saxell's *Europe* series thus ultimately responds to topical issues or, to use Ameel and Carracciolo's (2021, 314) words, "take[s] on direct real-world relevance." *Unenpäästäjä Florian* explores the status of the Roma people in the EU, which received widespread attention in Finland after the inclusion of Romania and Bulgaria to the Union in 2007, and the arrival of Roma beggars, now able to cross Schengen borders, to the streets of Helsinki. The Finnish media, unaccustomed to such public demonstrations of poverty, struggled to encounter the Roma unbiasedly (Oksanen 2012). The question of free mobility is significant in the series from the very beginning: in *Unenpäästäjä Florian*, Florian is involved in thwarting a plan to declare a state of emergency and suspend the Schengen Agreement in Finland. In *Sotilasrajan unet*, the very purpose of the Military Frontier is to keep the unwanted out of Europe, and the dissolution of Yugoslavia is a harrowing reminder of the potential consequences of reintroducing and reinforcing ethnic borders. *Tuomiopäivän karavaani* intensifies the political conditions contributing to the so-called "refugee crises" of 2015, during which refugees from the Syrian Civil War and the incursions of the Islamic State fled to the European Union. In the speculative present of the novel, the Islamic Caliphate has managed to annex large parts of the Middle East and North Africa under its despotic rule, and the Levant Confederation has been established in war-ravaged Syria as a puppet state of Russia. However, it is not the influx of refugees which is the crux of the crises, but the cynical policies introduced by the European Union to reinforce its borders and thwart the arrival of asylum-seekers. In this sense, Saxell's series aligns itself with the poetic activism of Finnish artists who addressed borders as physical, political, and mental boundaries during the "refugee crises" (see Kauranen et al. 2019, 22; Hiltunen et al. 2020, 172). In *Tuomiopäivän karavaani*, Daniela compares the refugees from the Balkan wars to those fleeing to Europe some 20 years later: "In the early years of the 1990s, Europe and the world found themselves in a pickle with two million Bosnian refugees. And similar measures were taken: quotas invoked, barbed wire drawn, visas cancelled, and border controls reintroduced" (TK 30). The only difference is that back in the 1990s, European politicians still felt some remorse for their passivity, when "directly beyond the southern borders of the EU, it was the 1940s, gorges of death, camps, and cattle wagons" (TK 31).

Conclusion: Redreaming History

To sum up, Saxell's *Europe* series defamiliarises the present reality to show glimpses of "the historical depth beyond the novel" (cf. Huber & Funk 2017, 158). It destabilises the ontology of its story world by conflating history, dreams, and actuality to explore the historically constructed political unconscious affecting European real-world politics and attitudes. The ontological gap between the story world and the actual world produces an epistemological backwash from the former to the latter, where the speculative elements acquire real-world significance. Rather than being a methodical scientific extrapolation or an allegory with systematic equivalence between fiction and actuality, the series develops into a fictional intensification of reality – or, like cyberpunk, a literalisation of narrative tropes (see McHale 2001, 246) – where an ambiguous substantiality is bestowed upon psychological phenomena, such as dreams, or metaphoric concepts, such as the collective unconscious.

The series's oscillation between ontology and epistemology is discernible in the tension between a speculative present and a historical past. On the one hand, the series explores how we are products of our history and how history, often unconsciously, affects our attitudes and decisions; on the other, it suggests that the present and the future are ours to reimagine. The key narrative device the series deploys to represent this tension is dream narration. By this, I do not mean the representation of dreams as surreal, subconscious fantasies; in fact, there are very few such representations in the entire series. Rather, I refer to sections of the novels that ostensibly are historical events narrated by an impersonal narrator but are in fact dreams or dream-like visions related by one character to another or to the reader. Dream narration represents a metamodern state of metaxy (see Akker & Vermeulen 2017, 11) that oscillates between an ontological and an epistemological interest. Ontologically, it invites the reader to imagine a world where dreams can be shared and subliminally transferred between subjects; epistemologically, it reinforces an understanding of history and how it becomes interwoven in the fabric of our dreams, aspirations, and attitudes.

In the series, dreams are a means to connect with the past and, more importantly, communicate a shared understanding of it. The reader first becomes privy to the history of the Bosnian city of Mostar in *Sotilasrajan unet* through Flavius's dream of the day when the Mostar Bridge, built by the Ottomans in the sixteenth century and *"an example of centuries of coexistence and interaction"* (SU 420, emphasis in original), was destroyed by artillery fire in 1993, as well as of the purging of Muslims from the city's west bank in the days that followed. More than 20 years later, Flavius's parents reacquaint in the very same city. During nights of drinking and sex, Daniela relates her past and Flavius's childhood to Florian by inducing a dreamlike state, in which Florian feels as if the paintings surrounding them come to life: "The future ripened in the past, the past decayed in the future – a harvest of decomposing leaves. And through the paintings, through Daniela's mind, windows opened" (TK 28). During these visions, "Florian felt what Daniela had felt, ran where she had run, queued where she had queued – glancing over her shoulder at the hills. Florian writhed in the labour of his child, gasped laughing gas through the mask" (TK 32). The first part of *Tuomiopäivän karavaani*, titled "1 425 Days" according to the length of the Siege of Sarajevo, alternates between scenes from Mostar, describing the tense tryst of Florian and Daniela, and scenes from the life of Daniela and Flavius in war-torn Sarajevo, shared to Florian by Daniela in this empathic state of shared dreaming. Instead of a direct view into history narrated by an objective, impersonal narrator, the reader is provided with an intersubjective view into the past experiences of Daniela, redreamed by Florian in the diegetic present.

This is but one on the series's many instances of oneiric transmission, described in *Unenpäästäjä Florian* as requiring "no words" (UF 199); it is communication unmediated by language. As such, it potentially provides a direct access to the authentic memories of others, an intersubjective experience of history. However, as literature necessarily must use language as its medium, the representations of this intersubjectivity available to the reader are mediated by words and arranged as a narrative. Thus, they are bereft of the unmediated authenticity of the original experience and its redreaming. Following the reasoning of Huber and Funk, the oneiric transmissions are metareferences, formal correlates of the irrepresentability of authenticity – but also signal the desire for sincere communication and an intersubjective understanding of history. The series oscillates between a realist and relativist stance towards history: while it acknowledges the past does not exist in the sense that it could be directly accessed in the present, it proceeds *as if* it were possible to access it beyond mediated narratives. As metamodern discourse, it "commits itself to an impossible possibility" (Vermeulen & van den Akker 2010), the possibility of shared experience and of dissolving the "Military Frontier" that cuts through the collective psyche and draws borders between us. It exemplifies an emerging corpus of socially and politically oriented, ontologically pluralistic works in Finnish contemporary literature – border discourses that make use of alternative realities to activate the readers' critical understanding of both history and the present as well as their ability to imagine different futures. At the time of writing of this chapter, when full-scale war, unlike anything seen in Europe since the dissolution of Yugoslavia, ravages Ukraine, killing thousands and driving millions into refuge, activating our historical understanding of the consequences of our choices has never seemed more crucial.

Notes

1 According to Saxell's publisher (www.wsoy.fi/kirjailija/jani-saxell), the novels belong to a "Europe tetralogy", but as the fourth part remains unpublished, I prefer to use the less speculative term *series* for now.
2 *Sotilasrajan unet* was nominated for the Tähtivaeltaja science fiction award, and *Tuomiopäivän karavaani* won it.
3 In fact, McHale (1992, 238) anticipates this very development.
4 Suvin (see 2016, 85) would no doubt argue that this very presumption amounts to ideology.
5 All translations of Saxell's novels are done by the author of this manuscript.

References

Akker, Robin van den & Timotheus Vermeulen. 2017. "Periodising the 2000s, or, the Emergence of Metamodernism." In *Metamodernism. Historicity, Affect, and Depth After Postmodernism*, eds. Robin van den Akker, Alison Gibbons & Timotheus Vermeulen, 1–19. London & New York: Rowman & Littlefield.

Ameel, Lieven & Marco Caracciolo. 2021. "Uncertain Ontologies in Twenty-First-Century Storyworlds." *Style* 55 (3), Special Issue: Uncertain Ontologies in Twenty-First-Century Storyworlds: 313–324.

Frelik, Paweł. 2011. "Of Slipstream and Others: SF and Genre Boundary Discourses." *Science Fiction Studies* 38 (1) Slipstream (March 2011): 20–45.

Fukuyama, Francis. 1992. *The End of History and the Last Man.* Harmondsworth: Penguin Books.

Gibbons, Alison. 2021. "Metamodernism, the Anthropocene, and the Resurgence of Historicity: Ben Lerner's 10:04 and 'The Utopian Glimmer of Fiction'." *Critique: Studies in Contemporary Fiction* 62 (2): 137–151.

Glaurdić, Josip. 2011. *The Hour of Europe. Western Powers and the Breakup of Yugoslavia.* New Haven: Yale UP.

Hiltunen, Kaisa, Tuija Saresma & Nina Sääskilahti. 2020. "Rajojen poetiikkaa ja politiikkaa. Taiteellinen aktivismi reaktiona 'pakolaiskriisiin'." *Media & viestintä* 43 (2): 150–175.

Huber, Irmtraud. 2014. *Literature after Postmodernism. Reconstructive Fantasies.* Houndmills, Basingstoke & New York: Palgrave Macmillan.

Huber, Irmtraud & Wolfgang Funk. 2017. "Reconstructing Depth: Authentic Fiction and Responsibility." In *Metamodernism. Historicity, Affect, and Depth After Postmodernism*, eds. Robin van den Akker, Alison Gibbons & Timotheus Vermeulen, 151–166. London & New York: Rowman & Littlefield.

Jameson, Fredric. 2007/2005. *Archaeologies of the Future. The Desire Called Utopia and Other Science Fictions.* London & New York: Verso.

Kauranen, Ralf, Olli Löytty, Aura Nikkilä & Anna Vuorinne. 2019. "Vuoden 2015 'pakolaiskriisi' ja sarjakuva-aktivismi Suomessa: Auttamishalu, antirasismi ja turvapaikanhakijoiden äänet." *Avain - Kirjallisuudentutkimuksen Aikakauslehti* 16 (1): 4–27.

Le Guin, Ursula. 1979/1974. *The Dispossessed.* London: Granada Publishing.

Levitas, Ruth. 2011/1990. *The Concept of Utopia.* Oxford: Peter Lang.

Levitas, Ruth. 2014/2013. *Utopia as Method: The Imaginary Reconstruction of Society.* New York: Palgrave Macmillan.

McHale, Brian. 2003/1987. *Postmodernist Fiction.* London & New York: Routledge.

McHale, Brian. 2001/1992. *Constructing Postmodernism.* London & New York: Routledge.

McHale, Brian. 2021. "Afterword: Earnest Ontology in the Year of the Flood." *Style* 55 (3), Special Issue: Uncertain Ontologies in Twenty-First-Century Storyworlds: 453–461.

Niemi, Marjo. 2012. *Ihmissyöjän ystävyys.* Helsinki: Teos.

Oksanen, Kimmo. 2012. "Kuinka media löysi kerjäläiset. Havaintoja romanikerjäläisten ja tiedotusvälineiden suhteesta vuosina 2006–2011." In *Huomio! Romaneja tiellä*, eds. Airi Markkanen, Heini Puurunen & Aino Saarinen, 248–273. Helsinki: Like.

Puikkonen, Emma. 2016. *Eurooppalaiset unet.* Helsinki: WSOY.

Pulkkinen, Riikka. 2016. *Paras mahdollinen maailma.* Helsinki: Otava.

Sandbacka, Kasimir 2021. " 'Me halutaan käsikirjoittaa toinen maailma.' Metamoderni utooppisuus Emma Puikkosen *Eurooppalaisissa unissa* ja Riikka Pulkkisen *Parhaassa mahdollisessa maailmassa.*" *Avain – Kirjallisuudentutkimuksen aikakauslehti* 18(1): 2237.

Saxell, Jani. 2010. *Unenpäästäjä Florian.* (UF.) Helsinki: Avain.

Saxell, Jani. 2014. *Sotilasrajan unet.* (SU.) Helsinki: WSOY.

Saxell, Jani. 2017. *Tuomiopäivän karavaani.* (TK.) Helsinki: WSOY.

Sterling, Bruce. 1989. "Slipstream." Originally published in SF Eye #5 (July 1989); reprinted through the Electronic Frontier Foundation. https://www.journalscape.com/jlundberg/page2. Accessed 1 March 2024.

Sterling, Bruce. 2011. "Slipstream 2." *Science Fiction Studies* 38 (1), Slipstream: 6–10.

Suvin, Darko. 2011. "Science Fiction and the Novum (1977)." In *Defined by a Hollow. Essays on Utopia, Science Fiction and Political Epistemology*, 67–92. Oxford: Peter Lang.

Suvin, Darko. 2016a. *Metamorphoses of Science Fiction. On the Poetics and History of a Literary Genre*, ed. Gerry Canavan. Oxford: Peter Lang.

Suvin, Darko. 2016b. *Splendour, Misery, and Possibilities. An X-Ray of Socialist Yugoslavia*. Leiden & Boston: Brill.

Vermeulen, Timotheus & Robin van den Akker. 2010. "Notes on Metamodernism." *Journal of Aesthetics & Culture* 2. http://www.aestheticsandculture.net/index .php/jac/article/view/5677. Accessed 1 March 2024.

Vermeulen, Timotheus & Robin van den Akker. 2015. "Utopia, Sort of: A Case Study in Metamodernism." *Studia Neophilologica* 87: sup 1 (2015): 55–67.

10

IMMIGRANT IDENTITY IN FANTASY FICTION

Russian Youth Culture in Contemporary Finnish Fantasy

Jenniliisa Salminen

During the last few decades, fantasy has been a popular genre in young adult fiction both internationally and in the Nordic countries. At the same time, the transnational turn in literature studies has inspired readers and scholars to pay attention to different cultural features in texts (Jay 2010; Grönstrand et al. 2016). For a while, Nordic fantasy writers have also striven to portray people from different cultural backgrounds, thus presenting Nordic countries as multicultural and better representing minorities – a well-known example is the Swedish *Engelsfors* trilogy (2011–2013) by Mats Strandberg and Sara Bergmark Elfgren. Since fantasy as a genre often addresses questions of identity, it offers tools for exploring immigrant identities. Secondary worlds are often used to examine, discuss, and negotiate identities since they have a strong potential for estrangement, giving the reader a comfortable distance to engage with the issues at hand. Fantasy literature has been seen useful even in teaching values due to its potential for estrangement (Alkestrand 2016, 83–91). To put it simply, secondary worlds detach problems from everyday life and the realistic framework; thus, fantasy provides the author and the readers with the means to address the sometimes complicated and even painful issues that the characters are facing.

This chapter examines how a fantasy novel series discusses immigrant identities and acts as a mediator between cultures by introducing elements of Finland Russian culture to Finnish readers, including Finland Russians reading literature in Finnish. The main subjects of study are the first two books of the fantasy trilogy *Neonkaupunki* by Susanna Hynynen and Dess Terentjeva. *Neonkaupunki* and its sequel *Neonkaupunki 2: Spiraalitie* came out in 2020 and 2021, respectively. The third book in the series *Neonkaupunki 3: Luutivoli* was published in the spring 2024 and thus is

DOI: 10.4324/9781003561101-15

also left out of the scope of this chapter. They are written in Finnish, and at least so far, no translations are available.[1] *Neonkaupunki* is the very first young adult fantasy with a strong focus on the identity of the young generation of Russian immigrants in Finland. The status of *Neonkaupunki* as young adult literature is open to question. The age of the target audience is hard to define, as often is the case in fantasy and speculative fiction, where the age barriers do not prevent cross-reading. The age of the protagonists varies from teenagers to young adults, which could indicate a youngish target audience. The *Neonkaupunki* series addresses such themes as identity, sexuality, and finding one's place in the world, which are often – but not exclusively – connected to young adult fiction. Yet, the books are marketed as adult fantasy and often placed in the adult section in libraries. One of the authors, Dess Terentjeva, calls her verse novel *Ihana* that came out after the first two *Neonkaupunki* books, her first young adult book thus defining the previous books as adult fiction (Neuvonen 2021; Tarsalainen 2021). On the other hand, Susanna Hynynen discusses the books in terms of young adult fiction (Leisiö 2023), and both authors note that the *Neonkaupunki* books also attract young readers (*Kulttuuriykkönen* 2021).

In the characters of *Neonkaupunki*, Russian ethnicity and Russian culture intersect with sexuality and gender. The potential of fantasy and science fiction in discussing and negotiating gender and sexuality have been noted in recent research (see, e.g., Tapionkaski 2021; Barbini 2017; Nilson et al. 2018; Pearson et al. 2008; Roberts & MacCallum 2016). Also, in the field of girl studies, the intersectional nature of depictions of fictional girls in youth literature has inspired research (Österlund 2011, 232–235). The position of *Neonkaupunki* as both fantasy and – arguably – young adult literature allows the authors to use the potential of both traditions. Two main characters of the books are certainly girls, and they can be seen as a part of the evolution of fictional girl characters, although as a whole, the characters of *Neonkaupunki* are not limited by binary gender categories. The authors have indeed stated that for them, the representation of minorities is an important goal and Terentjeva has also in her social media stressed her interest in the genre of *sateenkaarikirjallisuus* (literally, "rainbow literature"), a term that has lately established in Finnish language to mean literature discussing the diversity of gender and sexuality (Neuvonen 2021). Thus, in *Neonkaupunki* the Finland Russian minority is presented as a heterogeneous group of young people of different backgrounds and sexuality and gender identities.

In order to elaborate how Hynynen's and Terentjeva's novels are part of a wider phenomenon of introducing Russian culture to Western fantasy readers, I will first trace the use of Russian culture and mythology in non-Russian fantasy and present some examples of it, especially in Nordic fantasy. Then, I will analyse how *Neonkaupunki* introduces Russian culture to non-Russian readers: Russian elements are used and blended with elements of Finnish and international culture to form a specific Finland Russian youth culture. Since sexuality and gender are important themes in the books, I explore them as a vital part of the characters' identities.

Russian and Slavic Elements in Fantasy Fiction

Fantasy as a genre has drawn heavily on Celtic and Anglo-Saxon mythologies,[2] and fantasy authors also use imagery from their own national mythologies. In Nordic fantasy, there are traces of both ancient mythologies and Nordic folk beliefs. For example, Norwegian Siri Pettersen's trilogy *Ravneringene* (2013–2015; *The Raven Rings*) is set in a secondary world based on Scandinavian mythology, and several Finnish fantasy authors – for example, Johanna Sinisalo, Leena Laulajainen, and Sari Peltoniemi – draw on Finnish folk beliefs, mythologies, and fairytales (Sisättö 2006, 13; Halme 2006, 56). However, Russian folklore has been nearly absent from Nordic fantasy, which is interesting, especially in the case of Finland, which has a considerable Russian-speaking minority and a long shared cultural history with Russia, not to speak of their geographical proximity.

Before discussing Russian cultural elements in fantasy fiction, it is imperative to define how Russian culture is understood in this chapter. Russian culture is notoriously difficult to define both geographically and historically. The borders between Russian and Slavic culture are sometimes blurred, and Russian culture is cross-cultural in nature (see, e.g., Rzhevsky 2012). Unfortunately, this ambiguity is sometimes politically motivated and even used as an excuse to justify wars, as we have seen during the war between Russia and Ukraine. In this chapter, I use both terms, Slavic and Russian. "Russian" refers to explicitly Russian cultural material, whereas "Slavic" refers either to cultural material that is so old that it cannot yet be called Russian or to cultural material that is shared by several Slavic cultures. I also use the term "culture" itself in a wide sense, ranging from art and literature to folklore, religion, and everyday culture. Russian language is a vital part of Russian culture, although not all Russian culture is limited only to Russian speakers – nor is Russian language limited only to Russian citizens. For a closer analysis I have chosen those elements of Russian culture that are most prominent in the texts examined.

Very few original text sources on old Slavic mythology exist (Warner 2002, 7–8). Whereas little information on Slavic deities has been preserved, many folk traditions have lived on in both oral and written forms. Interest in folktales rose in late eighteenth-century Russia and intensified during the era of Romanticism, and from then on, folktale collections have been published for both scholarly and popular readers (Hellman 2013, 14; 41–42). The best-known collection of Russian folktales is probably Alexander Afanasyev's *Narodnye russkie skazki* (Russian folktales) first published in

1859. As in the rest of Europe, folktales have also provided material for children's books and culture, and their central characters like Baba Yaga are commonly known, especially in the sphere of Russian culture and, to some extent, internationally. During the Soviet period, folklore elements were also sometimes used in Soviet children's books that were often called fairy tales, yet some of them were similar to Western fantasy for children (Salminen 2009, 12–13, 93–95). Cinema and animated films have also been based on folktales (Wheeler Mjolsness 2020, 393–395). Folklore elements were occasionally used in Soviet literature for adults, but interest in Russian and Slavic mythology grew strongly in the 1990s: popular books on ancient Slavic folk beliefs were published, and with the rise of the Internet, pages and portals about Slavic pagan religions started to flourish.[3] Due to the lack of original source texts, the rise of the new pagan mythology was partly based on speculations and non-scholarly materials on ancient Slavic pre-Christian gods.

Soon the newly popular mythology found its way to fantasy literature as well. In Russia, the genre of Slavic fantasy (*slavianskoe fentezi*) became popular after the fall of the Soviet Union in 1991. Slavic fantasy is a subgenre of fantasy that combines elements from Slavic history and prehistory with characters from myths, tales, and Slavic pagan beliefs. Authors often strive to create a historically authentic milieu, and some texts have educational tendencies (about the genre of Slavic fantasy, see Safron 2012). The rising popularity of Slavic fantasy in Russia has been connected to the need for a new post-Soviet Russian national identity. Slavic fantasy with its representations of mythical heroes, more or less accurate historical events, and ancient Slavic beliefs combined with entertaining storylines provides a lucrative point of identification. Ideas presented by the authors of Slavic fantasy also converge with patriotic political ideas in Russia, for example, when speculating about the origins of the Russian nation or its place in the world (Abasheva & Krinicyna 2010). Thus, Slavic fantasy uses Slavic imagery partly for very different purposes than Western fantasy.

During the last few decades, Russian and Slavic imagery has also surfaced in international fantasy. Probably the best-known author that utilises Slavic fantasy imagery is Polish Andrzej Sapkowski, whose *Witcher* (*Wiedźmin*) series (1990–2013) introduces folktale characters including some Slavic ones. These characters can also be found in the popular television series (2019–) and video game adaptations (2007–) of the books. In English-language literature, Russian folktale characters have been seen, for example, in Neil Gaiman's comics *Books of Magic, Book III: The Land of Summer's Twilight* (1991), where the travelling hero ends up hanging upside down in Baba Yaga's hut. Gaiman's and Sapkowski's stories both borrow from a wide range of myths, so the Slavic stories are a part of a world wide web of mythologies. Also, Naomi Novik places her novels *Uprooted* (2015) and *Spinning Silver* (2018) in mythological Slavic and Easter European cultures.

Furthermore, authors like the Americans Catherynne M. Valente and Katherine Arden have based their stories especially on Russian folktales. Valente in the novel *Deathless* (2011) blends the storyline of the Russian tale Marya Morevna and the character of Koschei the Deathless with the events of the 1917 revolution and the early Soviet years (Magyarody 2017). Arden in the *Winternight Trilogy* (2017–2019) lets the heroine grow up in a mediaeval Russian village surrounded by traditional folktale characters and household spirits. In a slightly different vein, Leigh Bardugo has set their book series beginning from *Shadow and Bone* (2012; also, a television series from 2021) in "Grishaverse," a world inspired by Russian culture, and uses Russian-inspired vocabulary. The storylines have very few specifically Russian connections, yet the author calls their genre at least half jokingly Tsarpunk (Lazear 2012). Katherine Magyarody (2017, 360) attributes Anglophone fantasy literature's use of Russian imagery much to exoticisation. Yet more expansive research might also find other motivations behind the use of Slavic motifs in non-Russian fantasy. Several authors have mentioned their Russian-related roots or Russian-speaking relatives as their inspiration for integrating Russian material in their books (see, e.g., Valente 2013, 351).

In the Nordic countries, both the Swedish Peter Bergting and the Finnish Ilkka Auer have been inspired by the Slavic household spirit, the Domovoy. In Bergting's graphic novel *Domovoi* (2013), this spirit helps a young immigrant woman living in Sweden to find her Slavic heritage. In Auer's books, Russian or Slavic mythology and characters add to the milieu rather than mediating Russian culture to the Finnish audience. In Auer's *Domowik* (2018), a Polish version of the same spirit helps a girl to solve mysteries in her family history and in the surroundings of her new home that gives her access to a fantasy world. Unlike in Bergting's graphic novel, in Auer's story, Russian culture plays a minor role. Domowik is only one of several mythical characters in the story world – although a central one – and the "witch of Novgorod" in the sequel *Noidankiro* (2020) is not distinctively a Russian witch, despite her origins. In the horror novel *Anastasia* (2017), Auer introduces Russian and Soviet characters to the region around the former Soviet naval base, Porkkala in Southern Finland. As the title suggests, the plot circles around the historical tragedy of the Romanov family. The fate of Russia's last royal family has also inspired *The Waning Moon Duology* (*The Five Daughters of the Moon* and *The Sisters of the Crescent Empress* 2017) by Leena Likitalo. The books introduce a magical steampunk world with characters and events loosely drawn from Russian history. Since the Finnish author Leena Likitalo has written the books in English, *The Waning Moon Duology* can be called transnational literature: in this sense, the books compare interestingly to Hynynen's and Terentjeva's transnational text.

Russian and Slavic Elements in the *Neonkaupunki* Series

Whereas many authors using Russian elements seem to place their books in worlds inspired by the Russian past and not the present, Hynynen and Terentjeva introduce a dystopian world of urban horror. The books are set in contemporary Finland and a secondary world called Elm, an apocalyptic abandoned city where gangs fight for their right to exist. Elm is strongly inspired by the popular culture of the 1980s, especially by metal music and horror movies; the name Elm hints at the horror film *A Nightmare on Elm Street* (1984), and according to Susanna Hynynen, the title of the series *Neonkaupunki* is related to the visual atmosphere of 1980s music videos (Mankkinen 2021). The protagonists of the books are young Finland Russians who end up in Elm, where they have to find their way of surviving and come to terms with their Russian cultural heritage.

Hynynen and Terentjeva have stated in interviews that they write specifically about Russian and Finland Russian culture (Mankkinen 2021). One important source of imagery is Russian folktale, more accurately the genre of wonder tale (*volshebnaia skazka*). Russian wonder tales, examined in Vladimir Propp's structural studies, use different personage and imagery from their European counterparts. In their books, Hynynen and Terentjeva use both the structural aspects of the Russian wonder tale and its characters. Since Finnish readers are not necessarily familiar with Russian folktales, the novels offer short explanations of the folktale characters met in the text. Other forms of Russian folklore are hinted at: the text mentions bogatyrs, legendary heroes from Russian epic poems, or *bylinas*, and both books begin with a short introduction of Baba Yaga and Koschei the Deathless[4] and their roles in Russian tales. The introductory texts are composed so that they remind of the Russian folklore genre of *strashilka*, a horror story that children tell each other.

In the first part of the trilogy, the most prominent folktale character is Baba Yaga. She has kept the traditional attributes of the folktale witch: she is an old woman living in a chicken-leg hut with a traditional Russian stove. Yet she has more unique features. For example, she can transform into a metro train when needed and communicates with some of the characters in supernatural ways. Her function in the novel is partly similar to her function in folktales. Baba Yaga in folktales is a notoriously ambiguous character who can be a child-eating witch, a magical helper for the hero on the quest, or a tester and judge of the (false) hero.[5]

In *Neonkaupunki*, Baba Yaga is just as ambiguous. She is first introduced as a protector of a youth gang, the Gorkys, who sends her gang leader to kidnap young Finland Russians, like a folktale witch who snatches children. She punishes gang members who are not loyal to her – not unlike the folktale Baba Yaga, who rewards the good daughter and punishes the bad one. Baba Yaga also protects her own: when the Gorkys' headquarters is attacked, Baba Yaga as deus ex machina destroys the enemies like a monstrous horror story demon. Yet she also destroys and even eats her own gang members, showing cannibalistic traits that also suggest a folktale connection (Hubbs 1988, 47; Forrester 2013, XXXVI). In mythological readings of Baba Yaga, the old woman is often seen as a guardian between the land of the living and the land of the dead, and her image has also been connected to the idea of a rite of passage from childhood to adulthood (Propp 1986, 53–56; Johns 2004, 21–31). Both interpretations contribute to the novels' two-world structure and the young adult protagonists building their identities in a secondary world. However, Hynynen and Terentjeva's Baba Yaga also reminds readers of a wise old woman helping the characters in their quest: for one of the protagonists, Nikita, the witch is like the grandmother she misses. Baba Yaga calls Nikita her dear daughter (despite her male name, Nikita is a girl) and promises to help her gain power in the gang. Baba Yaga's role in the story depends on the point of view at the time, just as in folktales Baba Yaga's role in the plot depends on who she is dealing with. Baba Yaga has a special relationship with another protagonist, Vera, who can sense her presence in ways most other characters cannot. Despite the witch's ambiguous nature, Vera sees Baba Yaga as a thoroughly evil being. Unlike Nikita, Vera cannot see her as a nurturing grandmother. Vera does everything she can to escape her and finally succeeds in killing the witch in the end of the first novel.

In the second book *Spiraalitie*, Vera's friends want to find their way back to Elm and are involved when Vera gets kidnapped back there again, this time by the wizard Koschei the Deathless. If the first kidnapping by Baba Yaga represents the traditional folktale motif of stealing a child, the second one by Koschei represents another one, capturing a bride. Like Baba Yaga, Koschei the Deathless is a prominent character in Russian folktales, but unlike her, he is always the villain. The special characteristics of Koschei are his tendency to kidnap beautiful women and his deathlessness: he has hidden his death or soul in a secret place and cannot be killed until it has been destroyed – not unlike the wizard Voldemort in the Harry Potter series. Usually, Koschei's death is hidden in a needle inside an egg that is hidden inside several animals and buried in a box under an oak tree. Sometimes Koschei can get killed by a kick of a horse. The episode with Koschei the Deathless loosely follows the plot of the Russian wonder tale *Marya Morevna*.[6] Koschei kidnaps Vera, whom he calls Marya, and takes her to his estate to be his wife and a mother for his children – another group of young Finland Russians kidnapped to Elm. As in folktales, an excellent horse is essential to escape Koschei, and like a fairytale princess, Vera is saved using Koschei's horse. Yet perhaps the most crucial part of the folktale plot where Koschei's soul is sought and found to destroy him is not fulfilled in the second part of the trilogy.

The imagery of *Neonkaupunki* is strongly affected by Russian folklore, and it uses some typical plot devices from the Russian wonder tale. Of course, the plot motifs are present also in folktales of other cultures, yet the Russian imagery also ties the plot to explicitly Russian culture.

Cultural Mediators

In some interviews, Hynynen and Terentjeva have mentioned their different cultural backgrounds as a strength. According to them, Terentjeva's Russian background gives the authors a deep understanding of Russian culture and Hynynen's position as an outsider in relation to Russian culture helps them see which cultural traits need explaining to readers (Mankkinen 2021; Neuvonen 2021). The *Neonkaupunki* series can be seen as mediating Finland Russian culture in particular and Russian culture in general to non-Russian readers. Cultural mediation is thus vital for understanding the books. Russian cultural elements discussed here include linguistic features, traditions, and religion. Some cultural elements in the books are more traditional, whereas others are more typical for contemporary youth culture.

The Russian language is present in the texts in many ways. On the level of vocabulary, the books introduce several Russian words and expressions. Dess Terentjeva has said that the idea of using Russian expressions in Finnish text derives from Anthony Burgess using Russian words as the basis of the youth slang in *A Clockwork Orange* (1962; *Lohikäärmeradio* 2022). Since the books are written in Finnish but parts of the dialogues are supposedly in Russian, the Russian words used in the middle of the Finnish text sometimes imply that the conversation language is Russian. "Mam, I want to tell you about a girl. No, not Vera, another one" (*Neonkaupunki*, 343).[7] Here, the Russian word "Mam" signals that the conversation is in Russian – both Nikita and her mother's native language is Russian. Using Russian expressions puts readers from different linguistic backgrounds in different positions. For a Russian speaker, the Russian expressions are familiar, and through them, the reader can recognise aspects of Russian culture, whereas for a non-Russian speaker, Russian words might function as elements of estrangement. The Russian language is an instrument in worldbuilding and gives the secondary world Elm a specific atmosphere that for some readers might be familiar, and for others exotic.

Since for most Finns Russian is less well known than, for example, English, most Russian expressions have to be explained to the reader. Often this happens through one of the protagonists, Vera. She was born in Finland, and Finnish is the stronger of her two home languages. In the books, there are several scenes where Vera is pondering the meaning of some Russian expressions or where other characters explain words to her. For example, when Vera reminisces about her grandmother's funeral, she remembers a

Russian saying. "They had said to babushka: *Pust zemlja tebe budet perom.* Let the earth be like feathers to you. Sit tibi terra levis" (*Neonkaupunki* 108).[8] Some easily recognisable and understandable Russian words are presented without explanation, trusting that the reader will understand: "The door is locked, *idiotka*, thought Vera" (*Spiraalitie*, 17).[9] In other cases, the reader might not get the exact meaning of the Russian word, yet can guess close enough to understand the general idea: "She felt like vomiting and the feeling of *toska* was so bad that it hurt" (*Spiraalitie*, 18).[10] Here the word *toska* refers to Vera's hopeless longing or pining for Elm and her Russian friends. The word has a reputation of being untranslatable, and according to Vladimir Nabokov, "No single word in English renders all the shades of *toska*" (Nabokov 1990, 141). This gives Vera's feeling a deep undertone of "Russianness" that only a speaker of Russian language can truly understand. To appreciate some expressions requires deep knowledge of Russian culture, for example, when the Russian cultural concept of "Mother Moist Earth" (*Mat' syra zemlia*) is connected with a prosaic bodily function: "She took too deep a breath, felt a new wave of nausea coming and vomited onto the moist earth" (*Spiraalitie* 20).[11]

Russian culture has rich and varying traditions regarding names and forms of address that are vital in maintaining social relations. Readers of Russian literature often perceive the Russian naming system as complicated. It is one of the main linguistic features the authors of *Neonkaupunki* pay attention to and explain to the readers. A Russian person's name is made of three parts: first name, patronymic, and surname. Different combinations of these are used in different situations. First names have several forms, and their use depends on the relation between the speakers and the social situation. For example, Vera is often called Verotška or Verulja by her friends. They also call her by name and patronymic Vera Maksimovna, but never by surname. Nikita's name is a combination of Russian and Finnish elements. Her first name is Nikita, which is actually a male name, but Nikita has been named after her uncle; her Russian mother sees it also as a glamorous European girl's name (*Neonkaupunki* 321).

Nikita's last name, Tarkkinen, comes from her Finnish stepfather. She also has a Russian patronymic, Ivanovna. She is sometimes called by a nickname formed of her last name, Tarkkis, which in Finnish is also a rude slang word for a kid going to special classes often associated with bad or even dangerous behaviour. Through the conversation of the characters, the reader learns that in Russian, female and male patronyms differ from each other as for them the combination of a male name and female patronymic "Nikita Ivanovna" sounds strange (*Neonkaupunki* 260). Nikita's role as one who breaks the rules and Russian gender conventions is symbolically present even in her name. Thus, starting from the names of the characters, *Neonkaupunki* both presents Russian traditions to the reader and plays with the possibilities of breaking these traditions and giving the young characters a chance to define themselves.

Different forms of address include the use of informal and formal "you," in Russian "ty" and "vy." This informal and formal distinction is also drawn in Finnish, yet it is used differently and is less common than in Russian. If the names and forms of address are used incorrectly, Russian speakers often find the situation comical and see these mistakes as a sign of a non-Russian speaker. The Russian naming and addressing traditions are difficult for Vera, and she ponders them several times so as not to lose face in front of more fluent Russian speakers. For example, when Vera meets Ksenija for the first time, she wonders how to address her. She chooses the informal address since the girl she meets looks young. When Vera hears the girl's name, Ksenija Vladimirovna, she remembers that a typical nickname for Ksenija is Ksjuša (*Neonkaupunki* 34). Following Vera's thoughts gives this information to the Finnish reader, who might have had questions about the Russian name culture.

Yet another linguistic feature strongly present in the novels is Russian vernacular and swear words. In Elm, Russian speakers use quite a lot of expressions that in Russian are called *mat* or obscene language. In Russian culture, swear words or "Russian mat" are considered so rude they do not exist in common dictionaries and are currently forbidden in public use. The taboo status of swearwords in Russia can be seen in the government's attempts to restrict swearing in official situations: the use of swearwords in films was forbidden in 2014 and in social media in 2021 (*The Moscow Times*, 2021). Nevertheless, swearwords are abundant in speech, for example, in youth slang. In *Neonkaupunki,* swear words come up frequently in the dialogue and signal that the young characters do not speak according to the rules of traditional and formal language. Blurring the line between Russian youth culture and traditional Russian culture is the mascot of the Gorky gang, a talking raven called Puškin. Alexander Pushkin (1799–1837) was and still is the most iconic lyricist in Russia, considered a national poet and a master of Russian language. In the books, the bird's vocabulary consists mostly of swearwords, which builds a humoristic tension between expectations and reality. Yet the poet Pushkin also had lighter moments and used obscene vocabulary in some poems, and the raven's profanities challenge the high and pompous status of traditional Russian culture showing its more anarchistic side.

The *Neonkaupunki* series presents an abundance of Russian everyday objects that a non-Russian reader probably recognises as Russian, from various foods to samovars, balalaikas, and Russian rock band t-shirts. The second book, *Spiraalitie,* introduces a Russian village and its rural traditions with horror twists that recall the Ukrainian villages of the Ukrainian born Nikolai Gogol's nineteenth-century horror stories. In addition to creating a sense of Russian milieu, these details might motivate the curious reader to get acquainted with Russian culture: for example, one can easily find music by the rock bands mentioned in the books.

On a more abstract level, the most prominent aspects of Russian culture in *Neonkaupunki* are the feeling of community and the vertical concept of power. A strong sense of community is often seen as one of the most typical and valued qualities of Russian culture. Community is seen as a web of relations where family ties and friendship are the glue keeping the group together. In *Neonkaupunki*, it exists in the primary world of the books, a Finnish suburb, as mutual help and respect between Russian relatives, yet it has its dark side too, as the family covers up Nikita's mother's violence against her daughter. In the secondary world of Elm, there is a strong feeling of togetherness between the Gorky gang members, although conflicts and fights are not unusual either. The sense of community is linked to Russian ideas of *svoj i čužoj*, that is, "ours and theirs" or "us against the others" that in the books is most noticeable in the way the gangs fight each other, but sometimes also as solidarity between Russian speakers. Although for Vera, ending up in Elm is a personal tragedy, for the first time in her life she enjoys the Russian feeling of togetherness. Nikita, who has problems with her family, feels like she has found in Elm a proper home and a kind of new family. Vera and Nikita have different attitudes to the vertical power relations between people. Vera does not accept the Gorky hierarchy, in which the newcomers are at the lowest level and treated almost like slave workers until they graduate into soldiers. The gang is led by the first – sometimes also called the tsar[12] – who is supported by the second. The highest status is reserved to the god-like protector Baba Yaga. Resemblance to Russian power structures in different historical and political eras is obvious. Unlike Vera, Nikita thrives in this system and progresses up the hierarchy to become the first of the gang. Just as the hierarchical power relations are not only a Russian phenomenon, they are not presented as an entirely Russian feature in *Neonkaupunki*: the non-Russian gangs in Elm also have a hierarchy with a protector, first and second, and relations between the gangs are based on this hierarchy.

On the Gorky gang's territory in Elm there is an Orthodox church that represents yet another facet of Russian culture. According to legends, Russians – or rather the people living in Kievan Rus' – adopted the Eastern Orthodox form of Christianity in 988, and since then it has been the main religion in Russia, although its status has varied according to the historical and political situation (Korpela 2001, 9–11). For some of the characters, going to church is a natural part of life, whereas others like Vera see it more as a part of Russian culture and not of their own identity. The books briefly explain the Russian belief system that is based on both Christianity and folk beliefs: the Gorky gang has no problems believing both in the Christian

God and in Baba Yaga (*Neonkaupunki* 266).[13] Hynynen and Terentjeva also blend in traditional Russian religion features that are more familiar from horror films than from Russian Orthodoxy, like the unorthodox way of using the saints' bones as weapons to fight monsters.

Building an Identity as Young Finland Russians

Hynynen and Terentjeva have stressed the need for representation of minorities in fiction (Neuvonen 2021; Terentjeva 2021). The *Neonkaupunki* series is about two minorities: Finland Russians and LGBTQIA+ minorities. Terentjeva discusses minorities also in her later books. This chapter concentrates on the Finland Russian minority and treats sexuality and gender mostly in terms of negotiating Finland Russian youth identity, although the theme is so prominent in the books that it would deserve a study in its own right.

Finland Russians are a very diverse linguistic and ethnic minority that is not easy to define. According to Statistics Finland, at the end of 2021 almost 90,000 people in Finland had Russian registered as their native language and thus Russian was the biggest foreign language in the country (Statistics Finland a). The largest number of people living in Finland and born abroad were born in the former Soviet Union (Statistics Finland b). The background of Russians in Finland varies: some families have lived in Finland for generations ever since Finland was part of the Russian empire in 1809–1917, while some are more recent immigrants to Finland after the fall of the Soviet Union in 1991. In addition, some people from the former Soviet Union who are not ethnically Russian or do not have Russian as native language identify as Russian in some situations. In this text, the term "Finland Russians" is used for people with any level of Russian heritage living in Finland who themselves identify at least partly as Finland Russians.

Neonkaupunki both tells readers about minorities and provides an arena for representatives of those minorities to discuss their own identity. It is the first fantasy series depicting young Finland Russians from the minority's own perspective. The protagonists and one of the two authors are Finland Russians. Terentjeva names Russian as her native language, yet she also learnt Finnish as a child. She says that after living in Finland for 20 years she still feels she is Russian (Mangström 2021) and has also described Russian as her native language and Finnish as her "native writing language" (dessterentjeva 4.11.2022). For Hynynen, Finnish is the native language. In that sense, the series can be described as transnational literature. *Neonkaupunki* differs from other Finnish fantasy novels with Slavic elements, like Ilkka Auer's *Domowik*, where the protagonists are Finnish children who see the Slavic folklore elements from outside. As young Finland Russians are depicted from the minority's own perspective in *Neonkaupunki*, Russian culture is seen as "ours" and its meaning for the characters varies. The books blend Russian and Finnish culture with elements from Western pop culture – especially American metal music and 1980s horror and fantasy films. Even the name of the Russian speaking gang, the Gorkys, is derived from the English name of the Soviet Russian rock band Gorky Park (formed in 1987), although it also refers to the Russian and Soviet author Maxim Gorky and to Russian word meaning "bitter" (*Neonkaupunki* 124–125).

Some characters build their identity according to their taste in American 1980s heavy rock and play American Les Paul guitars in addition to balalaikas. One of the Russians in Elm even prefers the name Andy to his original Andrei. American pop culture has connotations to the ideological conflicts between the United States and the Soviet Union and contemporary Russia. In this context, American pop culture signals both freedom and resistance against or alternative to the Soviet or Russian government and official culture. It also signals conflicts between generations since American or international pop culture has often been seen specifically as youth culture – in both Russian and European contexts. Most importantly, it underlines the many facets of the characters' identity building. In the beginning of the series, the reader probably first notices the differences between Finnish and Russian culture and sees Vera as a key character searching for her place between these two. Yet as the story progresses, it becomes clear that Finland Russian culture is not just a combination of two existing cultures but takes influences from many different cultures and subcultures.

A vital instrument for writing about the Finland Russian minority is the two-world structure. The primary world of the books is a vaguely described suburb in contemporary Finland that provides a setting for a realistic mode of description. In the secondary world, Elm, a group of Russian-speaking young people have built their own community without the restrictions of the real world. The first two books, at least, do not tell a complete history of the world of Elm and its gangs or explain the rules according to which the magic works there. Most characters have ended up in Elm in their late teens or early twenties, but since time does not progress in Elm and people do not age, the readers – or even the characters themselves – do not know how long they have been there. Allusions to Joel Schumacher's film *Lost Boys* (1987) and the lost boys in J.M. Barrie's *Peter Pan* books are obvious. The Gorky gang is meant for Finland Russians, but also other gangs in Elm have at least some Russian-speaking members. The story illustrates the diversity of a minority group: first it looks like Vera arrives in a homogenous community of Russian speakers, but soon both Vera and the reader realise that all members are individuals who have ended up in Elm in their own ways. Although Elm and its protectors limit their choices, they have built their own community on their own terms and Vera too is able to influence how the Gorky gang's life develops.

The world of Elm introduces the reader and the characters to elements of Russian culture, yet it does not seem justified to interpret Elm simply as representing this culture, or Russia. It serves more as a space that enables the characters to realise and negotiate their ideas of Russian culture and their own identities. How the characters end up in Elm is parallel to their individual stories of how they have come to live in Finland and their relationships to Russian culture. Yet Elm is not a safe haven for young adults negotiating their identities: people get hurt, die in horrible ways, and suffer the consequences of their choices.

Neonkaupunki can be read as a story of growing up, although the characters do not age physically. Underneath the cruel realities, Elm seems to have a traditional nurturing motherly nature, not unlike the traditional feminine representations of Mother Russia. An abundance of feminine myths is connected to Russian culture, from Mother Earth to Mother Russia. For example, Joanna Hubbs (1988, 24–51) sees the folklore character Baba Yaga as one manifestation of the inherent feminine principle in Russian culture. Elm seems to provide the Gorky gang the necessities for life, and more. The Gorkys live in an abandoned hotel in nice rooms, and the bar and dining room serve Russian delicacies from pickled cucumbers and pastries to tea and vodka. The abandoned shops in Elm are full of clothes and accessories free of charge. When the hotel burns down during a gang war and Baba Yaga dies, the remnants of Gorky gang are left homeless and move into a metro train – a situation that brings to mind Dmitry Gluhovsky's *Metro* series (2005–2015) – until Nikita finds them a new home at a deserted metro station. Moving from the hotel to the metro station can be interpreted as taking more responsibility. In the hotel, the Gorkys were under the protecting wing and rule of Baba Yaga, but in the metro station, they have to take their fates in their own hands, although Elm still keeps providing them with everything they need from clothes to books of Russian classics.

The Gorkys also take more responsibility for constructing their own identities as the story progresses. In the beginning of book one, Vera and Nikita, who have a problematic relation to their Russian heritage, are offered Baba Yaga's version of a Russian identity. Nikita embraces this identity, although not completely without problems, whereas Vera rejects it. In a sense, Vera faces her fears related to Russianness in the form of the terrifying Baba Yaga, whom she manages to kill with the help of her Russian friends so she can return home more confident and accept herself as belonging to both Finnish and Russian cultures. The first book ends when Vera is home feeling safer and Nikita feels she's been robbed of everything Elm represented to her. In the beginning of the second book, Vera's uneasiness with her Finland Russian identity continues. This shows identity as a process or construction, not as something static and permanent that can be resolved once and for all (see, e.g., Hall 1992). Returning to Elm, Vera, Nikita, and their friend Slava get a new chance to continue building their identities and the book ends symbolically with Vera walking on the spiral road, not knowing where she is heading.

Furthermore, fantasy as a genre enables the authors to explore sexuality and gender identities both literally and metaphorically. Lenise Prater argues that in fantasy "magical queering, symbolic or metaphoric queering made available by the conventions of the genre, are often more radical than the literal engagement with sexualities carried out by these texts" (Prater 2016, 32). In *Neonkaupunki*, the depiction of different sexualities is quite literal, yet radical in the sense that the wide variety of sexual minorities get a chance to speak through the characters. The books introduce characters of different genders and sexualities; characters discuss their identities and have different forms of sexual relationships with each other. The authors themselves also identify as writers of LGBTQIA+ fiction (Neuvonen 2021; Terentjeva 2022). The sexuality and gender identity of some characters provide material for the plot, but in describing other characters, the emphasis is on representation: the theme of diversity and minorities inside minorities is strongly present. Identities are seen as intersectional: questions of culture and ethnicity are intertwined with gender and sexuality.

Characters are also affected by their family backgrounds; for example, Vera seems to have got a general feeling of security from his loving and caring *papa,* whom she seems to trust almost endlessly, whereas Nikita's mother is judgemental, unpredictable, and violent so that Nikita can only rely on herself. However, in the world of Elm, characters' economic backgrounds do not matter, since Elm provides them materially with everything they need from food to clothes; thus, the characters can express themselves freely through their appearances and clothing without economic problems restricting them. In *Neonkaupunki*, accepting people's right to define themselves – in terms of their sexuality, gender identity, and cultural identity – serves as a prominent defining feature of the Finland Russian youth culture. In *Neonkaupunki* it might even be seen as the main factor separating the Finland Russian youth culture from contemporary Russia, where sexual minorities currently have far fewer rights than they do in Finland.[14] In Elm, another Russian-speaking gang, the Martyrs are depicted as having conservative views on sexuality, which is presented as one reason for hostilities between them and the Gorky gang. It would be tempting to interpret the Martyrs gang as representing the ever more conservative contemporary Russia – although in *Spiraalitie* the reader gets some clues that the Martyrs might actually have arrived in Elm long ago, maybe in Soviet times or even earlier.

Although the young people in Elm have different opinions about each other's sexuality, the conflict mainly occurs between generations – for example, between Nikita and her mother in the real world – not between the young protagonists, which demarcates a line between youth and adult culture. The most prominent character representing sexual minorities is Nikita, who is described as a masculine lesbian with a boy's name. Her mother does not accept her sexuality, which leads to a physical conflict between them and to Nikita moving to live with a creepy cousin, which in its turn leads to Nikita being sexually assaulted. In Elm, she gets a chance to be herself and Baba Yaga reminds her of her own grandmother, who accepted her as she was. In Elm, the Finland Russian young adults freely combine elements from different cultures in terms of sexuality, too. When Nikita becomes the leader of the Gorky gang, her subjects want her to have a wife as a tsar should be married. Thus, Nikita gets married to another woman. In Elm, this is in perfect harmony with the demands of both Russian traditions and the characters' own sexualities, although Nikita's choice of *tsaritsa* does not make her happy in the end. Still, the wedding and marriage is in strong contrast with the official reality in contemporary Russia.

Conclusions

The *Neonkaupunki* series continues the international wave of using Russian and Slavic culture as an inspiration for fantasy texts, this time bringing the Russian folklore elements to contemporary settings. Russian elements in the story make the fantasy world familiar to a reader who is acquainted with Russian culture. At the same time, they bring into the fantasy world something fresh that differs from the well-worn Anglo-Saxon fantasy imagery. *Neonkaupunki* differs from most Slavic-inspired fantasies in the sense that it critically examines Russian culture from inside, through Russian characters. It is the first fantasy series to put young Finland Russians in the centre of the story and to see Finland Russian culture as a part of Finnish youth culture.

The series contributes to the contemporary cultural conversation about minorities' rights to define themselves and shows identity not so much as a rigid category but a unique blend of social and cultural positions. It also blends almost utopian elements in a dystopia by allowing the characters to do things they would not be able to do freely in their real world. The secondary world of Elm with all its horrors and cruelties provides protagonists with a chance to investigate their identities in settings that differ from their ordinary everyday life. Elm is characterised by ambiguity: the characters arrange their lives according to Russian ideals, yet they are very conscious about the stereotypes connected to Russian culture. They question and undermine the traditions, at the same time taking them very seriously. Same goes for their gender and sexuality: Elm lets them be who they really are, yet at the same time they have to negotiate their identities with themselves and others living in Elm. It would be tempting to read *Neonkaupunki* in terms of a Bakhtinian carnival where the characters get to play the role of the king – or the tsar – in the carnivalesque secondary world until the carnival is over and it is time to go back to their everyday roles.[15] Yet until we can read the third part of the trilogy, it is hard to see whether this particular carnival will lead back to normal or something else.

Notes

1 The word *neonkaupunki* in the titles means "neon city," and *spiraalitie* means "spiral road." For the sake of simplicity, here the novels are mostly called collectively by the name of the series, *Neonkaupunki*.

2 Fantasy as a genre has strong roots in English language cultures. For example, Lucie Armitt bases her introduction to fantasy genre mainly on Anglo-American books and identifies the tales of King Arthur as one of the primary sources of myth in them (Armitt 2005, 8–11). Dimitra Fimi names "Celtic" mythology as an important inspiration for especially children's fantasy (Fimi 2017, 1–2). Jyrki Korpua (2015, 17) sees *Beowulf*, Icelandic *sagas*, *Kalevala*, and the *Bible* as the main sources of myth in Tolkien's legendarium. Since Tolkien has had a defining effect on the formation of the modern fantasy genre, the Anglo Saxon and Northern European myths have found their way into a wide range of texts inspired by their work.

3 About Russian Rodnoverie, a religion based on pre-Christian Slavic beliefs, and its growing popularity during the last decades of Soviet Union and after that in Russia, see Aitamurto (2011).

4 In this text, Russian names are given in the form they are in the *Neonkaupunki* books, that is, in their Finnish transliterated form. The only exceptions are folktale figures Baba Yaga, Koschei the Deathless, and Marya Morevna and well-known Russian authors whose names are given in the forms somewhat established in English literature. Other transliterations are based on the ALA-LC romanisation.

5 For a thorough analysis of Baba Yaga in Russian folktales and culture, see Johns (2004). For a more concise introduction to Baba Yaga, see Jack Zipes and Sibelan Forrester's introductory chapters to *Baba Yaga: The Wild Witch of the East in Russian Fairy Tales* (2013).

6 Different versions of the fairytale exist. Probably the best-known version is tale number 159 in Alexander Afanasyev's collection of Russian folktales. The authors of *Neonkaupunki* are very conscious of the tradition; they present on their Instagram feed Catherynne M. Valente's novel *Deathless,* which also deals with the relationship between Koschei and Marya Morevna (neonkaupunki 25.2.2021).

7 English translations from *Neonkaupunki* and *Spiraalitie* by JS. "Mam, mä haluun kertoo yhdestä tytöstä. Ei, en Verasta, vaan toisesta."

8 "Babuškalle oli sanottu: *Pust zemlja tebe budet puhom.* Olkoon maa sinulle höyheninen. Kevyet mullat."

9 "Ovi on lukittu, *idiotka*, Vera ajatteli."

10 "Häntä oksetti ja hänellä oli niin kova *toska*, että häneen sattui."

11 "Hän veti henkeä liian lujaa, tunsi uuden pahoinvoinnin aallon ja oksensi märkään maahan." About Mother Moist Earth, see, for example, Hubbs 1988, 53.

12 Tsar was the official title for the Russian ruler in 1547–1721. After that, the official title was Emperor (*imperator*), yet tsar was widely used even after that. For a Russian speaker, the word "tsar" has a stronger Russian connotation than emperor, which is perceived as more European.

13 Double belief (*dvoeverie*), practicing simultaneously pagan and Christian religions, is a cultural concept often connected to Russian culture. For a thorough discussion of Russian double belief, see Rock (2007).

14 In their article, Eremin and Petrovich-Belkin (2022) present a short history of the legislation regarding homosexuality in Russia. They identify the current situation under Vladimir Putin's rule together with the Soviet era as the worst times in Russian history for LGBT rights. Like the Soviet regime, Putin's government treats homosexuality and Western values as an opposite of and a threat to traditional Russian values. The law against "propaganda for non-traditional relationships" was approved in 2013, and hate crimes against sexuality minorities especially in Chechnya have become notorious.

15 The idea of a Bakhtinian carnival has been connected to especially fantasy for children. See, for example, Nikolajeva (2000, 125–146).

References

Abasheva, Svetlana & Irina Krinicyna. 2010. "Problematika nacional'noj identičnosti v slavjanskih fentezi." *Vestnik Tomskogo gosudarstvennogo universiteta* No 332: 7–10.

Aitamurto, Kaarina. 2011. *Paganism, Traditionalism, Nationalism: Narratives of Russian Rodnoverie.* Helsinki: University of Helsinki.

Alkestrand, Malin. 2016. *Magiska möjligheter. Harry Potter, Artemis Fowl och Cirkeln I skolans värdegrundsarbete.* Svenska barnboksinstitutets skriftserie nr 137. Göteborg & Stockholm: Makadam.

Armitt, Lucie. 2005. *Fantasy Fiction. An Introduction.* New York & London: Continuum.

Barbini, Francesca T. (ed.). 2017. *Gender Identity and Sexuality in Current Fantasy and Science Fiction.* Edinburgh: Luna Press Publishing.

dessterentjeva. Dess Terentjeva's Instagram account. https://www.instagram.com/dessterentjeva/. Accessed 1 March 2024.

Eremin, Arkadiy & Oleg Konstantinovich Petrovich-Belkin. 2022. "State Policies Regarding Sexual Minorities in Russia: From Russian Empire to Modern Day Russian Federation." *Sexuality & Culture* 26: 289–311.

Fimi, Dimitra. 2017. *Celtic Myth in Contemporary Children's Fantasy: Idealization, Identity, Ideology.* London: Palgrave Macmillan.

Forrester, Sibelan. 2013. *Baba Yaga: The Wild Witch of the East in Russian Fairy Tales.* Jackson: University Press of Mississippi.

Grönstrand, Heidi, Ralf Kauranen, Olli Löytty, Kukku Melkas, Hanna-Leena Nissilä & Mikko Pollari. 2016. "Johdanto: Ylirajainen kirjallisuudentutkimus ja deterritorialisoiva lukutapa." In *Kansallisen katveesta. Suomen kirjallisuuden ylirajaisuudesta,* eds. Heidi Grönstrand, Ralf Kauranen, Olli Löytty, Kukku Melkas, Hanna-Leena Nissilä & Mikko Pollari, 7–37. Helsinki: SKS.

Hall, Stuart. 1992. "Question of Cultural Identity." In *Modernity and Its Futures,* eds. Stuart Hall, David Held & Tony McGrew, 273–326. Cambridge: Polity Press.

Halme, Jukka. 2006. "Esilukijan näkemyksiä ja kokemuksia. Kustantamon lukijan näkökulma." In *Ihmeentuntua. Näkökulmia lasten ja nuorten fantasiakirjallisuuteen,* eds. Anne Leinonen & Ismo Loivamaa, 56–69. Helsinki: BTJ.

Hellman, Ben. 2013. *Fairy Tales and True Stories: The History of Russian Literature for Children and Young People (1574–2010).* Leiden: Brill.

Hubbs, Joanna. 1988. *Mother Russia. The Feminine Myth in Russian Culture.* Bloomington and Indianapolis: Indiana UP.

Hynynen, Susanna & Dess Terentjeva. 2020. *Neonkaupunki*. Helsinki: Like.
Hynynen, Susanna & Dess Terentjeva. 2021. *Neonkaupunki 2 – Spiraalitie*. Helsinki: Like.
Jay, Paul. 2010. *Global Matters. The Transnational Turn in Literary Studies*. Ithaca & London: Cornell UP.
Johns, Andreas. 2004. *Baba Yaga: The Ambiguous Mother and Witch of the Russian Folktale*. International folkloristics, v 3. New York: Peter Lang.
Korpela, Jukka. 2001. *Prince, Saint, and Apostle. Prince Vladimir Svjatoslavič of Kiev, his Posthumous Life, and the Religious Legitimization of the Russian Great Power*. Veröffentlichungen des Osteuropa-Institutes München. Reihe: Geschichte 67. Stuttgart: Otto Harrassowitz.
Korpua, Jyrki. 2015. *Constructive Mythopoetics in J. R. R. Tolkien's* Legendarium. Oulu: University of Oulu.
Kulttuuriykkönen. Neonkaupunki-kirjasarja on paitsi väkivaltaista fantasiaa myös kurkistus suomenvenäläisyyteen ja naisen asemaan. Yle Areena 28.7.2021. https://areena.yle.fi/podcastit/1-50845302. Accessed 1 March 2024.
Lazear, Suzanne. 2012. "Genre Friction: What is Tsarpunk? by Leigh Bardugo." *Steamed! Writing Steampunk Fiction*. https://ageofsteam.wordpress.com/2012/04/25/genre-friction-what-is-tsarpunk-by-leigh-bardugo/. Accessed 1 March 2024.
Leisiö, Aapo. 2022. (Nuorten-)Kirjailijan tulee olla brändi. *Fantasiakirjailija Aapo Leisiö*. https://fantasiakirjailija.wordpress.com/2023/12/13/nuorten-kirjailijan-tulee-olla-brandi/ *Lohikäärmeradio*. Jakso 24 – Seppoversen salaisuus, vieraana Dess Terentjeva. Accessed 1 March 2024.
Magyarody, Katherine. 2017. "Translating Russian folklore into Soviet fantasy in Arkadi and Boris Strugatski's Monday Begins on Saturday and Catherynne Valente's Deathless." *Marvels & Tales* 31 (2): 338–369.
Mangström, Veera. 2021. "Ikuinen venäläinen." *Jylkkäri* 8/2021: 22.
Mankkinen, Jussi. 2021. "Kaksikko kirjoittaa väkivallan ja lesbosuhteiden kyllästämää fantasiaa, ja keskiössä on yllättävä ryhmä: Neonkaupunki-sarja kertoo suomenvenäläisistä." *Yle*. https://yle.fi/uutiset/3-11912932. Accessed 1 March 2024.
The Moscow Times. 2021. "Russians Post More Profanities After Social Media Swearing Ban." https://www.themoscowtimes.com/2021/04/05/russians-post-more-profanities-after-social-media-swearing-ban-a73466. Accessed 1 March 2024.
Nabokov, Vladimir. 1990. "Commentary." Alexander Pushkin: *Eugene Onegin. A Novel in Verse*. Volume II: Commentary and Index. Trans. Vladimir Nabokov. Bollingen Series LXXII. Princeton: Princeton UP.
neonkaupunki. Susanna Hynynen's and Dess Terentjeva's Instagram account. https://www.instagram.com/neonkaupunki/. Accessed 1 March 2024.
Neuvonen, Sini. 2021. "Kirjailijahaastattelu: Dess Terentjeva ja Susanna Hynynen." https://kirjavasatama.espoonkirjastot.fi/espoonfantasia/kirjailijahaastattelu-dess-terentjeva-ja-susanna-hynynen/. Accessed 1 March 2024.
Nikolajeva, Maria. 2000. *From Mythic to Linear. Time in Children's Fiction*. Lanham (MD): Scarecrow Press.
Nilson, Maria, Helene Ehriander & Emma Tornborg. 2018. *Feministisk fantastik. En läslustbok*. Lund: BTJ Förlag.
Österlund, Mia. 2011. "Kaunokirjallisuuden tyttölaboratorio." In *Entäs tytöt. Johdatus tyttötutkimukseen*, eds. Karoliina Ojanen, Heta Mulari & Sanna Aaltonen, 213–248. Tampere: Osuuskunta Vastapaino.
Pearson, Wendy Gay, Veronica Hollinger & Joan Gordon. 2008. *Queer Universe. Sexualities in Science Fiction*. Liverpool: Liverpool UP.

Prater, Lenise. 2016. "Queering Magic. Robin Hobb and Fantasy Literature's Radical Potential." In *Gender and Sexuality in Contemporary Popular Fantasy*, eds. Jude Roberts & Esther MacCallum-Stewart, 21–34. London: Taylor & Francis eBooks A–Z.

Propp, Vladimir. 1986. *Istoričeskie korni volšebnoj skazki*. Leningrad: Izdatel'stvo Leningradskogo universiteta.

Roberts, Jude & Esther MacCallum-Stewart (eds.). 2016. *Gender and Sexuality in Contemporary Popular Fantasy*. London: Taylor & Francis eBooks A–Z.

Rock, Stella. 2007. *Popular Religion in Russia: Double Belief and the Making of an Academic Myth*. London & New York: Routledge.

Rzhevsky, Nicholas. 2012. "Russian Cultural History: Introduction." In *The Cambridge Companion to Modern Russian Culture,* ed. Nicholas Rzhevsky, 1–16. 2nd edition. Cambridge: Cambridge UP.

Safron, Elena Aleksandrovna. 2012. *'Slavianskaya' fentezi: Fol'klorno-mifologicheskie aspekty semantiki*. Avtoreferat dissertacii na soiskanie ucheoj stepeni kandidata filosoficheskih nauk. Petrozavodsk: Petrozavodskij gosudarstvennyj universitet.

Salminen, Jenniliisa. 2009. *Fantastic in Form, Ambiguous in Content: Secondary Worlds in Soviet Children's Fantasy Fiction*. Turku: Turun yliopisto.

Sisättö, Vesa. 2006. "Tieteis- ja fantasiakirjallisuus Suomessa." In *Kotimaisia tieteis- ja fantasiakirjailijoita*, eds. Vesa Sisättö & Toni Jerrman, 9–18. Helsinki: BTJ.

Statistics Finland a: "Foreign-language Speakers." https://www.stat.fi/tup/maahanmuutto/maahanmuuttajat-vaestossa/vieraskieliset_en.html. Accessed 1 March 2024.

Statistics Finland b: "Persons Born Abroad." https://www.stat.fi/tup/maahanmuutto/maahanmuuttajat-vaestossa/ulkomailla-syntyneet_en.html. Accessed 1 March 2024.

Tapionkaski, Sanna. 2021. "Fantasia, sukupuoli ja seksuaalisuus." In *Fantasia: lajit, ilmiö ja yhteiskunta,* eds. Jyrki Korpua, Irma Hirsjärvi, Urpo Kovala & Tanja Välisalo, 433–454. Jyväskylä: Nykykulttuuri.

Tarsalainen, Anne. 2021. "Ilmavia säkeitä." *Kirjastolehti* https://suomenkirjastoseura.fi/kirjastolehti/ilmavia-sakeita/. Accessed 1 March 2024.

Terentjeva, Dess. 2021. "Vähemmistörepresentaatio: Kirjailija neuvoo." https://www.youtube.com/watch?v=tiH5uCxzNFo. Accessed 1 March 2024.

Terentjeva, Dess. 2022. "Kirjailija Terentjeva. Suomalainen sateenaarispefi." https://kirjailijaterentjeva.blogspot.com/p/suomalainen-sateenkaarispefi-koontilista.html. Accessed 1 March 2024.

Valente, Catherynne M. 2013. *Deathless*. London: Corsair.

Warner, Elizabeth. 2002. *Russian Myths*. London: The British Museum Press.

Wheeler Mjolsness, Lora. 2020. "Under the Hypnosis of Disney: Ivan Ivanov-Vano and Soviet Animation for Children." In *A Companion to Soviet Children's Literature and Film*, ed. Olga Voronina, 389–416. Leiden & Boston: Brill.

11

"WHAT IS LEFT BEHIND"

Extractivism in *Blå* by M. Lunde and
"The Satellite Charmer" by M.B. Diene

Marta Mboka Tveit

As the climate crisis deepens, there arises a pressing need to re-examine some of the obscured neoliberal and modernist premises that have, at the last instance, shaped our world into what it is today. The undeniable merit of large-scale resource extraction is one such premise. The contestation of such premises also comes to light in contemporary cultural texts from diverging parts of the planet, especially fictions of the future. Historically, Andrei Terian suggests, the idea of extractive fictions has been linked specifically to Latin America, post-1945, under what has been called "the great acceleration" (2021). However, Terian makes a forceful argument for expanding the application of the concept. Similarly, Imre Szeman makes a compelling argument for basing a new type of understanding of literatures and histories around energy or energy sources, in the study of petrocultures (Geleyn 2019, 140).

In this chapter, therefore, I contribute to expanding the application of extraction and extractivism as a basis for analysis. I will show how the theme of extractivism is co-located in two texts: the novel *Blå* by Maja Lunde from Norway (2017) and a novelette that can be classified as African speculative fiction – "The Satellite Charmer" by Mame Bougouma Diene (2020).

My endeavour over the past years has been to examine production sites of speculative fiction in relation to planetary issues, climate change in particular. In this effort, I have concentrated on the sub-genres African speculative fiction and Norwegian speculative fiction.

Focusing on these two sub-genres together was motivated by their recent explosive emergence on to the global stage, attracting global attention, and yet that both remain relatively understudied within academia. Afrofuturism, propelled into the spotlight by the blockbuster success of Marvel's "Black

DOI: 10.4324/9781003561101-16

Panther" movies, has gained worldwide recognition. Its themes and works have become subjects of extensive scholarly exploration, primarily in the United States (see Anderson 2020; Lavender 2019; Lavender 2020; Serrano 2020; Womack 2013; Steinskog 2018; Butler 2021; Hamilton 2023; Toliver 2022; Anderson and Fluker 2021; Anderson and Jones 2015; Ibaaku 2020; Wallace and Schwartz 2022; Walters 2022; Yaszek 2013, 2006; Guynes 2021; Neyrat 2020; Lavender and Yaszek 2020a, 2020b;). On the other hand, African speculative fiction has garnered less attention, though scholarly interest is on the rise (see Maurits 2020; Clarke 2019, 2019a, 2019b, 2020; Byrne 2004; Gaylard 2005; Quayson 2009; Osinubi 2009; Omelsky 2014; Bould 2015a, 2015b; Wood 2015; Zvomuya 2015; Barbini 2018; Emenyonu & Egbunike 2021; Bould 2013). This disparity might be attributed to historical and postcolonial structures of power that have marginalised African cultural research.

Norwegian speculative fiction is experiencing a revival, particularly driven by female authors. Maja Lunde, known for her climate-quartet, stands out with remarkable international success, while young and diverse writers are injecting new vitality into the sub-genre. This marks a departure from the male-dominated era of the 1960s–1980s, yet academic attention to Norwegian speculative fiction remains limited, except for the odd sporadic publications (see Berg 1998; Bing 2014; Bing 1967; Bambini 2023; Bøttcher 2003; Damsholt 1979; Eide 1992; Enger 2015; Ewo 2013; Fossum og Boasson 2022; Furuseth et al. 2020; Furuseth and Henning 2023; Johnsen 2021; Lindberg 1999; Lindholm 2008, 2018a, 2018b; Norheim 2011; Simonsen et al 2022; Omdal 2010).

Focusing on particular texts makes comparative analysis possible, despite obvious disparities in contexts and scale when it comes to production sites. I follow the entreaty of Gayatri Spivak in her infamous critique of comparative literature (*Death of a Discipline*, 2003). Spivak argues eloquently against the homogenising logic of globalisation, in particular universalisation and the "general equivalence" that is necessary in order to conduct literary comparison. This equivalence, Spivak argues, is a process of translation that has the effect of "flattening" texts. As such, comparative literature is caught up in the tensions between the politics of the local and the global, and in questions of origin and authenticity. There remains something in texts that cannot be translated into the general equivalence of the global. The question of alterity that Spivak touches upon always arises with cross-cultural comparative methods, also in relation to contexts. There is a danger of "flattening" by failing to observe the differences between contexts and intended readings. For practitioners of comparison, like myself in this chapter, it is a difficult balance to strike.

Spivak encourages instead a new way of practising comparative literature and teaching, one that is "responsible, responsive, answerable" (101) precisely in its non-negation and non-derivation of alterity: "If we imagine ourselves as planetary subjects rather than global agents, planetary creatures rather than global entities, alterity remains underived from us; it is not our dialectical negation, it contains us as much as it flings us away" (73). She explicates further:

> the "planet is, here, as perhaps always, a catachresis for inscribing collective responsibility as right. Its alterity, determining experience, is mysterious and discontinuous – an experience of the impossible. It is such collectivities that must be opened up ... when cultural origin is detranscendentalized into fiction.
>
> *(101–102)*

In this chapter then I strive to reflect such "textual planetarity" in my reading, holding here that these two texts and their sites of production are underivable different. Starting from this premise, I then argue that the theme of extractivism is *co-located* so to speak in both texts, the theme overlaps, saying nothing of their further characteristics. It is a small but significant distinction.

A comparative approach encourages valuable insights into how planetary challenges are perceived. In one way or another, imagined futures factor heavily into societal, political, economic, and environmental action (or inaction) in the present (Chattopadhyay 2021). In order to understand presents, therefore, we also need to understand imagined futures, how they function and the work they do in societies. Furthermore, shared planetary issues like climate change are experienced and conceptualised through cultural (g)local prisms. One way to approach future imaginings is through studying cultural texts. The comparative study of cultural texts can help us understand how those cultural prisms affect humanity's negotiation of shared global issues.

Moving to my reasons for choosing texts from these particular production sites: as mentioned, both African and Norwegian speculative fiction are emerging sub-genres that have come into their own on the world stage in the last two decades, yet they remain understudied. Both are in conversation with wider movements such as Indigenous futurism, New Nordic Magic (Kosmorama 2021), Afrofuturism, speculative climate fiction (Raipola 2019), and the general global blooming of climate fiction. Both make use of geographical markers that resist globalising tendencies within speculative fiction. Both signs move fluidly between the local and the global, have open channels for flows both horizontally and vertically, and have recognisable content that is not dependent on form or specific platforms.

Furthermore, the global position of both African and Norwegian speculative fiction is similar, since both are arguably minor sub-genres in the spaces of global cultural production. Looking at such texts together can be extremely fruitful because it can reveal aspects of each text and of each site of production, which would otherwise have remained hidden, argue cultural theorists Shu-mei Shih and Françoise Lionnet (2005). They advocate lateral comparisons, because looking at the transnational from the "minor" perspective can have theoretical and practical benefits "indispensable to a better understanding of the general logic of transcultural and transdisciplinary approaches, and it troubles the prevalent notion of transnationalism as a homogenising force" (2005, 11). In other words, these sub-genres are (g) local, dialoguing with the planetary without being global.

Finally, experiences of extractivism emerge from many parts of the planet, and it is of value to put this type of "peripheral writing" in conversation, as Spivak argues (16). This is especially true regarding the transnational phenomenon of extractivism as a worldwide phenomenon with varied reactions and consequences. Extractivism is the process of extracting natural resources from the earth to sell on the world market, a keystone in the neoliberal capitalist global economy that has dominated the Anthropocene[1] (Terian 2021). To economists the term specifically denotes the removal of large amounts of natural resources that are not processed or processed to a limited degree. There is no clear consensus on the term, yet its usage is usually in connection with resources that are not easily renewable, such as diamonds, coal, natural gas, lumber, oil, and minerals (Acosta 2013). 500 years ago, extractivism established itself on a massive scale as a mode of accumulation under the global capitalist system, tied closely to European and American colonisation and conquest of large parts of Asia, Africa, Oseania, and the Americas. Neo-extractivism, crudely summed up, refers to the continuation of extractivist practices in former colonies, in which post-colonial states and transnational corporations play a larger role.

Terian points out how the core/periphery binary does not necessarily coincide with geography or countries "and may include territories within countries otherwise not regarded as peripheral per se, such as the boreal forest in Canada or the *Arctic areas of Norway*" (497, emphasis added). In Norway, the debate on whether or not to end exploration for new oil and natural gas fields rages on, sprinkled with arguments that are built on a mindset of endless progress and bottomless resources, something I will return to. Similarly, since the Nigerian oil boom of the 1970s, West African citizens have been treated to a neo-extractivist discourse and policy, where development is linked to what is essentially extraction and selling off piecemeal, also to new actors like China, India, and Canada, or mysteriously untethered corporations with long names.

How do the two texts examined here, emerging from very different production sites, deconstruct and problematise extractivism, its consequences, and reactions? It is argued that these texts do so through portraying three dimensions of the theme: its inherent injustice, avenues of resistance, and finally widespread sense of complicity in relation to natural resource extraction.

Injustice

Both *Blå* and "The Satellite Charmer" expose the violence and injustices extractivism inflicts on communities, human and nonhuman. Further, both texts do so from the perspective of "normal, little people" struggling in the ruins of what is left behind. By doing so, the texts illustrate how "the personal is political," as the second-wave feminist slogan goes (Gupta 2015).

"The Satellite Charmer," by established writer Mama Bougouma Diene, first appeared in *Dominion: An Anthology of Speculative Fiction from Africa and the African Diaspora* (2020). In the story, we meet Ibrahima Ndiaye, living in a future-state called the Caliphate, probably in West Africa, probably akin to present-day Senegal, and part of the new Western Chinese economic Empire. In it we follow Ibrahima through his entire lifespan, from boyhood to adulthood to his final transformation into something else. He is orphaned at an early age and raised by his grandmother in an impoverished village, where he is "faced with the prospect of no prospects at all" (2020, 150). The Caliph, leader of the Caliphate, has allowed major satellite mining in Ibrahima's area by transnational corporations ChinaCorp and Han Industries. Besides being a story full of unexpected twists and turns, "The Satellite Charmer" illustrates the injustices of extractivism through the satellite mining beam and the powerlessness of its characters:

> Have you seen what is left behind when the beam is done mining the soil?"
>
> She nodded. They all had seen it. Entire swathes of the continent seared and bleeding with lava, like open arteries on a suicidal forearm. Soil ripped of every mineral and plant, cracked and fissured and void of life, leaking fluids like burned flesh. Earthquakes and death lingering long after the mining satellites had had their fill. Floods of displaced people fleeing the operations into the already overcrowded areas and cities.
>
> *(159)*

As exemplified in the quote above, it shows us the profound and devastating effects of large-scale extractivism on the environment and on communities. Ibrahima grows up hating the beam, with radical dreams and opinions for change, and plays bass guitar in a village band. Yet as he grows older, marries, and moves to Ikapa (Cape Town, South Africa), he eventually starts working for ChinaCorp, like most in his area, and is miserable.[2] Additionally, the text illustrates the "false promises" of extractivism:

We play with the toys we make out of scrap, light our homes and cook our food with them. We treat the leftovers as if they were gifts, but they're not. They're trash, and they're not even ours. And what does the Caliphate do? Give up even more, allow them to tear our wealth out of the ground. And what do we get in return? Empty promises and more junk.

(159)

Here, the "empty promises" of development and wealth are revealed as being just that. Terian points to the "myth of modernity," meaning the inherent promise of progress and development at any cost as a central premise for extractivism to exist (2021). Similarly, Michael Ziser, in his paper on petro-cultures, describes oil as being conceived of as a "free gift to capital" (Ziser in Yaeger 2011, 321), justifying almost any degree of fetishisation by earlier economic theorists (including Karl Marx). The massive surplus that materialised from oil extraction, the unbelievable overnight private fortunes, gives oil retrieval a mythical element (Yaeger 2011). Yet, as emphasised in the quote above, these "free gifts" do come at a price, especially at the sites of extraction.

The End of the Ocean (2017, *Blå* in original Norwegian) was the follow-up to Lunde's international best-seller novel *The History of Bees* (2015) and part of her "climate quartet." Similarly to *The History of Bees*, *Blå* plays with temporality. The text has a dual plot structure, following a father, David, and his daughter, Lou, from France in the year 2041, fleeing northwards from the city of Argelès in war-torn Southern Europe during a worldwide water shortage, and 70-year-old Signe, on a hazardous voyage southwards by sailboat in 2017. The three protagonists, David, Lou, and Signe, are moving in opposite directions through Europe, both driven by perplexing forces inside and outside themselves.

Through artefacts and locations, Signe's story is weaved expertly together with David and Lou's tale of survival and hope, to form a sort of parable of the climate apocalypse, that touches on the strength of the human spirit and the spectacular power of nature, fireworks for the end of the world as we know it. Lou and David end up in a refugee camp, one which is becoming more and more unliveable. Finally, they abandon the camp and go to live in a cabin near a sailboat in a parched garden, miles from shore. The boat named Blå and personal effects they find turn out to once have belonged to Signe, who will be the main focus character here. Signe is from a small village on the west coast of Norway. She has spent her life as an environmental activist. When we meet her, she is on her sailboat, named "Blå," with a load of stolen ice and an all-consuming mission to throw the ice at the feet of her former partner, Magnus. This happens following a return to her childhood village and to her beloved glacier "Blåfonna."

In *Blå*, Lunde thematises extractivism primarily through the conflict around ice mining in 2017, yet also through the "mining" of hydro-electricity in a local river. The text shows us the destructive and divisive effect of extractive industries, on families and social cohesion in a specific place. The animosity and high-feeling Lunde describes, around what to do with Norwegian waterways, is far from fictional in Norway. For instance, the major political conflict and massive mobilisation around the electrification of Alta-vassdraget in northern Norway continues to be a rift in collective memory (Berg-Nordlie 2023). Through Lou and David's story, the text additionally touches on the overarching consequence of continued large-scale extractivism, undermining the ecosystems that support life, human and nonhuman. The novel is deeply connected to "other places" yet by strictly adhering to the first-person narratives of Signe and David Lunde makes both extractivism and global warming painfully real and tangible for the reader. Signe observes how the glacier has been downwasting due to global warming, and the mining of ice is a kind of nail in the coffin:

> Dear, dear Blåfonna. All glaciers melt, I know that, but it's something else witnessing it. I stop, just breathe. The ice is still there, but not where it used to be. … I keep going and now I can see the extraction area, the gouges in the greyish-white glacier, and deep gashes in the blue interior, where the ice has been cut away. Nothing should surprise me anymore, all the things human beings do.
>
> *(Lunde 2018, 16)*

Signe has fought the glacier project her entire life, yet the ice is now being mined and sold off to rich buyers in the middle east, in order to have "pure Norwegian ice" in expensive drinks. Rich foreign powers are literally chipping away at the glacier, illustrating what Terian calls the triumph of the transnational over local capital, arguing that extractivism on a global scale corresponds to the stage of capitalist expansion which has "taken on the form of a world-system asymmetrically divided into core (which can extract, ship, and process resources by mastering technology) and peripheries (which can only supply unprocessed resources, since they lack technology" (497). Like in Diene's story, the injustice of extractivism is exposed, where the global rich benefit and local communities closer to the sites of extraction suffer.

Resistance

Neither of the protagonists in the two texts takes the injustices of extractivism lying down. Though she is battle-fatigued when we meet her, Signe's actions and words show tenacity to the last:

I am nearly invisible – a small, grey woman wearing a knitted cap covered with fuzz balls, I am old, old as stone, like Blåfonna.

I can't destroy everything, but I can destroy this.

I can't shout about everything, but I can shout about this.

I can dump the ice in the ocean and disappear.

(41)

The passage above is especially moving, since it reflects the sense of powerlessness and smallness many of us can feel, when faced with the great global forces of late-stage capitalism and modernity. Yet, Signe poignantly *chooses* to focus on the little she *can* do and takes action, though her actions are literal drops in the ocean. She is in the position of the underdog, the woman-on-the-street, and though faced with dire odds, she chooses to do what she can, announcing, "I can't shout about everything, but I can shout about this." She later celebrates her own agency, her small rebellion against the almighty "sheiks":

This ice can never be used as ice cubes – it can never, ever be served on a sheikh's table, in a crystal tumbler, in a drink, in Saudi Arabia or Qatar. Ice that melts, ice that melts in salt water, I am a part of it now, a part of what is taking place at all times. I am compounding the changes. I laugh, startled by the sound of my own laughter, an unfamiliar croaking, like a frog.

(47)

Signe's environmental activism began as a child when there was a plan to put a river near her home into pipes in order to produce hydroelectricity. Her father, a marine biologist, is vehemently opposed to the pipelining of the river, whereas her mother, a hotel owner, was for it, in the name of developing the region. This conflict eventually splits the family apart, her father and a neighbour almost blowing up a bridge for the pipeline workers with dynamite. As an adult, Signe has lost her life-long battle, both with climate change and with the "shambling jerry-built corpse-machine" of capitalism (Bould 2021, 31). She is a lonely warrior, a David against the goliath masquerading as "progress" and "development." In her internal monologue, she speaks to Magnus about her perceived failure:

everything I have done has been to no avail. I have really tried, I have been fighting for my entire life, but I have been mostly alone. There are so few of us, it was futile. Everything we talked about, everything we said would happen, has happened, the heat has already arrived, nobody listened.

(58)

She knows the battle is lost, yet she continues to resist. Her desperate acts, stealing ice and her ill-advised voyage alone, seems to be a way of externalising her own suffering, sense of helplessness, and fury at the state of the world. Not knowing what else to do, Signe is literally and figuratively at sea, yet continues to resist until the very end.

Ibrahima's resistance is perhaps more complex. At a young age he and his girlfriend vehemently oppose satellite mining and are part of an artistic community, resisting through music. He even advocated for a pan-African resistance at one point: "We should have stood our ground, not as the Massina Sokoto Caliphate. Not as the Yoruba Heartland. Not as the Congolese Brotherhood or the South African Confederacy. As Africa" (150). Later, however, Ibrahima becomes a part of ChinaCorp, having made a Faustian bargain for his son's prospects. Yet, one avenue of interpretation is that Ibrahima's resistance continues through his suffering. Much space is given in Diene's story to Ibrahima's suffering, throughout his life – expressed through a worsening alcohol dependency and general disinterestedness. He is eventually literally crushed by the external forces of a life in a future West Africa, illustrating how picking out a living in the ruins and crevices between crushing forces is anything but easy.

Furthermore, through portraying different forms of resistance, both these texts implicitly challenge the underlying assumptions buttressing the dominant modernist ontology of the nonhuman world. Taking from the earth is something human beings have always done and is, in and of itself, arguably value-neutral. Yet, according to Terian, the practice as the large-scale phenomenon we see today is made possible by the logic of modernisation tied to neo-liberal political-economic ideology centred on the accumulation of capital. The latter suggests an "extractivist discourse," one that hinges on certain underlying assumptions that Terian outlines.

They include the notion that the consideration of the ecological setting can be more or less disregarded during the extraction process, that the primary entitlement to benefit from these resources belongs to nations and entities with superior extraction capabilities, that indigenous populations are still in developmental stages and ought to pursue a particular developmental trajectory, that planetary resources are practically boundless, and "last but not least that the most efficient path is, at least for the moment, exploiting and exporting local natural resources" (498).

In the texts examined here, these underlying assumptions are challenged. For instance, David and Lou's near-future story in *Blå* contrasts in a very real way with the assumption that the planets' resources, such as fresh water, are unlimited and that "the (non)human environment can be ignored to a greater or lesser extent during this process of extraction" (Terian 2021, 498). Another example can be found at the end of Diene's story, where Ibrahima transcends earthly suffering – readable as a kind of resistance in and of itself. Terian argues how in magical realism, the magical element, animism, and quasi-mystical often represent a rhetoric of resistance. On his view, the natural world, the universe, and the resisting humans align, and magical elements represent a rhetoric of transspeciation, insisting on agency beyond capitalist consumerist citizenship. He writes: "Only by a consistent application of the Gaia principle, i.e. by the cooperation between humans and nature … can neocolonial capitalism be stopped" (2021, 497). Ibrahima has to transcend his human form (which he does) in order to truly face off with the satellite mining industry. The symbolic thrust of this lies in its implication, that the only force strong enough to face off against the mad drives of capitalism lies beyond the human social world in its current form – built on ontologies and epistemologies with underlying assumptions rooted in "modernity/coloniality" (Mignolo & Walsh's term 2018, 8).

The refusals presented in these texts resonate with contemporary discourses in the phenomenal world, where challenges are being posed to the notion of their being "one true nature" (Green 2013, 4), in academia, activism, art, and literature. Such contestations often emphasise the interconnectedness, "messy" entanglements, and interdependencies of all life (Haraway 2016). What is more, challenging the "One World World" as John Law calls it (2015) involves recognising heterogeneity and multiplicity – the "pluriverse" (Mignolo 2018) of the various ontologies, temporalities, and epistemologies coexisting on this planet.

Complicity

The undertone of complicity adds a layer of complexity to these extractive fictions. Both texts explore the idea of complicity inherent in extractivism, both societally and on the individual level through the ambivalence of the protagonists. To take the societal first: In both texts the forces behind the tearing-up of the protagonists' environment come from someplace else (Middle East, warring Chinese mega-corporations), and in both cases it is local leaders, the Caliph and the local council in Signe's Norwegian village, that have decided to let these forces in. In Diene's text the Caliphate is caught up in a tug-of-war between warring Chinas, playing a part of the power constellation allowing the laser-beam mining:

> Abdou shrugged. "… The Caliph only allows ChinaCorp to mine the Faso Subdivision, and the Caliphate gets paid for it. A lot."
> … Perhaps the Caliphate did get paid in return; perhaps the Caliph was sitting on velvet cushions drinking water teased from honey and dew. But just as the tingling in his veins made him feel like he owned the world, he knew something more sinister was at play.

"Your dad is a wise man, Abdou. But we're citizens of the Massina Sokoto Caliphate too. Have you seen any of that money here? I haven't."
(156)

Like in many African nations in the phenomenal world (former independence), leaders have become complicit in the continuation of praxises that harm local communities. Though European colonialism in its earlier political forms has ended, extraction, and for instance selling or shipping in cooperation with global transnational corporations, continue, though often alongside developmentalist policies that seemingly are intended to lessen the damage done to local communities. As mentioned, this is often referred to as neo-extractivism. It is tied to developmentalism and often justified with an idea of developing a struggling nation, along a set pathway, as outlined earlier as one of Terian's core assumptions belying extractivism.

A major flaw in the neo-extractivist logic is that the majority of value in a product, as well as capital accumulated, still ends up far from the peripheries and semi-peripheries that tend to suffer the most from the ills of extractivism (Acosta 2013). Terian argues how actors practising extractivism elsewhere have usually depleted their own resources of the materials in question. The main drivers of extractivism have indeed historically failed to deliver on promised development and redistribution of wealth to African societies. Former colonies are thus often, in a sense, a part of their own continued oppression, and it is this paradoxical condition in phenomenal Africa that Diene arguably gestures towards.

Similarly, in Blå it is the local council that has allowed for ice mining and local powers that allowed the river to be put in pipes, invoking similar developmentalist arguments based on an extractivist discourse. This discourse and these types of debates are present and highly charged in Norway today, with the added element that hydroelectricity and windmill parts provide clean(er) energy.

Furthermore, in Lunde's novel, societal complicity is deliberated through the motif of duality portrayed in sets of pairings, where one is interdependent on the other in order to produce the story world. There is the pairing of the imagery of a luscious and wild western Norway in Signe's memory, and the parched, torn-up landscape through which David and Lou labour and the ice and cool clean water of Norway next to the fire and dust ravishing David and Lou's hometown.

The most evident pairing is Signe and Magnus. The pairs also function as symbols for opposing ideologies. Signe the idealist and environmentalist is juxtaposed with Magnus the pragmatist and developer, paralleling the pairing of Signe's mother and father. Signe can be construed as a defender of mother earth, raging and uncompromising; she is like the wild ocean on which she sails. Magnus, on the other hand, is more passive, complacent, accepting what is and trying to live, not unsympathetic but essentially adhering to the more common and convenient view of things, seeking security.[3] When Signe finally asks him why he approved the excavation of Blåfonna, he answers:

> Because ... I'm the same person I've always been. Because the price of electricity has gone down. Because it was a chance to increase revenues. A chance for continued security.
>
> *(294)*

Reading between the lines, one can also see that Signe does have some understanding if not sympathy for both Magnus and the ideology he represents. Yet ultimately she chooses to take action against it and him.

The pairing begs the question of whether there can be any sort of reconciliation. There seems to be some evidence of reconciliation towards the ending, when Signe finally arrives at Magnus's home in France. It appears the ageing, ying-yang couple stay together for the remainder of their lives, finally finding some sort of balance. They discuss Signe's plan of destroying ice:

> "I know of a lot of other people who could have done something like that," I say.
>
> "In your world, sure. You live in another world."
>
> "We live in the same world."
>
> "Do we?" He smiles.
>
> "Do you think it's ridiculous?" I ask. "That I dumped the ice?"
>
> "No ... I don't think so. I don't think anything you've ever done has been ridiculous."
>
> "But it hasn't done any good," I say.
>
> "You don't know how the world would have been if you'd refrained," he says.
>
> *(292)*

This passage, and the pairing coming together at the end, are evidence that there is some hope for reconciliation. Signe and Magnus need one another and belong together, suggesting that the ideologies they represent can or should find ways of complementing one another as well. In a broader context, the much talked about "green transition" that needs to be implemented in the planetary struggle against climate change necessitates some kind of reconciliation (or at least alignment) between business interests and progress thinking, on the one hand, and environmental interests and activism, on the other. With this book, Lunde asks loudly whether or not such a reconciliation is possible, yet her answer also has a duality to it. Magnus and Signe do find each other again at the end of their lives. However, there is a carrying-on of that ended story through Lou and David, whose lives are shaped by the consequences of environmental interests having lost out, of the failures of both Signe and Magnus, of our generation.

Moving to the individual level, though the personal is of course political, struggling with complicity and ambivalence is central in shaping both protagonists and becomes a determining factor for their entire lives. The fact that there is this deep love and affection between Signe and Magnus can be read as symbolic of the interdependent and deeply entwined relationship between capitalism and human development in the so-called Global North. That development has lifted Norwegians to positions, through healthcare and education, where we are able to be aware of how humans are affecting the natural world and do something about it, which is what Signe in fact has the privilege to do. Her pain is testament to her awareness of her own privilege – her life and her activism would not have been possible without some degree of complicity. Signe is thus caught in the catch-22 of modern environmentalism, much like Norway as a nation is stuck in the cognitive dissonance of being both a progressive voice in the climate struggle and at the same time heavily entangled with the petroleum industry.

There are similar tensions in Diene's story, represented by Ibrahima's relationship to the mining beam. When Ibrahima works for ChinaCorp, he becomes everything he hates, a so-called "Satellite Hound" or "China rat" (165), evicting people from their homes, tearing up landscapes, and digging up ancient burial grounds, all in the name of profit. Yet, his relationship with the beam remains conflicted:

> The beam was death: he knew that; but to him it was life, in a way he couldn't quite understand. His senses heightened when it dropped, turning the clouds a deep red, every action anticipated by just a fraction. ...
>
> He tried to open his eyes but could not. It wasn't a dream. It was the beam. Somewhere it bore through the earth, mining out minerals from space, and whispering to him in a deep ululation. "You're mine Ibrahima. You have always been mine." It reverberated sensually, caressing him in his sleep.
>
> *(155, 157)*

The beam is destructive, yet it is also "deeply felt" and connected with Ibrahima. He is intellectually disgusted and "sensually" attracted to it all at once. In this passage the double meaning of "mine" is remarkable, where mine can be read both as something belonging to the speaker (the beam) and as an excavation in the earth. Ibrahima is both the miner and the mind. This doubleness is reminiscent of Du Bois's notion of double consciousness though with a slightly different connotation, simultaneously holding the consciousness of injured (thinking here of European colonial histories) and of injurer – re-creating systems, industrial practices, and institutions that in the last instance continue the oppression of both land and people. This postcolonial double consciousness is represented by Ibrahima's relationship with the beam, which is the force behind his transcendent bass guitar playing, and at least part of what keeps him and only him alive through the great explosion. Furthermore, the relationship is a neat way of illustrating the ambivalence inherent in many contemporary people's relationship to modern urban life, with all its comforts and all its horrors. We recognise that it is what is destroying us, yet at the same time, it is the source of much development, engendering many of our desires. Ibrahima's torn condition comes through in this following passage, from one of Ibrahima's visions:

> "Who are you?" he screamed. His voice sounded torn and he exhaled dirt back into the air.
> "We are the bedrock," the voices answered, now only a few.
> "We are the buried." …
> "We are the bones," the last voice concluded, the spinning sands shifting, slowly taking form in swirling static, and growing into a face. … The last of his flesh peeled off,
> leaving a statue of sand, eaten away by the beam. The beam that sounded like Mame Fatou.
>
> *(164)*

The fact that the beam voices speak in his grandmother's, Mame Fatou, voice is telling. A part of him seems to feel as if he has betrayed the land itself and with it the ancestors. Knowing that land is usually tied to ideas of belonging (LenkaBula 2008), Ibrahima's crisis is also one of identity. He is part of literally tearing up the land that made him. Signe, unlike David and Lou, has the privileged position of being able to have an impact on the system before the crisis becomes omnipresent. Ibrahima, on the other hand, is forced to be part of the system in order to sustain himself. Yet at what cost does one make this bargain, Diene seems to be asking in his text.

In the end Ibrahima physically merges with the beam. After the explosion in Ikapa, everything is desolated and there are almost no survivors, except Ibrahima. Then, the perspective shifts, and we follow two children exploring the desolated ruins of Ikapa many years later. They find Ibrahima, sitting in lotus position inside a building, glowing with radiation. He causes another massive explosion, melting the children, and becomes a kind of supreme being of the universe, perhaps comparable to the Starchild in *2001: A Space Odyssey,* original story by Arthur C. Clarke (1968).

The fact that Ibrahima literally has to become something other in order to both transcend his crushing sense of complicity and finally put an end to satellite mining (177) portrays how personally devastating and ultimately transforming resistance against the forces of capitalism continues to be.

Ibrahima's conflicted relationship with the beam is comparable to Signe's tormenting relationship with Magnus. The sense of ambivalence is described in both texts as something that is tearing the protagonist apart, holding within it a degree of complicity, and attraction.

Conclusion

As has been illustrated here, speculative fiction allows for deep critique of extractivism and its underlying modernist/colonial ontology of the nonhuman world. Such stories, whether they emerge from the so-called Global North or South, can function as tools for exploring the "pluriverse" (Mignolo 2018), of ways of relating to natural resources that make for more sustainable futures. Few other genres allow for so much experimentation, easy slippage between the real and its obverse, play with form and in-built challenging of conventional philosophy, and humanity's understanding of long and short processes of change (Otto 2012). As Donna Haraway writes: "SF [science fiction] is practice and process, it is becoming-with each other in surprising relays; it is a figure for ongoingness, [that encourages] staying with the trouble" (Haraway 2016, 3).

As scholars, putting such stories from different sites of production in conversation with one another, keeping in mind Spivak's "textual planetarity" (2003, 73), allows us to see with more clarity the planetary resonances in how omnipresent issues such as extractivism are conceptualised and reacted to. The texts examined in this chapter, *Blå* by Maja Lunde and "The Satellite Charmer" by Mame Bougouma Diene, thematise (neo-) extractivism, its devastating consequences, and its ambiguities. I have argued that these texts explore three planes of the theme: the injustice of extractivism in peripheries, avenues of resistance, and finally, the tensions complicity.

As discussed, there are similarities between the texts; the identities of both protagonists are tied up with their environments, and both need to make important life decisions because of the extraction happening near them. Yet, I would like to conclude this chapter by outlining two intriguing differences between the texts that could perhaps be a jumping-off point for further research. First, in *Blå* there seems to be discernible astonishment, both in Signe's reactions and in the tone of the novel more generally, in finding Norwegian environments being directly affected by extractivism. This discernible sense of astonishment pervading the novel might suggest an underlying assumption that Norway is somehow expected to hold itself to a higher standard than other societies, and refrain from pulling up, tearing apart, and selling off their environments (at least visibly).

The sense of astonishment at environments first and foremost being thought of in terms of use/commodity value is not present in Diene's text. Instead, large-scale and devastating extraction and its discontents is portrayed with an air of business-as-usual. Keeping in mind the diverging sites of production these texts emerge from, the difference is perhaps unsurprising. West African colonial histories are deeply entangled with histories of extraction – of palm oil, precious gems, coal, natural gas, and oil – and the kidnapping, enslaving, and transporting of human beings as commodities. In Diene's imagined future, therefore, there is a continuation of imbalances with deep historical roots, whereas in the Norwegian text there is a change, where large-scale extraction and its consequences is made visible and immediate in a different way than it is in the corresponding real-world context.

Second, there is a difference in tonality; there is a tone of end-times solastalgia in Lunde's story, which Diene's text does not contain to the same degree. *Blå* reflects "an atmosphere of gloom and melancholia ... which draws on a Nordic tradition of painting and literature, and which also often characterises the genre of Nordic noir" (Furuseth et al. 2020). The sense of end times and overhanging gloom and mourning pervades, one that is discernible in other Norwegian future fiction.

This type of apocalyptic future narrative, steeped in solastalgia, is in some senses a closed future. Closed futures come with their own dangers (Chattopadhyay 2018):

> the more closed the future and the more extreme its prediction, the less open and hopeful the present becomes. Take climate change and its dire apocalyptic presentations for instance. The crippling of hope in any possible positive future of the planet makes these the end times: we preempt the apocalypse by losing hope in any real possibility of change.
>
> *(7)*

I would argue that the future in Diene's text is more open, both in the story world and beyond the ending. In the end, greed wins in both texts. However, Diene's text reminds us of the tiny-blue-dot perspective. In cosmos Ibrahima plays the bass strings of the universe and wonders what to do next with his newfound power. Through this final scene, the text suggests that there is hope in something beyond human greed, hubris, and squabbles. One could take this to mean divine beings, the universe itself, death or nature's inevitable triumph; the point is the reminder that faced with the seemingly unassailable oppressive forces of modernity, there is still hope in the beyond, in imagining possibilities outside of existing systems and structures.

Notes

1 Chemist Paul Crutzen and biologist Eugene Stoermer coined the term "Anthropocene" in 2000. It has caught on as an unofficial geological epoch, a term used to describe the planet's recent history, where human activity began having a major impact. Since 2000 "Anthropocene" has flourished as an analytical concept. It has also met with challenges, also by posthumanist thinkers.

2 The beam's destruction of IKapa is forewarned in the story. Early on Ibrahima gets a vision of his childhood friend Abdou *"standing in front of him, wearing different clothes, terror in his eyes, his body disintegrating into shreds of skin and bone, trying to scream for help"* (154). Later, the citizens of Ikapa hear about a beam wiping up Ouagadougou. ChinaCorp and Han Industries blame each other for the accident.

3 One could argue further that both texts to some degree tie extractivism to masculinity. In Diene's story there is the obviously phallic "pounding beam," that Ibrahima cannot get out of his dreams. In *Blå* progressivism and developmentalism are represented by Signe's capitalist ex-partner Magnus, who had a hand in approving the ice-mining: *"Magnus, your grandchildren will not be able to skate across the lakes. Yet you have approved this, our glacier, the ice. You have dissociated yourself to such a large extent from everything that once was ours—or perhaps you have always been like this, you have just let it happen"* (58).

References

Acosta, Alberto. 2013. "Extractivism and Neo-extractivism: Two Sides of the Same Curse." In *Beyond Development: Alternative Visions from Latin America*, eds. Miriam Lang & Dunia Mokrani, 61–86. Amsterdam: Transnational Institute.

Anderson, Reynaldo & Clinton R Fluker. 2021. *Black Speculative Arts Movement: Black Futurity, Art + Design*. USA: Lexington Books.

Anderson, Reynaldo & Charles Earl Jones. 2015. *Afrofuturism 2.0: The Rise of Astro-Blackness*. USA: Lexington Books.

Bambini, Karl Kristian Swane. 2023. "Norwegian Futurisms: Posthumanism and the Norwegian Nordic Model in Tor Åge Bringsværd's "Du og Jeg, Alfred" and "Alfred 2.0"." *Ecozon@* 14 (2): 70–89.

Barbini, F. T., ed. 2018. *The Evolution of African Fantasy and Science Fiction*. United Kingdom: Luna Press Publishing: Academia Lunare.

Berg-Nordlie, Mikkel. 2023. "Alta-saken – Store norske leksikon." *Store Norske Leksikon*.

Berg, Johannes H.1998. "Kretsen fanzine." *Fandom.no*. Accessed 14.05.2023. http://www.fandom.no/kretsen/index.html

Bing, Jon. 2014."Fra skjermbrett til skjerm: Litterære forestillinger om fremtidens media." *Norsk medietidsskrift* 21 (4): 308–320.

Bing, Jon & Bringsværd, Tor Åge. 1967. "Fabelprosa Science fiction og dens bakgrunn." *Vinduet* 2: 83–89. https://docplayer.me/18370802-Fabelprosa -science-fiction-og-dens-bakgrunn.html.

Bould, Mark. 2021. *The Anthropocene Unconscious: Climate Catastrophe Culture*. New York: Verso.

Bould, Mark, ed. 2013. *Paradoxa: African SF*. Edited by Mark Bould. Vol. 25, *Paradoxa. Alt 39: Speculative & science Fiction - African literature tuday, African Litearture today*, eds. Emenyonu, Ernest N & Louisa Uchum Egbunike, USA: James Currey

Bould, Mark. 2015a. "African Science Fiction 101." *markbould.com* (blog).05.02.2015. https://markbould.com/2015/02/05/african-science-fiction -101/.

Bould, Mark. 2015b. If Colonialism Was The Apocalypse, What Comes Next? Accessed 22.06.2021.

Berg, Johannes H.1998. "Kretsen fanzine." *Fandom.no.* Accessed 14.05.2023. http://www.fandom.no/kretsen/index.html

Butler, Philip. 2021. *Critical Black Futures: Speculative Theories and Explorations.* Gateway East, Singapore: Springer.

Byrne, Deirdre C.2004. "Science Fiction in South Africa." *PMLA: Publications of the Modern Language Association of America* 119 (3): 522–525.

Bøttcher, Agnes. 2003. "Fantasy, litteratur og den norske virkeligheten." *Vinduet.* Accessed 20.01.2021. http://arkiv.vinduet.no/tekst.asp?id=333

Chattopadhyay, Bodhisattva. 2018. "Introduksjon: Alle grenser er midlertidige." *Alle Grenser er Midlertidige.* Oslo: Transcultural Arts Production (trAP). https://trap.no/uploads/10u-all-borders.pdf. Accessed 1 March 2024.

Chattopadhyay, Bodhisattva. 2021. "Manifestos of Futurisms." *Foundations* 139 50 (2): 8–23.

Clarke, Michelle Louise. 2019. "Ecocritical Frontiers in Sub-Saharan Anglo-African Speculative Fiction." Center for Cultural, Literary and Postcolonial Studies, SOAS, University of London.

Clarke, Michelle Louise. 2019a. "New Waves: African Environmental Ethics and Ocean Ecosystems." *African Environmental Ethics* 29: 153–172.

Clarke, Michelle Louise. ed. 2019b. *Vector 289: Special Themed Issue on African and Afrodiasporic SF.* Vol. 289.

Clarke, Michelle Louise. 2020. "Black Atlantic Futurism, Toxic Discourses and Decolonizing the Anthropocene in Nnedi Okorafor's *The Book of Phoenix*." In *African Literature Today: ALT 38 Environmental Transformations*, 106–121. Cambridge: Boydell & Brewer.

Diene, Mame Bougouma. 2020. "The Satellite Charmer." In *Dominion: An Anthology of Speculative Fiction from Africa and the African Diaspora*, eds. Oghenechovwe D. Ekpeki, Zelda Knight & Joshua Omenga. Louisbille: Aurelia Leo.

Damsholt, Torben.1979. "Ludvig Holberg: Niels Klims underjordiske rejse I–III, ved A. Kragelund (1970)" (book review). København: København: Danske Forening, etc.

Enger, Rolf. 2015. "Et blaff i horisonten. Et essay om fantastisk litteratur." In *Svolt – det som blir att kan villdyra ete.Skrivekunstakademiet 30 år.* Vigmostad Bjørke.

Eide, Øyvind.1992. *Fabelprosa:science fiction og fantasy på norsk.* Oslo: Biblioteksentralen.

Ewo, Jon. 2013."Intervju med Øyvind Myhre." 20.01.2021. https://jonewo.net/siste -nytt/intervju-med-oyvind-myhre/.

Fossum, Odin & Frode Lerum Boasson. 2022. Et annet sted: En litteraturgeografisk analyse av norsk science fiction-litteratur med nærlesing og fjernlesing som metode. NTNU: Master Thesis.

Furuseth, Sissel, Anne Gjelsvik, Ahmet Gürata, Reinhard Hennig, Julia Leyda & Katie Ritson. 2020. "Climate Change in Literature, Television and Film from Norway." *Ecozon@* 11 (2): 8–16.

Furuseth, Sissel & Reinhard Hennig. 2023. *Økokritisk håndbok: natur og miljø i litteraturen.* Oslo: Universitetsforlaget.

Gaylard, Gerald. 2005. *After Colonialism: African Postmodernism and Magical Realism.* South Africa: Wits University Press.

Geleyn, Rebecca. 2019. "On Petrocultures: Globalization, Culture, and Energy by Imre Szeman (Review)." *Ariel* 50 (4): 139–141.

Green, Lesley, ed. 2013. *Contested Ecologies: Dialogues in the South on Nature and Knowledge.* South Africa: HSRC Press.

Gupta, Rahila. 2015. "The Personal is Political: The Journey of a Feminist Slogan." *Open Democracy.* https://www.opendemocracy.net/en/5050/personal-is -political-journey-of-feminist-slogan/. Accessed 1 March 2024.

Guynes, Sean. 2021. "From Afrofuturism to afrofuturism." *Science Fiction Studies* 48 (1): 151–155.

Hamilton, Elizabeth Carmel. 2023. *Charting the Afrofuturist imaginary in African American art: the Black female fantastic.* New York: Routledge.

Haraway, Donna. 2016. *Staying with the Trouble: Making Kin in the Chthulucene.* North Carolina: Duke University Press.

Ibaaku. 2020. "L'afro-futurisme au-delà des frontières." *Hermès* (Paris, France: 1988) 86 (1): 257–260.

Johnsen, Ranveig Stende. 2021. "Futurismen er tilbake!" *Deichman Litteraturblogg* (blog). 20.01.2021. http://blogg.deichman.no/litteratur/book_reviews/ futurismen-er-tilbake/.

Kosmorama. 2021. "New Nordic Magic." *Kosmorama* #279. https://www .kosmorama.org/en/kosmorama/en/kosmorama-279-new-nordic-magic. Accessed 1 March 2024.

Lavender, Isiah. 2019. *Afrofuturism Rising: The Literary Prehistory of a Movement.* Columbus: The Ohio University Press.

Lavender, Isiah & Lisa Yaszek. 2020a. "The First Death of Afrofuturism." *Extrapolation* 61 (1/2): I–VIII.

Lavender, Isiah & Lisa Yaszek, ed. 2020b. *Literary Afrofuturism in the Twenty-First Century.* Columbus: Ohio State University Press.

Law, John. 2015. "What's Wrong with a One-world World?" *Distinktion (Aarhus)* 16 (1): 126–139.

LenkaBula, Puleng. 2008. "Beyond Anthropocentricity – Botho/Ubuntu and the Quest for Economic and Ecological Justice in Africa." *RT* 15 (3–4): 375–394.

Lindberg, Cato.1999. "Norwegian Fandom: Origins." *Mimosa* 23: 18–21. Accessed 24.08.2022. https://aniarasff.wordpress.com/archives/norwegian-fandom -origins/.

Lindholm, Audun. 2008. For aig veit existen af vorld. *Vagant.* Accessed 24.02.20201.

Lindholm, Audun. 2018a. Fra Algernon til Aardvark: norske science fiction fanziner på 1970-og 80 tallet. *fandom.se.*

Lindholm, Audun. 2018b. Fremtidslaboratoriet. Vagant 15.11.2018 https://www .vagant.no/fremtidslaboratoriet

Lionnet, Françoise & Shu-mei Shih. 2005. *Minor Transnationalism.* Durham: Duke UP.

Lunde, Maja. 2018. *The End of the Ocean.* New York: HarperCollins.

Maurits, Peter J. 2020. "Legacies of Marxism? Contemporary African Science Fiction and the Concern With Literary Realism." *African Identities* 18 (1–2): 64–79.

Mignolo, Walter D. & Catherine E. Walsh. 2018. *On Decoloniality: Concepts, Analytics, Praxis.* Durham: Duke UP.

Neyrat, Frédéric. 2020. "The black angel of history." *Angelaki: journal of theoretical humanities* 25 (4):120–134.

Norheim, Thorstein.2011. "Inne i fiktive verdner» - Allegori og dystopi: Thure Erik Lunds Inn (2006) og «critical dystopia." *Edda* 98 (2): 143–156.

Omelsky, Matthew.2014. "After the End Times: Postcrisis African Science Fiction." *Cambridge Journal of Postcolonial Literary Inquiry* 1 (1): 33–49.

Omdal, Gerd Karin.2010. *Grenseerfaringer.* Bergen:Fagbokforlaget

Osinubi, Taiwo Adetunji. 2009. "Cognition's warp: African films on near-future risk." *African Identities* 7 (2): 255–274.

Otto, Eric C. 2012. *Green Speculations. Science Fiction and Transformative Environmentalism.* Columbus: Ohio State UP.

Quayson, Ato. Irele,Abiola. 2009. "Magical realism and the African novel." In *The Cambridge Companion to the African Novel*, edited by F. Abiola Irele, 159–176. Cambridge: Cambridge University Press.

Raipola, Juha. 2019. "What is Speculative Climate Fiction?" *Fafnir – Nordic Journal of Science Fiction and Fantasy Research* 6 (2): 7–10.

Serrano, Andrea. 2020. "The Rise of the Afrofuturistic Novel: A Study of the Intersection of Science Fiction and African Environmentalism in Nnedi Okorafor's 'Lagoon' (2014)." Grau en Estudis d'Anglès i Espanyol, Facultat de Filosofia i, Lletres, Universitat Autònoma de Barcelona.

Steinskog, Erik. 2018. *Afrofuturism and Black Sound Studies: Culture, Technology, and Things to Come.* Cham: Springer International Publishing: Imprint: Palgrave Macmillan.

Spivak, Gayatri Chakravorty. 2003. *Death of a Discipline. Wellek Library Lecture Series at the University of California, Irvine.* New York: Columbia UP.

Terian, Andrei. 2021. "Neoextractivism, or the Birth of Magical Realism as World Literature." *Textual Practice* 35 (3): 485–503.

Toliver, S. R. 2022. *Recovering black storytelling in qualitative research: endarkened storywork.* Abingdon, Oxon, New York, NY: Routledge.

Wallace, Belinda Deneen, and Jesse W. Schwartz. 2022. "Afrofuturism: Race, Erasure, and COVID." *Radical Teacher (Cambridge)* 122 (122):1–12.

Walters, Wendy W. 2022. "Time in Afrofuturism, Classroom Time, and Carceral Time." *Radical teacher (Cambridge)* 122 (122):13–20.

Wood, Nick. 2015.Academia and the Advance of African Science Fiction - omenana .com. *Omeana.* Accessed 22.06.2021.

Womack, Ytasha. 2013. *Afrofuturism: The World of Black Sci-Fi and Fantasy Culture.* First edition. Chicago: Chicago Review Press.

Yaeger, Patricia. 2011. "Editor's Column: Literature in the Ages of Wood, Tallow, Coal, Whale Oil, Gasoline, Atomic Power, and Other Energy Sources." *PMLA: Publications of the Modern Language Association of America* 126 (2): 305–326.

Yaszek, Lisa.2006. "Afrofuturism, Science Fiction, and the History of the Future." *Socialism and Democracy* 20 (3): 41–60. https://doi.org/10.1080 /08854300600950236.

Yaszek, Lisa. 2013. "Paradoxa: Afro SF." *Paradoxa* 25 (1): 47–64.

Zvomuya, Percy. 2015.Science Fiction & Blackness: A Conversation With Raimi Gbadamosi On African Futures. Accessed 22.06.2021.

12

THE SEA AS A SITE OF CONTACT

A Hydrocolonial Reading of *Beforeigners*

Ruth S. Wenske

The Norwegian TV show *Beforeigners,* created by the veteran writing duo Eilif Skodvin and Anne Bjørnstad and produced by Rubicon TV AS for HBO Nordic, was an instant success when it was aired in 2019.[1] Set in Oslo, the show unfolds as time travellers from three distinct periods — the Stone Sge, the Viking period, and the nineteenth century — appear in the ocean in flashes of blue light, evoking contemporary scenes of migrants being pulled out of the Mediterranean sea, which have become an emblematic image of the current migration crisis in Europe (Guesmi 2017). *Beforeigners* is driven by a crime plot that unfolds against an imaginary future, in which a major concern is the integration of the involuntary time-migrants into society. The original Norwegian title *Fremvandrerne* ("forward-migrants") is a pun on the Norwegian word "innvandrere" (immigrants), and the creators have stated that the show and its "multitemporal" world are "an allegory of the refugee crisis and migration issues" (Pham 2019). This allegorical level constitutes the show's explicit engagement with contemporary social concerns, while also providing comic relief, as it plays on well-known tropes in current debates about migration, racism, and political correctness. For instance, it coins the terms "timesism" ("tidsisme" in Norwegian) as the temporal parallel to racism and humorously claims the word Viking – the "V-word" – as a derogatory term for people of Norse descent. And while carriages, cavemen, and goats peacefully roam the futuristic streets of Oslo, there is also hate-graffiti that reads "Beforeigners go home" and "Norway for present-day people,"[2] countered with the time-migrants' own slogan, "We were here first."

DOI: 10.4324/9781003561101-17

At the same time, *Beforeigners* is itself not free of race-inflected biases: its allegorical structure equates migrants with people from the past, thereby unwittingly perpetuating the stereotype of the global South – where most current migration comes from – as home to ossified societies that are "ancient" and "anti-modern" (cf. Gilroy 1993, 57, 74, 191). Moreover, the only non-white character in the show's first season is a sidekick in a criminal gang, and the Viking characters are all "pale and blonde" (Sibeko 2019, 52), even though there is some evidence to support, through DNA testing, that most Viking groups were diverse and with significantly darker hair than the majority of present-day Scandinavians (Margaryan et al. 2020). Taking *Beforeigners's* conflicted engagement with questions of migration and multi-culturalism as its point of departure, this chapter explores how the show fits within a larger framework of reckoning with colonial aftermaths through speculative fiction and traces how the *ocean* functions as an interpretive lens on *Beforeigners's* engagement with the socio-political issues it sets out to allegorise.

Hydrocolonialism and Hydroimperialism

The chapter's main framework of analysis is the recently introduced term *hydrocolonialism* (Bystrom & Hofmeyr 2017), which – like its precursor *hydroimperialism* – connotes the "fundamental connection between water, its management, and the colonial or neocolonial relations in the modern era" (Pritchard 2012, 591). Hydrocolonialism illuminates the historical and imaginative role of oceans in current world systems and, consequently, the critical purchase of the oceanic turn in cultural studies: "Just as *postcolonial* aims to understand a world shaped by European empires and their after-maths, so *hydrocolonialism* signals a commitment to understanding a world indelibly shaped by imperial uses of water" (Hofmeyr 2019, 13, emphasis in original). A recent special issue of *Interventions* (2022) explains hydrocolo-nialism's prism of "reading for water" (Hofmeyr, Nuttall, & Lavery 2022) as a "method that follows the sensory, political and agentive power of water across literary texts" (303). As Sarah Nuttall writes:

> water has been vividly and imaginatively rendered in fiction, not least the ways in which it inhabits our sense of memory and time, and itself gener-ates forms of feeling, knowing, and inhabiting both deep and future time that are colonising, decolonising, and full of fears and fantasies and the growing realities, too, of wet submergence.
>
> *(Nuttall 2021, 19)*

A focus on water is particularly salient in the current moment, when artistic and scholarly works seek to conceptualise links between oceanic slave trade and the Anthropocene (cf. Baucom 2020, 73–109, and the artistic works of Nyani Quarmyne and Jason DeCaires Taylor). In this context, hydrocolonialism takes bodies of water as elements that "routinely mediates [*sic*] between surface and depth, centre and periphery" (Bethlehem 2022, 343). Emblematised in the way the time-migrating "beforeigners" are being pulled out of the sea, much like migrants being pulled out of the Mediterranean, "reading for water" ties the current migration crisis to Norway's imperial and colonial past and the past's implications for the present/future.

By tracing the myriad and often unconscious connotations that the *ocean* evokes, I suggest that it becomes a mythological, haunting, liminal space that segues between past and present, time and place, enchantment, and disenchantment, as well as Norway and the world. I further suggest that on a narrative level, these intersections play out in the tension between form and content, and specifically what is known and unknown within the plot. Central in this regard is *Beforeigners's* speculative framework, and its dissemination through HBO, which allows it to interpolate mythologies – both folkloric and historical – that situate Norway within a global framework of references.[3] As Stephen Joyce (2021) notes in his analysis of *Beforeigners* (2021), the series's production by HBO allows for more elaborate (and expensive) worldbuilding than previous state-funded Scandinavian TV shows. According to Joyce, the series imbues the genre of Nordic Noir – Scandinavian crime fiction that has become hugely popular both in print and on screen (Koistinen & Mäntymäki 2020) – with fantastical elements from Norse mythology, creating a combination of sci-fi, fantasy, and crime that he terms "New Nordic Magic." Part of a larger trend in Scandinavian television discussed in a 2021 special issue of *Kosmorama*, "New Nordic Magic" functions to "re-enchant the Nordic everyday" (Joyce 2021), drawing on specific Nordic sensibilities in order to cater to global tastes. While building on Joyce's valuable insights into how *Beforeigners* navigates Scandinavia's embeddedness in metropolitan cultural production,[4] this chapter focuses on an aspect of Norway's global positionality that Joyce leaves unexplored: the way in which the sea implicitly sets up the Global South – and specifically the black Atlantic (Gilroy 1993) – as frames of reference for the show's engagement with referential history.

Beforeigners's main plotline revolves around the detective duo Lars Haaland (Nicolai Cleve Broch) and Alfhildr Enginsdottir (Krista Kosonen) – Oslo's first Viking police officer – who are paired to solve the murder case of a beforeigner woman whose body is washed ashore.[5] Joyce (2021) argues that the series's crime plot "encourages its audience to act like detectives, scanning the screen for clues and finding the world-building details," thus emphasising how its fantastical framework functions in tandem with its crime plot. Joyce uses Mittell's (2015) term "drillability" to describe how the series's forensic sensibility invites viewers "to dig deeper, probing beneath the surface to understand the complexity of a story and its telling" (Mittell 2015, 292). "Reading for water" extends this framework of analysis, as *Beforeigners*'s drillability moves beyond its worldbuilding clues and many humorous cultural references, foregrounding the ocean itself as a metaphoric space of archaeological depth and mystery, which is best understood through implicit references that need to be "drilled." Put differently, the show's "drillability" invites a reading that recognises the show's many oceanic references as clues to its engagement with Norway's embeddedness in oceanic world systems.

The framework of hydrocolonialism further draws on scholarship about the entwinement of speculative fiction (SF) with colonial histories and aftermaths. As John Rieder (2008) notes, colonialism was a ubiquitous frame of reference for science fiction from its inception in the nineteenth century, informing central tropes such as the alien invasion and the interlinkage of technology and conquest. Thus, "reading for water" also entails asking how *Beforeigners* "lives and breathes in the atmosphere of colonial history and its discourses" by "attempting to decipher the fiction's often distorted and topsy-turvy references to colonialism" (Rieder 2008, 3). Noting the latent aspects of the show's engagement with colonialism, and following recent interventions on the "unconscious" (see Bould's "Anthropocene unconscious" or Spain's "infrastructural unconscious" 2021), I suggest thinking of the show's engagement with the ocean as a "hydrocolonial unconscious." This has both historical and imaginative aspects, as the sea is the physical space of transporting people (in the show from past to present; otherwise from place to place), while also becoming a nexus through which various mythological narratives come together. This is not to say that the interconnection between migration and colonialism is an explicit theme on the show nor that migration is directly portrayed as an effect of colonial aftermaths. Instead, the significance of the sea in *Beforeigners* is most potent in gaps and silences, which embed hydrocolonialism as an undercurrent to the show's overt engagement with migration, much like slavery and colonialism itself remain a largely silenced part of Norway's history.

Norway's hydroimperial and hydrocolonial past

There is a widespread self-conception in Norway "that they were mere bystanders to European colonialism and slavery and are largely unscathed by racial worldviews" (McEachrane 2014, 1) and that the country has "no colonial history ... [since] Norway itself was subjected to colony-like relations [by Denmark]" (Bertlesen 2015, 1). Yet there is increasing awareness of Norway's layered history of imperial and colonial activity, which is inextricably linked to the sea. For instance, based on a large-scale research project on Norway's colonial history, Kjerland and Bertelsen argue that there is a

Crucial maritime aspect to these colonial ventures – a material dimension that concretizes the *flows* that characterized the colonial order. Geographically Norway has a long coastline, and historically it has been characterized by an expansive commercial and entrepreneurial seafaring orientation. Thus, in the era of white sails Norway was the third-largest nation globally in terms of tonnage in 1878, outranked only by the United States and the United Kingdom.

(Kjerland & Bertelsen 2015, 2, emphasis in original)

While Kjerland and Bertelsen (2015) focus on Norway's commercially driven colonial activities across Africa, Asia, and the Americas between 1850 and 1950, there is also increasing awareness of Norway's active participation in the trans-Atlantic slave trade in the seventeenth and eighteenth centuries. In the past, Denmark was seen as a major force in Scandinavian slave trade (Svalesen 1996), since Norway was effectively under Danish rule – the union now known as Denmark–Norway – from 1380 to 1814. Yet more recent scholarship shows that Norwegians were active partners in the triangle trade that connected Denmark and Norway with its slave forts on the West African coast and its Caribbean colonies in "Danish West India," the islands of St. Croix, St. Thomas, and St. Jan (cf. Løken 2020; for an overview of sources, see Hervik 2021). Hydroimperialsm and hydrocolonialism were thus two formative elements in Norway's maritime past, and the country's development into a modern nation (Andenæs 2021), much as slave trade was crucial for global industrialisation and modernisation (Gilroy 1993, 17).

Beforeigners's engagement with Norway's hydroimperial past is foregrounded by the centrality of the Viking era, arguably Norway's first – and certainly most famous – epoch of sea-bound conquests: "in the expansion of the Norwegian 'imperialism' in the mediaeval period of the Vikings, the likely half million inhabitants in Norway built colonies around the North Sea, in Iceland, in Greenland and in America" (Thorvaldsen & Østrem 2018, 238–39). On the show, the Vikings play a central part in the plot due to the protagonist detective Anfhildr, who was a shieldmaiden for the great warrior Tore Hund in the eleventh century. As a parallel plotline to the crime investigation, Alfhildr finds and reunites with Tore Hund, who had lost his memory when time-migrating. Portrayed as short flashbacks to the Viking past, Tore slowly regains an important memory at the end of the first season: he, along with a crew of Vikings, found Alfhildr at sea when they were returning from a raid (Season 1, Episode 6, 38:18). The flashback, set on a Viking battleship, culminates when the warriors notice a child floating in the sea, unusual due to her orange floating vest and modern garments. They fish her out in a gesture that foreshadows how the beforeigners – like migrants arriving in Europe by way of the Mediterranean – will be hauled out of the sea in the future. Through this memory, Alfhildr and Tore (and, implicitly, we) understand that Alfhildr is a child from the present/future who migrated *back* to the Viking era before returning to the future as an adult, showing that "time is not a one-way street, as government would like us to believe" (Season 1, Episode 6, 40:39) – a theme that sets the tone for the second season. The scene's centrality, and its foregrounding of Viking seafaring, illuminates the imaginative sway that the ocean – as a site of conquest and nation formation – holds in Norway.

Excavating a Hidden Hydrocolonial Past

Beforeigners's choice of location further relates to Norway's hydrocolonial history, but to a more recent epoch. In the show's opening scenes, the first beforeigners appear in the waters outside Oslo's iconic new opera house, which was opened in 2008 (Figure 12.1).

Located on the seashore, the opera house lies in a central area called Bjørvika, which has been a hub of urban development since the early 2000s, becoming a commercial and cultural centre associated with ultramodern urban architecture. Much of the show is set in Bjørvika's Barcode neighbourhood, a row of high-rises just behind the opera building, where detective Lars Haaland and his wife buy an apartment just seconds before the first time-migrants arrive in the sea, in a time/world that seems like our present in the twenty-first century, albeit without any mention of exact dates. The proximity to the sea allows Lars to be the first respondent on the scene, but it also becomes a liability when the beforeigners' continuous landings cause power failures in the area. Jumping to the future when the show is set – some 20 years after the first arrivals – Barcode has become a slum largely inhabited by people from the past, its ultramodern streets a mayhem of periodically dressed time-migrants and their relics. The contrast between the

FIGURE 12.1   Oslo Opera House (Ghirlandajo: Wikicommons, 2015)

area's architecture and the time travellers allows for an aesthetically potent contrast between the ancient and the modern (Figure 12.2).

At the same time, the area has a history – a hidden layer, quite literally – that is never mentioned on the show. The intensive constructions in Bjørvika led to some of Norway's most extensive archaeological finds, uncovering more than 60 shipwrecks, wharf constructions, and artefacts dated from the fifteenth century onwards, when Bjørvika served as Oslo's harbour (Vangstad 2011). In Barcode alone, 13 shipwrecks from the sixteenth and seventeenth centuries were excavated in 2008–2009, following the construction of the neighbourhood, and boats and structures from the eighteenth and nineteenth centuries were found in areas close by (Vangstad 2011, 137).

Even though Oslo (previously Christiania) was a secondary harbour to Bergen, and though there is no direct evidence linking these ships to slave trade, Norway's seafaring activities from the sixteenth through the twentieth century were inextricably linked to industrialisation and the burgeoning world order of capitalism, which relied on the trade of slaves and colonial goods (Løken 2020; Andenæs 2021). In addition to colonial trade, the nineteenth century also marked other important changes: Christiania became Norway's capital in 1814 and consequently experienced rapid urban growth. At the same time, mass migration from Norway to North America saw over 30% of the country's population leaving by sea to the new world, freeing up resources and land in Norway by effectively taking over lands of other native populations.[6] These changes meant that Oslo's modernisation was entirely dependent on its oceanic seascapes, as a site of both trade and travel that linked to colonial expansion.

Beforeigners is thus set in an area that is central to Norway's hydrocolonial history. To use Bethlehem's (2022, 344) beautiful description, this history can be equated to water, "mov[ing] between tiers, sometimes rising from the depths, sometimes sinking into the earth," thereby "generat[ing] powerful imaginaries that leak into the [city's] written and visual cultural

FIGURE 12.2 Oslo's Barcode area (Holmstad: Wikicommons, 2014)

representations." If the basic premise of the show is that Norway's history, embodied by the beforeigners, emerges from the past by surfacing in the sea, the Barcode neighbourhood becomes a literalisation of the metaphor (Rushdie 1991, 77). Put differently, Bjørvika is a place where Norway's maritime history has been submerged for centuries under layers of water and soil, only to re-emergence through modern development projects that seek to tame the seashore. The modern is thus literally constructed on the ruins of the past. As such, ironically, *Beforeigners's* basic premise of drawing parallels between Norway's past and current immigration discourses actually highlights the extent to which past and present in Norway are disconnected.

The View from above and the View from below

Much as Bjørvika's maritime history was paradoxically revealed – but also overshadowed – by Oslo's intensive urban expansion, so *Beforeigners's* mode of representing Barcode both reveals and obscures how the ocean relates to the pasts that the show excavates. The show's opening scenes have multiple panoramic shots of the Opera House and the Barcode blocks, including the view from Lars's Barcode apartment (Season 1, Episode 1, 01:22). This panoramic view of the Oslo fjord, filmed at night, creates a juxtaposition similar to what David Pike (2005, 8) calls "the view from above and the view from below": a contrast between the tall modern buildings and the deep dark sea. The binary of above/below is further emphasised by the show's opening footage, which starts with a long shot of the dark sea, then slowly moves upwards to the Opera House and seashore (Season 1, Episode 1, 0:15), as well as the repeated underwater shots of beforeigners' arrivals – human figures and gurgling bubbles – that serve as all the episodes' opening and transitional scenes.

Pike (2005, 1) considers the juxtaposition of "above and below" on land, in reference to subterranean urban spaces such as "drainage systems, underground railways, utility tunnels, and storage vaults," which have both material and imaginative functions in the modern city. Likewise, the juxtaposition between the Oslo fjord and Barcode contrasts *sea and surface* through a series of oppositions that are both physical and symbolic: between depth and height, past and present, known and unknown, as well as the visible with what remains hidden: the foundations of the old harbour that used to lie (and parts of which may still lie) right under Barcode's pavement. While Barcode's past as a harbour is a latent layer that needs to be "drilled" in order to be discovered, much like the archaeological excavations that revealed it, the show's second season sets up an explicit parallel between the sea and the underground, as the murder investigation moves from the sea to the subterranean city, and Oslo's subway becomes the primary location of the unfolding crime plot. In the first season, a woman's body washes ashore, murdered by a criminal network that "fishes" newly arrived beforeigner women out of the sea in order to use them as sex workers. In the second season, a mutilated body is found in a subway tunnel, the first in a series of murders by a fictionalised time-travelling Jack the Ripper.

This juxtaposition between the sea and the subway is further developed in the second season's climax: when Alfhildr fights Jack the Ripper in a subway tunnel, they create a space–time rupture that sends them into a dystopian parallel universe (Season 2, Episode 6, 45:00), where the second season's last chapter takes place. In the final fight scene between Alfhildr and Jack the Ripper, she finds him fishing on the Oslo wharf (Season 2, Episode 6, 33:55). The scene takes place on Aker brygge, Oslo's modern ferry quay and commercial centre (also the location where the body washes ashore in the first season) and is shot with the *Akershus fortress* in the background, a sixteenth-century military fort that separates Bjørvika from Aker brygge. Much like Barcode, the visual encoding of Aker brygge contrasts the ultramodern with the historic, showing how the sea brings the two realms together. Parallelly, the plot juxtaposes the "underworlds" of the sea and the city: as Alfhildr attacks Jack on the seashore, the two time-space continuums merge, and they fight simultaneously on the quay and in the subway tunnel.

This sets up a parallel between the ocean and subterranean urban spaces, in line with Bethlehem's (2022) convincing argument that underground infrastructures (she takes the sewers and mines of Johannesburg as an example) are continuous with the ocean in their evocation of hydrocolonial histories. The links between tunnels and oceans are not limited to their common "belowness" but, as Bethlehem shows, are tied to historical connections between industrialisation, urbanisation, and colonialism. While Oslo's colonial past is less apparent than that of Johannesburg, Oslo's many tunnels and subterranean spaces were also initially constructed in the nineteenth century, in the heyday of modern colonial seafaring, thus evoking the city's latent hydrocolonial history.

The "Magical" Vikings

Furthermore, the juxtaposition of subway and sea foregrounds the imaginative sway of maritime and urban "underworlds" as mythological spaces. As Pike (2005) explains, subterranean cities are associated both with evil – the underworld of the dead, legendary beasts, and even Satan himself (8–9) – and with "the more mythic or metaphorically underground spaces of poverty and crime" (11). These two interlaced aspects of the underworld come together in the first season, as a sex trafficking ring kidnaps beforeigners as they emerge in the sea, thereby evoking histories of gender violence entangled with imperial conquest, including the practice of kidnapping women from Viking landing places around Europe. The juxtaposition of the Transatlantic slave trade and European ancient slavery gestures towards the mythological aspects of these histories, in the sense of both historical mythologies and cosmological mythologies.

Firstly, when Lars and Alfhildr interview recent arrivals who might have known the murdered woman, a recently arrived Viking woman claims that she saw the murdered woman in the ocean and that the Norse sea monster Hafgufa had taken her (Season 1, Episode 1, 23:47). A debate ensues between Alfhildr, who wants to explore the Hafgufa theory, and Lars, who believes it to be utter nonsense. Alfhildr does some research and finds that "[t]he web is full of people who've seen strange things in the ocean" (Season 1, Episode 1, 29:09), supporting her belief in the possibility of a monster. As a prank to ridicule Alfhildr's beliefs, Lars lets her present the theory to the full police team. As expected, the team mocks the sea monster theory, stating that "we should stick to the scientific world view of our time" (Season 1, Episode 1, 34:41). Yet later – under the influence of the "temproxate" drug – Lars realises that the face composite looks like a fishing trawl, thereby prompting them to investigate sea-based criminal activity and solving the murder case.

Even though the Hafgufa theory is refuted, Alfhildr's belief in it is instrumental for the plots unfolding. It is thus part of the larger framework of "New Nordic Magic," in which Vikings and their Norse faith (Åsatro) infuse the show with magical elements that serve to "re-enchant the everyday" (Joyce 2021). A recurring trope of Viking religious practice in the series is shamans who cryptically but accurately predict the future, for instance when an eleventh-century shaman describes the futuristic Oslo to Alfhildr: "I see a place where the cities shine like stars, where the houses are as tall as mountains, and words can travel with the wind" (Season 1, Episode 2, 03:36). Further on, there are more explicit magical interventions, when Lars – first under the influence of drugs, later when sober – encounters paranormal persons from the Viking era who help him solve the murder cases: first a mysterious priest of Odin who turns out to be dead (Season 1, Episode 6, 40:20), then the Norse god Odin themself (c.f. Season 2, Episode 3, 31:30). As Joyce (2021) has it, "Norse history and mythology thus offers the storyworld a deep background that still fits within the fantasy genre [and] ... allows the world to feel immersive yet internally consistent." Yet in the context of the show's other evocations of hydrocolonial pasts, the ocean – and not just Norse mythology – offers an interpretive framework for understanding the show's negotiation of enchantment.

The association between the sea and the supernatural is evoked by the Hafgufa theory, by the sea as an "underworld" and by the arrival of the "magic" Vikings through the sea, even if the Vikings are only magic insofar as their uncanny presence is portrayed as being close to an urkraft based on Norse mythology. As such, the presence of the paranormal – combined with the show's portrayal of migrants being pulled out of the sea – illuminates the mythological role of the ocean in narratives of migration and colonialism. As Guesmi (2017) notes, the Mediterranean has become the emblematic site of twenty-first-century migration trauma due to the images of "bodies brown and black, declared dead or missing in its waters." This imaginary can hardly be understood outside of the context of the Middle Passage, which has made the "black Atlantic" (Gilroy 1993) an *urmetaphor* of the sea as a site of trauma and of human trafficking (Murphy 2012, 41). Much like Joyce's (2021) claims that "Vikings are both historical and mythical," Mbembe (2002, 259) describes the potency of the ocean as both historical and supernatural: "slavery is experienced as a wound whose meaning belongs to the domain of the unconscious – in a word, witchcraft." In literatures of African and African diasporic authors, the underworld of the ocean thus often takes on mythological meaning, combining supernatural phenomena with renditions of slavery and its aftermaths. I suggest that this significance, a crossover between historical and spiritual mythologies, is a form of a hydrocolonial unconscious and, as such, also offers an interpretive framework for the use of mythologies in *Beforeigners*.

The parallels between the time-migrants and the black Atlantic are subtle but significant. For one, slavery is evoked through the sea-based sex trafficking ring, which is a form of modern slavery. Secondly, the show explicitly thematises memory loss as parallel to the erasure of the past (see the next section), thereby evoking the haunting liminality of slavery within the capitalist world order. Thirdly, the Vikings echo the hydrocolonial networks of the black Atlantic in two ways: (1) they were the first Europeans to reach the Americas in their imperial seafaring networks and (2) their magical qualities – from a contemporary perspective – resonate an association between spirituality and indigenous cultures (Baker 2009, 11), even if this association is based on a stereotypical association of migrants, and indigeneity, with cultures of enchantment. This is most evident in the interventions of Odin and their priest, who mysteriously provide Lars with knowledge of otherwise-unknowable details in the murder cases, allowing him to solve them. Their supernatural assistance recalls the trope of the "magical Negro" (Glenn & Cunningham 2009, 138) that is widespread in American films: "the magical, mystical Negroes generally appear in the form of a spirit or angel [and] use their powers to help the White characters" (138). While the parallels between Odin (who is a god) and the "magical Negro" (who is a two-dimensional character) hardly capture the racism of the latter, both function, on a narrative level, to propel the story forward by playing on clichés. The use of "magical Vikings" likewise falls prey to stereotypical narratives: by equating migrants (here also: black people) with Vikings, it sets up a binary that likens the Global South to Europe's past and that evokes an image of the barbaric "other" and sets up a binary where *enchantment* is associated with the past/black cultures/Global South, and *scientific rationalism* is associated with the present/white Norway/the /Global North.

Consequently, other temporal and spatial hierarchies on the show put the modern-day white man on top, mirroring the basic premise of coloniality and racism rather than deflecting it. By replicating the mechanisms of classification that buttress coloniality and racism, the show reveals not only current manifestations of coloniality but also the submerged mechanisms that allow it to operate, both in the past and in the modern age.

Nevertheless, as I claimed at the beginning of this chapter, the fact that *Beforeigners* maintains certain racial biases does not diminish its engagement with the hydrocolonial. Quite the contrary, it merely shows how influential the narratives of hydrocolonialism are in the Norwegian context, even when not explicitly (or, as far as we know, consciously) addressed. The function of these parallels is therefore to illuminate Norway's embeddedness in histories and narratives that have a global span. The Vikings have a double function in this regard: for one, they evoke a specifically Scandinavian brand of magic, which is "indebted to indigenous myth and folklore" (Adejunmobi 2016, 267), much like SF from the Global South. Yet these magical elements also draw on historical mythologies of the black Atlantic and the trope of the "magical Negro." Put differently, *Beforeigners* demonstrates how the black Atlantic resonates with Norwegian sensibilities because of their common hydrocolonial mythologies and the way these take on contemporary meanings through parallels with migration narratives. Through this, the Norse mythology shows how Scandinavia is always already part of processes that connected the world into a single, albeit uneven, system (Warwick Research Collective 2015).

Fictionality and the Interpretive Choice

Joyce (2021) reads the show's instances of enchantment as open ended, claiming that they allow "sceptical viewers to dismiss these magical elements if they wish" by "always offer[ing] the possibility that there is a scientific explanation" – for instance the possibility that Lars is hallucinating. Yet ultimately, what grants viewers an interpretive choice is the show's speculative framework: as "New Nordic Magic" is a new genre, interweaving the fantastical (such as the sea monster), the science-fictional (such as the fictional temproxate drug), the fictional (invented characters and events), and the factual (real histories). Since the balance between the four aspects of the show is not yet fully defined, the viewers are granted an interpretive choice regarding the ontological status of the show's worldbuilding and certain events. Notably, the traditional ontology of Åsatro is still, or again, practised by some, further blurring the boundaries between referential and fictional or fictional and science-fictional. The final section of this chapter explores how narrative choices in *Beforeigners* reflect its "hydrocolonial unconscious." Central in this regard is the withholding of certain details, while humorously juxtaposing what is (un)known in the plot and in the fictional storyworld.

Memory and knowing – especially what is forgotten or not known – is a recurring theme on the show. As one of many humorous juxtapositions with contemporary culture that can be found in the "details in the background" (Joyce 2021), there are posters that repeatedly appear in the background (cf. Season 1, Episode 1, 07:34; 27:22), which show beforeigners' faces – a nineteenth-century woman and a Viking man – that are half-fading. The Viking poster reads, in runic font and (ostensibly) Old Norse, "Hefir dū minni?," while the nineteenth-century poster uses the Norwegian equivalent "Har du minner?," meaning "Do you have memories?" These posters play on road safety signs that are common in Norway, where people's faces are likewise half blurred. These figureposters, also in black and white, read "over the speed limit?," the fading faces thus equating speed with death. By contrast, the posters on the show seem to be equating forgetting with death (or remembering with life?), as the semi-pixelated faces connote the memory loss that many beforeigners have suffered during time travel. Much like the "hydrocolonial unconscious" evoked by the Vikings scenes, the subway/sea parallels, and the location of Barcode, the posters point to the erasure of the past even while foregrounding its importance.

The tension between the known and the forgotten is likewise emphasised by a series of narrative choices that equate memory loss with details that remain unknown about time travel: much like the beforeigners themselves remember little about their migration process, there are few clues as to why and how people migrate. Media announcements are used to explicate that this ambiguity is part of the show's worldbuilding premise, for instance when a TV news broadcast announces that "the centre for memory registration" is closing because scientists cannot figure out how or why time travel takes place (Season 1, Episode 1, 27:27). Though in the second season, scientists in a top-secret supertemporal agency called "Project 19" have found a way to create artificial time travel (Season 2, Episode 6, 41:12), the show's basic premise remains that time travel is a hidden – albeit scientific rather than supernatural – phenomenon. The show thus challenges the line between science and what we call magic, between fact and belief, complexifying our conceptions of both.

The viewers – like the characters on the show – thus have to make sense of time travel without knowing its practical mechanisms: how and why it takes place. Because this knowledge is withheld from characters and viewers alike, it complicates the binary relation between "the world in which one tells [and] the world of which one tells" (Genette 1980, 236), creating metalepsis – slippages – between what is known and unknown in the fictional and real worlds. As if setting up the discourse as an "underworld" of the plot, this metalepsis functions to emphasise the significance of the show's latent layers.

A similar metalepsis is created by the show's ambiguous temporality: the year in which the plot unfolds is never mentioned, though based on the age of Haaland's daughter, we can infer that there is approximately a 20-year time gap between the first beforeigners' arrival (the opening scene) and the futuristic Oslo, where the series takes place. In line with Joyce's (2021) claim that the show is characterised by its setting in the mundane everyday, its fictional world seems much like the present-day Oslo, thereby blurring the line between the fictional and referential worlds. By making the show's setting inconspicuously everyday-like, its speculative premise allows its time travel to function much like narrativiation, as Wittenberg writes:

> [Narratives] set out to modify or manipulate the order, duration, and significance of events in time – that is, since all narratives do something like "travel" through time or construct "alternate" worlds – one could arguably call narrative itself a "time machine," which is to say, a mechanism for revising the arrangements of stories and histories.
>
> *(Wittenberg 2013, 2)*

Narrative time is foregrounded by the use of flashbacks, which are often fragmented, with loud sounds and elaborate costumes, which allows the inclusion of minimal details while creating an immersive effect. Alternately, flashbacks are only audible, for instance when Tore Hund picks up a life-jacket and hears the sounds of the Viking ship (Season 1, Episode 6, 46:58), thus using the audiovisual framework to underscore temporal playfulness and ambiguity. In this framework, the 20-year time leap mimics the premise of the show, allowing us – the viewers – to travel in time, much like the flashbacks to the Viking era do, thereby leaving us somehow dazed, not knowing where (or why) we have ended up. Since the show's premise is both fictional and fantastic, it may well be that the opening scene takes place in the past and that its "future" is in fact the present. This speculation is emphasised by the fictionalisation of Barcode: while there is repeated footage of the real Barcode, its hallmark buildings are a mirror image of the real Barcode and include a burnt-out building, giving viewers an interpretive choice regarding the extent of fictionalisation.

This fictionalisation foregrounds James Phelan's (2018, 113–114) premise that audiences have an "awareness not only that the characters and events are invented but also that they have been invented for some reason," which offers "the practical payoffs of relating those experiences to the actual world." In other words, foregrounding the constructedness of the story (the "discourse" in narratological terms) strengthens the awareness of the show's allegorical level, which – as I have argued – is equally tied to hydrocoloni-alism as to the current migration crisis. In this regard, another important yet unexplained narrative choice is the choice of *only* three time periods – the Stone Age, the Viking era, and the nineteenth century – which share common characteristics that tie seas and mythologies together and embed Norway in global hydrocolonial processes. For one, all three periods were characterised by migration, where people either settled Norway or left it, mostly through the sea (for the Stone Age, see Jørgensen 2020). Secondly, these were all periods of radical changes in worldviews – from hunter/gath-erers to permanent settlements, from pagans to Christians, and from a faith-based society to scientific empiricism. Finally, all the periods are intelligible to an international audience, either because Norway's history in that epoch is well known (the Vikings) or because it has continuities with the rest of Europe (the Stone Age and the nineteenth century).

Conclusion

Beforeigners offers its viewers multiple interpretive choices through its foregrounding of unknowability (both as a topic matter and as a narrative choice) and through its interpolation of Norwegian and global mytholo-gies –both spiritual and historical. The sea is the site where all this comes together; as the juxtaposition between sea and surface highlights the ten-sion between the latent and obvious parallels, the show draws between the current migration crisis and Norway's hydrocolonial past. These parallels are scaffolded both by the show's choice of location, the Barcode neigh-bourhood, which was built on the ruins of Oslo's old harbour, and through its representation of Vikings in reference to both historical and ontologi-cal mythologies. While *Beforeigners's* "hydrocolonial unconscious" seems to thematise Norway's seafaring past as a latent layer of the present, the show's speculative framework emphasises that the past is crucial for envi-sioning the future. The ocean, and water in general, are crucial resources in the era of the Anthropocene, and new oceanic exploitation – such as North Sea oil drilling –shows that social and environmental justice cru-cially depends on the use and management of water. A hydrocolonial per-spective to SF thus bridges historical narratives and future imaginaries, while demonstrating how the world remains connected through its oceanic routes.

Notes

1 It was nominated for the 2020 *Seriekritikerprisen* (the Norwegian Series Critics' Awards) and the 2020 *Gullruten* ("Gold Screen") in the categories Best Drama and Best Actress. Internationally, it received positive reviews from the *Chicago Tribune*, *Variety*, the *Indie Wire*, *Pajiba*, and more.

2 In the original, "Norge for nåtidsfolk." In quotes from the series, I use the translations from the subtitles. Otherwise, translations from Norwegian are mine.

3 When comparing these two forms of mythologies, I refer to (1) folkloric mythologies that Irele (2001: 236) describes as the "mythological registers" of literatures, connoting the amalgamation of folkloric (often oral) traditions, living religions, and narrative epistemologies, and (2) the historical and political mythologies that Barthes (1993) describes as the reification of events/concepts into simplified narratives with an ideological function.

4 Joyce focuses on the surge in Scandinavian fantasy film and television as part of the growing popularity of successful high-budget productions such as *Harry Potter* and *Lord of the Rings,* calling it a case of "glocalization," in the sense of infusing global genres with offering context.

5 I alternately use the terms "beforeigners" and "time migrants" to refer to individuals who have time travelled. In the subtitles, the series also uses the term "timeigrants" for the Norwegian *fremvandrere.*

6 Current estimates suggest that close to one million Norwegians left for North America (some also to Australia and New Zealand) between the 1860s and 1929 (Thorvaldsen & Østrem 2018). The mass migration was conductive in the development and urbanisation of those left behind, as it freed up land and resources: "Instead of dividing the land they owned in order to feed the entire household, they could travel across the ocean and grab the lands that melanin-rich people had been expelled from or massacred on" (Sibeko 2019, 53).

References

Adejunmobi, Moradewun. 2016. "Introduction: African Science Fiction." *Cambridge Journal of Postcolonial Literary Inquiry* 3 (3): 265–272.

Andenæs, Ulf. 2021. "Da Den Nye Verden Åpnet Seg." In *Tidsrom 1600–1914 Timescape,* 25–35. Oslo: Norsk Folkemuseum.

Baker, Geoffrey. 2009. *Realism's Empire: Empiricism and Enchantment in the Nineteenth-Century Novel.* Ohio: Ohio State UP.

Barthes, Roland. 1993/1957. *Mythologies.* Trans. Annette Lavers. London: Vintage.

Baucom, Ian. 2020. *History 4° Celsius: Search for a Method in the Age of the Anthropocene.* Durham: Duke UP.

Bethlehem, Louise. 2022. "Hydrocolonial Johannesburg." *Interventions* 24 (3): 340–354.

Bould, Mark. 2021. *The Anthropocene Unconscious: Climate Catastrophe Culture.* London: Verso.

Bystrom, Kerry & Isabel Hofmeyr. 2017. "Oceanic Routes: (Post-It) Notes on Hydro-colonialism." *Comparative Literature* 69 (1): 1–6.

Genette, Gérard. 1980. *Narrative Discourse.* Trans. Jane E. Lewin. Ithaka: Cornell UP.

Ghirlandajo. "File: Oslo Barcode.JPG." Photo. Wikicommons, 08.02.2015. https://commons.wikimedia.org/wiki/File:Oslo_Barcode.JPG. Accessed 1 March 2024.

Gilroy, Paul. 1993. *The Black Atlantic: Modernity and Double Consciousness.* London: Verso.

Glenn, Cerise L. & Landra J. Cunningham. 2009. "The Power of Black Magic: The Magical Negro and White Salvation in Film." *Journal of Black Studies* 40 (2): 135–152.

Guesmi, Haythem. 2017. "Next Time You See the Mediterranean." *Africa is a Country,* August 13. https://africasacountry.com/2017/08/next-time-you-see

-themediterranean?fbclid=IwAR013wXkZz5PFizNwY60zQMD6SF3e0oZl EEG9Ll95hCArgS-g5mwUTmmTRc. Accessed 1 March 2024.

Hervik, Anders. 2021. *Transatlantisk Slavehandel og Kolonialisme: En Undersøkelse av dens Plass i Norsk Historie og det Kollektive Minnet.* Bacheloroppgave. Trondheim: NTNU.

Hofmeyr, Isabel. 2019. "Provisional Notes on Hydrocolonialism." *English Language Notes* 57 (1): 11–20.

Hofmeyr, Isabel, Sarah Nuttall & Charne Lavery. 2022. "Reading for Water." *Interventions* 24 (3): 303–322.]

Holmstad, Øyvind. "File: Oslo Opera House Barcode Bakgrun 2014 2.JPG [SIC]." Photo. Wikicommons. 06.17.2014. https://commons.wikimedia.org /wiki/File:Oslo_Opera_House_Barcode_bakgrun_2014_2.JPG. Accessed 1 March 2024.

Irele, Abiola F. 2001. *The African Imagination: Africa and the Black Diaspora.* Oxford: Oxford UP.

Joyce, Stephen. 2021. "Re-Enchanting the Nordic Everyday in 'Beforeigners'." *Kosmorama*, February 24, 2021. https://www.kosmorama.org/kosmorama/ artikler/re-enchanting-nordic-Everyday-beforeigners. Accessed 1 March 2024.

Jørgensen, Erlend Kirkeng. 2020. *Maritime Human Ecodynamics of Stone Age Arctic Norway.* PhD Dissertation, Tromsø: The Arctic University of Norway.

Kjerland, Kirsten Alsaker & Bjørn Enge Bertelsen (eds.). 2015. *Navigating Colonial Orders: Norwegian Entrepreneurship in Africa and Oceania.* New York: Berghahn Books.

Koistinen, Aino-Kaisa & Helen Mäntymäki. 2020. "Affective Estrangement and Ecological Destruction in TV Crime Series Fortitude." In *Transnational Crime Fiction: Mobilities, Borders, and Detection*, eds. Maarit Piipponen, Helen Mäntymäki & Marinella Rodi-Risberg, 261–277. New York: Palgrave Macmillan.

Kosomora. 2021. "#279: Ny Nordisk Magi." *Kosmorama*, February 24. https:// www.kosmorama.org/kosmorama/artikler/279-ny-nordisk-magi. Accessed 1 March 2024.

Løken, Roar. 2020. *De Dansk–Norske Tropekoloniene – Sukker, Krydder, Slaver og Misjon.* Oslo: Solum Bokvennen.

Margaryan, Ashot et al. 2020. "Population Genomics of the Viking World." *Nature* 585 (7825): 390–396.

Mbembe, Achille. 2002. "African Modes of Self-Writing." Trans. Steven Rendall. *Public Culture* 14 (1): 239–273.

McEachrane, Michael. 2014. *Afro-Nordic Landscapes: Equality and Race in Northern Europe.* New York: Routledge.

Mittell, Jason. 2015. *Complex TV The Poetics of Contemporary Television Storytelling.* New York: New York UP.

Murphy, Laura T. 2012. *Metaphor and the Slave Trade in West African Literature.* Athens: Ohio UP.

Nuttall, Sarah. 2021. "The Time Sea." *Wasafiri* 36 (2): 13–21.

Pham, Annika. 2019. "'Beforeigners' Anne Bjørnstad on HBO's First Norwegian Original Series." *Variety*, August 23, 2019. https://variety.com/2019/film /festivals/beforeigners-anne-bjornstad-hbo-first-norwegian-original-series -1203310317/. Accessed 1 March 2024.

Phelan, James. 2018. "Fictionality, Audiences, and Character: A Rhetorical Alternative to Catherine Gallagher's 'Rise of Fictionality.'" *Poetics Today* 39 (1): 113–129.

Pike, David L. 2005. *Subterranean Cities: The World Beneath Paris and London, 1800–1945.* Ithaka: Cornell UP.

Pritchard, Sara B. 2012. "From Hydroimperialism to Hydrocapitalism: 'French' Hydraulics in France, North Africa, and Beyond." *Social Studies in Science* 42 (4): 591–615.

Rieder, John. 2008. *Colonialism and the Emergence of Science Fiction.* Middletown: Wesleyan UP.

Rushdie, Salman. 1991. *Imaginary Homelands: Essays and Criticism 1981–1991.* London: Granta Books.

Sibeko, Guro Jabulisile. 2019. *Rasismens Poetikk.* Oslo: Ordatoriet.

Spain, Andrea. 2017. "Shining Girls and Forgotten Men in Lauren Beukes' Urban 'America.'" *Safundi* 18 (3): 258–278.

Svalesen, Leif. 1996. *Slaveskipet Fredensborg og den Dansk-Norske Slavehandel på 1700-Tallet.* Oslo: Cappelen.

Thorvaldsen, Gunnar & Nils Olav Østrem. 2018. "Migration and the Historical Population Register of Norway." *Journal of Migration History* 4.2: 237–248.

Vangstad, Hilde. 2011. "De Siste Års Arkeologiske Funn i Bjørvika fra Perioden 1570 Til 2000 – Lange Linjer, Flyktige Episoder." In *1537 – Kontinuitet eller Brudd?*, eds. Tor Einar Fagerland & Knut Paasche, 135–151. Trondheim: Tapir Akademisk forlag.

Warwick Research Collective. 2015. *Combined and Uneven Development: Towards a New Theory of World-Literature.* Liverpool: Liverpool UP.

13

LIVING IN SPACE(S) WITHOUT A FUTURE

Depictions of Mental Illness in *Aniara*

Josefine Wälivaara

The Swedish science fiction film *Aniara* (2018, directed by Pella Kågerman and Hugo Lilja) is a story about human despair and distress. In the film, humans are forced to leave Earth due to the devastation of the natural environment. Shortly after its departure, the spaceship Aniara – bound to take its passengers to a new life on Mars – is knocked off course. Unable to control the ship, the crew and passengers are forced to spend the rest of their lives on the ship as it drifts further and further away from Earth and into the vast darkness of outer space. The film is permeated by a sense of growing despair, and the distress and eventual demise of the characters lie at the centre of the narrative. It follows the protagonist Mimaroben (Emelie Jonsson) and her ultimately futile struggle to retain a sense of hope for others and herself when the people around her have lost the will to live. One film reviewer has remarked that "this is a movie that simulates the experience of losing the will to live, a daunting premise even for the bravest voyagers" (Bugbee 2019). *Aniara*, possibly derived from the Greek word *aniaros* (ἀνιαρός), meaning "in distress" (Klass & Sjöberg 1999, 151), is thus a fitting name for the ship.

This chapter explores the central theme of distress in *Aniara* by analysing how the film depicts mental illness. It traces how the growing feeling of despair onboard the ship – which leads to mental illness, expressed primarily as anxiety, depression, and eventually suicide – is related to space and time. Representations of mental illness often (re)produce misconceived stereotypes and contribute to an Othering of people with mental illness (Heath 2019; Pugh 2022). Throughout this chapter, I argue that the connection between space-time and the characters' mental state serves to avoid such

DOI: 10.4324/9781003561101-18

Othering.[1] Instead, the film depicts despair, distress, and mental illness as intrinsic parts of being human.

Othering of Mental Illness

Cultural representations of mental illness often (re)produce stereotypes and misconceptions of such conditions and those who experience them. For example, certain frequently used stereotypes in cinema reinforce the belief that people with mental illness are dangerous. Another misguided belief is that they themselves are to blame for the onset of their condition and are similarly responsible for ending it (Heath 2019, 2). Hollywood films, for example, continuously depict people with mental illness as "crazy people that cinema confines, pities, and kills" (Heath 2019, 86). Mental illness is often conflated with madness in textual representation. However, "[m]adness lacks the complexity and individuality of mental illness, instead embodying a far more explosive, erratic, and dramatic set of behaviours" (Pugh 2022, 131). These representations feed into an Othering of people with mental illness (cf. Heath 2019, 5–6; Pugh 2022, 132). The separation of groups of people into "us" and "them" also serves as a central component of stigma (Rüsch, Angermeyer, & Corrigan, 2005, 30).

While textual representations are, by no means, the only source of Othering of mental illness, they constitute a potent site for the (re)production of ableist beliefs. Ableism is dependent on "[a] *constitutional divide* – a division enforced between the 'normal' = human and the aberrant (and sometimes pathological) = subhuman" (Campbell 2012, 215). What is at stake here is not only how certain groups are Othered but also how such divides dehumanise them. In speculative fiction, dehumanisation can take on literal forms. Characters can, not only symbolically or metaphorically, be made into monsters or sub-humans. One common way of representing disability in science fiction is to use "disability as a defining quality of the non-human" (Allan 2014, paragraph 10.1). In her discussion of the horror genre, Catherine Pugh asserts that

> the non-normative (mentally-ill) mind is twisted into madness with an equal expectation of deviance as the non-normative (disabled) body is transformed into a monster […]. Mad characters not only become representatives of the mentally ill, but also of the monstrous; the excessive nature of madness mutates mental illness into monstrosity.
>
> *(Pugh 2022, 132)*

My analysis shows that *Aniara,* in contrast, does not depict its characters as mad by pathologising them as "crazy" or "insane." The characters in the film are not blamed for their condition, nor are they depicted as dangerous, erratic, or monstrous. Instead, the film portrays a world and context of distress to which the only possible human response is despair. Mental illness is thus depicted as an integral part of what it is to be human. In *Aniara*, the world is mad; people are not.

A Review of Man in Time and Space

The film is based on Swedish writer Harry Martinson's epic poem or "space-epic" (*rymdepos*) entitled *Aniara: A Review of Man in Time and Space (En revy om människan i tid och rum)*, which was published in 1956, during the Cold War. The epic poem not only thematises the nuclear anxieties of the period but also describes environmental destruction and the human tendency to exploit planet Earth (Stenström 1994, 7). The film from 2018, written and directed by Pella Kågerman and Hugo Lilja, is a rare example of a feature-length Swedish science fiction film aimed primarily at an adult audience. Films of this genre in Sweden are few and far between but not non-existent, with previous titles including *Rymdinvasion i Lappland* (Virgil W. Vogel, 1959), *Storm* (Björn Stein & Måns Mårlind, 2006), and *Metropia* (Tarik Saleh, 2009). *Aniara* also falls into the sparsely populated category of European films set in space (Power 2021, 50).

Humanity's relation to space and time plays a crucial role in the story. This is particularly evident when one considers the title of Martinson's epic poem: *Aniara: A Review of Man in Time and Space*. Although the film's creators chose to name it simply *Aniara*, Martinson's title expresses the central theme of the epic poem and of the film. Kågerman and Lilja have made a quite deliberate decision to diversify the story by casting female actors in the prominent leading roles of protagonist Mimabroben and the Astronomer (played by Anneli Martini), even though these characters in Martinson's epic are male.[2] By not changing the gender of the other significant characters, most notably MR's love interest Isagel (Bianca Cruzeiro), the result is a cast dominated by female voices and a story that expresses lesbian and bisexual experiences. Only a few male characters play major parts in the film, most notably the character of Captain Chefone (Arvin Kananian). Through these casting choices, it is emphasised that the film is not merely a review of "Man" in time and space.

In an interview before making the film, writer and director Kågerman commented on the relationship between humanity and the spaces we inhabit:

> It's about humanity without its earthly setting. What is humanity without planet Earth? No human has ever lived elsewhere. All we know and everything that has ever happened to humans has taken place on this little blue dot in the universe. To imagine humanity without Earth is vertiginous.[3]
>
> *(Åsell 2016)*

The film offers a bleak vision of a future where humanity is forced to abandon Earth.[4] The film thus emphasises increasingly urgent questions regarding the future of humanity in the wake of the ongoing climate crisis. It depicts a future world where the present-day climate crisis has become a catastrophe of apocalyptic scope, forcing humanity to leave the planet. Thematically, the film is aligned with the growing trend of "climate fiction," that is, speculative fiction that is focused on the effects of climate change (see, e.g., Streeby 2018; Svoboda 2016; Goodbody & Johns-Putra 2019; Sperling 2019–2020). Reviewer Wendy Ide has called the film a "sci-fi eco parable" (2019), and scholars have primarily approached the film through the analytical lenses of ecocriticism, climate crisis, and the Anthropocene (Nielsen 2020; Power 2021; Wennerscheid 2021).

Read solely from an ecocritical perspective, the film can be interpreted as a cautionary tale of the horrors to come if we do not counteract ongoing climate change. In this reading, portrayals of despair, depression, and anxiety are reduced to a simple moral lesson in an eco-parable, thus serving as an example of an unwanted future and urging the contemporary viewer to take action before it is too late. The film invites viewers to a future where they can perform a *review* – "a looking back" – of humankind's actions (OED Online 2022). For example, Power (2021, 50) has argued that *Aniara* portrays "a future that requires us to rethink the past that got us there. As such, it is faithful to the spirit of its source text that reads above all as a plea for humankind to change course." Nielsen (2020, 33) also refers to *Aniara* as an example of a dystopian artwork that uses fear to "[compel] me to act against climate collapse." This perspective echoes how Hollywood cinema frequently uses mental illness as "a magnifier by which social, political, or economic problems become enlarged in order to critique societal conditions" (Heath 2019, 1).

The film thus reinforces its ecocritical message by portraying feelings of despair and existential anxiety as intrinsically connected to the physical environment in which the characters find themselves. The depiction of the destruction of the Earth's natural environment and its dire consequences for humanity provides a source of eco-anxiety through connecting human well-being and human distress to the characters' immediate environment – the spaces they inhabit. For example, in one emotionally loaded scene, a character desperately cries out: "I don't want to live here!"[5] The problem is not that the passengers and crew of Aniara do not wish to continue living, but rather, they do not wish to live *here*, on Aniara. It is the space, and as I will argue, its temporality, that produce mental illness in *Aniara*. This chapter interrogates this connection between mental illness and space-time in the film in an attempt to move beyond those eco-critical readings in which portrayals of mental illness mostly serve to underscore a sense of eco-anxiety and work to compel the audience to act against clime change.

Shifting Temporalities

In the following, I delineate how the space-time of Aniara is connected to the increasing sense of despair and distress that is felt onboard the ship. I argue that in *Aniara*, it is not changes in the crew and passengers' space that bring about their increasing despair but the shifting temporality of the space in which they find themselves.

During the first hour of its journey, the spaceship Aniara proves to be an unproblematic space for its passengers and crew. It is a transitional space on a route controlled by human agency and governed by human time. It meets expectations of what such a space should be, and the passengers interact with it as such. Within the first diegetic hour, the expected duration of the journey is announced to the passengers. Aniara will dock on Mars in 23 days, 7 hours, and 25 minutes. During this time, and despite the dire conditions on Earth, the passengers are provided with the comforts of excessive consumption and luxury. Aniara is portrayed as a cruise ship with many opportunities for consumption and entertainment. For a Nordic audience, the aesthetics of the Baltic Sea cruise ferries that run between Sweden and Finland is hard to miss. In fact, parts of *Aniara* were filmed on such a ferry, but also on location at a congress centre and large shopping mall (cf. Power 2021, 53; Åsell 2016). With its decks filled with restaurants, shopping facilities, entertainment, bars, spas, and gyms, the spaceship's environment invokes in the crew and passengers the very same habits that brought Earth to the brink of destruction and forced humanity to leave. The passengers are soon engaged in shopping and settle in for a comfortable three-week cruise during which they will "want for nothing," as announced by the ship's many screens.[6]

When the ship is forced off course and it is revealed that it cannot turn around, the captain ensures the passengers that as soon as they encounter a celestial body, they will slingshot themselves back onto their initially intended route. Once again, the estimated duration of the journey is highlighted. The captain promises the passengers that they will return to their original course within a maximum of two years. However, this is a lie to keep the passengers calm until they adapt to their new circumstances: the captain states: "Once the passengers have got used to eating algae ...we'll be straight with them."[7] Since the ship is no longer a transitional space, the crew is forced to manage the changed temporality and attempts to create a long-term inhabitable environment onboard the ship. Fortunately, the ship did not suffer significant damage to its life-support systems when it was struck off course. However, since they are unable to restock their supplies, the crew and passengers are forced to ration the finite food supply that is available from the onboard restaurants and start producing algae for sustenance. The ship itself provides a physical environment that, for all intents and purposes, supports human life. The characters have food (or at least basic sustenance), water, fresh air to breath, gravity, and a place to live. Once the crew and passengers realise they must spend at least two years on the ship, they create a society that includes a labour market, a school, and access to recreation. At one point in their journey, the captain proudly declares that "we've built our own little planet."[8] This statement underscores the impression that he believes that Aniara could provide an alternative to planet Earth, that Aniara could be a human-made place where people could live. In the three years that follow, the crew and passengers manage to make Aniara an inhabitable place. However, everything depends on Mima, a form of artificial intelligence or sentient machine that is overseen by Mimaroben (MR), the film's protagonist.

Mima's hall is portrayed in the film as a place of utmost importance for the survival of humanity on the ship. Three weeks into the ship's journey, that is, about the same amount of time Aniara was supposed to reach Mars, people begin to interact differently with the space. The passengers abandon the entertainment areas and seek out Mima's hall, the room within the ship containing Mima. At the beginning of the journey, only a few passengers showed any interest in learning how to use Mima. But soon after the ship is taken off course, Mima's hall is overrun with people desperately waiting for their turn to spend time in the room, compelling MR to ask the captain for more staff to manage the situation. Mima provides the passengers with an escape from the cold darkness of outer space and their growing despair.

Already within the first hour of diegetic time, following the announcement that Aniara has been struck of course, Mima's hall becomes a therapeutic site where those who experience anxiety are taken to be soothed. The hall is as white and sterile as the rest of the ship, bathed in a cold, blue light. However, whenever Mima is activated, she spreads a warm, yellow light throughout the hall. Mima displays visions of the Earth's natural environment lit in natural light from the sun for those inside the hall. But Mima provides more than images; she provides a doorway, an escape from the darkness of outer space, from despair, and the artificially illuminated ship. Mima can mentally "transport us back to the Earth how it once looked," as MR explains.[9] During the passengers' experience in the hall, their physical body remains on the ship, but the sensations are indistinguishable from "real life."

After three years since Aniara left its trajectory, Mima is lost. Viewing human memories and experiences becomes too horrific for the sentient machine because soon, "people are starting to want to see terrible things."[10] Mima cannot stand looking into the darkness of humankind's memories anymore. She adopts a human voice and begs MR for escape: "Deliver me from this vision!"[11] Despite MR's plea to the captain, like planet Earth, Mima is continually exploited and is ultimately spent, ending in her self-destruction, or suicide. For Mima, humanity, rather than space-time, makes her continued existence impossible: "Now, in the name of all things, I want peace. I shall display my visions no longer. There is protection from almost everything. But there is no protection from humankind."[12] In their discussion of Mima, Wennerscheid contends:

> She is a sentient machine, programmed by humans, that nevertheless does not show empathy with humanity but rather with the suffering of nature, ...Instead of distracting humans from their guilt towards the nature they have destroyed, Mima identifies with it so much that she first weeps over the devastation and finally, in an act of solidarity and despair, destroys herself.
>
> *(Wennerscheid 2021, 45)*

Mima sides with nature, not with her creators, and by doing so, she brings about the slow demise of every human being on the ship. Self-destruction becomes the only way out for Mima, who would otherwise remain trapped inside her hall. Similarly, for many of the humans onboard, suicide offers their only escape from the ship.

By the fourth year of the journey, darkness prevails throughout the ship. With Mima gone, the humans are left to the confinement of Aniara. Suicide becomes commonplace. On one occasion, the captain matter-of-factly notes that the dead man in front of them is the 48th suicide this month, including an entire family. In the years that follow, Aniara's remaining inhabitants turn to drugs and follow cults, worshipping the light and proclaiming that Mima was a saint. By the 24th year of their fateful journey, in one short scene, MR and a few others sit in the dark confines of Mima's hall, praying for the light to return. This is the viewer's last glimpse of humanity onboard the ship.

In the next scene, 5,981,407 years have passed since the ship's departure from planet Earth. This temporal shift, almost six million years in the blink of an eye, offers an ending to the narrative and its final eco-critical conclusion. Aniara has continued to move across space without a living human presence onboard, and time has continued to pass. Aniara drifts in outer space above an Earth-like planet and the light of a sun finally flows through its windows, but only the desiccated bones and dust of humans remain inside the ship. In this ending of the film, as far as the viewer is concerned, humankind is long gone.[13] As the slightly upbeat music at the end of the film suggests, the possibility of a future for a new planet exists, but not for humanity. The ending thus implies that the planet that Aniara has approached, and perhaps the rest of the universe, might be better off without the destructive impulses of humankind, who, not only once but twice in the film, has destroyed the very things that sustained them, planet Earth and Mima.

Living without a Future

The two central spaces of the film, planet Earth and Aniara, are associated with opposite temporalities in the narrative. Earth is a space where time has ended – there is no more time left for its human inhabitants. The film's opening sequence showcases the end of human existence on the planet. We observe a small dot of light travelling across empty space towards the centre of the screen over which the opening credits fade in and out. As the small dot of light reaches the centre, it disappears behind and seemingly merges with the letter "I" in a single word that occupies the screen in capital letters: ANIARA. The small dot of light is the ship Aniara, drifting endlessly in the darkness of deep space. The letters of the film's title then fade away, and the opening credits continue but change in form; they now move over the screen from the bottom to the top, as is typically the case when a film's closing credits are presented. But this does not signify the end of the film, but the end of planet Earth, instead. Behind the credits the screen fades from black into a documentary-styled montage of the ongoing destruction of the planet including devastating hurricanes, floods, tornados, and wild-fires. These are the reasons why humanity was forced to abandon Earth and journey into space. The narrative thus starts at the end of time, with those who can leaving the devastated and soon-to-be-uninhabitable planet Earth.

Aboard Aniara, on the other hand, time and space eventually become eternal, without end, beyond human perception. As Aniara deviates from the plotted trajectory and thereby takes the humans with it, they deviate more and more from normative, anthropocentric time. As the crew loses control of the ship, they also lose control over time as they are thrown into the eternal space-time of outer space. The further they drift into outer space, the further away the crew and passengers are from human perceptions of time since they have left behind the very fundamental way in which we measure time, namely by observing the relationship between the Earth and the sun. For the rest of the journey, artificial light serves as the only reminder of the diurnal rhythm. MR, for instance, turns off a small bedside lamp and informs her child: "Look. It's night-time!"[14] The very structure of the film also emphasises this notion of temporality. The film is divided into episodes of time-marked sequences highlighting the passing of time aboard the ship after it was struck off course, explicitly referring to the first hour, the third week, the third year, and so forth on screen. This temporal structure contributes to how the film conveys a sense of despair. Hours spent aboard the ship become weeks, weeks become years, and years become aeons. The film thus evokes to the viewer a sense of the eternity of time and space.[15] The Astronomer explains their movement in space by invoking the visual metaphor of the imperceivably slow movement of a bubble of air in a drinking glass, suggesting that the ship is moving infinitely slowly in the vast space-time of outer space.

However, while planet Earth and Aniara are associated with opposite temporalities, both constitute space-times in which humankind has no future. Neither Earth nor Aniara provides any future for humanity. Earth can no longer physically sustain human life, and Aniara does not provide a viable substitute. Humans have no future in either. Aniara, as described by the Astronomer, is a sarcophagus, a space for the dead, for those without a future. The darkness of outer space and its threatening presence materialise and make tangible the sense of overwhelming inner turmoil and despair that Aniara's crew and passengers feel. The outer darkness of deep space serves as a metaphor for the darkness within the passengers when they are confronted with the knowledge that they will spend the rest of their lives on the ship, for example, in the scene when the Astronomer reveals to MR that they cannot change the ship's course. Following this revelation, the viewer is provided with a lingering close-up of MR's facial expression. The Astronomer asks her to turn off the light, and MR complies. MR lies in darkness in her bunk until she can bear it no more and leaves the cabin. In another part of the ship, she stands in front of the floor-to-ceiling windows looking out at outer space, trying to deal with the realisation that they will never return. The camera work and music suggest a sense of vertigo, of outer space pushing against her as her anxiety grows until she screams out in panic. Similarly, a few scenes later, after MR has calmed down a passenger experiencing a panic attack, the mere sight of outer space through the window pushes the passenger back into a state of fear and anxiety, compelling the passenger to flee from the view. While the hull and windows of the ship enforce the physical separation between outer space and the passengers, the windows fail to shut off its threatening darkness. Aniara and the surrounding outer space become intimately connected to passengers' sense of darkness, despair, and (most importantly) the conclusion that they do not have a future.

This is also why Mima is so important to the crew and passengers. Using Mima allows the film's characters to experience being immersed in nature and light and, more importantly, experience an alternative space-time. Once the passengers understand that they are on a voyage of no return, they desperately seek out Mima, who provides a doorway to the past in which a future for humanity was still possible. Mima contrasts the darkness and despair that permeates Aniara with light, hope, and the memory of having a future. The manner in which Mima displays images of the past, of memories, emphasises the importance of temporality to the film. All that is left for the characters is their past, idyllic memories of planet Earth. The only way they can deal with the despair of not having a future is by escaping to a past when a future was still possible.

The Possibility of Another Future?

The experience of living on the ship is mediated through the protagonist MR. Her point of view, her experience, and her emotions are shared with the audience. This narrative perspective plays a vital part in how the film conveys a sense of despair and depictions of mental illness. It portrays her struggle to retain hope in the face of the despair that abounds onboard the ship and her relentless attempts to assist people in distress as she tries to transform Aniara's space-time. For a great deal of time, she effectively manages the impact of living aboard the ship by keeping the darkness at bay.

Throughout the journey, MR tries to help those around her as more and more people fall into depression and experience anxiety attacks. This work appears to be one of her professional duties in her role as "Mimarob" or may be a self-imposed duty that has fallen upon her because of the lack of counsellors or therapists onboard. On several occasions in the film, MR rushes to assist passengers with anxiety by bringing them into Mima's hall. But her concern is not limited to her fellow humans. She also takes care of Mima and immediately responds to her pleas for rest, begging the captain that Mima be given a chance to recuperate. However, her care for Mima could also be read as an anthropocentric response to the possible loss of Mima for the sake of humanity, not as a plea for Mima herself. MR, like the other humans onboard, is dependent on Mima's resources and the comfort they provide. For example, when she learns that the ship will not be able to turn back, she immediately turns to Mima for solace.

MR has a different relationship with Aniara's space-time than most of the other characters in the film. Already prior to the accident that forced the ship off course, she lived in accordance with a different temporality. As a crew member, she was already accustomed to spending long periods of time on Aniara. From the very beginning of the film, we see that she has decorated her cabin with images of nature in an attempt to transform her somewhat sterile living quarters into a more homely place. It is also revealed that she has lived outside of normative time, without any family or people waiting for her on Earth or Mars. Unlike most passengers, who are only confronted with the realisation of what living in outer space without Earth really entails once the ship is struck off course, MR has already come to that conclusion. She knows there is no other place for humanity once Earth is lost. MR knows Mars offers an equally hostile environment as Aniara's: "What do you think it's like on Mars? Do you think it's paradise there? It isn't. It's cold. Nothing grows. Just a little frigitulip … we might as well live here as anywhere else."[16] Like the humans onboard, the tulip flower survives in this environment but does not flourish. For a tulip to grow large and bloom, it needs sunlight, water, soil, manure, bees, and the changing seasons; it needs Earth. Likewise, humans need more than just physical space and sustenance.

In contrast to the captain, who believes that a suitable physical environment is all that is needed for survival and claims that they have successfully created their own little planet on Aniara, MR understands that something more is necessary for human survival. Throughout the film, MR works resolutely to find something that would substitute for a lost Earth. Mima functions as such a substitute. But with her gone, MR searches for alternative solutions, a process hastened on by her relationship with Isagel.

The romantic relationship between MR and Isagel provides a focal point of the narrative after Mima's self-destruction in the fourth year of the ship's journey. Dramatic tensions intensify by moving the protagonist's attention to a loved one (and later, a child), thereby replacing the more impersonal and professional relationships that MR had with the passengers. More is at stake as MR tries to create a better place to live for her family. Meanwhile, however, she is forced to witness how her beloved Isagel loses hope and falls deeper and deeper into depression as she spends increasingly more time staring out the window into outer space. Through MR's perspective, the audience is provided with an intimate view of the events that led to Isagel killing their child and then committing suicide.

For most of the passengers, personified in Isagel, turning the ship back on course offers the only prospect of having a future. The storyline centring on the birth and death of MR and Isagel's child, in particular, highlights this. The child is a figure that frequently serves as the very symbol of the future (cf. Kafer 2013, 20). Isagel's inability to imagine a future drives her to kill their child and herself. When Isagel's pregnancy is revealed in the fifth year of their journey, it is clear that she does not want to have the child on the ship: "There's no hope here. I'll give birth to a prisoner. ... It will be born to eternal night."[17] In a moment of solitude in the final scene of the fifth year, Isagel briefly holds the baby underwater, thereby foreshadowing its eventual death. At that moment, she is hindered by the news of the discovery of an object approaching the ship. When the ship encounters the object hurtling through space towards them, hope is momentarily restored, and even Isagel is seen outside of the solitude of the cabin, at work and playing happily with her child. The possibility of a future is momentarily restored for her. The object is believed to be an emergency probe sent from Earth containing the means which would enable the crew to change the ship's course. However, this temporary spark of hope is soon extinguished when it is shown that the object offers no hope of salvation.

Throughout most of the film, MR is conscious of the possibility of living an alternative future, of living in time differently. Even as the film portrays her struggles and her own sense of despair, she continues with her attempts to transform the environment. This enables a continued existence, a possible future. Her ability to imagine a future for her family drives MR's efforts to transform the environment. When Isagel falls pregnant and expresses her unwillingness to have the baby, MR responds by promising to remove the darkness. She initiates work to construct a system of screens to cover the ship's windows with images of nature and light, thus removing the darkness of outer space and, by extension, Isagel's inner darkness. After the revelation that the object that approached the ship cannot help them, MR continues to work relentlessly on the screens in a desperate attempt to get rid of the darkness, to make Aniara a better place for her family. She is in search of a paradise, a new beginning for humanity. Meanwhile, back in their cabin, Isagel drifts further into her inner darkness. When MR finally finishes the screens, Isagel has drowned their child and hung herself. After their death, MR gives up on her attempts to transform Aniara and loses hope for a future.

Conclusion

I have demonstrated throughout this chapter that *Aniara* deals extensively with the impact on humans while being forced to live in space. Specifically, the film explores the psychological impact of being aboard Aniara, far removed from planet Earth.[18] It highlights the profound psychological impact spending time in space has on humans, which includes, for example, an increased risk of mental illness and changes in behaviour and cognition (NASA 2021). *Aniara* thematically lingers on such psychological effects directly connected to the space-time they inhabit, and the absence of planet Earth, to an extent that is seldom seen in audio-visual science fiction.[19] The film uses despair as its major narrative concern. Even though Aniara, much like many other science fiction spaceships, provides an environment suited to human survival, it becomes a space where most humans cannot bear to continue to exist. Life onboard the ship is portrayed as horrific, not because of familiar science fiction tropes, such as alien threats, hostile relationships between groups of humans or rival organisations, a lack of supplies, malfunctioning machines, or a life-threatening AI, but by the insufferable space-time the characters inhabit. A brief comparison to another narrative focusing on characters "lost in space" can showcase the very importance of the space-time they inhabit. The starship Voyager from *Star Trek: Voyager* (1995-2001) is portrayed with a significantly different space-time compared to Aniara. Voyager is a space designed for deep-space exploration, in contrast to Aniara, which is a line cruiser between Earth and Mars – intended as a temporary and transitional space. Perhaps more importantly for this comparison, Voyager is en route back to Earth. While Voyager's journey might take a very long time, planet Earth remains their destination. Thus, a future for Voyager's crew (or any future generations) awaits them once they return, a future they travel towards.[20] The two central spaces in *Aniara*, however (Aniara and planet Earth), both fail to provide a future for humanity.

Aniara depicts mental illness by connecting a growing sense of despair (leading to mental illness, depression, and anxiety) to the tangible relationship between humans and space-time. I argue that this connection between space-time and mental illness serves, at least in part, to depict mental illness as an inherent human trait. *Aniara* highlights that our interactions with the spaces we occupy, including the changed environment brought about by the present climate crisis, have a profound effect on our bodies and minds. Experiencing mental illness following a traumatic event or from being in distressing situations like the one portrayed in the film is a very human reaction. However "normal" that reaction is, cultural representations of mental illness, as noted at the beginning of this chapter, tend to present mental illness as deviant or even monstrous, thus locating it firmly within the realm of the individual. By the connection between human distress and space-time established in the film, *Aniara* avoids such Othering of mental illness. The film also locates this distress, not in individual characters but in all its characters. Some are portrayed as more susceptible to the hostile space-time and others less. This way of portraying mental illness as intertwined with space-time acknowledges that the future might hold new ways of thinking about what it means to be human. For example, to imagine that the physical and mental variations we currently call "disabilities" or "mental illnesses" are not fixed categories with inherent meaning but that such categories and current beliefs about them are based on sociocultural norms and are thus subject to change across time and space. Ableist beliefs uphold the view that such variation is inherently tragic, dangerous, and even monstrous – by positioning "them" as a clearly defined Other in contrast to those considered able-bodied/able-minded rather than an intrinsic aspect of being human.

The film does not offer a depiction of mental illness that provides hope, either for MR or for the audience. Instead, it uses the characters' confinement aboard Aniara and the sense of not having a future to convey an unyielding exploration of both outer and inner darkness. The film's very structure plays a role in conveying this sense of despair. The film's dramaturgy is structured episodically in sequences rather than according to the more traditional Aristotelian dramaturgy of, for example, Hollywood cinema with a distinct beginning, middle, and end (see, e.g., Thompson 2003, 10). Expectations connected to traditional dramaturgy entail that each action and event is supposed to be followed by an appropriate effect, one that in *Aniara* does not occur. For example, the object Aniara encounters initially promises the possibility of a literal turning point or peripety, namely by providing the crew with the means to turn the ship around and thus save the crew and passengers. The expected peripety fails to occur because it is only a random object in space, encountered by chance. Instead, the discovery of the object is the turning point that pushes the story further into despair, leading to MR losing her family. Through its form, the film thus highlights the fact that life, unlike traditional film plots, is random. Events can take place without being meaningful to the larger story in which everything makes sense. It is the hope of a closed, intelligible narrative with a clear beginning, middle, and most importantly, an end that enables the characters to go on living. However, it transpires that the story that unfolds on Aniara has no heroes, no antagonists, or no final justification for the awful destiny that befalls the film's characters. Thus, the film effectively simulates a sense of living without a future, without hope, and in despair.

Acknowledgements

This chapter is part of a project headed by Lotta Vikström: "Ageing with disabilities in past, present and future societies: Risks and loads from disabilities and later life outcomes." It has received funding from the Wallenberg Foundation (Stiftelsen Marcus och Amalia Wallenbergs Minnesfond, MAW 2019.0003).

Notes

1 Throughout this chapter, I use the term *space-time* to indicate that space and time are inseparable entities. I draw inspiration from literary theorist Mikhail Bakhtin, who emphasises the inseparable relationship between space and time in literature by means of the term *chronotope*, where "spatial and temporal indicators are fused into one carefully thought-out, concrete whole. Time, as it were, thickens, takes on flesh, becomes artistically visible; likewise, space becomes charged and responsive to the movements of time, plot, and history" (Bakhtin 1981, 84).

2 Throughout this chapter, I use pronouns to refer to characters according to the performance of gender in the film. However, the character of Mima, a sentient machine that does not have a humanoid body, is voiced by a female actress. Consequently, I refer to Mima as *she/her*.

3 "Det handlar om människan utan sitt jordiska ramverk. Vad är människan utan jorden? Ingen människa har ju någonsin bott någon annanstans än här. Allt vi känner till och allt som någonsin har hänt människor har utspelat sig på den där lilla blå punkten i universum. Att föreställa sig människan utan jorden är svindlande" (author's translation).

4 The writer/director duo have stated that the film is set in a parallel time. However, throughout this chapter, I discuss the film in terms of the future. While, aesthetically, the film connotes the present, it also situates itself in a discourse about the future. Kågerman and Lilja also suggest this when they argue that future speculations are always rooted in the present, an idea they wanted to highlight throughout the film. Regarding this, they state: "The future is here, now" ("Framtiden är här, nu") (Åsell 2016, author's translation). The film thus brings the future closer to the present, thereby merging two temporalities.

5 "Jag vill inte leva här!" The analysis is based on the Swedish dialogue. Henceforth, I include my transcript of the original dialogue in footnotes. Neil Betteridge's translation into English, as provided by the film's subtitles, is used in the text above.

6 "Här kommer ingenting fattas dig."

7 "när passagerarna har vant sig att äta alger så ska vi gå ut med hur det ligger till."
8 "Vi lyckades bygga vår egna lilla planet."
9 "förflyttar hon oss tillbaks till jorden så som den en gång har sett ut."
10 "folk börjar vilja se väldigt, väldigt hemska saker."
11 "Befria mig från synen."
12 "Nu vill jag i tingens namn ha frid. Nu vill jag inte förevisa mer. Det finns skydd mot nästan allt som är. Men det finns inget skydd mot människan."
13 While it is possible that humanity still exists in the solar system, the film does not suggest this.
14 "Titta här. Nu blev det natt."
15 This could be considered a representation of how a realisation of the vastness of "deep-time" creates a new relationship to "our personal count, the intimate passage of time we experience and mark in our own bodies as we grow and age, [which] now occupies a vanishingly miniscule segment of the overall timescape" (Shoshitaishvili 2020, 129). From this perspective, a human lifetime is insignificantly brief.
16 "Hur tror du att det är på Mars egentligen? Tror du att det är härligt där? Det är inte det. Det är kallt och ingenting växer. Bara en lite köldtulpan. ... Vi lika gärna kan leva här som någon annanstans."
17 "Det finns inga möjligheter här. Jag kommer att föda en fånge. ... Jag kommer föda nån till evig natt."
18 However briefly, the film also establishes the idea that the hostile environment of Earth has had physical effects on the human body. In the first minutes of the film, a series of close-ups on the passengers embarking on the journey to Mars includes people with facial injuries, possibly caused by radiation. However, these characters remain peripheral to the central storyline and are limited to minor roles. None of these characters display extensive physical impairments.
19 Such themes are of course not absent in science fiction cinema. That there is an affinity to such films that take as its starting point questions concerning human psychology to a certain degree is notable. For example, during an interview, the writer and director-duo expressed a fondness of science fiction films such as *Gravity* (Alfonso Cuarón, 2013), *Interstellar* (Christopher Nolan, 2014), and *Solaris* (Andrei Tarkovsky, 1972) (Åsell 2016).
20 Likewise, in *Battlestar Galactica* (2004–2009) while the ship's crew travel away from the destruction of their home planets, they travel towards a still imagined planet Earth.

References

Allan, Kathryn. 2014. "Disability in Science Fiction." In *SF 101: A Guide to Teaching and Studying Science Fiction,* eds. Ritch Calvin, Doug Davis, Karen Hellekson & Craig Jacobsen, np. Kindle Edition. Medford: Science Fiction Research Association.

Aniara. 2018. Directed by Kågerman, Pella & Lilja, Hugo. Meta Film Stockholm AB. https://viaplay.se/film/aniara-2018. Accessed 1 March 2024.

Åsell, Jakob. 2016. "Aniara' - Svensk rymdodyssé i shoppingmiljö." *Moviezine,* December 11, 2016. https://www.moviezine.se/intervjuer/aniara-svensk-rymdodysse-i-shoppingmiljo. Accessed 1 March 2024.

Bakhtin, Mikhail. 1981. *Dialogic Imagination: Four Essays.* Trans. Michael Holquist. Austin: University of Texas Press.

Battlestar Galactica. 2004–2009. Created by Glen A. Larson. R&D TV et al.

Bugbee, Teo. 2019. "'Aniara' Review: A One-Way Ticket into the Abyss." *The New York Times*, May 16, 2019. https://www.nytimes.com/2019/05/16/movies/aniara-review.html. Accessed 1 March 2024.

Campbell, Fiona Kumari. 2012. "Stalking Ableism: Using Disability to Expose 'abled' Narcissism." In *Disability and Social Theory: New Developments and Directions*, eds. Dan Goodley, Bill Hughes & Lennard J. Davis, 212–230. Basingstoke: Palgrave Macmillan.

Goodbody, Axel & Adeline Johns-Putra. 2019. *Cli-fi: A Companion*. Oxford: Peter Lang.

Gravity. 2013. Directed by Alfonso Cuarón. Warner Bros., Esperanto Filmoj, & Heyday Films.

Heath, Erin. 2019. *Mental Disorders in Popular Film: How Hollywood Uses, Shames, and Obscures Mental Diversity*. Lanham: Lexington Books.

Ide, Wendy. 2019. "*Aniara* Review – Stunning Sci-fi Eco Parable." *The Guardian*, August 31, 2019. https://www.theguardian.com/film/2019/aug/31/aniara-review-stunning-swedish-sci-fi-parable. Accessed 1 March 2024.

Interstellar. 2014. Directed by Christopher Nolan. Paramount Pictures, Warner Bros., & Legendary Entertainment.

Kafer, Alison. 2013. *Feminist, Queer, Crip*. Bloomington: Indiana UP.

Klass, Stephen & Leif Sjöberg, trans., 1999. "Notes." In *Aniara: A Review of Man in Time and Space* by Harry Martinson, 151–155. Ashland: Story Line Press.

Metropia. 2009. Directed by Tarik Saleh. Atmo Metro AB.

NASA. 2021. "The Human Body in Space." Last updated: November 14, 2022. https://www.nasa.gov/hrp/bodyinspace. Accessed 1 March 2024.

Nielsen, Kim Skjoldager. 2020. "The Role of Dystopian Art in the Climate Crisis." *Peripeti* 17 (32): 32–34.

OED Online. 2022. "Review." Last modified: December 2022. Oxford: Oxford UP. www.oed.com/view/Entry/164850. Accessed 1 March 2024.

Power, Aidan. 2021. "Eurocentrism, the Anthropocene and Climate Migration in Aniara." *Foundation* 50 (140): 45–61.

Pugh, Catherine. 2022. "Such Pretty Things: Madness in the Whedonverse." In *Slaying Is Hell: Essays on Trauma and Memory in the Whedonverse*, eds. Alyson R. Buckman, Juliette C. Kitchens & Katherine A. Troyer, 131–155. Jefferson: McFarland.

Rüsch, Nicolas, Matthias C. Angermeyer & Patrick W. Corrigan. 2005. "Mental Illness Stigma: Concepts, Consequences, and Initiatives to Reduce Stigma." *European Psychiatry* 20 (8): 529–539.

Rymdinvasion i Lappland. 1959. Directed by Virgil W. Vogel. Gustaf Unger Films and AB Fortuna Film.

Shoshitaishvili, Boris. 2020. "Deep Time and Compressed Time in the Anthropocene: The New Timescape and the Value of Cosmic Storytelling." *The Anthropocene Review* 7 (2): 125–137.

Solaris. 1972. Directed by Andrei Tarkovsky. Mosfilm & Chetvyortoe Tvorcheskoe Obedinenie.

Sperling, Alison. 2019–20. "Climate Fictions: Introduction." *Paradoxa* 31: 7–21.

Star Trek: Voyager. 1995–2001. Created by Rick Berman, Michael Piller, and Jeri Taylor. Paramount Television.

Stenström, Johan. 1994. *Aniara: från versepos till opera*. Malmö: Corona.

Storm. 2006. Directed by Björn Stein and Måns Mårlind. Breidablick Film Produktion AB.

Streeby, Shelley. 2018. *Imagining the Future of Climate Change: World-making through Science Fiction and Activism*. Oakland: University of California Press.

Svoboda, Michael. 2016. "Cli-fi on the Screen(s): Patterns in the Representations of Climate Change in Fictional Films." *WIREs Clim Change* 7: 43–64.

Thompson, Kristin. 2003. *Storytelling in Film and Television*. Cambridge: Harvard University Press.

Wennerscheid, Sophie. 2021. "Things don't Cry, do they? Emotional Attachment between Humans, Technology and Nature in Harry Martinson's Epic Space Poem *Aniara* and the Science Fiction film *Aniara*." *Journal of Scandinavian Cinema* 11 (1): 31–48.

PART IV

Art, Games, and Beyond

14

EXAMINING GENDER IN THE GAMEPLAY AND RECEPTION OF HOUSEMARQUE'S *RETURNAL*

Maria Ruotsalainen

In this chapter I examine the Finnish video game *Returnal* (Housemarque 2021) and its reception amongst players and in video game critiques. *Returnal* is Housemarque's first big title and was published for Playstation 5 on 30 April 2021.[1] The game is commonly classified as belonging to the third-person shooter *roguelike* or *roguelite* genre of games.[2] Furthermore, *Returnal* is a psychological horror/science fiction game taking place on the planet Atropos, showcasing its alien flora and fauna. The game has had a highly favourable reception: it has been acclaimed by the critics, and won, for instance, the British Academy Game Award in 2022 for the music, narrative, performer in a leading role, and best game of the year.

In my analysis of *Returnal* and its reception, I utilise the concept of intersectionality to analyse how age and gender and the intersections of the two are discussed via Selene, the protagonist of the game, a white middle-aged woman. Intersectionality as a theoretical framework highlights the importance of examining different social categories together and recognising how these intersections produce difference (Crenshaw 1990). Thus, for instance, the experience of being a white woman can differ radically from an experience of being a woman of colour, as can the experience of a young woman from that of an older one. I furthermore approach gender as *performative*. According to Judith Butler (1988), gender is not a given, but always a construct. This construction is performative and takes place through repetition of gendered performances. These performances always have a social dimension as they are repeated in a historical and cultural context. They are scripted to signal appropriate (or non-appropriate) ways of being of a certain gender, and they are both encouraged and sometimes enforced upon

DOI: 10.4324/9781003561101-20

gendered subjects. Simultaneously, they also construct gender as an idea itself and enforce the imaginary gender binary (1988).

In my analysis, I am also interested in the reception of *Returnal* and how age and gender *are* and *are not* discussed in critiques as well as by players. As Selene is a middle-aged woman, she is rather unique as a video game protagonist, particularly for an AAA[3] game. Female protagonists are (still) relatively uncommon in video games, where most characters are male (Salter & Blodget 2017, 76). Furthermore, when characters are female, they are mostly sexualised, young, fit, and able-bodied (Cote 2018; Downs & Smith 2010; Ivory 2006). The tendency to portray women in this way extends beyond games in game culture, and many women engaged with gaming and game culture feel considerable pressure on how to present themselves, for instance when streaming their gameplay (Ruberg et al. 2019). In terms of representation, *middle-aged women* in particular continue to be an anomaly both as game characters and in the media representations of gamers and gaming women, even though games are increasingly made by women who are middle-aged, to other middle-aged people – including women.

In my earlier work, I have argued that middle-aged women represent a sense of threat to masculine gamer identity, as they diversify the representation and presence of women in game culture (Ruotsalainen 2022). As such, the lack of diversity in game characters is not an isolated phenomenon, but part of a larger set of issues both in the ways that video games are designed and in the way women and minorities are positioned within game culture (Consalvo 2012). Much of game culture has been defined and constructed as masculine space, and the figure of the geek has played an important role in that (Cote 2018; Kirkpatrick 2017; Taylor 2012). Geek masculinity has historically offered space for men to perform a type of masculinity which is subordinate to hegemonic masculinity in everyday life, but which forms hegemonic masculinity within the context of game culture and geek cultures more broadly (cf. Taylor 2012; Taylor & Voorhees 2018; Scott 2019). As a result, geek masculinity transforms hegemonic masculinity in the context of geek and gamer culture and secures the position of patriarchy (Lockhart 2015; Taylor 2012). According to Salter and Blodgett, gaming "embodies many of the contradictions between geek culture and masculinity, as avatars are often hypermasculine (athletic, militant, and violent) while the act of playing a video game is not inherently physical or masculine" (2017, 75). Furthermore, they note that the overwhelming presence of male avatars, and thus males as active actors, constructs women as passive in game culture (2017).

Against this backdrop, I will first analyse how age and gender are present in *Returnal* at the level of both interaction (e.g. game mechanics) and representation (e.g. as character, game world, story). Through my analysis, I seek to show how Selene's gender is a meaningful part of *Returnal* as a whole and how the game showcases the interplay of gender and age, but also trauma, societal expectations, and motherhood, through not only the representation of the protagonist or the story of the game but how also the game mechanics and the game world can be read as extensions of these themes.

Second, I will analyse the reception of the game by looking at the critiques of *Returnal* as well as online discussions surrounding the game. My analysis highlights how almost none of the aforementioned elements – gender, age, trauma, societal expectations, and motherhood – are present in the writings of game critics, but instead Selene's gender and its implications to the game are fully pushed aside. By drawing from Bo Ruberg's (2018) earlier research on straightwashing queer elements in the reception of the video game *Undertale* (Toby Fox 2015) by game critics – in favour of gatekeeping the hypermasculine game culture – I demonstrate how similar tendencies of *doing away with* are present in the critics' reception of *Returnal*. I show how the elements related to Selene being a middle-aged woman are either rarely mentioned or not mentioned at all in the analysed game reviews and are thus sidelined from focus by other aspects of *Returnal*, aspects that can traditionally be seen coded as masculine in game culture, such as game mechanics and genre conventions (Kirkpatrick 2017). Graeme Kirkpatrick (2017) discusses how in the 1980s, particularly the difficulty of a given game became to be seen as highly important – the harder the better – and this was directly tied to the emerging techno-masculine values (see also Kocurek 2012) in game culture: the measure of manhood became that of mastering the (hard) games.

However, whilst in the game reviews Selene as a character is overlooked, I will demonstrate through my analysis of multiple online discussion threads by players that Selene's gender as well as her age do matter to the players. To put it simply, player discussions reveal that for many players Selene's gender and age *are a meaningful* part of the game. For them, Selene represents a type of character (a middle-aged woman) that players rarely see in games. The discussions show that players appreciate the diversity, and for some particularly, seeing themselves in Selene invokes a sense of being recognised and seen. I therefore argue that player reception acknowledges Selene as a middle-aged female character and finds this meaningful. Moreover, the player reception occasionally brings forth the potential queer readings of the *Returnal*'s narrative, thus queering the reception rather than straightwashing or negotiating away the meaning of Selene's character (and her age/ gender).

Materials and Methods

I use multiple different types of materials in my analysis. For analysing the intersections of gender and age in *Returnal* the game, I have utilised notes recorded during my own gameplay of the game as well as public game play-through videos. I chose two videos, both available on Youtube. The first video selected is from a channel named *Shirrako* (2021).[4] The playthrough video is five hours and ten minutes long and showcases a playthrough of the whole game, excluding the downloadable content (DLC), an extra material to the game released after the official release. The second video I included in the data is a collection of all the cutscenes in the game, in the chronological order they are shown to the player. Cutscenes in games usually function as narrative devices which advance the game plot and during which the player has no or limited interactive agency, meaning that the game play is either altogether paused or altered. In addition to clear cutscenes with no player agency, the video also contains sections which are clearly different from the rest of the game and where the gameplay has been altered. These sections, like cutscenes, function to further the narrative. This video is from a channel named *Gamer's Little Playground*[5] and is 1 hour and 50 minutes long. The first video selected contains the full playthrough of the game without any commentary, because I wanted to focus on analysing the game content and the narrative of the game, rather than the reception of the game by the content creator, the player of the game in this case. The second video that contains all the cutscenes from *Returnal* is also with no commentary, and my focus is on the in-game content displayed on it. Utilising diverse ways of accessing the game highlights the multiple ways games and game cultures can be accessed (Friman 2022; Meriläinen & Ruotsalainen 2023).

For the analysis of the reception of *Returnal*, I have collected two different types of materials. The collection of the data was done between 1 May 2022 and 15 June 2022. Firstly, I gathered a total of 28 game reviews written in English. All of the reviews were publicly available online. The reviews were found in Reddit by utilising subreddits r/Returnal and r/games as well with searches conducted via the Google search engine (with search words "Returnal," "game," and "review"). The second type of materials I analyse are discussion threads from Reddit, found by the subreddits r/Returnal and r/games. I gathered these by first familiarising myself with the subreddit r/Returnal to find out what kind of themes and topics were discussed there. After this, I collected discussion threads connected to Selene's age or gender, or both, by using search words "gender," "woman," and "middle-aged." In this chapter, I avoid using direct quotes from the discussion threads to protect the privacy of the discussants.

Different data sets also require different analytical methods. In practice, I made notes while playing and watching playthroughs aiming to create thick descriptions of both what I see and what I experience and utilise these as part of the analyses. Thick description is a way of describing phenomena or events so that the description is rich and contextualised (Freeman 2014). In my analysis I have traced the ludonarrative elements of the game, meaning that I have paid attention to both the narrative of the game and its game mechanics (cf. Hocking 2009), while focusing on the narrative of the game and Selene as a character. I have furthermore organised my notes in themes by utilising thematic analysis. For analysing the game reviews and player discussions, I have used critical discourse analysis (Wodak & Meyer 2001). Critical discourse analysis enables examining the data beyond themes and rather allows connecting it to larger societal discourses, thus also making it possible to see not only what is present in the data but also what is missing, hidden, and done away with, in other words, what are the meaningful absences in the given data (von Münchow 2018).

Returnal the Game and Selene as an Atypical Game Character

In what follows, I first describe the game and its central themes to the readers, in order to make it easier to follow my arguments afterwards. *Returnal* starts when Selene, the protagonist of the game, crashes on a planet called Atropos, which she has been sent to investigate by the corporation called Astra. The game thus has a clear science-fictional setting. After crashing, Selene soon realises that her ship Helios has been damaged beyond repair and she cannot contact Astra. She decides to venture outside and follow a signal she calls the "white shadow," apparently convinced that this will help her to get in contact with Astra. The player plays Selene from a third-person perspective. As Selene leaves her ship and moves in a jungle-like environment, full of hostile fauna (different types of animal-like creatures with tentacles) and old ruins, she stumbles upon a lifeless body which she first thinks belongs to another Astra scout. When she checks the identification tag, she nevertheless realises it is her own body. Thereafter, the aspects of speculative horror become evident in *Returnal* as, from this point on, the realisation – that is, finding her own dead body – occurs more often, as Selene continues to venture deeper in the new world. During her venture, Selene realises that every time she dies, she is sent back to the moment of the crash in a new body whereas her lifeless bodies remain on Atropos. As she finds more bodies, she also finds audio logs next to them, containing her own recordings before dying. In the first found audio log, Selene recounts that the forest rearranges itself every time she returns (returning is the word she chooses to use rather than talking about herself dying). This is connected to *Returnal*'s gameplay as every time Selene (and thus, in a sense, the player) dies, the map is procedurally generated again and changes. This ties together the narrative and gameplay elements of the game, creating a sense of ludonarrative consonance, as opposite to ludonarrative dissonance where the narrative and gameplay elements clash together (Saldivar 2022). The way the narrative unveils via the audio logs also adds to this sense of coherence, as does the disorienting feeling resulting from the character/player dying and the world reorganising itself around Selene (and the player) as similar but never quite the same.

As the player advances in the game, Selene discovers more about not only Atropos and its apparently disappeared sentient civilisation (in contrast to the planet's hostile fauna, which is at that point not seen as sentient) but also her own house on Earth, that is, somehow now on Atropos. The house stands in stark contrast to the rest of the game world, as it is wooden and clearly human-made and evokes a sense of familiarity in an unfamiliar world. To access the house, the player has to first find a key. When the player as Selene moves inside the house, the perspective changes from the third perspective to first. This happens every time Selene returns to the house. When exploring the house, the player starts to learn more about Selene. During the game, Selene returns to the house multiple times, and one time, the player is no longer Selene, but a child in the house. The game strongly suggests that the child is Selene's, but this is never completely clear. In addition to Selene and the child, there appear to be two other beings in the house: something or someone hidden in the basement and an astronaut, who is referred throughout the game as "the Astronaut" and who appears to be in turns both a malignant and a friendly presence.

The world of *Returnal* consists of four different biomes, meaning that there are different types of areas to venture through. As Selene moves through the biomes, the audio logs reveal that she becomes increasingly disoriented. This sense of disorientation and urgency, however, is present throughout the gameplay as in order to advance in the game the player has to be almost continuously on the move and try to survive in the hostile environment filled with belligerent fauna and environmental danger. Dying comes with a high cost as not only does the world regenerate itself, but the player loses almost all their weapons and other gear, with few expectations: thus, not only the world that has gained familiarity is lost, but the player has to start the grind (finding weapons and gear) from the beginning. However, new iteration of the world can also reveal new aspects of the narrative, as narrative in *Returnal* is mainly present via cutscenes and as embedded (Brand & Knight 2005), thus told via audio logs, writings in the environment (such as scripts on the statues left behind by the humanoid civilization), and different items the player can find in the gamewold and interact with.

By the end of the third biome, Selene finally finds the source of the "white shadow," which seems to be a form of transmission from inside an ancient city. With its help, she is finally able to contact her employer, Astra, that sends a vessel to pick her up. Here onwards the player sees a cutscene of news on television reporting on Selene being found, and then sees her growing old, spending time with a person that seems to be her partner, and playing piano with a ring on her left ring finger, suggesting she is married. Finally, we see the scene cutting to a funeral and a close-up on Selene's casket in a grave.

Then, the screen turns black. After a while, Selene wakes up – in her crashed ship again, like when she dies in the game. She is back on Atropos, returned, and the cycle has not been broken.

From here on the player advances to the last biome, which mainly takes place under water. Now Selene is no longer following the "white shadow," but rather music. The song she keeps hearing is "Don't Fear the Reaper," by the band Blue Öyster Cult. As Selene descends under water, her logs become increasingly incoherent. Finally, she reaches what is lying deep in the water, a giant octopus-like creature, the last boss of the game, that she needs to fight. After Selene wins the fight, a cutscene begins. In these cutscenes, a middle-aged woman, looking much like Selene, appears to be driving a car over the bridge. There is a child in the backseat. Suddenly, an astronaut is standing on the bridge, and while trying to avoid crashing into them, the woman ends up driving off the bridge, into the water. When the car is sinking, the woman reaches towards the child and tries to open their seatbelt but fails and is pulled out of the car and towards the surface by shadowy tentacles.

There is also an alternative ending to the game, depending on whether the player collects all the car key fragments from the house before facing the last boss. If they do, after defeating the last boss, a different kind of cutscene begins. In this scene, Selene is facing a humanoid in a wheelchair. The humanoid is pregnant, looks very old, and has tentacles in place of hands. This humanoid attacks Selene, and Selene must fight her. After defeating the humanoid, she is back on the site of the crash, but as the astronaut this time. After this, she is transported back to the water, swimming towards the surface again. The game ends when she reaches the surface and cries out "Helios."

As said before, simply the fact that Selene is a middle-aged woman makes her a rather atypical game character. For a long time, video games suffered from the lack of protagonists other than white, straight men (Cote 2018; Salter & Blodget 2017, 75–78). One of the most iconic video game characters is Mario, a white man on a mission to save princess Peach, who is in turn depicted as an extremely passive woman with no agency of her own. According to Anastasia Salter and Bridget Blodgett, "in gaming, straight white male is the default avatar, which brings with it a different set of assumptions and consequences that make it difficult for games to break out of the straight white male gaze" (2017, 75). They continue to state that "in most video games, particularly in genres associated with the hardcore title, straight white male is often the only avatar presented" (75). While this is still not that uncommon in video games, and many video games still portray characters and their gendered agency in this manner, there have been some notable exceptions. The most famous is most likely Lara Croft from *Tomb Raider* (Core Design 1996). Lara Croft can be seen as part of a larger movement introducing female protagonists to films and games (Kennedy 2002). She, however, like many following female protagonists in video games, showcases a kind of femininity that is very much preferred in the patriarchal society: fit, (hetero)sexually appealing, and young, as women's value is often tied to age and ageing is seen differently for men and women (Schubart 2019). That said, games like *Last of Us* (Naughty Dog, 2013) offer more diverse female protagonists and alter the way gendered agency is represented in games. However, middle-aged and ageing women as protagonists remain a rarity.

What kind of characters are included in games and how much diversity is afforded is not inconsequential: they function as a way to negotiate belonging within game culture and, in that sense, also function as horizons of belonging. They showcase the kinds of belonging – and whose belonging – is even imaginable within the context of game culture. For instance, some of the LGBTQ+ players of the game *Overwatch* (Blizzard 2016) found the game's queer characters extremely important for them. In this sense, belonging is always a privileged activity, and locations of belonging are both created and not created by game designers through character diversity – or lack of it thereof. Simultaneously, players do have interpretive power over characters (Välisalo & Ruotsalainen 2022).

While the representation of age is slowly changing at least for male characters as middle-aged men are increasingly a more visible part of video game culture, particularly older women are still rare as video game characters. As I have argued in my earlier work, middle-aged women are negotiated in the margins of game culture both as players and as characters (Ruotsalainen 2022). Furthermore, even now, when we have characters in video games that differ from the "norm" (heterosexual, white men and later young, able-bodied women), they often tend to be different only in their appearances, thus bearing little or no consequences to the gameplay or story of the game (Bohunicky & Youngblood 2019; Cullen et al. 2018). Thus, Selene, already by value of being a middle-aged female character, adds diversity to video game characters.

Two Worlds, Two Stories, Two Selenes: Female Masculinity and the Struggles of Femininity

When playing *Returnal*, the player first gets a sense of partaking in two different worlds, two different stories, and playing through two different Selenes. One Selene is strong and capable and navigates the hostile environment of Atropos with speed (albeit not without difficulty, especially in the hands of a more inexperienced player). When killing the enemies, she uses expressions like "dispatched," rather than talking about killing them. She often seems to have a nonchalant attitude towards the bodies of herself that she constantly comes across. She dryly notes that she has become used to them and can either repurpose them or take revenge for them. Revenging activates a game mechanic, where the player combats whatever killed Selene's earlier iteration and receives a reward if they are successful. In my opinion, Selene's character can be understood through the notion of female masculinity, showcasing how female bodies can perform masculinity and adopt traits and habits, such as strength, speed, and a nonchalant attitude, associated with men (Halberstam, 1998). This is also evident in the way Selene interacts with the world – through shooting. The only way for the player to advance in the game is by killing a continuous stream of enemies, using a variety of weapons discovered from Atropos. Themes such as violence are traditionally associated with masculinity in games (Kirkpatrick 2016), and shooting is a very common mechanic in games (in comparison to photographing, for example).

However, Selene's voice in the recorded logs, found next to her decaying bodies, portrays vulnerability unlike the played character of Selene, for whom the bodies of other Selenes become merely a resource and who moves past them swiftly. Selene moves in the world fast and effortlessly, the efficiency of her actions measured by a game mechanic called adrenaline level. However, when Selene enters her house – a home, traditionally considered as a female sphere – her movements change, as does the perspective she is played from, from a third-person perspective to a first-person perspective. The player therefore becomes more intimate with Selene. She is now slow, and her movements make sounds – one can hear the floorboards under her creaking as she steps on them. Moreover, the only time Selene's primary interaction with the world is not shooting is when she enters the house.

Once the game advances, the third-person Selene continues moving fast and effectively, but her voice lines start to reflect the fact that these "two Selenes" are coming closer to each other. Elements that first were only present in the house start to become present outside on Atropos as well. She talks about how the astronaut, first only present in the house, is following her. The two stories, and consequently the two Selenes, start merging. This is particularly notable in the audio logs. Whilst playing, passing Selene's decaying corpses becomes a mundane activity, but this is occasionally disturbed by the audio logs found by the corpses. These jolt the player back to having a relationship with a corpse, reminding the player that they (Selene) are the corpse, dead and violated. The application of *uncanniness*, typical for horror (Schneider 1999), is present here, and for the player, the affective power of this reminder, repeated multiple times, does not fade but begins to strengthen the idea of the inevitability of Selene's death and eternal resurrection, the suffering of the battered body. Thus, throughout Returnal, *Selene* is both the one who does violence and also the one to whom the violence is done. Re-living the trauma of physical (and mental) violence and amplifying it become the key to success, and the pain this causes is evident in the recordings. This also adds emotional depth to Selene's character, including vulnerability. Vulnerability also adds a feminine layer to Selene, as it is traditionally coded as a feminine trait (cf. Koistinen 2015). This also brings closer the two different representations of Selene.

The precarious relationship Selene's body has with her environment is not limited to discovering her bodies, but other aspects in *Returnal's* game mechanic evoke this as well. Selene can attach parasites from Atropos to her spacesuit. The parasites have both negative and positive effects (in other words, they make Selene stronger in some ways and weaker in others). In the same way, Selene can use the technology from the deceased civilisation. These encounters and fusions with the environment are inherently risky but are needed to advance in the game. They showcase Selene's hybridity and fusion with the world around her. Eventually Selene herself notes that she has lost a part of herself and has become irreversibly contaminated, acknowledging this hybridity.

Examining the two Selenes reveals how Selene's gender is negotiated within the game and how she is breaking gender norms via performative repetitions (see Butler 1988). On the one hand, Selene is represented wearing attire and engaging in activities often coded as masculine within Western contemporary culture: she is wearing a uniform almost throughout the game and is physically battling the monsters around her. Her presentation also differs from the eroticised femme fatale-like figures through which women's violence and agency are often presented in fiction (Deery 2008) and the sexualised way women are often presented in games (as discussed before). Here, I argue, two interconnected factors play an important role: Selene's age and the lack of other humans in the science-fiction setting of Atropos. Amongst the non-human beings of Atropos, Selene's humanity is momentarily allowed to be defined beyond traditional human gender roles. It is in the sequences where Selene visits her house, the feminine sphere of the home that she expresses more common feminine traits, which is mainly done through representation of motherhood and remembering, but also via game mechanics, as she is no longer shooting. The home does not belong to the sphere of the alien and the other but rather to the known and the familiar, and Selene's existence becomes negotiated via recognisable feminine traits.

The child who appears to be Selene's arguably makes Selene appear more feminine. It has, indeed, been claimed that motherhood functions as a way to feminise women otherwise portrayed in a "masculine" way in popular science fiction/action TV and films, and a notable example of this is Ellen Ripley (played by Sigourney Weaver) from the *Alien* franchise (e.g. Inness 2021; see also Koistinen 2015), to whom Selene is also compared in the game's reception. However, whereas Ellen Ripley accepts the child trusted in her care and creates a positive relationship with her, Selene's child seems to embody her struggles with being a mother and occupying this position coded both as feminine and as valuable for women (Zanin 2017).

This struggle is furthermore portrayed in the alternative ending, where Selene strangles the pregnant humanoid. In the very beginning of the game, Selene says, "Helios did not survive" in the crash. At this point, the player knows only the spaceship as Helios. However, if the player unlocks the alternative ending, they learn that the child who drowns in the car accident is most likely called Helios. It also seems that this same child is present the fourth time the player visits the house, and this time the player experiences the house from the child's perspective. Here the child listens to a message from the home phone, where Selene's voice says, "hi sweetheart, I'm not coming home," explaining she has to stay at work until late. She also gives instructions on how to warm food. The child moves to the kitchen, and there, by the dinner table, is the astronaut. Whilst eating (cereal rather than warming the food Selene talked about), the child tells the astronaut a story. The astronaut stares back, their face hidden by the helmet.

The way that *Returnal* depicts the mind of a middle-aged woman and a mother is something groundbreaking in games. Indeed, Atropos might be read as a creation of Selene's mind, or at least Selene's perception of it is strongly influenced by her past trauma. This trauma seems to be linked to her child, who appears to be dead or otherwise absent, and Selene seems to be blaming herself (and especially her wish to be an astronaut) for this. Motherhood is therefore a site of conflict and what Selene ultimately tries to reject but what also ultimately leaves her stranded and stuck on the planet. This conflict is between the traditional role of a woman and the role that is more transgressive, functioning beyond the intimacy of home. This is present also in how Selene eventually finds something that resembles sentient beings in Atropos who she thought were extinct. But instead of becoming extinct, the individuals she encounters have gone insane, and she repeatedly has to battle them in order to survive. Their quasi-sentient state and descendance into madness, rather than creating a sense of assurance that Selene is not alone, highlight how alone Selene is throughout the game. It seems to suggest that her rejection of motherhood (even if this was only emotional rejection before the death of the child), the traditional female role, has severed a fundamental bond to that which is humane and sentient, as to be that for woman is to be a mother (see Zanin 2017 about pressures of motherhood for women) and she is now left aligned with only those who have equally severed this bond – the deranged humanoids.

Reception of *Returnal*

In this section, I will focus on the reception of *Returnal*, starting by analysing how the game is discussed in game reviews and paying attention to which aspects of *Returnal* are mainly dealt with in these discussions. However, I also examine the aspects left out, thus focusing on what Patricia von Münchow (2018, 6) calls the "meaningful silences and absences" that encourage us to pay attention to those elements which are not immediately apparent in the text but can be important for the wider context. After discussing the game reviews, I will move into analysing the player reception of *Returnal*.

Only two of the analysed 28 reviews mention Selene's gender: *Gamesradar*'s Ben Tyrer (2021) brings up her likeness to the character of Ellen Ripley from the *Alien* film series, while *Spieltimes*'s Caleb Wysor (2021) brings to the fore also her age by noting that it is

> refreshing to see a game with a slightly older lead, especially a woman, as we've seen many middle-aged dad stories pop up in gaming like the recent "God of War," but very few stories about women at that same stage in life. But Selene is a character that never quite grapples with the conflicting forces acting upon her character. She feels too detached from the horrors surrounding her, and her surprisingly aloof tone and occasionally awkward writing can make it tough to empathize with her struggle.

Other reviews mention Selene's character only in passing, or not at all, and when they do mention her, they bring up neither her age nor her gender.

In addition to gender, the story of *Returnal* is not discussed much in the reviews, at least not in detail. While it is understandable that reviewers do not want to spoil the whole story for the player, one would have expected them to discuss it more. Mostly the reviewers mention the story in terms of liking or disliking it (both were present). For instance, *Eurogamer*'s Chris Tapsel notes that "[i]n *Returnal* the story and setting are so compelling that it feels like reading a good book, or binging a show on Netflix," while *Egmnow*'s Josh Harmon (2021) argues that "[b]eyond the effective structuring of the horror atmosphere, it's not like this game is telling a story worth following, for a start."

Although Selene and the plot are not discussed widely or in detail – and thus everything that makes Selene as an interesting character in terms of representation is left aside – there are certain main themes that are repeated across the reviews. First of these is the attention to genre and genre definition. The reviewers constantly look to place *Returnal* in a certain game genre or game genres and discuss it in the context of these genres. What is notable here is that the genres the reviewers discuss are first and foremost defined by game mechanics. Thus, by discussing *Returnal* as roguelike or roguelite game, or as having the elements from the "Bullet hell" type of games,[6] the reviewers also bring to forefront the importance of game mechanics and knowledge of game genres, a type of gamer capital that is considered for masculine gamer identity (Consalvo 2007), over representation.

Another constant theme is the high difficulty of the game: most of the reviewers talk about this in length, often through detailed descriptions of their own gameplay, and with rhetoric that can evoke affective responses in the reader. For instance, Eric Hauter (2021) from *Gaming Nexus* points out that they, as an average gamer, could not finish *Returnal*. Many of the reviewers highlight how unforgiving and hard the game is, often talking about how this also contributes to a sense of threat. David Burdette from *gaming trend* expands on this: "What *Returnal* does manage to accomplish however is a general feeling of uneasiness. What's around the next corner? What creatures may be waiting to tear my head off in the next area?" While it is true that *Returnal* is a very hard game and the overt focus on that again places emphasis on the mastery of the game, this review echoes the normative masculine gamer position where the values of the game and gamer are measured by how hard a game is to master and who can master it.

Graeme Kirkpatrick (2017) argues that gaming has primarily been constructed as a masculine activity, and consequently gamer identity has become understood as male. By analysing computer and gaming magazines from the 1980s United Kingdom, and game reviews in them more specifically, Kirkpatrick establishes that gamer identity has become increasingly coded as masculine and that certain aspects of games have become coded as masculine and thus more valuable. According to Kirkpatrick, with time, aspects such as story and graphics in video games have started to be considered as feminine "fluff." They are therefore seen as less valuable than the more "masculine" aspects, such as the game mechanics, certain themes in games (e.g. space and war), and particularly the difficulty of a game: a true gamer and a true man is one who can master the hardest games as well as the technology. Consequently, the games highest in hierarchy are those which are hard to master (Kirkpatrick 2017). As demonstrated above, a similar tendency can be seen in the game reviews about *Returnal*.

Another important meaningful absence can be traced by looking at the way Selene's character is largely absent in the game reviews. Whilst Kirkpatrick's research focuses on the gaming and computer magazines in the 1980s, Bo Ruberg (2018) analyses the reception of the game *Undertale*, published in 2015. Thus, while Ruberg too focuses on game reviews, the material they use is considerably more contemporary. Ruberg aptly demonstrates how *Undertale* has a considerable amount of queer content, from non-binary characters to same-sex relationships between characters. *Undertale* also differs from many contemporary video games by the game design that allows using other ways than violence to complete the game. This can also be understood as a form of "queer game mechanics," or queering the gameplay, as it alters the typical game mechanics of shooting and killing which are intimately tied to masculinity (Engel 2017).

Despite the visible queer content and LGBTQ+ presentation in *Undertale*, Ruberg notes that game reviewers largely ignore this, choosing instead to focus on *Undertale's* level of difficulty as a game, on the mastery of the game mechanics (even those which do not include killing) and on the nostalgic appeal of the game. They thus establish *Undertale* as a heteronormative space (as this nostalgia is directed to a time when the issues of diversity were largely ignored in game culture) and effectively *straightwash* it. Similar practice of *doing away* can be seen in the reviews of *Returnal*: by focusing on the aspects of the game that are coded as masculine and ignoring Selene's character's gender and age as well as the complex story present in the *Returnal*, the game reviewers place the game firmly in the hypermasculine traditions of game culture.

Player Discussions on *Returnal* and Selene

I analysed nine discussion threads where players of *Returnal* scrutinised specifically Selene as a middle-aged woman character and what that meant to them. It is important to note that these discussions are a minority of all discussions taking place around the game. Most discussants in these threads who disclosed their own gender were women.

The discussants say it is important to them to be able to see themselves in the game: Selene makes them feel represented and gives them someone to identify with. The discussants praise both Selene's appearance and her personality. They highlight how important it is to have female characters in video games – as well as female characters that embody diversity in terms of age. Moreover, the discussants praise the way Selene is depicted as a middle-aged woman, drawing attention to the visible lines on her face: she is not only middle-aged but is also allowed to have visible signs of ageing. As mentioned previously, Schubart (2019), for instance, notes that ageing women are culturally preferred not to have any signs of their age. One discussant even discloses that their first thought upon seeing Selene was thinking how brave the developer is, making such an unusual character. The discussants also compliment the story and Selene's personality, noting how multidimensional she is, and how Selene is neither a hero nor a villain, but simply a deeply flawed person. Some discussants also compare her, like one of the reviewers, to Ellen Ripley from the *Alien* film series, noting that she even sounds the same. It would not be surprising if these similarities are not accidental.

Selene is also seen as a well-made character, rather than a "token female," and her gender and age are argued to be an important part of the game. Selene is seen as extremely fitting for the game, as the game deals with themes of motherhood in so many ways. One discussant even suggests that the whole of Atropos is an extension of her mind. Simultaneously, it is also stated that it should not be an issue even if she would just be a middle-aged woman and her age and gender would have nothing to do with the plot of the game as this is, in the end, how it often is with characters who are men. This brings forth how men still continue to be the default characters in games and how women and gender minority characters are often expected to have particular reasons for their existence in the game.

In some of the discussions the focus is on speculating what *Returnal*'s ending means and the discussants share different interpretations of the game's story. These also function as sites of *queering* the game and as bringing forth the *queerness* already inherent in *Returnal;* one of the discussion threads even focuses on the possibility that Selene is actually a trans character. Queering here is understood not only as queering sexuality and gender but also as a practice of creating spaces of possibility: "queerness as a 'horizon' of potential toward which we continually strive" (Harper, Taylor & Adams 2018, 2).

These player discussions demonstrate that at least for some of the players Selene's gender and age – the representation of a middle-aged woman she offers – are highly meaningful, and through different readings and interpretations, they open the space of possibility and create new horizons. By doing this, these discussions also contest the creative authority of the game developer by bringing forth an interpretation of Selene that is, if not intended, at least not explicitly stated by the developers. Similar interpretative authority and creation of new horizons of belonging can be seen in how some of the self-identifying queer *Overwatch* players hailed one of the *Overwatch* characters as queer and gay icon, even if this was never the intention of the developers (Välisalo & Ruotsalainen 2022). Similarly, the player reception of *Returnal* contests the institutional authority the game reviewers have, bringing forth different readings of the game and different understandings of what is important in *Returnal* and thus in games in general. In that way, they create a discourse of resistance for a hypermasculine, heteronormative game culture.

Conclusion

Women and marginalised groups continue to negotiate and fight for their position in game culture. Gaming continues to be seen as mainly masculine activity, and people who are not white, straight men continue to struggle with having their presence acknowledged and accepted within game culture. One of the ways in which toxic game culture has been maintained is making only certain types of games with only certain type of characters. *Returnal* is a needed change from that, being an AAA game with a middle-aged woman as the protagonist. Examining the game reveals that the character's age and gender, as they intersect in the game, are meaningful for both the gameplay and the story of the game.

Player discussions, particularly by female players, also affirm the importance of having a varied representation of people in games. Earlier research has time and time again established the importance of representation for marginalised players. However, in the game reviews, Selene's gender is effectively negotiated away and barely mentioned. This can be seen as a way for game culture to stay loyal to its roots and maintain the hegemonic position of geek masculinity and gamer identity. However, this interpretation is resisted by the players of the game who forefront Selene's age and gender as meaningful to them – and for the way they negotiate their belonging to game culture.

Notes

1 The PC version of *Returnal* was released 15 February 2023.
2 What is typical for these games is the presence of perma-death: every time a player dies, they will have to start playing the game from the beginning without their equipment or from a set spot. What is also typical for roguelikes is that the levels are procedurally generated; thus, the map changes after each death.
3 AAA games are usually made with a big budget and typically produced and distributed by well-known publishers. These games tend to have a high visibility.
4 https://www.youtube.com/watch?v=mX58Z_ct-ow&ab_channel=Shirrako
5 https://www.youtube.com/watch?v=HmDlHjYjLCw&ab_channel=Gamer%27sLittlePlayground
6 In bullet hell games (also known as manic shooter games), one of the central mechanics is evading incoming bullets as a player. These games tend to have a very high level of difficulty.

References

Blizzard Entertainment. 2016. *Overwatch*. PC.
Bohunicky, Kyle & Jordan Youngblood. 2019. "The Pro Strats of Healsluts: Overwatch, Sexuality, and Perverting the Mechanics of Play." *Gender Studies*: np.
Brand, Jeffrey E. & Scott Knight. 2005. "The Narrative and Ludic Nexus in Computer Games: Diverse Worlds II." In *DiGRA Conference*, np.
Butler, Judith. 1988. "Performative Acts and Gender Constitution: An Essay in Phenomenology and Feminist Theory." *Theatre Journal* 40 (4): 519–531.
Consalvo, Mia. 2007. *Cheating: Gaining Advantage in Videogames*. Cambridge & London: MIT Press.
Consalvo, Mia. 2012. "Confronting Toxic Gamer Culture: A Challenge for Feminist Game Studies Scholars." *Ada: A Journal of Gender, New Media, and Technology* 1 (1): 1–6.
Cote, Amanda C. 2018. "Writing 'Gamers' the Gendered Construction of Gamer Identity in Nintendo Power (1994–1999)." *Games and Culture* 13 (5): 479–503.

Crenshaw, Kimberle. 1990. "Mapping the Margins: Intersectionality, Identity Politics, and Violence against Women of Color." *Stanford Law Review* 43: 1241–1299.

Cullen, Amanda L. L., Kathryn E. Ringland & Christine T. Wolf. 2018. "A Better World: Examples of Disability in Overwatch." *First Person Scholar*, np.

Deery, June. 2008. "The Biopolitics of Cyberspace. Piercy Hacks Gibson." In *Future Females, The Next Generation. New Voices and Velocities in Feminist Science Fiction Critisism*, ed. M. S. Barr, 87–108. Lanham: Rowman & Littlefield.

Downs, Edward & Stacy L. Smith. 2010. "Keeping Abreast of Hypersexuality: A Video Game Character Content Analysis." *Sex Roles* 62: 721–733.

Engel, Maureen. 2017. "Perverting Play: Theorizing a Queer Game Mechanic." *Television & New Media* 18 (4): 351–360.

Freeman, Melissa. 2014. "The hermeneutical aesthetics of thick description." *Qualitative inquiry* 20 (6): 827–833.

Friman, Usva. 2022. *Gender and Game Cultural Agency in the Post-gamer Era: Finnish Women Players' Gaming Practices, Game Cultural Participation, and Rejected Gamer Identity*. Turku: University of Turku.

Gamer's Little Playground. 2021. "RETURNAL All Cutscenes (Game Movie) PS5 4K 60FPS Ultra HD." https://www.youtube.com/watch?v=HmDlHjYjLCw&ab _channel=Gamer%27sLittlePlayground. Accessed 1 March 2024.

Halberstam, Jack. 1998. *Female Masculinity*. Durham: Duke UP.

Harmon, Josh. 2021. "Returnal Review." *Egmnow*, April 29, 2021. https://egmnow .com/returnal-review/. Accessed 1 March 2024.

Harper, Todd, Meghan Blythe Adams, Nicholas Taylor & Gerald Voorhees (eds.). 2018. *Queerness in Play*. New York: Palgrave Macmillan.

Hauter, Eric. 2021. "Returnal Review – Gaming Nexus." *Gaming Nexus,* April 29, 2021. https://egmnow.com/returnal-review/. Accessed 1 March 2024.

Housemaque, 2021. *Returnal*. Playstation 5, PC.

Inness, Sherrie A. 2021. *Tough Girls: Women Warriors and Wonder Women in Popular Culture*. Philadelphia: University of Pennsylvania Press.

Ivory, James D. 2006. "Still a Man's Game: Gender Representation in Online Reviews of Video Games." *Mass Communication & Society* 9 (1): 103–114.

Kennedy, Helen W. 2002. "Lara Croft: Feminist Icon or Cyberbimbo?" *Game Studies* 2 (2): 1–12.

Kirkpatrick, Graeme. 2016. "Making games normal: Computer gaming discourse in the 1980s." *New media & Society*, 18 (8): 1439–1454.

Kirkpatrick, Graeme. 2017. "How Gaming Became Sexist: A Study of UK Gaming Magazines 1981–1995." *Media, Culture & Society* 39 (4): 453–468.

Kocurek, Carly Ann. 2012. "Masculinity at the video game arcade: 1972–1983," (UT Electronic Theses and Dissertations) (Doctoral dissertation). University of Texas. Texas ScholarWorks. Available online at: https://repositories.lib.utexas .edu/handle/2152/22133

Koistinen, Aino-Kaisa. 2015. "Maskuliinisuuksia ja vaarallista seksuaalisuutta: naiset ja väkivalta *Taisteluplaneetta Galactica* -televisiosarjassa." In *Uhri, demoni vai harhainen hullu? Väkivaltainen nainen populaarikulttuurissa*, ed. Tiina Mäntymäki, 153–170. Vaasaa: Vaasan yliopiston julkaisuja.

Lockhart, Eleanor Amaranth. 2015. *Nerd/Geek Masculinity: Technocracy, Rationality, and Gender in Nerd Culture's Countermasculine Hegemony*. Collage Station: Texas A & M University. OAKTrust.

Meriläinen, Mikko & Maria Ruotsalainen. 2023. "The Light, the Dark, and Everything Else: Making Sense of Young People's Digital Gaming." *Frontiers in Psychology* 14: Article 1164992, np.

Naughty Dog. 2013. *Last of Us*.

Ruberg, Bonnie. 2018. "Straightwashing Undertale: Video Games and the Limits of LGBTQ Representation." *Journal of Transformative Works and Cultures* 28: np.

Ruberg, Bonnie, Amanda L. L. Cullen & Kathryn Brewster. 2019. "Nothing But a 'titty Streamer': Legitimacy, Labor, and the Debate Over Women's Breasts in Video Game Live Streaming." *Critical Studies in Media Communication* 36 (5): 466–481.

Ruotsalainen, Maria. 2022. "'Cute Goddess is Actually an Aunty': The Evasive Middle-Aged Woman Streamer and Normative Performances of Femininity in Video Game Streaming." *Television & New Media* (5): 487–497.

Saldivar, Diego. 2022. "Cyberpunk 2077: A Case Study of Ludonarrative Harmonies." *Journal of Gaming & Virtual Worlds* 14 (1): 39–50.

Salter, Anastasia & Bridget Blodgett. 2017. "Come Get Some: Damsels in Distress and the Male Default Avatar in Video Games." In *Toxic Geek Masculinity in Media*, 73–99. London: Palgrave Macmillan.

Schneider, Steven. 1999. "Monsters as (Uncanny) Metaphors: Freud, Lakoff, and the Representation of Monstrosity in Cinematic Horror." *Other Voices* 1 (3): 167–191.

Schubart, Rikke. 2019. "'How Lucky You Are Never to Know What It Is to Grow Old.' Witch as Fourth-Wave Feminist Monster in Contemporary Fantasy Film." *Nordlit* 42: 191–206.

Scott, Suzanne. 2019. *Fake Geek Girls*. New York: New York UP.

Shirrako. 2021. "RETURNAL PS5 Gameplay Walkthrough FULL GAME (4K 60FPS) No Commentary." https://www.youtube.com/watch?v=mX58Z_ct-ow&ab_channel=Shirrako. Accessed 1 March 2024.

Taylor, Tina Lynn. 2012. *Raising the Stakes: E-sports and the Professionalization of Computer Gaming*. Cambridge: MIT Press.

Taylor, Nicholas & Gerald Voorhees (eds.). 2018. *Masculinities in Play*. New York: Springer.

Toby Fox. 2015. *Undertale*.

Tyrer, Ben. 2021. "Returnal Review: 'Sony's Most Beguilingly Weird Blockbuster in a Long Time." *GamesRadar*, April 29, 2021. https://www.gamesradar.com/returnal-review/. Accessed 1 March 2024.

von Münchow, Patricia. 2018. "Theoretical and Methodological Challenges in Identifying Meaningful Absences in Discourse." In *Exploring Silence and Absence in Discourse*, eds. M. Schröter & C. Taylor. London: Palgrave Macmillan.

Välisalo, Tanja & Maria Ruotsalainen. 2022. "'Sexuality does not belong to the game': Discourses in Overwatch Community and the Privilege of Belonging." *Game Studies: The International Journal of Computer Game Research* 22 (3): np.

Wodak, Ruth & Michael Meyer. 2001. "Multidisciplinary CDA." In *Methods of Critical Discourse Analysis*, eds. Ruth Wodak & Michael Meyer, 95–121. London: SAGE Publications Ltd.

Wysor, Caleb. 2021. "Returnal Review — There's Joy In Repetition." *Spieltimes*, April 29, 2021.

Zanin, Andrea. 2017. "Ellen Ripley: The Rise of the Matriarch." In *Alien and Philosophy: I Infest, Therefore I Am* eds. Jeffrey A. Ewing, Kevin S. Decker & William Irwin, 153–165. John Wiley & Sons.

15

ONCE AGAIN YOU VOTED THE WRONG WAY!

Atorox Award, Short Fiction, and the Finnish SFF Fandom

Oskari Rantala

One exceptional aspect of the Finnish speculative fiction field is the prominence of short fiction and the fan activities surrounding and supporting it. A central institution in this respect is the country's oldest speculative fiction award Atorox, awarded annually to the best speculative short story by a vote among fans. The award is grounded in the participatory science fiction and fantasy fan culture that in Finland is a rather highly organised network of interlinked fan associations and communities.

Due to its focus on short fiction as well as its logic of participation, the Atorox award is quite exceptional even in international comparison. The fact that it has survived and thrived in the ever-shifting scene of science fiction and fantasy fandom for four decades makes it an interesting topic for examination. More expansive formats such as novels, films, and television series have unquestionably become more prominent than short stories in the science fiction and fantasy culture at large. However, Atorox has succeeded in driving interest towards speculative short fiction, and, in fact, the number of dedicated voters has increased year by year.

In this chapter, I offer an overview of the history of the Atorox award and the related debates in Finnish SFF fandom as well as the developments in participation and the makeup of the winners during the last decade. My main data consists of Atorox-related fandom discussions in magazines published by Finnish science fiction associations during the 1980s and 1990s and a corpus of ten Atorox-winning stories from 2011 to 2020.[1] This canon of awarded stories sheds light on what kind of stories the current Finnish speculative fiction fandom considers the best and most engaging short fiction.

Atorox has been discussed and debated by fans throughout the course of its existence, during which the small, nascent science fiction fandom

DOI: 10.4324/9781003561101-21

evolved into a significant and established literary subculture. The chapter thus inquires what the history of the Atorox award and the debates around it reveal about the development of the Finnish SFF fandom, its current state, and the aspects that perhaps set it apart from other national fandoms.

Background

There has been little academic interest in Finnish science fiction culture, the only exception being a doctoral thesis by Irma Hirsjärvi (2009) based on fan interviews. The Atorox award and the connected speculative short fiction field have received no attention, as the research on Finnish SFF literature has focused on novel-length works or, in the case of short stories, on singular commercially published authors (e.g. Ollikainen 2017; Kankkunen 2021; Toikkanen 2022).

Arguably, short fiction has been and continues to be important in the global Anglophone science fiction and fantasy culture as well. Organised science fiction fandom originally came into being by coalescing around pulp era[2] short fiction magazines such as *Amazing Stories* in the 1920s and the 1930s (Hellekson 2018, 66–67; Moskowitz 1974, 5). Historically, publishing short speculative fiction has often been a profitable business in the English language context. Even though the publishing field has decisively shifted towards long-form prose, contemporary English language magazines and anthologies have sufficient audiences to be commercial, albeit often small press, enterprises (see Sanford 2019; Locus 2021).

In Finland, the publishing landscape is markedly different. There is a strong tradition of publishing short stories of varying lengths in magazines and anthologies (Matilainen 2014, 51), yet almost none of them are commercial in any meaningful way. Even though short fiction has kickstarted the careers of some internationally renowned Finnish authors – such as James Tiptree Jr. Award winner Johanna Sinisalo – the writers, readers, and publishers can all be considered fans rather than professionals working primarily for pay. This is not to suggest that there would not also be professionally published authors engaged in these activities, but as the field is concentrated around magazines published by and writing contests organised by not-for-profit associations, money seldom changes hands. Even when it does, it is rarely if ever the main motivator for creators.

Before going further, one terminological point is in order. Many major international speculative fiction awards draw distinctions between short fiction of different lengths. The Hugo Awards[3] and the Nebula Awards,[4] to name but two, have different categories for short stories (under 7,500 words), novelettes (7,500–17,500 words) and novellas (17,500–40,000 words). In Finland, however, such categories have never been used, and word counts designed for fiction in English would not work for obvious linguistic reasons.[5] Therefore, the term "short story" refers to all lengths of short fiction in this chapter. To be exact, most of the recent Atorox-winning stories tend to be rather extensive works, perhaps closest to long novelettes of the Anglophone SFF field.

Lastly, it is worth pointing out that I am myself a participant in the Finnish SFF fan culture, even though I belong to a later generation. As an active SFF fan and researcher as well as an occasional Atorox voter, I am hardly an outsider in this subculture. However, I was not involved with fandom during any of the fan debates discussed here, and my viewpoint is limited to what can be observed from fan magazines. A relative inside perspective on the subculture is in some instances important for deciphering the complexities of fan interactions.

A Short History of the Atorox Award

First awarded in 1983, the Atorox award is given annually to the best speculative short story published in Finland during the previous year. The award is administered by the Turku Science Fiction Association (Turun Science Fiction Seura; later TSFA), a pioneering actor in the Finnish science fiction field in many respects. Founded in 1976, it is the first SFF fan association in the country as well as the publisher of the first Finnish speculative fiction magazine *Spin*.

The late 1970s and especially the early 1980s were formative years for Finnish science fiction fandom, as several other fan associations emerged and launched their own magazines (Hirsjärvi 2009, 161–163). At the time, these were perhaps best described as fanzines, even though some of the ones still operating have evolved into publications that appear highly professional. These magazines were the first stable venues for short-form speculative fiction that were otherwise few and far between – in fact, very little Finnish science fiction or fantasy literature of any length was published at the time (Ijäs 1990, 35).

Organised science fiction fandom was born significantly later in Finland than in many Anglophone countries or the closest Nordic neighbours. In comparison, the history of Swedish science fiction clubs and Norwegian fanzines goes back to the 1950s (e.g. Määttä 2006, 182–183; Cato 1999). Despite the late start, the Finnish fandom has been one of the more vibrant and active science fiction and fantasy fan communities in Europe since the turn of the millennium. When it organised the 75th Worldcon (World Science Fiction Convention) in Helsinki in 2017, Finland became one of the few non-Anglophone countries that have ever hosted the global event.[6]

The Atorox award is one of the early institutions formed in the Finnish fandom. When it was first awarded in 1983, the award did not have a title other than "Scifi prize" (TSFA 1983, 12–13). At the time, TSFA had not yet secured the rights to use Atorox, the name of the robot protagonist who visits different planets in the 1940s pulp science fiction novels by Finnish author Aarne Haapakoski. This happened the following year, and since then, the winner has received a clay head of the robot (TSFA 2022a). There is no monetary aspect to the award, and the stories compete only for prestige and recognition.

If the first unnamed award is counted, a total of 41 short stories have won the Atorox award to date.[7] The list of winners reveals conclusively that the fan magazines have been the primary venue for short speculative fiction in Finland. More than three quarters of the award-winning stories originally appeared on the pages of magazines *Portti*,[8] *Tähtivaeltaja*,[9] *Aikakone*,[10] or *Kosmoskynä*,[11] published by the Tampere Science Fiction Association, Helsinki Science Fiction Association, Ursa Astronomical Association (later Aikakone Association), and the Association of Finnish Science Fiction and Fantasy Writers, respectively.

The quality of these magazines can be considered high or professional, but none of them are strictly speaking commercial publications, as they are created by fans and anchored in the Finnish speculative fiction fan culture.[12] Before becoming defunct after issue 4/1995, *Aikakone* was the standard bearer for quality short fiction and the venue for most Atorox-winning stories. Since then, *Portti* by Tampere Science Fiction Association has taken its place and stories published in the magazine have been awarded as many as 22 times during the 41 years of the award's history. The main reason for this domination is likely the magazine's annual short story contest with a gracious monetary prize for the winner. In addition to Atorox, this long-running competition can be considered another major institution supporting short Finnish speculative fiction.

In total, there have been only nine Atorox winners that were initially published in a venue other than the four magazines mentioned above. Four of them appeared in anthologies published by either Ursa Astronomical Association[13] or Osuuskumma,[14] a cooperative formed by tens of Finnish speculative fiction writers. Therefore, only the last 5 of the 41 winners might be considered commercially published in the traditional sense. Three of them appeared in anthologies containing stories by multiple Finnish authors and two in short story collections by a single author.

This quick rundown of Atorox award winners aptly captures the Finnish speculative short fiction market during the last four decades. An overwhelming majority of Finnish short SFF stories are published in semi-professional magazines or anthologies put together by committed fans and active writers themselves, and only in rare instances do corporate publishers show interest in short-form speculative fiction. For some writers, however, literary success in the speculative fiction fandom has contributed to the launch of a professional writing career – examples include frequent Atorox winners Johanna

Sinisalo (awarded in 1986, 1989, 1991, 1993, 1994, 1997, and 2001), Pasi Ilmari Jääskeläinen (awarded in 1998, 1999, 2000, and 2012), and Anne Leinonen (awarded in 2004 and 2007).

Negotiating the Rules for Participation

As mentioned before, Atorox is an award for Finnish speculative short fiction. Defining Finnish speculative fiction, however, is a complicated issue, and the current Atorox rules have intricate criteria for the nationality of the author, the language of the story, and the publishing venue (see TSFA 2022b, 2022c). Stories written by Finnish authors in Swedish or by foreign authors in Finnish as well as stories appearing, for example, in self-published zines are eligible under certain conditions. However, these considerations have remained theoretical. All the winning stories have been written in Finnish by Finnish writers and published in established Finnish fan magazines, anthologies, or collections. More contested parts of the rules are the ones setting voting procedures: who gets to vote and how the votes are counted. The rules have changed at least ten times in 40 years, ranging from extensive overhauls to minor modifications.

A complete set of up-to-date rules for the award have often not been made available, but their evolution can be traced from fan magazines. The Atorox award, its significance, voting procedures, and rule changes have indeed been frequent topics of discussion in fandom forums. As editor-in-chief Erkki Lindholm wrote in *Spin* in 1988: "The award has been hotly debated. Without going further into this, I just point out that the rules have been modified, but it seems like there is no more than one person satisfied with the Atorox guidelines each year"[15] (Lindholm 1988, 3). Especially in the 1980s and the early 1990s, discussion among fans was at times intense and conflicts between different actors and associations were visible on magazine pages.

At the time of writing the present chapter, Atorox voting has been completely open for everybody for over 15 years. Anyone can sign up to become a voter, and all readers can nominate stories to be included on the list of finalists. One does not have to be a member of any organisation or even Finnish to participate. Although newer Atorox voters might take this democratic approach for granted, it was actually implemented as late as 2007. Prior to that, there were certain safeguards in place against completely open participation – or, in other words, to ensure that Atorox reflects the tastes of committed fans and enthusiasts of the organised Finnish science fiction fandom. Indeed, Atorox was originally conceived as an award of knowledgeable fans who were active in the newly founded fan associations. The early Finnish fandom had a need for distinguishing itself from the general public, emphasising its own subcultural literacy and protecting its institutions from outsiders.

In *Spin* 2/1982, the TSFA chair Pekka Hernejärvi informed the readers for the first time about "a nationwide writing and drawing competition for Finnish science fiction stories and comics" (Hernejärvi 1982, 27), even though it was later decided that the first "Scifi Competition" would only have a category for prose stories (TSFA 1983, 12). "Now begins the difficult and dutiful work of the juries," commented *Spin* editor-in-chief Harri Haarikko (1983, 2) when releasing the list of all stories published in fan magazines during the previous year. The juries, it turned out, consisted of active members of the science fiction associations of Turku and Tampere and a single fan from Oulu. In 1984, the award was officially named Atorox, and the Science Fiction Association of Helsinki formed a jury as well. Next year, the editors of *Aikakone* magazine were added as the fourth jury (Roimola 1996, 9–10). Each of these juries put together their own list of best stories which were then compiled to decide the winner.

After three years, it was already recognised that some changes would be necessary. When the third winner had been awarded, TSFA acknowledged that "[b]ecause the selection process of the ATOROX award has been rightly criticised, we will seek to clarify the award rules in the future and possibly increase the number of selectors" (TSFA 1985, 8). The rules were modified, and anybody who wished could now take part in voting. There were the juries of five associations, and all other votes would be combined into a sixth list (TSFA 1986, 47). Even though the number of eligible voters increased, the rules preserved the strong influence of established fan associations. Due to the jury system, even a huge number of outside voters would not be able to heavily influence the process. The issue was discussed regularly, and in 1987 TSFA secretary Ben Roimola announced again that "[i]t has been decided that ATOROX will remain an award by the so-called active hobbyists" (1987, 4) instead of a more popular vote.

Fears of a strong outside influence proved to be unwarranted, however. The participation of readers not belonging to fan associations remained minor and the open vote was scrapped in 1991. Another stated reason was that voters were now explicitly required to read all eligible stories, and this was deemed something that the general public outside the active associations would not do – "[w]e do not want them distorting the results" (Pajunen 1991, 11). Voting procedures were changed, and the associations would no longer compile their own lists. Instead, all associations could name up to five voters whose votes would be counted equally in the final count (Pajunen 1991, 10–11). The public vote was restored but limited to ten voters in 1998. In the last major overhaul in 2007, all the limits were lifted: all associations could have as many voters as they wished, and all interested fans outside them could vote as well.

Since then, the voter numbers have been steadily growing. In 2000, there were 31 voters, whereas in 2020, there were 83. Voters are generally committed fans, however, since all of them pledge to read over 20 stories comprising the shortlist, which is a significant commitment. In short, it appears that the award has remained an effort of the organised fandom, but the organised fandom has grown. The traditional associations have been joined by more informal web communities and fan groups that have been incorporated into the Atorox award process.

Debating Atorox Voting

Even though the rules governing the Atorox voting were openly discussed in Finnish fandom, a topic of even more heated debate has been the way voters and nominators act within these parameters. Judging by the concerns raised by fans in *Spin* and other magazines, there have been two major bones of contention. On the one hand, some fans voted (or nominated) "the wrong way," while, on the other hand, some fans did not participate at all even though they were expected to.

The fact that Atorox results have brought up criticism in a community of opinionated and outspoken fans is hardly surprising. Already after five Atorox awards in 1988, it was suggested in the fan press that the award tends to favour a certain kind of pretentious stories (e.g. Ijäs 1988, 29; Lehtinen 1988, 29), whereas others vehemently disagreed with this criticism (e.g. Jerrman 1987, 27). Twenty years later, some concerns raised were quite similar: why do not "good old-style science fiction and fantasy" stories do as well as they should in the Atorox vote (Henriksson & Karppanen 2007, 11)? In fact, some fans' dissatisfaction with the voting results was almost a running joke in the fandom. In Finncon 2007, a panel discussion on Atorox awards was titled "Once again you voted the wrong way!"

Certain patterns of voting or nominating were considered more of a breach of etiquette than others, however. In 1993, TSFA chair Hannu Pajunen admonished fans whose nomination choices they did not consider sufficiently objective:

> To tell the truth, one must be taken aback by nominators who have not read short stories worthy of nomination from anywhere other than the publication of their own association ... there are such persons in more than one SF association. Already last year, my opinion was that the voting process should be completely public (otherwise this favouritism will never end), but my position lost.
>
> *(Pajunen 1993, 2)*

Voters who seemed to favour the stories in magazines they were themselves producing was a frequent grievance. As Atorox vote was conducted with preferential lists containing several stories in ranked order, it was possible to game the voting system to some extent. Voting only for one's own favourites and leaving the rest of the ballot empty was reportedly not an uncommon practice (see comment by Suntila in Karppanen 2001, 28).

It is perhaps debatable whether the voters in actuality intended to mathematically maximise the impact of their votes, but tactical voting was considered a serious enough problem to warrant a rule change in 2007. At the time, TSFA argued explicitly that it sought to "increase the fairness of the process and remove the possibility for tactical voting" (TSFA 2007). The ranked lists were replaced by a system of instant-runoff voting, which eliminates some issues that were considered problematic.[16]

Even though several stakeholders in the fandom held strong opinions about the award and had invested a lot of time and effort in it, it is worth pointing out that not all discussion around it was entirely serious. The tone of discourse in the fandom has always been informal and irreverent. While describing the modified vote counting method for the tenth Atorox in 1992 in the official TSFA bulletin, Hannu Pajunen wrote: "This method seems to work: this year, nobody griped about the system [didn't they now? -ty] which wouldn't have done them any good anyway" (Pajunen 1992, 2). Pajunen's humorously aggressive tone or bulletin editor Tero Ykspetäjä's (-ty) sarcastic comment in the middle of the sentence is not something that one would expect to see in the context of the literary field's most prestigious award in most other genres.

A prank that a group of fans from Helsinki conducted in the Atorox nomination process in 1993 illustrates the attitude in fan communities as well as the effort they were willing to make to prove a point. Previous year, the group had published a booklet titled *Kaikkien huijausten äiti ja muita Atorox-voittajia* ("The mother of all hoaxes and other Atorox winners") under the name Jukka Laajarinne – he was (and still is) a real writer who at the time acted as the chair of the Association of Finnish Science Fiction Writers. Only a couple of the included stories were written by Laajarinne, whereas other fans wrote for the booklet several intentionally bad stories that were credited to him. As three nominations were enough to get a nominee on the final ballot, three fans sent in identical photocopied ballots nominating all the 24 stories in the booklet. The prank was not well taken by Atorox organisers, and the stories were described as "pieces of junk" (Pajunen 1993, 2) in *Spin*, but they were admitted on the list of finalists because no rules were violated. The crux of the prank was to draw attention to the fact that the requirement for three nominating votes was arbitrary and the system could easily be gamed in case somebody sought to do that.

As the prank illustrates, there were those with something of a carnivalistic approach to fandom, while others took the fan matters more seriously, and this dynamic led to some minor conflicts. On the whole, however, the Atorox process and the culture around it were informal and ad hoc compared to the rigorous rules of many international awards. Even though the people behind the prank did intend to raise an issue concerning the Atorox nomination, it is safe to assume that it was more about having fun in a creative and communal way rather than organising an earnest influencing campaign.

In the early Finnish fandom, there were also Atorox-related conflicts that were caused by fans not voting at all instead of voting the wrong way. The Tampere Science Fiction Association, which was the second oldest Finnish fan organisation (Hirsjärvi 2009, 161), dropped out of the Atorox voting and became the only active fan association not involved in it in the late 1980s and early 1990s. Apparently, the reason for this fandom feud was that the fans from Tampere felt that fans from Turku did not take part actively enough in a reader poll of their own magazine (Haarikko 1988, 5). As the Atorox award was intended to be a joint effort of the whole Finnish fandom, a major association being absent was met with quizzical and snarky commentary in the fan magazines. "Looking at the list of Atorox voters, one is astonished by the passivity of the association publishing the biggest SF magazine in Finland. What's the matter now that the Tampere SF association board doesn't vote?" wondered *Spin* editor-in-chief Ben Roimola (1989, 3). Two years later, Hannu Pajunen reported on the Atorox results with more sarcasm: "Tampere Science Fiction Association did not react to our invitation in any way – maybe the mail lost the letter?" (Pajunen 1991, 11). The Aikakone Association also boycotted the Atorox in 1995, when stories published in *Aikakone* issue 1–2/1994–1995 were not accepted on the final ballot until the next year due to the unusual cover date (Pajunen 1995, 6; Hinkkanen & Peltonen 1995, 4).

Atorox was clearly a matter of great importance for many in the Finnish fandom, and questions about winning it or being eligible for it were not taken lightly. Fans also took the projects and activities of their own associations very seriously and were ready to intervene when they felt that those were slighted by other actors in the fandom. Various discourses around the award show that there was an idealised conception of what an Atorox voter should be like. In addition to being an active, committed fan and a member in a fan association, they were expected to use tens of hours to read all the works in the final ballot and vote objectively, without favouring magazines they are themselves associated with. Before a nomination phase was added, an Atorox voter in practice had to be a reader of all the fan magazines, including some obscure fanzines. Obviously, only a person well-connected and involved in the fan community could fill these expectations.

These shared assumptions defined a certain fandom elite but, on the other hand, also made clear to prospective fans how one could join it: as different associations and organisations were founded, those were welcomed into the organised fandom and into the Atorox vote as well. In the mid-1990s, there were already nine fan groups or associations taking part in the Atorox vote, even with one major association abstaining. It is not unreasonable to assume that the Atorox award played at least some role in shaping this model for fandom participation. Therefore, one can consider SFF fan culture open and inclusive while also acknowledging that there are certain hierarchies at play.

The claims that, for example, the award-winning stories would have become too far removed from core science fiction at one time or another do mirror interestingly some arguments made in the global SFF fandom. In 2013–2017, specific fan groups aimed to influence the Hugo Awards of World Science Fiction Society with tactical voting campaigns. Motivated by the supposed high-brow aesthetics and progressive politics of many fiction writers and editors, these campaigns managed to politicise the Hugo Award vote and polarise the fan community (Oleszczuk 2017; Canavan 2017). One can ask, why nothing of this scale and intensity has ever taken place in Finland despite certain amount of fan quarrels. A possible answer might be that even though its organisation is decentralised, the Finnish national fandom is highly interconnected. This interconnectedness is bound to produce shared values and uphold expectations of accepted behaviour. Attacking other fandom factions too harshly or importing culture war rhetoric into fandom discussions would not be considered acceptable, as opposed to the more heterogeneous Anglophone SFF fandom.

Atorox on the Planet of the 2010s

The 2010s were the first full decade of voting with the current system, with all the limits on voter participation lifted in 2007. As a matter of fact, that was the first decade of no significant procedural changes whatsoever. In the 1980s, 1990s and 2000s, the rules were being constantly modified, especially earlier on. Therefore, years 2011–2020 saw a rise in voter participation that was not caused by rule changes. Instead, it seems that the interest in the award and short Finnish speculative fiction was on the rise.

In 1992, as few as 33 jury members were enough to set a new record. When the rules were amended in 1998, the number of voters rose to 42. Between 2001 and 2010, the number of voters mostly remained below 50, but it has been steadily rising since. Between 2016 and 2020, a new highest number of Atorox voters was recorded almost every year. The field has grown markedly, and there are now more publications, more published short fiction, more semi-professional authors and more readers willing to participate. The number of voters, which has been in a constant upward trend, surpassed 80 individuals for the first time in 2020. Against this background, it is interesting to discuss the works and writers that were awarded during the past decade (see Appendix 1 for complete list).

Compared with the preceding ten years, some shifts are immediately apparent from the list of awarded stories, writers and publishing venues.

As far as the Atorox award is concerned, *Portti* magazine had overshadowed everything else between 2001 and 2010, having published nine out of ten Atorox winners. In the 2010s, its dominance was somewhat less overwhelming and stories in *Portti* were awarded a total of six times. The rest of the winners appeared in anthologies exploring various themes: cheating, pirates, steampunk, and ecological science fiction. Thematic anthologies have offered the writers a new option for getting published and added diversity into the SFF scene. As most of them are publications by the writer cooperative Osuuskumma, the producers of fiction are themselves becoming more active in shaping the publishing landscape of short fiction alongside associations which publish the traditional fan magazines.

The list of Atorox-winning writers has become more diverse as well. Earlier, it was not uncommon that certain writers would almost monopolise the field. Pasi Ilmari Jääskeläinen, for example, won three Atorox Awards in a row in 1998–2000, while Johanna Sinisalo has been awarded as many as seven times in total. During the last decade, however, there were nine separate winners, as only prolific short story writer Maiju Ihalainen managed to win twice in 2015 and 2017.

Of the nine winners, all are writers of some renown. Magdalena Hai, Janos Honkonen, Pasi Ilmari Jääskeläinen, Jenny Kangasvuo, Anne Leinonen, and Anni Nupponen have all published at least one and in many cases several novels before winning the Atorox Award. The rest of the winners – Maiju Ihalainen, Jussi Katajala and Reetta Vuokko-Syrjänen – are well established in the speculative fiction scene for their output of short fiction. Atorox winners seem to be distinguished writers with notable careers already, but the number or successful authors in the genre has grown and none of them overshadows the others in quite the same way Jääskeläinen or Sinisalo were able to do earlier. This is another indication that the Finnish short speculative fiction scene is broadening and attracting more active writers and readers.

Atorox-winning stories also reveal some directions in which the tastes of the Finnish speculative fiction fandom have been shifting. For example, the winners tend to be fantasy instead of science fiction, a clear break from the stories awarded during the previous decade. There is no one particular subgenre of fantasy that would dominate the list, however. Anne Leinonen's "Nahat" ("Skins," 2011) takes place in a pre-mediaeval fantasy setting and Anni Nupponen's "Joka ratasta pyörittää" ("The One Who Turns the Cogwheel," 2013) in a steampunk world, whereas Jenny Kangasvuo's "Musta otsa" ("Black Forehead," 2018) is urban fantasy dealing with the challenges that indigenous minorities face in a post-industrial society.

Very few of the winners are set in a completely fantastical milieu explicitly separate from the primary world of the readers. More often, the stories are situated in a world otherwise resembling our current or historical world with one speculative element, be that a species of squids that attains consciousness and turn to ecoterrorism in "Mare Nostrum" (2014) by Jussi Katajala or a medical condition that makes a person remember the things that will happen to them in advance but forget them as soon as they occur in "Kirje Lethelle" ("A Letter to Lethe," 2012) by Pasi Ilmari Jääskeläinen. Among the ten stories, the only ones that seek to extensively describe and establish a secondary world are Nupponen's tale set in a quirky steampunk city where a cogwheel has been installed on every person and "Kaunis Ululian" ("Beautiful Ululian," 2016) by Magdalena Hai in which air-borne pirates fly over deadly crystal seas raiding towns.

Perhaps interestingly for a science fiction and fantasy award, none of the stories take place in space or on other planets. The sample is arguably small, but space exploration and space opera do not seem to be subgenres that would hold the interest of current Finnish speculative fiction fans. Ten years earlier, such stories were commonplace among the Atorox winners, and it remains to be seen whether they are just temporarily out of fashion or have fantasy and science fiction more firmly grounded in our world become the predominant subgenres in the Finnish speculative fiction scene. Any kind of Tolkienesque, mediaeval-inspired, or epic fantasy is another subgenre that is completely absent from the list of winners, even though it dominates novel-length fantasy. This can be associated with the conception of Finnish Weird as an alternative to situating Finnish SFF writers works inside the established popular genres of science fiction and fantasy (see also chapter by Raipola in this volume). Originally, the multiple Atorox-winning author Johanna Sinisalo (2011) presented Finnish Weird in her essay as a more suitable umbrella term for Finnish speculative fiction that does not fit the stereotypes of either Tolkien-inspired heroic fantasy or technology-heavy space opera – which is how she argues many readers still view these genres.

All ten stories are written by Finns for a Finnish audience, but only four take place specifically in Finland. In addition to stories by Jääskeläinen and Katajala mentioned earlier, "Emma Halmin vaihtoehdot kuolemalle" ("Emma Halm's Alternatives for Death," 2020) by Reetta Vuokko-Syrjänen is situated in postapocalyptic Tampere and "Sadan vuoden huuto" ("Hundred Year Scream," 2019) by Janos Honkonen in Jyväskylä. In contrast, both Atorox-winning stories by Maiju Ihalainen are set in a milieu reminiscent of Ancient China, featuring some fairy-tale elements such as the ability to breathe life into terracotta sculptures or dragon tears that heal any sickness. Even though several stories take place in Finland, the story by Honkonen is the only one seriously entrenched in Finnish culture and history. In it, a time-traveling protagonist is sent from the future back to year 1918 and the Finnish Civil War to prevent atrocities committed by the victorious White Army. They become stuck in time, though, and must live the next hundred years disguised as an ordinary Finnish citizen.

In terms of themes or plot elements, the ten stories have little in common. However, two general points can be made. Atorox winners tend to be conventional, straightforward classical narratives: the storylines are linear, writing style is lucid and the stories offer little in the way of narrative innovations. They also often espouse social commentary instead of focusing on more personal issues or sheer sense of wonder. Jääskeläinen's story, which deals with remembering future events and then forgetting them, may be seen as the one exception. Its narrative is somewhat complex as it strives to demonstrate the perplexing temporal experience of the protagonist and its scope is more personal than societal.

Whether this reflects the reading preferences of an average Finnish speculative fiction fan is an interesting question. During the same decade, for example, the annual Tähtivaeltaja Award for the best science fiction novel has been awarded to works such as *Lomonosovin moottori* by Antti Salminen, *Blindsight* by Peter Watts and *The Quantum Thief* by Hannu Rajaniemi, all of them unconventional and innovative works. Even if the winner is selected by a jury instead of a popular vote, the selectors belong to the same network of dedicated speculative fiction fans, and it is safe to assume that the award reflects (and influences) the tastes in the fandom.

The social issues and societal tensions that the Atorox winners foreground are diverse. In stories by Ihalainen, the protagonist has to act against immoral authorities, whether it is an emperor abusing their consorts or a greedy temple abbot inflicting drought and sickness on people. In the technothriller story by Jussi Katajala, nature and underwater creatures are turning on humans for our crimes against the planet. Reetta Vuokko-Syrjänen explores on the one hand the rights of artificial humans and on the other a society in which people are so estranged and mentally stressed that the healthcare system cannot cope — therefore, the protagonist is assigned an artificial friend to make their life more tolerable. In the story, the plan works, but the characters and the readers get to consider whether personhood and human rights belong to technologically reappropriated human bodies. Anni Nupponen deals with the same issues from a steampunk perspective. In their story, the people are enhanced with cogwheels that cause complications in the relationships between characters.

The legacy of the violent Finnish Civil War of 1918 and the welfare-turned-unwelfare state in Janos Honkonen's and Reetta Vuokko-Syrjänen's stories are grounded in contemporary Finnish society, even if they are discussed through the lens of science fiction. The atrocities carried out during the Civil War and the disintegration of social safety nets are frequent flashpoints in Finnish political discourse. The indigenous people and their right to preserve their own culture examined by Jenny Kangasvuo are further removed from contemporary Finland, as the story takes place in an undefined country with an invented native people with black bones. The history of racialisation and discrimination of the indigenous Sámi people are, however, often discussed in Finland, and readers are aware of this context.

It will be interesting to see whether these national trends will be visible in the Atorox-winning works of future decades, since the speculative fiction culture is becoming more global. Today, science fiction and fantasy content dominate the international entertainment industry to a degree that early Finnish fans of the 1970s and 1980s could never have imagined.

In Conclusion: Finnish Fandom in Comparison

All things considered, the focus on short stories in the Finnish speculative fiction scene is an intriguing phenomenon. The Atorox award is, on the one hand, its product and, on the other, a reinforcing institution that keeps short fiction at the forefront of Finnish fandom activities. During the last 40 years, the Atorox award has offered a meaningful way for different fan associations to cooperate and form networks, even if it has at the same time stirred up debate and conflicts. It has also given new fan groups a model for activities and encouraged fans to organise, because it has always been first and foremost an award given by organised fandom.

One exceptional aspect of the Finnish speculative short fiction field and the Finnish speculative fiction fan culture overall is its uncommercial nature. Magazines are published by fan associations and fans writing for them are doing so without compensation save the occasional prize from a writing competition. However, the quality of the prose is high and has arguably improved over the years. In the Atorox vote, stories in fan magazines continue to beat professionally published short fiction. Many successful novelists have emerged out of this cultural undergrowth, however, and today none of the Atorox award winners can be described as amateurs.

Especially during the last ten years, the Atorox-winning writers have become more professional, fantasy has superseded science fiction and the very top of the Finnish speculative fiction has broadened so that single authors do not stand out as clearly as before. The prominence of fantasy, classical narrative structures and social themes instead of science fiction, experimentation and more personal stories are recognisable phenomena. Whether these trends will last in the 2020s and 2030s is another matter.

Examining the peculiar aspects of the Finnish speculative fiction fandom leads one to contemplate whether there is something substantial setting the Finnish fan culture apart from other national fandoms and how these differences have developed. It is worth pointing out that organised SFF fan culture took hold in Finland relatively late, and in practice it was imported from Sweden. Despite all the small-scale fan activities in the late 1970s, a significant milestone was the very first fan convention held in May 1982. As many of the organisers and audience members were Swedish and the event started in a ferry from Stockholm to Helsinki (Hirsjärvi 2009, 169–170), it can almost be considered a Swedish convention held in Finland. Compared to Sweden, the beginnings of Finnish fandom were strikingly modest. At the time when the high points of Finnish science fiction culture were photocopied fanzines, professional science fiction magazines such as *Jules Verne-Magasinet* and *Häpna!* had already been appearing in Sweden for half a century and there were science fiction clubs with history going back for decades (Määttä 2006, 63, 69–70, 143–144). On the other hand, one could argue that the directions in which the Finnish fandom developed are connected to these differences.

As there was practically no commercial science fiction culture, the fandom concentrated on organising itself into associations and producing fan magazines. In time, this led to the emergence of a participatory fan culture that is constantly looking to recruit new active members. This might never have happened in case the commercial infrastructure had already existed, and prospective fans could have more easily assumed the position of a consumer instead of that of a participant.

In addition, the Finnish SFF fan culture has always been decentralised. There has never been one large national science fiction association that would dominate the field. Instead, the associations based in different cities have engaged in different activities, co-operated, influenced, and mainly promoted but at times also criticised each other. Lively conversations have shaped the fandom, and one of the hot topics debated has been the Atorox Award, as this chapter has sought to demonstrate.

Appendix 1: Atorox Awards 2011–2020

Year[17]	Writer	Story[18]	Published in	Voters
2011	Anne Leinonen	Nahat ("Skins")	*Portti* 3/2010	46
2012	Pasi Ilmari Jääskeläinen	Kirje Lethelle ("A Letter to Lethe")	*Valhe & viettelys* (Teos)	35
2013	Anni Nupponen	Joka ratasta pyörittää ("The One Who Turns the Cogwheel")	*Steampunk! Koneita ja korsetteja* (Osuuskumma)	53
2014	Jussi Katajala	Mare Nostrum	*Huomenna tuulet voimistuvat* (Osuuskumma)	51
2015	Maiju Ihalainen	Terrakotta ("Terracotta")	*Portti* 4/2013 [2014]	52
2016	Magdalena Hai	Kaunis Ululian ("Beautiful Ululian")	*Kristallimeri* (Osuuskumma)	62

Year[17]	Writer	Story[18]	Published in	Voters
2017	Maiju Ihalainen	Itkevän taivaan temppeli ("The Temple of the Crying Heaven")	*Portti* 1/2016	47
2018	Jenny Kangasvuo	Musta otsa ("Black Forehead")	*Portti* 4/2016 [2017]	62
2019	Janos Honkonen	Sadan vuoden huuto ("Hundred Year Scream")	*Portti* 4/2017 [2018]	66
2020	Reetta Vuokko-Syrjänen	Emma Halmin vaihtoehdot kuolemalle ("Emma Halm's Alternatives for Death")	*Portti* 1/2019	83

Notes

1 Furthermore, some individuals have graciously answered my questions. I would like to thank especially Irma Hirsjärvi, Jukka Laajarinne, Simo Suntila, and Jukka Halme as well as Katja Juusela of Turku Science Fiction Association for providing me with Atorox voting statistics.

2 Pulp magazines refer to cheaply produced and inexpensive fiction magazines that were an important medium for genre-based popular literature especially in the first half of the twentieth century.

3 Awarded by World Science Fiction Society.

4 Awarded by Science Fiction and Fantasy Writers Association.

5 Compared with English, a text written in a language such as Finnish that employs no articles or prepositions has significantly fewer individual words.

6 The other ones being West Germany (1970), Netherlands (1990), and Japan (2007).

7 All award totals and percentages in this chapter include the awards from 1983 until 2023.

8 Awarded in 1983, 1984, 1988, 1998, 2000–2004, 2006–2011, 2015, 2017–2020, 2022, and 2023.

9 Awarded in 1987, 1995 and 1999.

10 Magazine now defunct, awarded in 1985, 1986, 1990, 1991, and 1996.

11 Awarded in 2021.

12 Commercial considerations were perhaps most relevant for *Aikakone*, which was first published by the Ursa Astronomical Association. However, it was turned over to a fan association formed by the staff in 1989 (Hinkkanen 1991, 15–16; Peltonen 1991, 20).

13 Awarded in 1989.
14 Awarded in 2013, 2014, and 2016.
15 All translations from Finnish by the author.
16 Instant-runoff voting allows the voters to vote for multiple candidates in order of preference without their second choice decreasing their first choice's possibility of winning. The vote counting mechanics are somewhat complicated, but a similar system is used by World Science Fiction Association for selecting the winners of Hugo Awards, and therefore many Finnish fans are familiar with it. For further information, see World Science Fiction Association 2022.
17 The year when the award was given, not the year when the awarded story was originally published.
18 Approximate translations from Finnish by the author of this chapter.

References

Canavan, Gerry. 2017. "New Paradigms, After 2001." In *Science Fiction. A Literary History*, ed. Roger Luckhurst, 208–234. London: The British Library.

Haarikko, Harri. 1983. (Untitled editorial.) *Spin* 1/1983: 2.

Haarikko, Harri. 1988. "Puheenjohtajan palsta." *Spin* 3/1988: 4–6.

Hellekson, Karen. 2018. "The Fan Experience." In *A Companion to Media Fandom and Fan Studies*, ed. Paul Booth, 65–76. Hoboken: Wiley-Blackwell.

Henriksson, Saara & Pasi Karppanen. 2007. "Finncon 2007. Huonon onnen con?" *Kosmoskynä* 2/2007: 6–12.

Hernejärvi, Pekka. 1982. "Puheenjohtajan palsta." *Spin* 2/1982: 27.

Hinkkanen, Juhani. 1991. "Olin kaksi vuotta *Aikakoneen* päätoimittajana ja jäin henkiin." *Aikakone* 3/1991: 15–17.

Hinkkanen, Juhani & Leena Peltonen. 1995. (Untitled letter on the letter column.) *Spin* 6/1995: 4.

Hirsjärvi, Irma. 2009. *Faniuden siirtymiä. Suomalaisen science fiction -fandomin verkostot*. The Research Centre for Contemporary Culture: University of Jyväskylä.

Ijäs, Jyrki. 1988. (Untitled letter.) *Kosmoskynä* 1/1988: 29.

Ijäs, Jyrki. 1990. "Suomalainen tieteiskirjallisuus." In *Science Fiction*, eds. Juhani Hinkkanen & Kai Ekholm, 11–38. Helsinki: Kirjastopalvelu.

Jerrman, Toni. 1987. (Untitled letter.) *Kosmoskynä* 2/1987: 27.

Kankkunen, Sarianna. 2021. *Harassing Habitats: Experienced Space in Finnish Contemporary Fiction, A Study on Maarit Verronen*. Helsinki: University of Helsinki.

Karppanen, Pasi. 2001. "Suuri Atorox-keskustelu." *Kosmoskynä* 1/2001: 26–34.

Lehtinen, Vesa. 1988. (Untitled letter.) *Kosmoskynä* 1/1988: 29.

Lindberg, Cato. 1999. "When Fandom Came to Norway." *Mimosa*, No. 23: 18–21. http://www.jophan.org/mimosa/m23/lindberg.htm. Accessed 1 March 2024.

Lindholm, Erkki. 1988. "Toimittajan höpinöitä." *Spin* 1/1988: 3.

Locus. 2021. "Year-in-review: 2020 Magazine Summary." *Locus*, February 15. https://locusmag.com/2021/02/year-in-review-2020-magazine-summary. Accessed 1 March 2024.

Matilainen, Hanna. 2014. *Mitä kummaa. Opas kotimaiseen spekulatiiviseen fiktioon*. Helsinki: Avain.

Moskowitz, Sam. 1974/1954. *The Immortal Storm. A History of the Science Fiction Fandom*. Westport: Hyperion Press.

Määttä, Jerry. 2006. *Raketsommar. Science fiction i Sverige 1950–1968*. Lund: Ellerströms förlag.

Oleszczuk, Anna. 2017. "Sad and Rabid Puppies: Politicization of the Hugo Award Nominating Procedure." *New Horizons in English Studies* 2/2017: 127–134.

Ollikainen, Minttu. 2017. "Dreams and Themes in the Texts of the 'Reaalifantasia' Group: Unnatural Minds in Anne Leinonen's *Viivamaalari* and J. Pekka Mäkelä's *Muurahaispuu*." *Fafnir – Nordic Journal of Science Fiction and Fantasy Research* 4 (2): 45–55.

Pajunen, Hannu. 1991. "Atorox-kilpailun viralliset tulokset." *Spin* 3/1991: 10–12.

Pajunen Hannu. 1992. "Atorox X on ohitse!" *Spin Extra* 1/1992, *Atorox-tiedote Turun Science Fiction Seura ry:n jäsenille*: 2.

Pajunen, Hannu. 1993. "Puheenjohtajan mietteitä." *Spin* 3/1993: 2.

Pajunen, Hannu. 1995. "Finncon-special." *Spin* 4/1995: 4–6.

Peltonen, Leena. 1991. "Kun se parasta on ollut..." *Aikakone* 3/1991: 18–20.

Roimola, Ben. 1987. "Sihteerin sivu." *Spin* 3/1987: 4–5.

Roimola, Ben. 1989. "Puhelu päätoimittajalta." *Spin* 3/1989: 3.

Roimola, Ben. 1996. "Pikakelauksella läpi TSFS:n vuosien." *Spin* 1/1996: 9–11.

Sanford, Jason. 2019. "#SFF2020: The State of Genre Magazines." Jason Sanford's website, December 30. https://www.jasonsanford.com/blog/2019/12/sff2020 -the-state-of-genre-magazines. Accessed 1 March 2024.

Toikkanen, Jarkko. 2022. "Sanallisen kauhun intermediaalinen kokemus. Marko Hautalan *Leväluhta*." *AVAIN - Kirjallisuudentutkimuksen Aikakauslehti* 19 (1): 64–73.

TSFA. 1983. "Scifi-kilpailu." *Spin* 1/1983: 12–13.

TSFA. 1985. "Atorox 1984." *Spin* 3/1985: 8.

TSFA. 1986. "Atorox 1985." *Spin* 1/1986: 46–47.

TSFA. 2007. "Uudet Atorox-säännöt." Turku Science Fiction Association website, 27 February 2007. The site used at the time is no longer online, archived version accessed 31 January 2022. https://web.archive.org/web/20070715213748/http:/ /www.tsfs.fi/blog/2007/02/27/uudet-atorox-saannot. Accessed 1 March 2024.

TSFA. 2022a. "Atoroxin historiaa." Turku Science Fiction Society website. http:// www.tsfs.fi/?toiminta/atorox/historia.html. Accessed 1 March 2024.

TSFA. 2022b. "Atorox-säännöt." Turku Science Fiction Society website. http://www .tsfs.fi/?toiminta/atorox/saeaennoet.html. Accessed 1 March 2024.

TSFA. 2022c. "Kelpoisuus Atorox-ehdokkaaksi." Turku Science Fiction Society website. http://www.tsfs.fi/?toiminta/atorox/saeaennoet/kelpoisuus-atorox -ehdokkaaksi.html. Accessed 1 March 2024.

World Science Fiction Association. 2022. "The Voting System." The Official Site of the Hugo Awards. http://www.thehugoawards.org/the-voting-system. Accessed 1 March 2024.

16

TRACING "CHTHULUCENE ENVIRONMENTAL IMAGINATIONS" IN CONTEMPORARY ART

The Speculative in the Work of Larissa Sansour and Johannes Heldén

Caroline Elgh

Reality sometimes seems stranger than fiction: humans are destructively terraforming planet earth on a rapid and global scale, and what is often merely described as climate change is under the surface a far more complicated and wide-ranging ecological crisis. Whilst the effects of climate change have become increasingly clear, a growing number of international visual artists have during the past two decades turned towards environmental and speculative practices. Through the lens of speculation, artists have found new strategies of exploring possible futures and creative imaginations that open up new understandings of the world. In this chapter I seek to highlight the relationship between visual art, ecology, and speculative practices through the work of two contemporary artists with connections to the Nordic countries. Thinking through the speculative work of Larissa Sansour and Johannes Heldén, the chapter aims to trace *Chthulucene* (Haraway 2016, 5) types of *environmental imaginations* (Yusoff & Gabrys 2011, 1) in art and to reflect on these imaginations as utopias, dystopias, or simply worlds that might be more ethical to live in. What potential worlds are embedded in these specific artworks and in what ways do they relate to the Nordic context? Through a feminist visual analysis, the chapter approaches the two-channel film installation *In Vitro* (2019) by Sansour, made in collaboration with Søren Lind, and the sculptural installation *Extinction Archives (Part 1)* and *Meditations* (both 2019) by Heldén. The analyses are performed as visual *close readings* (Lykke 2010, 187), which in this case implies a focus on the ecological aspects of the artists' work.

  In the context of this chapter, the term "Nordic" is seen through the lens of *situated knowledges* (Haraway 1988, 575–599), an epistemological take

DOI: 10.4324/9781003561101-22

that challenges disembodied scientific objectivity. The concept implies that knowledge is as much a social phenomenon, as it is embedded in a specific cultural and political setting, as it is material: a form of feminist embodied objectivity (Haraway 1988, 581). Consequently, the Nordic is seen here as a sociopolitical, geographical, and environmental site, at the same time as it is understood as a social construction in the form of an imagined community (Anderson 1983, 6), within which the artists operate, remotely or more directly. This chapter therefore investigates how these entanglements are articulated in the works of Sansour and Heldén. The chapter begins with a theoretical framing, followed by a short overview of the connections between Nordic speculative fiction and art. This is, then, succeeded by analyses of Sansour's and Heldén's work and concluded by a discussion on what reflections these "Chthulucene environmental imaginations" – a concept I derive from Haraway and Yusoff & Gabrys – might evoke in audiences, and why such reflections are of crucial importance at the current juncture.

"SF," Planetary Crises, and Imaginations

Donna Haraway's neologism Chthulucene[1] constitutes an alternative to the more frequently used term "Anthropocene," popularised by Paul Crutzen and Eugene Stoermer (Crutzen & Stoermer 2000, 17–18). With the concept Chthulucene, Haraway criticises the anthropocentrism embedded in the concept Anthropocene and introduces the idea of "multispecies assemblages," meaning the envisioning of the possible survival for humans and nonhumans alike in the current ecological crisis. For Haraway, "[o]ne way to live and die well as mortal critters in the Chthulucene is to join forces to reconstitute refugees, to make possible partial and robust biological-cultural-technological recuperation and recomposition" (2015, 160). But what can this approach mean in practice? Ecofeminist pioneer Val Plumwood (2007, 1–4) writes:

> If our species does not survive the ecological crisis, it will probably be due to our failure to imagine and work out new ways to live with the earth, to rework ourselves and our high energy, high consumption, and hyperinstrumental societies adaptively … We will always go onwards in a different mode of humanity, or not at all.

Plumwood thus emphasises that we urgently need to find new ways to imagine life on earth including more sustainable ways of living as humans in constant entanglement with the nonhuman world (see also Haraway 2016, 4). Art has a long tradition of testing the boundaries of the realistically depicted, to speculate and to imagine new worlds. How do contemporary imaginations in art, then, relate to our present condition? How can imaginations be used to inspire action towards more sustainable living conditions for humans and nonhumans alike?

Haraway declares that all beings on Earth are living in disturbing and troubling times where the Chthulucene constitutes a timeplace for "staying with the trouble" (Haraway 2016, 1–2). This "staying with the trouble" implies learning to be truly present, "not as a vanishing pivot between awful or edenic pasts and apocalyptic or salvific futures, but as mortal critters entwined in myriad unfinished configurations of places, times, matters, meanings" (Haraway 2016, 1–2). Unlike the dominant narrative of the Anthropocene discourse that places humans at the centre of both the destruction and the salvation of planet earth, the Chthulucene is made up of ongoing multispecies stories, practices, and entanglements in current precarious times where humans can no longer be considered the only important life form (Haraway 2016, 55). In the Chthulucene there is no good God or advanced technology that will come to the rescue; instead Haraway suggests that we need to start from the present situation and engage in "SF," which they see as a method of tracing science fiction, speculative fabulation, string figures, speculative feminism, and science fact (Haraway 2016, 2–3, 10). Through the SF method, Haraway identifies the world as a kind of multispecies assemblage in which people, plants, insects, bacteria, and animals tangle together in innovative ways: basically, a practice and process for ongoingness in the Chthulucene (Haraway 2015, 160; Haraway 2016, 3, 16, 38).

The SF method is strongly related to Haraway's concept of *worlding* as a worldbuilding practice (Haraway 2008; Spivak 1988; Hellstrand 2015, 2020), where the suffix -ing shifts the world from a being to a doing, a process of setting up the world that according to Haraway is a practice of entering a world which relies on species interdependence (Haraway 2008, 19). This Harawayian world-making connects to the aforementioned science fiction as well as to speculative fiction more broadly, Ursula Le Guin's work in particular, as it allows for abstractions to be built up and then broken down so that richer and more responsive invention and speculation – worlding – can go on (Haraway 2008, 92–93). The abbreviation SF in the context of this chapter thus refers to the Harawayian worlding of which speculative, environmental, and Chthulucene-like imaginations – including imaginations presented in speculative fiction – are part and not to the genre of science fiction (typically called "SF") or the broader category of speculative fiction as such.

I argue that the works by Sansour and Heldén include speculative elements that operationalise as part of the Harawayian SF worldbuilding method. In this sense, Haraway's method invites us to think through the work of Larissa Sansour and Johannes Heldén and their host of "companions" – flowers, trees, seeds, and speculative-fictional clones or AIs – present in their works as speculative worlding practices.

Kathryn Yusoff and Jennifer Gabrys's introduction of the *environmental imagination* as a concept aligns with Haraway's SF method and the Chthulucene timeplace. Here, I touch upon two concepts: imagination and the imaginary. The relationship between them is not often sufficiently problematised (an exception being, e.g., Lennon 2015). The imaginary has frequently been discussed in philosophy, psychoanalysis, and cultural theory (e.g. Foucault 1998; Dawson 1994; Bryld & Lykke 2000; Braidotti 2006; Shildrick 2009) and is characterised by the way fantasy images and discursive formations coincide (Åsberg 2005, 30) or as "a realm of imagining the future, and reimagining the borders of the real" (Franklin 2000, 198). In this chapter, I see imagination as a speculative and creative power, system, or process that generates new ideas and perspectives, whilst the imaginary relates more to what is in fact already present in the phenomenal world and how this can be transformed. I prefer to discuss both concepts in plural, since I believe that a multitude of perspectives exists at the same time. Yusoff and Gabrys highlight imagination as a site of interplay between material and perceptual worlds and a way of seeing, sensing, thinking, and dreaming the formation of knowledge (2011, 1–2).

Today several academic disciplines have begun to pay attention to climate as a dynamic, cultural, and societal force capable of reshaping societies and environments (ibid.). This brings us to the realm of the emerging transdisciplinary research field of environmental humanities, starting from the premise that environmental problems are not just technical problems that require technical solutions, but we also need to take into account the human desire, motivation, and values in relation to what we call "nature" or "environment" (Neimanis, Åsberg & Hedrén 2015, 80). The environmental humanities in the feminist registers identify environmental imaginaries as a crucial concern – as sites of negotiation that can orient material action and interaction and further guide us to increase our responsiveness to nonhuman nature not only locally but in various temporal and spatial modes (Neimanis, Åsberg & Hedrén 2015, 80–82). Basically, then, the environment cannot be divorced from humans' social and cultural imagination, something that, I argue, becomes strikingly clear in the work of Sansour and Heldén. Art that imagines the unimaginable through speculative fiction may in this way mobilise imaginative acts that open new spaces and practices for dealing with the effects of living with uncertain futures (Yusoff & Gabrys 2011, 3).

Yusoff and Gabrys argue that the imagination of climate-change landscapes is an entry point for examining environmental relations to identity, place, practices, and nonhumans. This can be referred to as the *environmental imagination* (Yusoff & Gabrys 2011, 6), where the "mental" draws specific attention to the psychological and speculative. As such, one can think of environmental imaginations in the context of this chapter as cultural speculative landscapes – based on situated, real, and experienced events or scientific facts – comprising a collection of visualisations and ideas of the environment that forms a site of negotiation that can orient material action and interaction (Dawson 1994, 48; Van Dijk 1998, 12; Åsberg 2005, 30; Stacey 2010, 25; Yusoff & Gabrys 2011, 6).

Therefore, what is at stake in this chapter is to work through the SF method that brings attention to how Chthulucene environmental imaginations are formulated within the artistic and speculative practices of Sansour and Heldén. Haraway cites scholar Sha La Bare, who writes: "What I call the 'sf mode' offers one way of focusing that attention, of imagining and designating alternatives to the world that is, alas, the case" (cited in Haraway 2016, 213). Haraway's SF method thus curiously and creatively sutures my writing practice where the artworks in question will be highlighted and immersed with feminist and environmental knowledge epistemologies.

Speculative Arts in the Nordic Context – An Overview

The ongoing interactions between visual art and speculative fiction are lively in a global context: artists use, for example, speculative methodologies, themes, topics, images, and devices in artworks crossing borders and genres. From an art-historical perspective, speculative fiction and its complex networks of ideas have influenced both surrealists of the 1920s and land artists of the 1960s (Byrne-Smith 2020, 1).[2] In the Nordic context, the interplay between visual art and the speculative is discernable in, for instance, Sten Eklund's series of hand-coloured etchings *The Secret of Kullahuset* (1971), Monica Sjöö's painting *The Goddess at Avebury and Silbury* (1978) and in experimental film works such as *Altisonans* (1966) by Karl-Birger Blomdahl and *Främmande planet* ("Alien Planet," 1960) and *EMS NR. 1* (1966) by Ralph Lundsten. Both Blomdahl and Lundsten were composers, and a vital part of Sweden's 1960s music scene, where experiments crossing boundaries between music, art, film, astronomy, natural science, and technology made a clear mark.

In the realms of Nordic speculative fiction, art, and ecology, Harry Martinson's space epic *Aniara* (1956) has had a great influence on artists' work. It is not only a key work of Nordic speculative fiction but also an early work of *climate fiction,* making it an important text to think with in relation to the work of Sansour and Heldén. Over the years, *Aniara* has taken many different shapes: an opera by Karl-Birger Blomdahl in 1959, a sound installation by visual artist Susan Philipsz at Bonniers Konsthall in Stockholm 2017, a choral-theatre work by composer Robert Maggio in 2019, and a feature film by visual artists Pella Kågerman and Hugo Lilja also in 2019. These new portrayals show *Aniara's* ongoing relevance, and its ability to adopt many different visual and musical representations. However, since *Aniara's* first release, the ecological crisis have become increasingly dire, and the speculative fiction of later years has been dominated by climate fiction dystopias that try to imagine all the different ways in which our societies are about to transform because of global warming (Määttä 2019, 33; Wälivaara in this anthology).

In the Nordic countries, contemporary visual artists like Ann Lislegaard (DK), Sandra Mujinga (NO/CG), Lea Porsager (DK), Jennifer Rainsford (SE), Jenna Sutela (FI), Jakob Kudsk Steensen (DK), Tora Wallander (SE), Niclas Wallenborg (SE), Ylva Westerlund (SE), and Lundahl & Seitl (SE) have all since around 2010 utilised speculative fiction in their works. They share an interest in speculative fiction and ecology that takes shape through installation, film, photography, sculpture, drawing, performance, and text. As it is obviously impossible to cover all these ambitious outlooks within a single book chapter, I will now shift my focus to the work of Sansour and Heldén. These two artists are brought together in this chapter because of the way their works connect with environmental imaginations and multispecies assemblages where speculative fiction is used as a strategy to test possible future scenarios.

Larissa Sansour was born 1973 in East Jerusalem, Palestine; was raised and studied in Copenhagen; and currently lives in London. In techniques such as film, performance, installation, and photography, Sansour employs speculative fiction as a tool to address social, political, and ecological issues. Memory, trauma, identity, and belonging are central concerns in her work that often balances on the border between reality and fiction. Sansour's artistic collaborator for many years, Søren Lind, was born in 1970 in Copenhagen, has a background in philosophy, and works as a writer and visual artist. Sansour and Lind set the overall artistic approach and do research together; Sansour visualises, while Lind writes the script, and they both direct the films. Since the duo conceptually work from Sansour's experience of being Palestinian, living in exile in Copenhagen and London, Sansour's name usually appears as the heading of the exhibitions they participate in, while Lind appears as the co-creator of the specific artworks. Therefore, this is also the approach in this chapter. Johannes Heldén, born in 1978 in Katrineholm, Sweden, is a Stockholm-based visual artist, writer, and musician. His interdisciplinary works unite speculative fiction, poetry, ecology, and artificial intelligence. In what follows I will investigate the entanglements of speculative fiction, ecology, and visual arts in the artistic work of Heldén and Sansour/Lind, situated in the expanded field of the Nordic.

Climate Apocalypse and Cloning as Survival

Ecology might not be the first thing one comes to think of in relation to Larissa Sansour's work. Even though their work has most often been acknowledged for addressing social and political matters in relation to the diverse geography of Palestine, it is important to point out the ecological aspects

FIGURE 16.1   Larissa Sansour & Søren Lind, *In Vitro*, 2019. Installation shot, the Danish Pavilion, 58th Venice Biennale 2019. Photo: Ugo Carmeni.

as part of the same mattering; emphasising the entanglement between the social, political, and ecological crises. Environmental humanities research has indeed highlighted that the ecological crisis is entangled with other crises and that it is no longer adequate to imagine humanness and culture as distinctly separate from nature, matter, and the planetary (Alaimo 2010, 2; Neimanis, Åsberg & Hedrén 2015, 68). In works such as *A Space Exodous* (2009), *Nation Estate* (2012), and *In the Future They Ate from the Finest Porcelain* (2016) – which together form a speculative fiction trilogy – Sansour explores identity, statehood, and political agency through a variety of futuristic settings. However, in *Heirloom* (2019) (Figure 16.1), made by Sansour and co-produced by Lind for the Danish Pavilion at the 58th Venice Biennale 2019, ecological considerations form the very starting point of the project. Given this, it is justified to concentrate the analysis in this chapter on a close reading of the ecological aspects of *Heirloom* – without forgetting its political and geographical implications, the context of the Danish pavilion, and the wider Nordic context.

In relation to climate change and speculative fiction (here specifically science fiction), Sansour declares as follows:

As for the eco-disaster aspect, sci-fi frequently turns to tropes to facilitate the clean slate, the tabula rasa, which clears the way for new structures and systems to emerge. Climate change presents the most imminent threat to our civilization at this point, and that makes the setting relatable, which is why it is important for the world-building element of sci-fi not to appear too farfetched and get in the way of the conceptual reworking I set out to accomplish.

(Sansour & Downey 2019, 62)

The above quote underlines that Sansour wants their storytelling to be relatable at the same time as it stretches the boundaries of the possible. So rather than speculating about defamiliar worlds, Sansour's approach to speculative fiction is one that stays on Earth where science fact is combined with speculative fabulation. This aligns Sansour's worldbuilding with a Harawayian understanding of storytelling – as well as with the wider scope of science-fictional storytelling, for instance, Le Guin's work – which allows for a conceptual reworking of present scenarios describing what is happening now and what could happen in the future.

Heirloom is a project consisting of the two-channel video installation *In Vitro*, the sculpture *Monument for Lost Time,* and a series of floor tiles that (during the exhibition) interacted with the architecture in the Danish pavilion. It is a large-scale production, and in total around 120 people contributed to its making. The film installation *In Vitro* (Figure 16.1) is the core of the project since it sets the narrative structure to which the other two works relate. What Sansour and Lind portray is a world where people have been forced to go underground after an overwhelming ecological disaster. The powerful opening scene of *In Vitro* shows a giant tidal wave of black oil flowing through the iconic building of the Church of the Nativity in the West Bank in Bethlehem. The wave completely destroys the city, including its historical and religious landmarks.

After the opening scene of the oil wave, *In Vitro* shifts focus to the main story that takes place 30 years after the catastrophe (Sansour & Downey 2019, 59). Here we meet Dunia and Alia, two female scientists in an underground bunker (a former nuclear reactor) where they debate the value of memory and the loss of their world above. The conversation in Arabic (subtitled in English) highlights the psychological implications of erasure relating to the ongoing climate crisis but also to the occupation of Palestinian land. Alia is a construct, a clone, a monster,[3] a genetic manipulation or an embodied other engineered by Dunia from salvaged DNA and therefore has no real memories of the environment she seeks to describe. Dunia, on the other hand, is a survivor of the catastrophe and holds memories as an existential link to who she is. The name Alia is reminiscent of *inter alia*, Latin for "among other things," which links back to the point that the clone Alia certainly is a multispecies assemblage. Human clones are a common theme through the history of science fiction and appear, for instance, in Le Guin's novelette *Nine Lives* (1968). Sansour visualises the separation between the clone Alia and the human Dunia through black-and-white imagery on a split screen, where Dunia lies on her deathbed and Alia struggles with her identity as a human/nonhuman hybrid. In Sansour's representation, Alia looks indistinguishable from humans, but in the course of the speculative storytelling, it becomes clear that she is tormented by the fact that her memories are false.

FIGURE 16.2   Larissa Sansour and Søren Lind. Film still from *In Vitro*, 2019.

Alia and Dunia live in a bunker under the city of Palestine, which is sustained by an orchard. Like Alia, the orchard with its trees, birds, and bees is produced in a laboratory where high-tech botanists work to keep the regional vegetation alive, with the aim to replant the soil above ground in the future (Sansour & Downey 2019, 66) (Figure 16.2). The laboratory is never really visually present in the film; however, it hovers like a ghost over the rest of the imagery and the conversation between Alia and Dunia, but also within the title of the film itself. *In Vitro* refers to the cloning and the life in the bunker (Sansour & Moore 2019, 116) and more specifically to the laboratory vessel in which the biological cloning process occurs. As such the title raises questions on what is real and what is fiction and brings further attention to Alia as a clone and Dunia as a human being and the entanglement between the characters portrayed as mother and daughter in the film. On a geographical and political level, their life in the bunker echoes the reality of many Palestinians living under occupation and therefore cut off from historical Palestine by strict barriers, permits, and checkpoints (Muller 2019, 13).

At the same time, the film addresses future scenarios of climate change when Earth has become uninhabitable and humans need to find other solutions for continuing life, something that climate fiction texts like *Aniara* have previously addressed. By depicting oil instead of water in the opening scene, Sansour conveys the entanglement between various environmental problems and focuses on the chain reactions between the extraction of oil, burning of fossil fuels, oil spills, warming temperatures, and flooding. Oil is a natural resource, and its extraction is a huge part of the global economy. Extraction, transport, and refining of crude oil can account for anywhere between 15% and 40% of the total greenhouse gas emissions from transport fuels such as petrol and diesel (Masnadi et al. 2018, 851). The imagery in *In Vitro* therefore shows that nature is far from passive; instead it is active and embedded in humanity itself. In its full force, the visual imagery of the wave is a speculative multispecies assemblage, a Chthulucene monster, and an awakening that asks us to reclaim vision to unpack complex planetary entanglements and interconnections, yet also to look ahead to what is to come (see Haraway 2016, 162). As Haraway would put it, *In Vitro* is "storytelling and fact telling; it is the patterning of possible worlds and possible times, material-semiotic worlds, gone, here, and yet to come" (2016, 31).

In an interview with Anthony Downey, Sansour asserts that the apocalyptic setting of the film first took its cue from the looming climate catastrophe and more specifically its implications for Palestinian agriculture (Sansour & Downey 2019, 66). With this in mind, we can follow two main research strands that Sansour and Lind engaged with while working on the film, namely, the preservation of native crops and heirloom seeds and the idea of inherited trauma. Both threads connect with biology where the vanishing of original Palestinian crops helped the artists to shape the overall approach to the climate apocalypse but also to define the development of the underground orchard (Sansour & Downey 2019, 75). The research was set up as a collaboration with the Palestine Heirloom Seed Library (PHSL) and Sansour's cousin Vivien Sansour. The PHSL is an interactive art and agriculture project with the attempt to recover ancient seeds and the stories around them. It aims to provide a conversation for people to exchange seeds and knowledge and to tell the stories of food and agriculture that may have been buried away for a long while (Sansour n.d.). In the current challenging time, *In Vitro* highlights the entanglements between history and future, politics and ecology, subject and object, collective and individual, human and nonhuman. The shifting of scale in the film – going from micro to macro, from local to global (where the Palestinian focus also is transferable to other locations in the world) – illustrates in its sound and visual imagery that the environmental crisis is not just a technical problem for environmental science to solve, since we also need to take into consideration its psychological, political, social, and cultural dimensions.

In line with Haraway's SF method, Sansour therefore applies speculative fabulation, string figures, speculative feminism, science fact, and science fiction in a way that opens an urgent and critical reflection about the state of local-planetary politics and environments and all their complex entanglements. The speculative feminism approach in particular is highlighted in the sense that Sansour clearly avoids one-dimensional and Eurocentric master narratives of control, domestication, and beliefs in nature as a phenomenon "out there." Instead, as an artist, Sansour insists on multi-layeredness and hybridity, where the story in *In Vitro* is told from the perspectives of a human and a clone portrayed as female: an approach that is also notable through the course of the artist's oeuvre.

Plant and Animal Meditations from the Future

Johannes Heldén's speculative worlds are often set in a near future where images, animation, text, and music are combined into installations, performances, or digital works. Thus, like Sansour, the speculative aspects of Heldén's work operate especially in the framework of science fiction. As a poet, Heldén has published 12 books where the written word often connects with the artist's visual and oral manifestations in exhibition spaces. Ecological speculations, but also themes related to artificial intelligence, are at the very core of Heldén's works such as *First Contact* (2019), *The Extinction Archives (Part 1)* (2019), and the series *Meditation* (2019). To begin with, the poetry book *First Contact* and the animated video installation *The Extinction Archives (Part 1)* (Figure 16.3) both relate to the same worldbuilding, namely how life would be if humans no longer inhabited the Earth. The video may be seen as a continuation and prolonging of the book where the video's imagery and soundscape give the text a visual and audial shape, at the same time as the two elements, the book and the video, evidently function separately from each other. This captivating and intricate interplay and blurring of boundaries between text, sound, and image makes these works particularly relevant for analysis in this chapter. Taking the year 2037 as the starting point, Heldén invites the viewer, in the book as well as the video, to follow what seems to be a survivor from a spaceship that has crashed on a planet in a distant solar system. As the survivor walks along the spaceship, we encounter plants and insects that seem to be hybrids, as life forms from Earth have mutated with extraterrestrial ones into what Haraway (2016, 41) would describe as multispecies assemblages.

Heldén is an artist whose speculative storytelling leaves room for interpretation, and even though we are not completely sure where we are located

FIGURE 16.3   Johannes Heldén, *The Extinction Archives (Part 1)*, 2019. Animation, sculpture, mixed media. Duration 3:49 min loop. Courtesy Cecilia Hillström Gallery.

(on what planet, solar system, etc.), it is always a place where nonhuman life forms are the focal point, whereas humans are placed in the periphery, and time seems to be non-linear. Utilising speculation to reimagine the relation between humans and the environment, as proposed by Haraway, Heldén challenges the hierarchical order between nature and culture integral to traditional European thought (Tuhiwai Smith 2021, 55). As such, their work gestures towards the Chthulucene that is made up of ongoing multispecies stories and worlding practices (Haraway 2016, 55); the *Chthulucene environmental imagination* offers tools for how to mobilise imaginative acts that open new spaces and practices for dealing with the effects of living with uncertain futures (see Yusoff & Gabrys 2011, 3).

The last chapter in the book *First Contact* is titled "Field Guide to Future Planets" and contains a list of 11 new species, like the Exoplanetary sticky alder, described by Heldén (2019, 129) as a "tree/weed hybrid" that "Grows best on rock shelves, in fog. Every forty-seven hours the silver-green mottled bark fell off in large, poisonous flakes that drifted like snow on the wind." Other species are Sylvian's ship's moss, neo-honeysuckle, cricketorium, and the red skeleton leaf, all with their own speculative species description.[4] Here, Heldén brings ecology to the very centre of the work, imagining how plants might crossbreed in a world where humans are rare and perhaps even extinct. This recalls Martinson's *Aniara* discussed above (and of course many other speculative fiction stories and worlds in literature, film, television, and games): a dystopia where humans have ruined planet earth. Feasibly *First Contact* and *Aniara* thus envision the kind of scenario described by Val Plumwood (2007, 1–4): the consequences of what will happen if humans fail to imagine and work out new ways to live with the earth.

The texts in *First Contact* are combined with dark and blurred watercolour paintings of cloudy landscapes. The painting printed on the book cover, where we see a single streetlight against a dark landscape background, is extended to the installation *The Extinction Archives (Part 1)* – an animated film with sound composed by the artist, projected on a physical copy of a book hanging on the wall (Figure 16.3). Poetry fragments from *First Contact* reappear in the animation and across its surface drifts a mixed media sculpture depicting a small, possibly fire-damaged tree with naked branches and uncovered root system, reminiscent of the displacements in Robert Smithson's *Upside Down Trees* (1969). Heldén continues the work with hybrid species in another piece titled *Encyclopedia* (collaboration with artist Håkan Jonson, 2015–2021), an installation taking the shape of an old school library stand (that was used to catalogue books before digitalisation), where small cards in drawers tell the stories of new animal species that we might encounter in the future. This work is made of a database created by the artists where an algorithm combines descriptions of animal species, alive and extinct, into new hybrid species. This algorithm also gives the animal a date of extinction, between 10 and 300 years into the future, and this text – in combination with about six sentences describing the hybrid species – is printed on cards and placed in the drawers. At an exhibition at Cecilia Hillström Gallery in Stockholm in 2019, visitors were allowed to bring one card home to become carriers of the memory of one specific hybrid in what can be considered as an act of care, responsibility, and mourning in relation to the animal in question.

Therefore, my reading of Heldén's work calls forth the Chthulucene as a timeplace, since it embraces the webs of speculative fabulation, science fiction, and scientific fact to identify the world as a multispecies assemblage where to entangle with each other in surprising "tentacular" ways (see Haraway 2016, 31–32, 101). This practice brings attention to species interdependence on Earth as something that comes out of response and respect (Haraway 2008, 19). Because "to be one is always to become with many" (Haraway 2008, 4), just consider the fact that human bodies are occupied with loads of nonhuman lives in the form of bacteria. It also includes the mourning of irreversible losses in the age of the sixth mass extinction on planet Earth. The new hybrid species created by the computer algorithm may be considered "nonsense fact" where fortuity is at stake as a way to let a nonhuman machine decide the outcome, but they may also be read as a critique against the anthropocentric Linnaean[5] order of categorising plants and animals. In both cases it constitutes an artistic critique of human exceptionalism that moves towards an understanding that humans and nonhumans are always entangled in the timeplace of the Chthulucene (see Haraway 2016, 1–2, 13).

Plant species are central to Heldén's multimedia installation series *Meditation* (Figure 16.4). Here the artist thinks with existing species that frequently appear in the Nordic countries. In four sculptural pieces taking

FIGURE 16.4   Johannes Heldén, *Meditation (Broadleaf Plantain)*, 2019. Suitcase in aluminium, future suede, two animations, watercolour collage. 48 × 53 × 33 cm. Courtesy Cecilia Hillström Gallery.

the shape of field kits for the collection of species, this installation includes animation, sound, text, and watercolour collage, arranged in aluminium suitcases. The idea for this particular series came from a herbarium that Heldén's aunt compiled in the 1940s–1950s (Heldén 2022). In Swedish schools around 1850–1950 it was a common task in summertime to collect plants in a vasculum, press and dry them, and then paste them in a herbarium. The pupils were supposed to follow in the footsteps of Linnaeus, as part of their education in botany. In Heldén's compilation we meet the species water avens, yarrow, marsh cinquefoil, and broadleaf plantain: species that are not yet endangered but could be so in the future as the temperatures increase. The purpose of the field kits is consciously made slightly obscure by the artist (Heldén 2022); however, in my reading, they appear as small-scale portable archives of more-than-human worlds coming from the future, where each suitcase constitutes a system of communication where the plants are the active agents.

The title of the work *Meditation* suggests that the artist sees themselves as a mediator or speculative storyteller in between worlds and different communication systems where the plants speak through sound, painting, text, and animation. The knowledge the plants bring is something beyond scientific fact: knowledge systems that may have been lost and forgotten within present generations of humans, concerning how it is to live as a plant on earth, to experience their aesthetics, entanglements, needs, and struggles. As portable field kits, the suitcases can also be carried along as the ecological disasters get closer, as a container or carrier bag that saves the knowledge about these specific plants for future generations, like an heirloom seed archive within a museum setting. As such the *Meditation* series is a multi-species worlding practice (Haraway 2008, 92–93) situated in the Nordic context in the time of the Chthulucene, remapping and redescribing worlds in a great variety of creative and speculative practices.

Discussion: Tracing Chthulucene Environmental Imaginations

That Sansour's and Heldén's practices are embedded in Harawayian SF, ecology, science-fictional futurities, and hybrid and nonhuman worlds has already been established in the above visual close readings. The analysis shows how, through the SF method as proposed by Haraway, we can do away with anthropocentrism and imagine new worldings where human and nonhuman life forms co-exist on more equal terms. Art is often identified as a visual category, and in this realm of visualisation, Sansour and Heldén use imagination as a site where science fact and speculative/science fiction, human and nonhuman, nature and culture, subject and object, blend into physical and material manifestations in the exhibition space. In this way the imaginations envisioned in their art are, as Kathryn Yusoff and Jennifer

Gabrys (2011, 2) propose, "a site of interplay *between* material and perceptual worlds, where concepts cohere, forces pull and attract, and things, discourses, subjects and objects are framed, contested and brought into being." What *is* brought into being, I argue, are Chthulucene environmental imaginations about worlds to come, if not already here. The oil wave in *In Vitro,* for instance, is an environmental imagination based on current floodings all over the world, and Sansour has also clearly expressed that the looming climate catastrophe was the film's starting point. The storytelling of the film thus becomes relatable because it is "staying with the trouble" at the present moment (Haraway 2016, 1–2) at the same time as it proposes new worldings. In this way, I suggest that through engaging with the film, viewers can develop new ways of noticing, seeing, and feeling and thus also ways of thinking differently, which may clear the way for new multispecies structures of care and responsibility to emerge (Puig de la Bellacasa 2017). Alia, the underground orchard, and the lab are also Chthulucene environmental imaginations where ecology and technology merge with psychology, politics, and ideas about what constitutes human and nonhuman lives. Seeing how Alia struggles with her identity and memories as a nonhuman hybrid created in the lab – including the point that the eco-disaster put them in this situation in the first place – the film may be considered a critical dystopia (Moylan 2000), containing fractions of hope, as Alia and Dunia carry the confidence that in the future the orchard will be replanted on earth.

Both Sansour and Heldén also work with multiple temporalities and the relations between, understanding the dichotomies of human and nonhuman, nature and culture as something fluid rather than fixed (see Haraway 2008, 16). Heldén's worlding practice is one where plants and animals are the storytellers, a speculative fabulation where Heldén as a poet, artist, and musician uses artistic tools to open up new scales of sensation and forms of representation by which to imagine the world. As such, the Chthulucene environmental imagination at stake here is a worlding practice communicated via plants as in the *Meditation* series or animal hybrids as in the library archive. All the works by Heldén clearly depict dystopic future scenarios of extinction, where humans have created destruction and therefore have been forced to leave Earth to find other ways of sustaining life and to archive the memory of plants and animals that have become extinct.

As for tracing the Nordic from the perspective of situated knowledges, it is important to clarify that this is a methodological viewpoint that asks us to take responsibility for what we learn to see since vision is always embedded in a socio-politically situated body, which affects what is seen and what is excluded from that particular vision (see Haraway 1988, 581, 583). The vision represented by Sansour's work is politically, socially, and geographically shaped from her experience of being a Palestinian living in exile in Copenhagen and London, but also the reality of Palestinians living under occupation as the climate changes. Therefore, *In Vitro* deals with local-planetary interconnections, operating simultaneously on local and global scales. Thus, the collaboration of Sansour and Lind also connects to the Nordic even if this specific linking is clearer on a structural and production-based level, as *Heirloom* was commissioned by the Danish Arts Council for the 58th Venice Biennale, than on the level of the narrative. Heldén's worldbuilding also takes place on a local-planetary level, whereas this knowledge production is more specifically formed within the Nordic landscape. The herbarium of his aunt and the plants Heldén thinks with in *Meditation* are species that are widely spread in the Nordic countries. Within this specific work, Heldén also situates himself as a storyteller of nonhuman worlds, where plants bear witness to future eco-disasters.

When thinking through the SF method in order to trace Chthulucene environmental imaginations, it becomes clear that both Sansour and Heldén put emphasis on the fact that humans need to find more sustainable ways of living in constant entanglements with the nonhuman world. Therefore, their speculative worlds may be transferred to many other geographical contexts since floods, droughts, agriculture, forestry, overfishing, mining, fires, toxins, drainage of lakes and rivers, air pollution, and mass extinction now indicate a systemic collapse on a global level. In Sansour's and Heldén's works, we are all entangled as humans and nonhumans living on Earth as multispecies assemblages. Meeting these works in an exhibition space may increase the visitors' felt responsiveness to environmental bodies, not only locally but also on a global and planetary scale. As such they constitute an urgent critical reflection that also envision possible survival for humans and nonhuman alike.[6]

Conclusion

This chapter has highlighted how the speculative is articulated in the work of Larissa Sansour and Johannes Heldén in the form of what I call Chthulucene types of environmental imaginations, as they examine environmental relations to identity, place, practices, and nonhumans. These Chthulucene environmental imaginations exist on multiple levels: as a giant oil wave, a clone, and an underground orchard in Sansour's work and as hybrid plant and animal species as storytellers of nonhuman worlds in the practice of Heldén. For both artists, their entry point is the looming climate disaster leading to floods and extinction – the main ecological dilemmas addressed in their works. Following Haraway, the works of Sansour and Heldén can thus be defined as multispecies assemblages that envision possible survival in times of ecological and social crises for both humans and nonhumans alike. Thus, through their works, the artists can be seen as creating possible biological–cultural–technological recuperation and recomposition in the Chthulucene, as they ask, for instance, how cloning and species hybridization may affect life in the future.

The Chthulucene types of environmental imaginations present in Sansour's and Heldén's work are primarily dystopic, leading to the question of what we can learn from such dystopian fiction or, rather, what we can learn from dystopian climate fiction in general. As an umbrella term, dystopian fiction gathers thematically close genres that often intertwine in individual works of fiction, where art can be the medium and climate fiction the category (Isomaa, Korpua & Teittinen 2020, xi). Feminist theorist Rosi Braidotti has criticised the trend in popular culture featuring dystopian fiction as a "narrow and negative social imaginary" because it signifies anthropocentrism, panic, and human exceptionalism where the broad appeal and success of the genre is embedded in contemporary capitalism (2013, 64). I argue, however, that this is not the case in the work of Sansour and Heldén, whose art is far from the storytelling and commercialism of, for instance, Hollywood blockbusters. Rather, their dystopian fiction does not hide away from the multispecies entanglements on Earth but engages with it by finding ways for staying with the trouble on a damaged planet (see Haraway 2016, 1–2; c.f. Tsing et al. 2017). Consequently, what becomes clear is that the imaginations at stake here not only shape the perceptions of climate change but also co-fabricate it in ways that affect action in the present. With this said, I claim that the art of Sansour and Heldén generates feelings and thus provokes the viewer to think about what it might be like to endure and survive, both emotionally and practically, in a changed environment. As Yusoff and Gabrys highlight, much has been said about the "doom-laden" narratives of climate change as being unhelpful, but this single-sided conception misses the point of the creative role of fiction and cautionary offerings of the disaster (Yusoff & Gabrys 2011, 5). The dystopic scenarios mediated through the artworks analysed in this chapter illustrate means to rethink a radically new environment and how to survive with it. They open a space for critically reflecting upon how humans treat the planet we live with – and urge the viewer to find new sensibilities of living in the world.

As practicing artists, one could say that both Sansour and Heldén are digging deep into the ground in a timeplace where their speculative worlding is a practice that engages with humans as mortal critters entwined in myriad unfinished configurations of places, times, matters, meanings. As artists their work is truly tentacular, also in relation to production, since Sansour works with many specialised collaborators, and Heldén's work combines visual artistry, music, and poetry. It is an artistic practice of situated and embodied knowledge production where the artists unpack the complex planetary entanglements, interdependencies, and interconnections. The imagery and narratives highlighted by Sansour and Heldén depict climate change and its difficult emotions and dilemmas present in the Chthulucene. In these perspectives of dystopian speculative storytelling within art rests hope for learning to shape better multispecies futures.

Notes

1 Chthulucene is a compound of two Greek words (*khthôn* and *kainos*). *Kainos* means now as a time for beginnings and *khthôn* or chtonic means "of, in or under the earth and seas," something that Haraway relates to replete beings with tentacles, fellers, digits, cords, whiptails, spider legs, and very unruly hair, luxuriating in manifold forms and names in all the airs, waters, and places on earth (Haraway 2016, 2, 55).

2 Land artists such as Robert Smithson, Nancy Holt, and Michael Heizer sought to move out from museum and gallery contexts, including its economic and aesthetic value systems, to rural areas.

3 In this context I see the monster as a hybrid and boundary figure through the lens of feminist scholars Margrit Shildrick and Donna Haraway. Shildrick turns to the monster "in order to uncover and rethink a relation with the standards of normality" where the concept of vulnerability works as an "existential state that may belong to any of us": thus, the encounter with the strange is a constant condition of becoming (Shildrick 2002, 1). In relation to monsters, Haraway highlights science fiction as "generically concerned with the interpretation of boundaries between problematic selves and unexpected others where the monster incorporates the possibility to work against fixed positions and train humans to more subtle visions" (Haraway 1992, 70).

4 The book *First Contact* was published in Swedish by Albert Bonniers Förlag in 2019. The same year I curated the exhibition *Cosmological Arrows – Journeys Through Inner and Outer Space* for Bonniers Konsthall in Stockholm, with Johannes Heldén as one of the invited artists. The exhibition included (among others) the video *The Extinction Archives (Part 1)*, and the last chapter of Heldén's book *First Contact* was translated into English by the artist to be published in the accompanying publication edited by myself in collaboration with Jerry Määttä. Therefore, only the last chapter of *First Contact* is translated to English.

5 Carl Linnaeus (in Swedish Carl von Linné, 1707–1778) was a Swedish botanist, zoologist, taxonomist, and physician. Linnaeus was professor of medicine and botany at Uppsala University and conducted journeys through Sweden to classify plants and animals. The scientific results were published in *Systema Naturae,* which came out in several editions. Generally, Linnaeus is known as the "father" of modern taxonomy to which one of the origins of scientific racism also can be traced. The Linnaean large-scale visions and order of things have been criticised from feminist perspectives by, for instance, Donna Haraway (1989), Londa Schiebinger (1993), and Cecilia Åsberg (2009). For a discussion on Linnaeus, race, and sex, see also https://www.linnean.org/learning/who-was-linnaeus/linnaeus-and-race.

6 While saying this it is important to recognise that art historians (e.g. T.J. Demos) and museologists (e.g. Laurajane Smith) have pointed towards the imbalance across visitor demographics in museums. In a recent study performed at American, Australian, and British museums and heritage sites, Smith confirms that the visitor profiles tended to be dominated by people from politically dominant ethnic groups within the respective countries with high education attainment and holding "higher" socially valued occupation (Smith 2021, 6). T.J. Demos thus suggest that the most ambitious artistic engagements today are those that can enact an intersectional politics of aesthetics, where art no longer

prioritises the gallery-enclosed experience of aesthetic contemplation alone, but rather emerges in close proximity to field research, creative pedagogies, political mobilisation, and civil society partnerships and solidarities (Demos 2016, 13).

References

Alaimo, Stacy. 2010. *Bodily Natures. Science, Environment, and the Material Self.* Bloomington: Indiana University Press.

Anderson, Benedict. 1983. *Imagined Communities: Reflections on the Origin and Spread of Nationalism.* London: Verso.

Åsberg, Cecilia. 2005. *Genetiska föreställningar. Mellan genus och gener I popular/vetenskapens visuella kulturer.* PhD dissertation. Linköping: Linköping University.

Åsberg, Cecilia. 2009. "Looking at Science, Looking at You!: the Feminist Re-visions of Nature (Brain and genes)." In *Teaching Visual Culture in Interdisciplinary Classrooms: Feminist (re)interpretations of the Field*, eds. Elżbieta H. Oleksy & Dorota Golanska, 95–121. Utrecht: Athena.

Braidotti, Rosi. 2006. *Transpositions: On Nomadic Ethics.* Cambridge: Polity Press.

Braidotti, Rosi. 2013. *The Posthuman.* Cambridge and Malden: Polity Press.

Bryld, Mette & Nina Lykke. 2000. *Cosmodolphins: Feminist Cultural Studies of Technology, Animals and the Sacred.* Chicago: University Press of Chicago.

Byrne-Smith, Dan. 2020. *Documents of Contemporary Art: Science Fiction*, ed. Dan Byrne-Smith, 12–19. London: Whitechapel Gallery.

Crutzen, Paul & Eugene Stoermer. 2000. "Have we Entered the Anthropocene?" *International Geosphere-Biosphere Program Newsletter* 41: 17–18.

Dawson, Graham. 1994. *Soldier Heroes: British Adventure, Empire, and the Imagining of Masculinities.* London: Routledge.

Demos, T. J. 2016. *Decolonizing Nature: Contemporary Art and the Politics of Ecology.* Berlin: Sternberg Press.

Foucault, Michel. 1998. *Aesthetics, Method, Epistemology: The Essential Works of Michel Foucault, 1954–1984.* Harmondsworth: Allen Lane, Penguin.

Franklin, Sarah. 2000. "Life Itself: Global Nature and the Genetic Imaginary." In *Global Nature, Global Culture*, eds. Celia Lury, Jackie Stacey & Sarah Franklin, 188–217. London: SAGE.

Haraway, Donna J. 1988. "Situated Knowledges: The Science Question in Feminism and the Privilege of Partial Perspective." *Feminist Studies* 14 (3): 575–599.

Haraway, Donna J. 1989. *Primate Visions: Gender, Race, and Nature in the World of Modern Science.* New York: Routledge.

Haraway, Donna J. 1992. "The Promises of Monsters: A Regenerative Politics for Inappropriate/d Others." In *Cultural Studies*, ed. Lawrence Grossberg, Cary Nelson & Paul A. Treichler, 295–338. New York: Routledge.

Haraway, Donna J. 2008. *When Species Meet.* Minneapolis: University of Minnesota Press.

Haraway, Donna J. 2015. "Anthropocene, Capitalocene, Plantationcene, Chthulucene: Making Kin." *Environmental Humanities* 6 (1): 159–165.

Haraway, Donna J. 2016. *Staying with the Trouble: Making Kin in the Chthulucene.* Durham: Duke UP.

Heldén, Johannes. 2019a. *First Contact.* Stockholm: Albert Bonniers Förlag.

Heldén, Johannes. 2019b. "Field Guide to Future Planets." In *Cosmological Arrows*, ed. Caroline Elgh Klingborg & Jerry Määttä, 25–33. Stockholm: Art and Theory Publishing.

Heldén, Johannes. 2022. Interview by Caroline Elgh, February 19. Audio 31:30.

Hellstrand, Ingvil. 2015. *Passing as Human. Posthuman Worldings at Stake in Contemporary Science Fiction.* Stavanger: University of Stavanger.

Hellstrand, Ingvil. 2020. "Innovasjon i science fiction: perspektiver på endring og nyskapning." In *Samskaping – grensebrytende samarbeid og innovasjon,* ed. Elisabeth Willumsen & Atle Ødegård. Oslo: Universitetsforlaget.

Isomaa, Saija, Jyrki Korpua & Jouni Teittinen. 2020. "Introduction: Navigating the Many Forms of Dystopian Fiction." In *New Perspectives on Dystopian Fiction in Literature and Other Media,* eds. Saija Isomaa, Jyrki Korpua & Jouni Teittinen, ix–xxx. Newcastle upon Tyne: Cambridge Scholar Publishing.

Lennon, Kathleen. 2015. *Imagination and the Imaginary.* New York: Routledge.

Lykke, Nina. 2010. *Feminist Studies: A Guide to Intersectional, Theory, Methodology and Writing.* New York: Routledge.

Martinson, Harry. 1956. *Aniara: en revy om människan i tid och rum.* Stockholm: Bonnier.

Masnadi, S. Mohammad et al. 2018. "Global Carbon Intensity of Oil Crude Production." *Science* 361 (6405): 851–853.

Moylan, Tom. 2000. *Scraps of the Untained Sky. Science Fiction, Utopia, Dystopia.* Boulder: Westview.

Muller, Nat. 2019. "Before and after a Disaster. Unsettling Representations in Larissa Sansour's 'Heirloom'." In *Larissa Sansour. Heirloom,* ed. Anthogy Downey, 6–22. Berlin: Sternberg Press.

Määttä, Jerry. 2019. "Science Fiction 101." In *Cosmological Arrows,* eds. Caroline Elgh Klinborg & Jerry Määttä, 25–33. Stockholm: Art and Theory Publishing.

Neimanis, Astrida, Cecilia Åsberg & Johan Hedrén. 2015. "Four Problems, Four Directions for Environmental Humanities: Toward Critical Posthumanities for the Anthropocene." *Ethics & the Environment* 20 (1): 67–97.

Plumwood, Val. 2007. "A Review of Deborah Bird Rose's Reports from a Wild Country: Ethics of Decolonisation." *Australian Humanities Review* 1 (42): 1–4.

Sansour, Larissa & Anthony Downey. 2019. "Epigenetics and Speculative Research." In *Larissa Sansour. Heirloom,* ed. Anthogy Downey. Berlin: Sternberg Press, 58–77.

Sansour, Larissa & Lindsay Moore. 2019. "Suspended between the Past and the Future." In *Larissa Sansour. Heirloom,* ed. Anthony Downey, 110–130. Berlin: Sternberg Press.

Sansour, Vivien. n.d. "Palestine Heirloom Seed Library". https://viviensansour.com /Palestine-Heirloom. Accessed 1 March 2024.

Schiebinger, Londa. 1993. *Nature's Body: Gender in the Making of Modern Science.* Boston: Beacon Press.

Shildrick, Margrit. 2002. *Embodying the Monster. Encounters with the Vulnerable Self.* London: SAGE.

Shildrick, Margrit. 2009. *Dangerous Discourses of Disability, Subjectivity and Sexuality.* London: Palgrave Macmillan.

Smith, Laurjane. 2021. *Emotional Heritage: Visitor Engagement at Museums and Heritage Sites.* Abingdon: Routledge.

Spivak, Gayatri Chakravorty. 1988. *In Other Worlds. Essays in Cultural Politics.* New York: Routledge.

Stacey, Jackie. 2010. *The Cinematic Life of the Gene.* Durham: Duke University Press.

Tsing, Anna, Heather Swanson & Nils Bubandt. 2017. *Arts of the Living on a Damaged Planet: Ghosts and Monsters of the Anthropocene.* Minneapolis: University of Minnesota Press.

Tuhiwai Smith, Linda. 2021. *Decolonizing Methodologies: Research and Indigenous Peoples*. Third edition. London: Zed.

Van Dijk, Jose. 1998. *Imagenation. Popular Images of Genetics*. London: McMillan Press.

Yusoff, Kathryn & Jennifer Gabrys. 2011. "Climate Change and the Imagination." *WIREs Wiley Interdisciplinary Reviews Climate Change* 2 (4): 516–534.

17

CODA

Speculative Conversation (a Poetic Inquiry)

Aino-Kaisa Koistinen and Line Henriksen

—

> lækija 5
> message 105

—

&&& to answer your question, i looked for indications of space travel in my parts of the book + it seems it was a common practice but at a cost: "With its decks filled with [indecipherable] bars, spas, and gyms, the spaceship's environment invokes in the crew and passengers the very same habits that brought Earth to the brink of destruction" (Wälivaara, J.) i'm on the train between the moons of Ai + Mi. it's cold, i cannot feel my toes. the lights went out as they so often do + space is both outside + in, all dark. i wish for a spa + a bar, even (especially?) if it brings me to the brink of destruction. &&&

—

> lækija 8
> message 106

—

&&& i myself have been stuck on the station for too long.

as we agreed, i have been searching for signs of advanced technologies in augmented reality. this strongly indicates that they had access to such technologies:

"The dynamic of the interpretive quest changes
[indecipherable]
narrator's account of it."

(Kuusisto, P.)

DOI: 10.4324/9781003561101-23

or what do you make of it?
i hope you have found your spa + bar. &&&

—

> lækija 5
> message 107
—

&&&
when i think of ancient augmented realities i almost get a little dizzy, like it sets reality spinning. i have a book snippet saved onto my *vade mecum*, it says that "the opening scene takes place in the past, and [indecipherable] its 'future' is in fact the present" (Wenske, R. S.). we have stopped, suspended between the two moons, the train awaiting permission to continue, the compartment so eerily quiet. here, between one thing + another, in the cold + the dark, my feet numb, i can almost imagine that the past is indeed the present is the future. i read to think of something else.

"the major political conflict
[indecipherable]
continues to be a rift in collective memory," (Mboka Tveit, M.)

how far do collective memories go? + their rifts? &&&

—

> lækija 8
> message 108
—

&&&
there seems to be a tension between the subjective + the collective, as another snippet states that: "Reality is subjective and depends on the point of view." (Korpua, J.) what do you fathom they mean by subjective point of view here? as they seem to have access to augmented reality, would they have also experimented with shared subjectivities?

jumping to a completely different issue, i am quite excited about my next finding:

"we have encouraged all authors to [indecipherable] pronoun 'they' when referring to people" (Korpua et al.)
even though some if it is not readable, this quote seems to confirm our hypothesis that they sometimes used other pronouns than 'they' when referring to people.&&&

—

> lækija 5
> message 109

—

&

      our hypothesis

             ancients

there is
&&&

      between th e moons

           i have a book

"For a while, Nordic fantasy
writers have
[indecipherable]
   striven to portray peopl e from d

           ifferent cultural backgrounds" (Salminen, J.)

       you think?

&

&

   "do [indecipherable] research together [indecipherable]
   writes the script, and
   [indecipherable] they both
   [indecipherable] direct" (Elgh, C.)

         direction? where or when they ended up

cannot see
   hands
    o   feel feet

        direction?

—

> lækija 8
> message 110

—

&&&
   you're breaking up.

i am getting an uncanny sensation that the book is now communicating something through us in a manner that my training has not prepared me for.

just read these snippets, if you can:

"bifurcation, back to which the divergences of past, present and, speculatively, future events could be traced" (Sandbacka, K.)

"In [indecipherable] the bourgeois saloon in the 19th century, people are
spending time with arithmetic games, mathematical needlecraft, reading
and short lectures" (Godhe, M.)

"Selene's voice in the recorded logs, found next to her decaying bodies, portrays vulnerability unlike

[indecipherable] Selene for whom the bodies of other Selenes [indecipherable]

moves past them swiftly" (Ruotsalainen, M.)

had they figured out a way to duplicate, to be both dead and alive at the
same time? can we reclaim these knowledges? &&&

—
> lækija 5
> message 111
—

&&&

we're through the tunnel, i always forget how it scrambles the signal. the
light just blinked back to life, i think the heat is back on. it's easier now, in
the warmth + the light, to dismiss your concern about the book + how it may
communicate, but my toes are still cold.

"... an imaginary municipality somewhere
     [indecipherable]
     attracts mutants, outsiders and misfits" (Sandbacka, K.)

what imaginary places pull us in, you think, while reading? us, the outsiders,
at least from the book's perspective? the wagon rattles, i almost dropped the
vade mecum + my fingers still stiff + cold called up a random text snippet –

"they often tend to be different only in their appearances, thus bearing little
or no consequences to the
[indecipherable]
story" (Ruotsalainen, M.)

– should we take this personally?&&&

—

> lækija 5
> message 112

—

&&&
almost at the station now, gotta go but leave you with this:
"sarcastic comment in middle of the sentence" (Rantala, O.)
will send you the rest when at the office &&&

—

> lækija 8
> message 113

—

&&&
i think it may very well be that their texts are pulling us closer with them,
closer to their time, and also pulling us closer together, you + i, i think i can
almost feel your cold feet. or perhaps the texts that i read are longing for the
ones you are reading?

this quotation suggests, indeed, that they embarked on projects where such
connections were imagined:

"[indecipherable] Sitra joins companies and governmental agencies [inde-
cipherable] the purpose of drawing possible links to the future from the
present" (Roine, H-R.)

have you heard of this sitra? my *vade mecum* does not recognise it.

the next quotation suggests a different relationship to temporality than what
we are accustomed to:

"vi har alltid vært her" [*vade mecum* transl. from old norwegian "we have
always been here"] (Schrattenholz, M. D.)

what if they are still here, accessible through the texts as some sort of astral
beings, influencing us?

i thought that their play with identity suggested knowledge of augmented
reality, but what if it is something different, something embodied?

"she every autumn exchanges her identity with this mysterious animal."
(Wennerscheid, S.)

it also seems that they valued art and literature greatly:

"Their common ground can be found in [indecipherable] literary devices and what might be called [indecipherable]." (Piippo, L.)

imagine common ground to be based in literary devices. the possibility of being contacted by such beautiful creatures now almost scares me.

there now
something with my vade mecum with my vade mecum with my
 a glitch, i cannot the correct the corr
 like texts spilling and there is
hope hope you can

what is that sound?
if you doooo not hear from

& & & & & & & & & & & & & & & & & & & & & & & & & & & & & & & & &
& & & & & & & & & & & & & & & & & & & & & & & & & & & & & & & & &
& & & & & & & & & & & & & & & & & & & & & & & & & & & & & & & & &
& & & & & & & & & & & & & & & & & & & & & & & & & & & & & & & & &
& & & & & & & & & & & & & & & & & & & & & & & & & & & & & & & & &
& & & & & & & & & & & & & & & & & & & & & & & & & & & & & & & & &
& & & & & & & & & & & & & & & & & &

Notes from the present

The coda is inspired by the concepts/practices of place-based writing (Case 2017; Galleymore 2020) and site-specific reading and writing (Heimonen & Rouhiainen 2022; Cocker & Séraphin 2021), where the writing process is influenced by spaces and places – usually one's immediate surroundings. With this coda, we wanted to examine how speculative spaces and places work in place-bound writing practices (cf. Galleymore 2020 on writing about other than one's immediate surroundings), that is, how site-specific writing might be developed within the context of speculative worldbuilding – or *worlding* (Haraway 2016; Elgh in this anthology). Our idea was to have two researcher-readers (here: *lækija*, based on the Finnish and Danish words for 'reader', *lukija* and *læser*, to acknowledge an aspect of our own site-specific speculations) from the future read and discuss surviving snippets from this collection, unsure of what is fact and fiction, speculation and reality.

The coda is in the format of a found poem/collage, where the readers cite parts of the texts to each other to try to make sense of them. Our method resonates with the practice of live action role play, which has been used in futures thinking (Fast45), but also with an understanding of conversation as collaborative method (Lykke et al. 2024, 93–96). The conversation we invited here is, however, a speculative one where each of us tried to get a feel of who our character was and how they would respond in a given situation, using the collage/poem as a method of inquiry (see Faulkner 2019; Richardson 2000). In practice, we created a Discord channel to simulate a future instant message platform, where the researchers could discuss. To emulate how the characters only have access to parts of the book, we applied a virtual dice: the first throw showed what chapter we were reading from; the second throw what page, and the third throw showed what sentence or line to cite from (though sometimes we 'cheated' and threw the dice again).

With this method of speculative site-specific writing and conversation, we hope to offer a playful method of sensing, feeling and looking at present reality through a different experience of space, time and embodiment. How might one's understanding of the present moment change (or not) if approached through the embodied, site-specific position of readers/writers from the future? We share this method with you as an opening up of the speculative conversation and an invitation to test and develop it further.

—

> lækija 5
> message 114

—

&&& "we have always been here" is uncanny indeed. shapeshifters. common ground through literary devices, i worry that we are starting to spook ourselves, friend, it's easy in these dark research stations to let the imagination get the better of oneself, not least when sifting through these fragments from the past. but that is what they are. that is WHEN they are. "The [indecipherable] polar explorer [indecipherable] is talking to a journalist with no experience in the Arctic" (Nierste, C.) sorry don't know where that came from. i am readying the documents, uploading now. if what you say is true – that the book longs to be put together again – i guess we are soon to find out what that means&&&

Acknowledgements

We wish to thank all the authors of the present collection for granting us permission to use their texts as material for this coda.

Koistinen's work on this text is part of the project *Artistic thinking driven artist pedagogy* (funded by the Academy of Finland, no. 353305) and their sub-project *Writing-with Others as Artist Pedagogy – Feminist Practices of Creative, Collective Writing in Times of Polycrisis* (University of the Arts Helsinki Research Institute).

References

Case, Jennifer. 2017. "Place-Based Pedagogy and the Creative Writing Classroom." *Journal of Creative Writing Studies* 2 (2): 1–14.

Cocker, Emma & Leena Séraphin (in association with writers Andrea Coyotzi Borja, Alexander Damianisch, Cordula Daus, Sepideh Karami & Vidha Saumya). 2021. "Site-Reading – Site Specific Writing and Reading." https://www.researchcatalogue.net/view/1184609/1222743. Accessed 2 May 2024.

Faulkner, S. L. 2019. *Poetic Inquiry: Craft, Method and Practice*. 2nd edition. New York: Routledge.

Fast45. "Summer School. Live Action Role Play for Futures Thinking in Art Education." https://learningplatform.fast45.eu/larp/#worlding. Accessed 2 May 2024.

Galleymore, Isabel. 2020. *Teaching Environmental Writing: Ecocritical Pedagogy and Poetics*. London: Bloomsbury Academic.

Haraway, Donna. 2016. *Staying with the Trouble: Making Kin in the Chthulucene*. Durham: Duke University Press.

Heimonen, Kirsi & Leena Rouhiainen. 2022. "In the Shadows: Phenomenological Choreographic Writing." *Choreographic Practices* 13 (1): 75–96.

Lykke, Nina, Katja Aglert & Line Henriksen. 2024. *Feminist Reconfigurings of Alien Encounters: Ethical Co-Existence in More-than-Human Worlds*. New York: Routledge.

Richardson, L. 2000/1995. "Writing: A Method of Inquiry." In *The Sage Handbook of Qualitative Research*, ed. Norman K. Denzin & Yvonna S. Lincoln, 9–49. Newcastle upon Tyne: Sage.

INDEX

For Product Safety Concerns and Information please contact our EU
representative GPSR@taylorandfrancis.com
Taylor & Francis Verlag GmbH, Kaufingerstraße 24, 80331 München, Germany

www.ingramcontent.com/pod-product-compliance
Lightning Source LLC
Chambersburg PA
CBHW071531110726
47908CB00007B/1833